"This is my kinc
and guts thrill ri
well, getting the
got sunburned. Ungerman is an excellent
gifted writer who gives readers a good dose of the hard stuff."

—*Charles Henderson,*
author of Marine Sniper *and* Silent Warrior

"A fast-paced journey through the killing fields found only where good and evil battle for domination. *The Devil's Finger* pulls you willingly in for a ride into the dark halls of the mind, seeing men at their worst, where ego and ambition rule and where men of good will often face their harshest decisions. Once you pick up this book you will not put it down until finished."

—*Scott Powers,*
SniperCountry.com

"A sizzling read. A brilliant, complex anatomy course in weaponry, the sinew of love, and necrosis of mortality. What Ungerman does to these pages, these pages will do to you. Try to forget what this author writes and you will fail."

—*Bill Branon,*
author of the New York Times *Notable Book* Let Us Prey

"*The Devil's Finger* is a grab-you-by-the-throat thriller, filled with betrayal, danger, and exotic locales. What truly sets it apart is the pervasive sense of justice, and the author's knowledge of the world he describes. This is a vivid insight into the world of the killer elite, and it's a powerful and compelling read."

—*Robert Ferrigno,*
author of Scavenger Hunt *and* The Horse Latitudes

THE DEVIL'S FINGER

WILLIAM UNGERMAN

J

JOVE BOOKS, NEW YORK

THE BERKLEY PUBLISHING GROUP
Published by the Penguin Group
Penguin Group (USA) Inc.
375 Hudson Street, New York, New York 10014, USA
Penguin Group (Canada), 10 Alcorn Avenue, Toronto, Ontario M4V 3B2, Canada
(a division of Pearson Penguin Canada Inc.)
Penguin Books Ltd., 80 Strand, London WC2R 0RL, England
Penguin Group Ireland, 25 St. Stephen's Green, Dublin 2, Ireland
(a division of Penguin Books Ltd.)
Penguin Group (Australia), 250 Camberwell Road, Camberwell, Victoria 3124, Australia (a division of Pearson Australia Group Pty. Ltd.)
Penguin Books India Pvt. Ltd., 11 Community Centre, Panchsheel Park, New Delhi—100 017, India
Penguin Group (NZ), Cnr. Airborne and Rosedale Roads, Albany, Auckland 1310, New Zealand (a division of Pearson New Zealand Ltd.)
Penguin Books (South Africa) (Pty.) Ltd., 24 Sturdee Avenue, Rosebank, Johannesburg 2196, South Africa

Penguin Books Ltd., Registered Offices: 80 Strand, London WC2R 0RL, England

THE DEVIL'S FINGER

A Berkley Book / published by arrangement with the author.

PRINTING HISTORY
Jove mass-market edition / October 2004

Cover design and illustration by Pyrographix.
Book design by Kristin del Rosario.

ISBN: 0-515-13841-X

JOVE®
Jove Books are published by The Berkley Publishing Group,
a division of Penguin Group (USA) Inc.,
375 Hudson Street, New York, New York 10014.

PRINTED IN THE UNITED STATES OF AMERICA

10 9 8 7 6 5 4 3 2 1

AUTHOR'S NOTE

The Devil's Finger contains some esoteric military and intelligence community terminology, including acronyms, jargon, and slang. One will also find technical weapons references as well as some foreign language utilized in dialogue. In any instance where a satisfactory interpretation is not possible within context or where a specific meaning is not self-evident, the reader may consult the glossary.

ACKNOWLEDGMENTS

I'd like to thank my informal editors and readers who took their time to read the manuscript of *The Devil's Finger* and provide feedback and input: Foremost, my mother, Wanda Ungerman, and of course Frank Barilla, Helen Michels, Jerry Laffey, and Gunnery Sergeant Robert L. Barham (rest in peace, Marine). Viet Nam claimed him thirty years after the fall. *Semper fidelis*.

Special thanks to B. Grant Gelker, a great friend.

Heartfelt appreciations to my agent, Diana Finch, for her consummate professionalism and her belief in me. Lastly, my grateful acknowledgment of my editor, Samantha Mandor of The Berkley Publishing Group, for her tireless efforts in pursuit of perfection. *The Devil's Finger* is a better book because of her.

Thank you all.

William Ungerman
Santa Ana, California

For my wife, Frances Ungerman,
who stood by me, encouraged me, and sacrificed.
I owe it all to her.
Without her unflagging support,
this novel would not have been possible.
And thanks for letting that drunk at the sushi bar
know the damn book wasn't about
a crazed proctologist!

Out to about nine hundred meters shooting, as a skill, can be taught as a science. From there to approximately twelve hundred meters it becomes art. Beyond that . . . it's Zen.

THOMAS W. MUZILA, sniper, U.S. Army Special Forces

Fire seldom, but accurately.

FIELD MARSHAL PRINCE ALEKSANDR V. SUVOROV, 1796

PROLOGUE

THE Root . . .

It smelled just like all the rest of those Third World shit holes: Guat City, Whore-ez, Mog, Moresby, Port-o-Piss, the Dom Rep, and a dozen others. The stench couldn't be concealed, but a city's essence has a lot of false fronts. Daylight veneers and facades foster the chamber of commerce images. Its true character is revealed at night, exposed by a conspiratorial agency of shadows and sounds. There, the Root had its own signature: ghosts with guns slipping through alleyways, the midnight wail of jihad survivors, moonlight filtering through Swiss cheese buildings, skinny dogs feeding on dead dogs, and funeral pyres by Goodyear and Michelin creating an eternal pall of caustic smoke. The odors of acrid urine, rotting garbage, putrefying corpses, raw sewage, garlic, armpits, and decaying fish became chemical and biological warfare, a sensory weapon of mass destruction. Only Mog more or less mirrored the Root.

From his elevated position on the top floor of the destroyed Excelsior Hotel, Myles Rawlings could see half of Beirut. The Med, stretching aquamarine, segued seamlessly into an azure/cobalt interface at an indecipherable horizon. He could identify the old American embassy building, parts of the Beirut-Sidron Road, and the soccer stadium. He could also see the target building towering over the tenements, tin shacks, the Shit River, and the *shuk* with its facade of gaiety, its veneer of normalcy in a city that mocked the concept. *The Republic of Lebanon . . . kiss my ass.*

Rawlings drew his breath in through his nose and extended the effort by sucking in the parched air through his mouth, using his abdomen for full effect. Now he could taste the Third World, too. He was definitely back. He'd been to places like this before and—Odin willing—he'd be to others. He pulled his eyes away from the Steiner binoculars he held in two hands, his elbows propped up on a splintered table in the center of the space, and surveyed the three other men who occupied the shattered semblance of what once must have been the tony veranda of an observation deck. His eyes slid across the lines and shadows of the room. Habib, the Lebanese guide, fidgeted in the far corner, nervously biting his narrow lips while wringing his prayer beads with sweaty hands. Floyd Cruickshank, the surly spook, was pacing restlessly, wearing a trough in the dry-rotted floor. Grainger, Rawlings's shooter, remained motionless, half visible in the shadows of the interior wall, the killing tool hidden in its case cradled on his lap.

"Time check, Ace."

Cruickshank was talking to no one in particular, and that was good. No one but Cruickshank gave a rat's ass about the time. When—and if—it happened, it happened. Rawlings shot him a bored look. "Three minutes later than the last time you asked . . . Ace." The monotony of Cruickshank's demands for time checks were becoming imperious; an ongoing interrogation. A first impression of Cruickshank was an Easter Island monolith. His bullet head was shaven close and sunburned. His muscular neck disappeared into massive trapezius muscles that made him look like a walking pyramid, an NFL linebacker gone to seed or the missing link.

Lon Grainger remained motionless as he had for the last hour, now contemplating a bead of sweat that slowly elongated and broke free of his fingertip. He sat on a wooden crate against the fractured wall. His angular face surrounded wide-set eyes and was capped with close-cropped hair. His muscles were lean and sinewy. In Mississippi they would have called him "rawboned." He balanced a Weapons Container, Parachutist, Model 1950 on his lap. The heavy, padded, olive drab canvas case was used as a drag bag during stalks and as transport for the principal tool of his trade.

Grainger was still wearing his jellaba, the traditional, floor-length Arabic robe favored by the majority of Beirut's male population: Sunni, Druze, Shiite, Alawite, Isma'ilite, the dominant Islamic contenders for the soul of the city. But even the minority Christian groups wore them. The garment looked like a high school graduation gown somebody made out of grain bags. The cloaks were obtained from Cruickshank and Habib, who had met them on the beach following the mission insertion by a SEAL team and their Zodiac RIB boat. Now, the temperature was a smelting furnace and, even in the waning afternoon sun, seemed to be climbing. Grainger shuffled off the caftanlike robe. He slipped the heavy-barrel rifle from the case into his hands, a surgeon examining his scalpel.

Yussuf Akram Habib gripped his slippery prayer beads tightly and watched the sniper pull the long rifle from its container and wondered what kind of man this was. He imagined a white darkness, a bloodless killing machine. Habib thought of himself as a practical man. He regarded his own morality as . . . fluid. Perhaps *flexible* was a better word. Survival required a certain amount of elasticity. When he wasn't providing hard-to-come-by information for Western intelligence services or the Israeli *Shabac,* he was splashing *llyaawm Al-Quds, Ghadan Falasteen* in whitewash on walls to please the minions of HAMAS—*Harakat Muqama al-Uslamiyya*—the Islamic resistance movement.

He had guided the Americans to this spot, true; but he worked for anybody who would pay him: The Syrians and the PLO, the Israeli *AMAN* and *Mossad* and their surrogates, and the disorganized remnants of what used to be the South Lebanese Army. Even for the CIA and their man Cruickshank and that other, unknown man to whom he had sold information on this adventure. Who that man was remained a mystery. Ultimately it was unimportant, because the more the better, and at the same time was best. Life was very short. Information was a transactional commodity. He was a broker. But it was the time of Ramadan, the ninth month of the Islamic year, and he should be fasting. This was the Islamic *Hijazi* land and that was the *Shari'ah* law. After, he could play his *halil*—the reed flute he had mastered—titillate and hopefully seduce the desirable Zakia, even though she was from Jezzine and therefore probably a Christian. But that was all secondary now. *What these men plan to do . . .* It made him shudder. Yussuf squeezed the peanut butter from the MRE foil container directly into his mouth, strained the crunchy mix through his teeth, and masticated the grit like a famished bovine. He hoped this would soon be over. *Then* he'd fast.

Lon Grainger's practiced eyes swept the enclosed roof terrace of the abandoned hotel. Shattered window glass and ceiling plaster littered the floor, and a few brazen rats stared at him in defiance. There was no stairway access to this top floor—the tenth—inasmuch as the fourth and fifth floors had collapsed. They had roped up. It was a mixed blessing; secure, but providing no rapid egress should they need an emergency back door. They'd been there before. *This place must have been on Fodor's and Bimbaum's four star list. Fielding's gave it a five, but they were a CIA front and never got it right.*

Grainger examined the rifle in his hands, a Mauser-Werke Model 66SP precision sniper weapon. An already superb tool of long-range killing, it had been modified. This rifle had been rechambered from the original 7.62 × 51 millimeter NATO caliber cartridge to the far greater ranging .300 Winchester Magnum. The usual accompanying Swarovski 6 × 42 Bullet-Drop-Compensator rifle scope had been removed. In its place was a Bausch & Lomb 6-24 power variable magnification telescopic sight. This rifle was the weapon of choice of Israeli Defense Force snipers and in fact had IDF proof marks. He studied Rawlings, his spotter and security man, who was setting up a collapsible shooting platform that had been pre-positioned for them.

Cruickshank massaged his sweat-glistened head, considering the two other Americans. As far as he was concerned, Habib was a nonentity. "Any time you prima donnas want to get ready, it'd be appreciated."

Grainger stared right through Cro-Magnon man like he wasn't even there. He figured Cruickshank for a Defense Intelligence Agency PM, a paramilitary operative from the Department of Defense's intelligence apparat. This was, as he understood it, an exclusive DIA operation. They had received the mission through usual DoD channels. Granted, no one had asked for or volunteered any specific employer information. There was no "need to know." As briefed, Cruickshank and Habib, the indigenous guide, had met them and the SEAL insertion team at the landing site. Cruickshank had the password, and that's all that mattered. In any case, this was their show, his and Rawlings's. Cruickshank, whoever he worked for, was just an observer.

"Hold on to your nuts. We'll be ready," said Rawlings. "There hasn't been a soul on the balcony all day."

Cruickshank stalked over to a spot equidistant between the two men. "Let's get one thing straight. I call the shots. You're here to make 'em. Savvy?"

Rawlings turned back to observing through the paneless window openings. "Yeah. No problem, Ace. Same team. Same war." *Same team, maybe, but you're the second string. There will always be a war. But foolish people thought we were at peace. "They cry, 'Peace, Peace,' but there is no peace." It's okay. Peace is overrated. Fuck it; peace sucks.* Certainly, even the sheltered ignorant were aware that there were occasional minor diseased conditions in the world body politic that needed specialized surgery; minor disturbances in the universal force that required quelling or rectification. Well, that's what they did: make necessary adjustments in the equilibrium, bring balance to the planet, tweak the status quo, vanquish evil, champion justice, and revenge the little people. There was no such thing as "excessive violence." They were specialists for hire for whatever vexing problem needed solving, messenger boys when Sam—or some allied surrogate—wanted to make a statement. *Red, white, and blue only, please.*

Sure, he was an adrenaline junkie, but he made no excuses nor rationalized his addiction. There was just something about living on the edge. Maybe it was knowing where the edge was. Some people bungee jumped. He ventilated bad guys. "Politics by other means"; he was just playing his part. Rawlings refocused on the balcony.

Blood-thick sweat dripped onto Cruickshank's Serengeti sunglasses. He jerked them away from his face, squinting even in the mixed shadows and sun of the room. He suppressed a yawn. "We used to call this place Hooterville. You know, I was here in '83 with the Crotch, 24th MAU; an eighteen-year-old stud billeted at BIA. The fucking camel jocks blew the building to hell. Twenty-three October '83, and I was there for the largest nonnuclear explosion ever recorded." He thumped his chest. "I survived. This towel head we're gonna tag today was part of the plot. So, you see, I got a personal interest. Plus, a lot of intel went into this op. We've invested a lot of years in locating this bastard Saleem and nothing—I mean nothing—is going to keep me from taking him down. I'm here to see things are carried out to specifications."

So that is it. Habib didn't know why the Americans wanted to come to this spot or who they wished to kill. Now he understood it was Muhammad Malik Saleem, the Fire of Allah. *Yes, he is their target for today.* Saleem was also the one who had kidnapped the American Marine Colonel Higgins from the streets of Beirut ten years ago and accused him of being CIA. He hung the man and sent the Americans the videotape of the execution. Saleem, a hero to the Muslims, was *Dajjal,* the Antichrist, to the Christian Lebanese. Habib had forgotten about the killing. It had been so long ago. *Maybe some Americans have longer memories than others . . . If I had this information, I might have demanded more.*

"I got movement on the balcony," Rawlings stated matter-of-factly. He continued to observe with his binoculars.

Cruickshank moved to the edge of the window and peered out. "It's about time."

"Two men; Arabs, with a Scorpion and an Uzi. It's just the muscle, not the package," Rawlings muttered, turning sideways toward Cruickshank.

Cruickshank slipped back into his sunglasses and thrust out his arms, drawing back his sleeves as he slid up next to Grainger. "So tell me. How many?"

Grainger ignored him and inserted the tine of a Bushnell bore-sighter scope into the muzzle of the Mauser.

Cruickshank bore in closer. "One hundred kills? One fifty? I heard about Somalia. 'Citations classified,' 'erasure,' and all that shit. How many tags, triggerman? How's it feel?"

Grainger looked through the rifle scope, insuring that the reticles of both scopes were coincident, verifying the continued alignment of the telescopic sight with the axis of the bore. Cruickshank was only a voice. He removed the bore-sighter from the muzzle. "Like having the cure for cancer."

Cruickshank gnawed on his lower lip. "Yeah, I'll bet."

"Got a bitch on the balcony." Myles's voice was up one octave, but still flat and emotionless.

Cruickshank dropped the subject and moved back to the window. He looked out, swinging the binoculars up to his face. "That's our Judy Goat; our Scheherazade, Lady of Fatima, and Mata Hari all rolled into one. She has done the dirty deed and given up her sugar daddy. Lesson learned: Never trust a woman. But I'd still skull-fuck her." He whirled around to a startled Habib. "Time check, Goddamn it."

Habib trembled. He looked at his knockoff Rolex he bought for ten pounds in the *shuk*. "*As-sa'a had'ash*—it is fifteen hundred, *Shaikh* Cruickshank. Sir." He gazed at the sun-reddened hulk who spoke and thought his face reminded him of Ron Jeremy, his favorite American movie star he would watch in those smoky rooms no one dared mention to the fundamentalists. *Only the face, for sure.*

Grainger moved the rifle to the platform and set up the commercial rifle sandbags that cradled the fore end. "Rawlings and I will take it from here. Myles, what's the temperature?"

Rawlings peered at an instrument gauge. "Ambient air,

ninety-seven degrees in the shade; except there ain't no fucking shade. So, that makes it one hundred and six."

Grainger eased behind the rifle like he was part of the nomenclature. "Wind speed and direction?"

Rawlings raised the binoculars to his eyes and scanned across the city. "I have a boiling mirage with a Syrian flag seven hundred meters out showing a ripple; maybe ten, twelve degrees of lift. Street trash is pretty still." He looked at the digital readout sent by the remote wind velocity meter they had placed on the roof. "The hardware indicates a two-point-six-knot breeze at full-value angle to the target line."

"Roger that," said Grainger softly. He removed the scope caps from the B & L telescopic sight and turned the adjustment knob on the ocular lens piece until it indicated twenty-four magnification power. "There still could be some wind-shear factor crossing the stadium."

"That's affirmative. But at least there's no appreciable up or down angles," said Rawlings. He stepped away from his line of sight through the window.

Grainger moved his eye to the scope and found the balcony of the target building in his view. At twenty-four power, the optical sight made the target appear as viewed at fifty yards by the naked eye.

"Did you know she's giving up Saleem for a hundred thousand Lebanese pounds? A hundred thou lousy P! Some kind will sell you out for a fucking nickel." Cruickshank's face wrinkled into a sneer as he turned to Grainger. "Or shoot you for a dime." If he was looking for an argument, he didn't get one.

"Range, one more time," said Grainger.

"I make it—"

"I told you, it was one-zero-niner-eight meters on the HALEM," Cruickshank snarled. His reference was to the Hensoldt Zeiss laser range finder he was holding. "This thing is accurate to within five meters at that range."

"I make it eleven hundred fifty in the Steiners," Rawlings drawled laconically.

"We go with the Steiners," said Grainger.

Cruickshank slammed a balled-up fist into an open palm.

"Have it your way, Ace. Suit yourself. But fuck this up, and I'll be all over you like stink on shit."

The abandoned theater was nine hundred meters away—ten football fields—to the northeast of the Excelsior Hotel. It was the tallest structure in that direction, rising above the slums of the surrounding city. It shimmered in the heat-generated mirage and smoke rising from the nearby outdoor crematorium and garbage dump. Eighty feet above the pestilence, on the open, walled roof, two men watched, one with a rifle and the other with a spotting scope and a radio. And they waited for orders.

CRUICKSHANK eased a Buck BMF fighting knife from its sheath strapped to his leg. He twisted the blade in front of his face. He lowered the knife, pitching it from hand to hand, while pacing back and forth like a caged animal. He swaggered over to Grainger who was *doping in,* inputting range data information, into the rifle scope. "I know all about you, hero. The Long Ranger. The Distant Death. Fate's Finger, and all that other horseshit. The man, the myth, the legend. Robin Hood with a scope. I say you ain't in the club until you gut a man up where you can smell him. You ever get blood on your hands—up close and personal—sniper?"

Grainger returned a deadpan. "Only when I eat my meat raw."

"Hey," Rawlings hissed. "I got me beaucoup people here. Two. Three . . . The woman's back, and she has a kid with her. Damn! It's him. Saleem."

Cruickshank raised his binoculars to his eyes. His mouth spread open, and his face radiated a precoital anticipation. "That-a-girl." He spun on Grainger. "Time to earn your blood money. Step up to the plate, sport. Make it a home run. I've been carrying you two long enough. Take this bastard down."

Grainger removed a single round of ammunition from a felt-lined wooden case and slid it into the maw of the chamber. He closed the bolt slowly. It made the rick*rack* sound of a lubricated ratchet. Grainger's dominant eye closed in on the scope and obtained proper relief. He regarded the target dispassionately, like it was a metal silhouette of Class A armor that was impervious to pain or death.

ACROSS the tin huts, over the soccer stadium, past the alleys, garbage dumps, dead dogs, and empty shell casings, Nabilia Tibi removed her *hijab* and veil and stood next to Muhammad Saleem, the child of their union—Khizar—between them. Muhammad leaned down, patted the boy's head, and placed his fingertips on the woman's lips.

WITH the binoculars still to his eyes, Cruickshank uttered, "Well, ain't that fucking touching." He dropped the 10 × 50 binoculars on their neck strap and whirled toward Grainger. "Come on; what are you waiting for? Ice that fuck."

Rawlings pretended to spit. He was too dry to do it for real. "This isn't a contact sport, asshole. That's twelve hundred meters you're looking at; almost three-quarters of a mile, last I checked. This is art in progress. Plus, people are supposed to shut up when it's your turn to bowl." He turned back to his binoculars. "Wait one. I got somebody else; a white guy talking on his sat phone with a shit-eating grin like he's ordering pizza."

Grainger studied the newcomer through the rifle scope.

"Who in the fuck . . . ?" Rawlings turned around.

"Don't mean nothing," snarled Cruickshank.

Grainger continued to consider the new subject in silence. For the first time, he agreed with Cruickshank. His finger moved inside the trigger guard, and the first joint of his index finger molded to the curve of the metal.

Habib shivered.

Grainger's breathing slowed. His breath expelled like a sigh. His head jerked up.

Cruickshank whipped around. "Nuke him, Goddamn it. Erase that raghead."

Habib peered at the target through the tripod-mounted spotting scope positioned in the shadow of another window. "*La'. Mish mumkin.* He cannot."

Grainger's eye went momentarily back to the scope; then he pushed away from the rifle.

Cruickshank turned slowly back to the window and raised his binoculars to his eyes. Saleem had the boy in his arms. Cruickshank backed up a step and spun, his mouth gaping open, his voice a rictus of rage. "The fuck you can't. Whack that son of a bitch before the window closes. Now."

Grainger's voice was edgeless. "We wait until—"

Cruickshank drew a Beretta M-9 pistol from his Safariland shoulder holster and jammed it against Grainger's head. "I say we don't. And like I said, I'm calling the shots."

In the oppressive heat another man waited, this one a lone hunter. One hundred and ten feet above the rubble-strewn street and three-quarters of a mile away from the Excelsior Hotel, he lay alone in silence among the shifting shadows cast by the minaret of the old mosque. He had but one thought, one goal, and one objective. He knew his target was out there someplace to the southwest, estimated somewhere along azimuths running between 190 and 250 degrees magnetic from his position. The target he sought to eliminate would be attempting to make—for even the most accomplished—an incredibly long shot. It was of necessity, for in this, the Fakahani district of West Beirut, HAMAS and the PLO reigned supreme. His target would not venture inside that perimeter. The lone hunter had drawn a circle with a compass on the military grid map and, utilizing the estimated factors of distance, required elevation, ballistic limitations, politics, mission, skill assessment, and the requirements of personal survival, he used a shorthand version of a mental exercise based upon Bayes' theorem of subjective probability. The lone hunter used it to quantify the values of his possibilities. They had once taught him well. Now, looking at the infrastructure of the city, he put an X on the Excelsior Hotel. That is where the target would be. That is where his target waited to kill. And where the target would die.

RAWLINGS set the binoculars down on the splintered table. A SIG Sauer P226 pistol sprang into his hand. He raised it to eye level, pointing right at Cruickshank. "It'll be the last fuckin' shot you ever call. Ace."

Cruickshank ignored the threat, like Rawlings wasn't even there. He cocked the Beretta, the hammer rearing back in three distinct, staged clicks. He again pressed the barrel into Grainger's temple. "Now."

Rawlings took a step forward.

Grainger raised a calming hand. "It's okay, Myles." He slid forward back into position, his eye locked on the rifle scope.

Rawlings and Cruickshank lowered their weapons.

Habib released the grip on the Tokarev pistol he kept under his shirt. *Total madness!*

"Time to target?"

Rawlings was in animated suspension. "About—"

"Exactly." Grainger's voice had an ice edge.

"Two-point-oh-nine seconds." *Who's the white guy?*

On the theater roof, the sniper's spotter put down the Stratos Iridium radiotelephone, which provided secure communications for SIWF protocol at 4.8 kbps over the INMARSAT-M. "Stand by for plan B."

The sniper nodded and hoped it wouldn't come to pass. But he was first of all a man who followed orders. He snapped down the bipod on the Giat Industries Fusil a Repetition Modele F2, a world-class French sniper rifle, and looked into the advanced optical world of the Modele 53 bis telescopic sight. He would switch to thermal sight imagery most likely after the first shot. Duty. Honor. Country. Two out of three was all there was. He had to settle for that or abdicate. He brought the triple-post horizontal crosshair NATO sniper reticle to bear on his target and began the final ritual.

A done deal! I made it happen. On the balcony with Saleem, Roger Blankenship Carruthers turned his satellite communications radio to standby and congratulated himself. *I pulled it off. Meritorious promotion, yeah man. The rewards of success. G-S Thirteen, here I come. There isn't a thing money can't buy. Friendship. Information. Maybe not loyalty, but fear could insure that. Muhammad Malik Saleem, you're my man.* Politics was fascinating.

Saleem picked the boy up in his arms and rocked him back and forth, his own upper body rotating from the effort. Uzi and Scorpion stood Sphinx-like behind him. Nabilia reached desperately for the boy but was ignored by Saleem. Helplessly she stared straight out across the expanse of her city, anticipating with limp dread. Her heart beat with love, her head with hate. The resultant mix was resignation.

CRUICKSHANK'S stubbled face was caressing Grainger's, his voice a viper's hiss. "You got the green light, Magic Man. Now, reach out and cancel that stench."

Grainger was confident he could make the shot. The mil-dot reticle centered on Saleem's throat. *Timing. Time it right.* He squeezed the trigger, and the rifle muzzle erupted. Grainger imagined he could see the tiny missile climb to the peak of its parabola where it began its decent to the target. Saleem was laughing now. So was the boy, a dusky, curly-headed child.

The 180-grain pointed soft-point boat-tail bullet hit the laughing boy in the chest and punched out his back. Undeterred, it drilled through the neck of Muhammad Saleem and scattered blood like rain on his woman, Nabilia, whose agony at that moment transcended all worldly hurt. Blood splattered, cascading over the YSL sunglasses, snow-white Eddie Bauer bush jacket, and dreams of G-S Thirteen of Roger B. Carruthers, servant of the people.

At the sound of the rifle's report the lone hunter confirmed the origin and turned to the distant balcony. He had always known where the balcony was and that Saleem would be the target. He observed the unanticipated result, allowing himself a moment of professional reflection on the majesty of the kill shot. Collateral consequences notwithstanding, it was extraordinary. He turned back to where he had been observing. His estimate of the hotel had been accurate. The time had come. He had the precise position. He eased the Dragunov SVDS folding stock, semiautomatic sniper rifle into the hollow of his shoulder like he was cradling a familiar lover. He sought his target in the PSO-1 telescope and found him, supported by three others in the lair. The target would understandably be still gloating—although his face was indistinct—over the kill. The target would soon celebrate no more. The Russian pointed triple-post reticle searched for the aim point.

GRAINGER slumped over the laminated stock of his rifle. Rawlings lowered his binoculars slowly. Habib backed away from the spotting scope.

"Not bad, Ace; a two-for-one day for you. Now, that's *real* economy. This is one for the books," Cruickshank cackled.

Grainger staggered up and reeled away from the shooting bench.

The sniper spoke softly to his spotter, telling him what his partner already knew. "He made the shot."

The spotter nodded. "It wasn't your fault. They didn't allow for this or give us any time. The contingency in the OPLAN was too tight." The spotter raised the radio, made his report, and waited for the order. Thirty seconds later, it came.

CRUICKSHANK strode to his rucksack and removed a cheap portable radio, pretuned to *Galei Tzahal*, the Israeli military radio network. He scattered about a few sheets of *Maariv*, an Israeli newspaper. "We'll leave the PLO and the Hezbollah some giveaways. Give your friends credit whenever you can." His radio trembled, announcing a call. Cruickshank pulled the Motorola LST-5D SATCOM radio, which was embedded with COMSEC and DAMA capability, from the built-in carrier on his black, one-piece jumpsuit. He activated the radio, made contact, and cradled the handset between his jaw and shoulder. Eight seconds later he replaced the radio, said, *"Ma'a assalama,"* and shot Habib three times.

Habib staggered backward from the multiple impacts and collapsed onto the front page of *Maariv* with a look that said, *It figures* on his face.

Cruickshank looked momentarily at the dead body before regarding the shooter and spotter. "I kinda liked old Habib. He smoked a little too much hash, but he wasn't bad for a fucking

A-rab. But I just got the word this is going to be a sanitized op. No prisoners. You know what the IRA saying is: 'Leave one witness, and make sure it's yourself.' " He chuckled mirthlessly, the Beretta still dangling loosely in his hand. His lips tightened into a hard line, skinning back over his teeth. "It's too bad you couldn't have popped the female, too; could have saved Uncle Sugar fifty large."

Rawlings watched him, caught in a quicksand of paralyzing uncertainty.

Grainger understood the end game.

Cruickshank grinned. "If I was you, I wouldn't take this personal, sport. That fucking kid you snuffed was probably already a *HAMAS* terr making bombs up in the Krum al-arz mountains or the Shuff to kill the Phalange, the SLA, and our good buddies, the Israelis. Anyway, what's another killing or two to someone like you?" He scratched his head with the muzzle of the M-9. "Or me?" The gun came off his head.

The bullet struck with a vicious slap. Cruickshank was still standing, but his skull was shattered, and his face was missing a forehead. A distant rumble of thunder rolled across the city. Reflexively, Rawlings dove for the floor.

Grainger knelt down and followed Cruickshank, sinking to his knees, the latter's eyes wide with disbelief and incomprehension. The Beretta clattered to the floor, and Cruickshank's body covered it. Two more shots cracked convulsively in rapid succession, somewhere out across the expanse.

Rawlings rolled onto his back. "Jesus Christ!" His eyes locked on Grainger, who seemed inanimate. "Come on Lon, we got to extract, unass this AO." He started for Cruickshank and then stopped. *What for? The top of his head is gone.* "Let's get out of Dodge. Now."

Grainger stared at him. "Those were two different long rifles."

Rawlings low-crawled toward him. "No shit. You can't tell who the players are anymore. This place has turned into a sniper's convention."

The lone hunter arrested his breathing, and the wings of the angel of death stopped beating. The trigger of his rifle was eas-

ing rearward when his target stepped back from view. The angel's wings resumed their hypnotic, slow-motion rhythm, and the hunter resumed watching and waiting. Then he heard a second shot emanating elsewhere. Springing swiftly to identify the origin, he found two armed men on the roof of a theater, three city blocks away. Who? *He smoothly shifted position and brought his Russian-manufactured rifle around to target this new, unknown threat.* What? *The lone hunter was unable to fathom what this all meant except he had to kill them before they killed him or drove him from his aerie. He saw the glint of glass and steel and sighted confidently. The master sniper fired twice in quick succession. He watched his rounds impact. The head of one exploded. The other appeared to take a mortal wound in the torso. He turned back to his original objective but found the tide had passed. He had lost the initiative. He pondered the events. Who were those two men on the theater roof? Where had they come from? What was their intent? He would get no answers here. Perhaps it didn't matter. Whoever they were, they no longer existed. His original target would have to wait for another inevitable day. Then the lone hunter, the master sniper, was gone, a shadow among shadows.*

GRAINGER low-crawled to the stairwell. Rawlings had said it before: *The best thing you can do for the dead is not to join them.* Behind him, a thermite grenade melted everything they had brought with them to molten metal and ash. And the destruction he wrought on a balcony eleven hundred and fifty meters across the tin roofs, the garbage dumps, the Shit River, dirty alleys, and the soccer stadium, incinerated Grainger's heart and turned it to dust. *I'll do whatever is necessary.* The words had come back to haunt him.

ONE

IN some places the temporal sense stands still. Time passes more slowly. Maybe it's because some geophysical meridians overlap, creating a geomagnetic anomaly, perhaps a time warp. It could be just the heat that slows everything down. Then again, maybe this twilight zone is only in the imagination, a state of mind; like Zapata, Texas. Zapata dangles on the edge of civilization's abyss, a nodule on an umbilical cord called U.S. 83. From Laredo, you take the highway east forty-seven miles, past the outpost of San Ygnacio, to the town that everybody forgot. Once there, you can continue on the highway to McAllen and Harlingen. Or you can bypass the town and go north, on County Road 16, but it only runs to Bustamante and Escobas, which means it runs to nowhere.

Zapata's citizenry is a collective manifestation, a living embodiment of the Greek legend of Sisyphus, who was condemned by the gods to push a boulder up the mountain, only to have it roll down again. The monotonous repetition of that eternal sentence was played out in the reality of everyday life's toil and strife. It is also a place where Darwinian theory is showcased. In 1999 the *National Geographic* planned a piece focusing on the effects of physical and cultural isolation of towns in Texas and among the villages of the Bedamini tribe in the highlands of Papua New Guinea. Zapata was to be the Texas location. The New Guinea piece played alone. Local folks figured the magazine blew its wad in PNG, shot their financial bolt, leaving nothing left for the domestic angle. But there were other reasons why they never got around to researching in Zapata.

Zapata's sidewalks roll up before dark and, as residents say, cars would rust, but there isn't enough moisture in the air. Try as you might, you won't find a cigar bar, personal trainer, or a McDonald's. Neither will you see a proliferation of cell phones or pocket pagers. No nights at the Roxbury or seven-buck martinis. No four-dollar Mocha Frappuccinos from Starbucks. (The local farmers are glad when the coffee at the Red Barn coffee shop is brewed the same day it's served.) No one's heard of tofu or sushi. Franchised convenience stores or BMW dealerships? Hardly. Zapata is so poor, people rush into Mexico to escape the crushing poverty. There is no industry, no business, no recreation, and no future. The town defined *hardscrabble.*

Zapata lies on the border with *Punta Roja,* Mexico, each town sharing a horseshoe bend of the mother river, the *Rio Grande.* The river was their front porch, toilet, bathtub, swimming pool, and kitchen sink and sometimes their graveyard. Across *el rio,* the village of *Punta Roja* stares back at Zapata, and, but for the river, would be a seamless extension of that town of 1,530 residents. A narrow bridge connects the two countries. There is a border checkpoint and immigration building on both sides of the river. Neither is occupied or manned. Vehicles and pedestrians pass unimpeded, in both directions, with impunity. The Mexicans don't care if the gringos want to spend their money on their side. For their part, the Americans have a resident border patrolman, but his perception of the job had been modified over the years. He operated in a suspended animation mode known as *in-service retirement.*

Zapata's single main street—*Calle Verdugo*—cuts the town in half on a diagonal. A circle road skirts the perimeter, creating a silent, symbolic boundary, a prison wall from which there is no real escape. The perimeter road appears as a route exiting the town, a doorway in the collective prison of Zapata. It's illusory. The road circles back on itself. Viewed from the air, the town looks like the universal sign for *no,* a circle with a slash through it. Because the main highway circumvents the town, Zapata doesn't even serve as a speed bump for the transient. Most pass without a thought of its existence.

The heat is constant and, in the summer, oppressive; but people say they're lucky. *It's a dry heat.* Zapata is essentially invisible to the rest of the world. Some people like the isolation and would do whatever is necessary to keep it that way.

BUCK Downs leaned back in his chair and hitched up the sagging Sam Browne gun belt over his tumultuous belly. The formerly black basket-weave leather was bleached white from wear and lack of care. The chrome belt buckle was corroded. His boots looked like they were polished with a melting Hershey bar, but the Ruger Super Blackhawk .44 Magnum revolver glistened from its coat of WD-40. It was a single-action piece because Buck fancied himself the spiritual heir to Wyatt Earp and Bat Masterson. He would have preferred to tie the rig's holster down, low on his leg, like he did his fast-draw leather, but he was chief of police of Zapata, and he figured he owed his constituents something.

But, it was Estaban Rios to whom he owed everything. Rios owned the whole damn town and—though he hated to admit it—he owned Buck, too; lock, stock, and barrel. Well, there were worse fates. *I could have been born a Mexican, and then where would I be?* Buck became chief by default. He owed Rios twenty thousand in gambling markers that he could never pay, and the choices were to play along or have the NRA boys come over and break him into kindling. Or that spooky bitch Rios kept around might put the mojo on him. No, that wasn't going to happen. Instead, Rios had him appointed chief. *Christ, besides me, Rios owns the alcalde and the city council—for what they're worth—and that isn't much.* Of course, Estaban didn't actually absolve him of his obligations, but he at least suspended enforcement of the lien or the alternate payment plan.

Surveying his domain from the front steps of the police station, Buck spat a chunk of wintergreen Skoal out into the street. The station was actually a storefront operation located in the former hardware store. He watched two kids argue on the sidewalk in front of the post office, which was inside Garcia's drugstore. *Gawd damn orphanage brats.* Buck would have arrested them for vagrancy, truancy, highway mopery, or murder, but it was Saturday and what the hell. No matter, the law was a wonderful thing. If you could find the section, you could do anything you wanted. In Zapata, Estaban Rios made whatever municipal ordinance he wanted. And Buck was his enforcer, although he was saddled with that Negro with the college education and the uppity attitude. Levon Butler was a thorn in his side, an inherited fixture, employed before he was appointed, and he couldn't fire him. The nigger would probably file an EEOC complaint, and the last thing Mr. Rios wants is a federal look-see down around here. Plus, there was nothing the Zapata County sheriff would like better than some excuse to obtain jurisdiction in Zapata city. Buck scratched his belly. He looked at the two boys again. *They get into the street, I'll bust 'em for impeding traffic and warn those priests they better get their shit together and quit bucking Buck and the system.* He spat again into the street and, using his tongue, released another piece of chew that had been mellowing between his lower teeth and lip.

"**HOW** many times you gonna read that thing?" Enrique "Ponce" De Leon looked at his friend.

Joey Painter sat on the curb, his dirty, bare feet in the gutter, his skinny arms hugging his spindly legs. He brushed a lock of unruly hair from his face and stared at a piece of yellow paper he held in his hand. "I don't know. I jest wanna make sure we said the right stuff, I guess." He looked at the envelope hidden behind the yellow, lined tablet paper, then set them both down on the curb. He removed a rolled-up, dog-eared magazine—*New Breed*—from his back pocket. *New Breed* was self-proclaimed as "The Professional Adventurer's Sourcebook—The Bible of Mercs, Spooks, and International Warriors."

Ponce tapped the tattered magazine. "Just check the address and make sure it's right, will you?"

Joey opened the magazine and flipped to the classified ads in the back. He found the one he was looking for and placed the envelope next to it. "It looks the same."

"Well," the older boy said, "it doesn't matter; no one is going to come."

"Yes they will. I know they will." Joey searched his pockets and displayed twenty-seven cents.

"That ain't enough. Stamps is thirty-seven cents." Ponce chewed on his gum and blew a lopsided bubble.

Joey now knew where his friend's absent contribution toward the required thirty-seven cents went. He got to his feet and brushed back his hair. He looked over at the drugstore.

"I know what you're thinking, but if Buck Downs sees you panhandling, he'll bust us for sure." Ponce blew an even larger bubble that burst over his nose.

Joey wiped his hands on his pants and handed Ponce the letter and magazine. "Hold these."

Joey marched into the drugstore and inspected the customers in line. He made his choice. " 'Scuse me, ma'am, but would you like to invest a dime in a young man's future? Please. I'll help you cross the street."

The woman looked like she had hiked all the way to Zapata from Saint Louis behind a Conestoga wagon. Her deeply lined, pioneer woman's face accented the world-weariness in her shuffle. She regarded the kid and frowned. "I live on this side of the street, and there ain't been a car pass since I've been in line."

"Please."

The woman moved forward one in line. "I normally don't cotton to street urchins begging for a stipend, but . . ." She opened her purse and fetched a dime. She put it in his hand. "Now don't y'all spend that on dope or nar-a-cotics."

Joey gave her back the dime and twenty-seven cents. "I need a stamp."

The antediluvian woman purchased a stamp at the counter

and handed it to Joey with a sigh. He thanked her and ran to Ponce, who was still sitting on the curb pulling bubble gum out of his eyebrows. "Got it."

Joey led the way to the mail receptacle on the corner.

Ponce took the stamp from Joey, swiped at it with his tongue, and stuck it to the envelope. Joey took the letter and pulled open the pivoting door. The letter disappeared inside. Joey slapped his hands together as Ponce made the sign of the cross. The two boys walked down Verdugo Street and waved to Buck Downs as they passed the police office.

"I'm smarter than you, Ponce. That stamp had its own glue. It didn't need you licking it."

"That don't make you no smarter." Ponce cuffed the younger boy with his open hand across the back of the head, friendly like.

Joey knew better. He *was* smarter. He knew they would be coming.

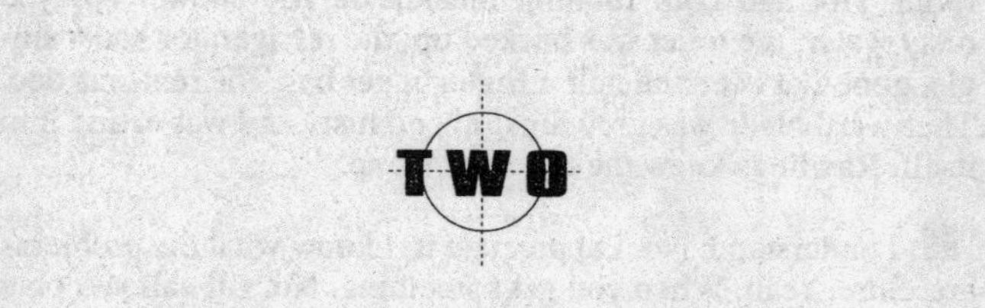

TWO

PLACA. Graffiti. It spoke of defiance. It was the Thomas Guide to the hood and the *Wall Street Journal* of the block. It was also the ultimate expression of the territorial imperative, cultural-normative sociology, and aggressive capitalism. A Hispanic kid finished the last, loving touches on his personal moniker and gang symbol on the sidewall of the welfare office and scurried off, letting the empty spray can of black Rustoleum roll into the gutter.

THE Third World.

Damn rights it was all the same. Wall-to-wall poverty. A fierce sense of "fuck you." This place was a little different, though. It had freeways. The tagger wasn't writing, Death to Israel. Free Palestine on the wall, but still, it *was* all the same. Rawlings stared out from the second-story window of his rented apartment in East Los Angeles. A low-rider Chevy cruised down the street, hydraulics making the car prance like a Clydesdale walking on hot coals. The passenger, wearing a do-rag and colors, eyeballed Rawlings and threw him a sign; maybe it was only the finger. The car's radio drowned out all other ambient sound. Ice Cube was letting the hood know, "It was a good day 'cause I didn't have to use my AK." Rawlings turned back to his room. Hot and cold running bleakness. The shower sprayed rusty water; the toilet was backed up; the refrigerator had a single, gone-flat beer and half a Butterfinger bar. The rent was due. The sword blade was growing dull and rusty and was eating into itself. Rawlings knew the time had come.

"NO. I understand. No. I appreciate it. I know what the problems are. Sure. Yeah. When you get something. No. I'll call you on a cold line. If I move, I'll fax you a PO box or a general delivery address. Forget it. You don't owe me anything. I'll be around." He dropped the telephone from his ear to his opposite hand and stared at it for a while before disconnecting.

Lon Grainger left the phone in the kitchenette, on the grimy, cigarette-burned, canary-yellow linoleum floor that looked like it had suffered the death of a thousand cuts. He moved slowly to the only other room and sat back down on the tattered, brown cloth chair. Drawn shades and dirty windows insured the motel room's half-light. He regarded the bottle of Calvert's bourbon on the floor by the door. Its open mouth and emptied interior pointed straight at him as he slumped in the chair. The television set sent attenuated flashes of light throughout the room. The Home Shopping Network offered real—no imitations or faux here—CZ tennis bracelets for $29.95 plus tax and shipping of an additional $29.95. A copy of *Soldier of Fortune* and *Gung Ho* magazines lay on the floor, partially covering the July issue of *New Breed.* Lon Grainger appeared inert, only his eyes betraying a life force within. A passing eighteen-wheeler on Long Beach's Pacific Coast Highway shook the small motel room like a 5.7 Richter scale quake. Grainger never felt it. He stared straight ahead, his mind a merciful void. The remaining numbing effect from last night's intake of blended whiskey was abandoning the vessel. He was facing another day. That's the way things were, now. . . .

After the shot they managed to make it to the street below and mingle with the crowd. Their jellabas made them feel like

Jedi knights walking alone on Tatooine among an alien community, but no one seemed to take notice. In the dark, all women are fair, all men are Arabs. Reaching the safe house, they were met by a Lebanese guide chain-smoking Gauloise cigarettes. He took them outside the city, south to the sand dunes, where the SEAL team was signaled. They were picked up an hour later and motored back to a diesel sub that surfaced to take them on board. Miles out to sea, they were picked up by helicopter and whisked to a destroyer, which took them home.

Their debriefing took place in Alexandria five days later. They continued to be held incognito, allowed no contact with anyone. Interviewed separately, Grainger told the DIA debriefing team what happened. They appeared satisfied with his role but pressed him for details on the death of Habib and Cruickshank, including times, conversations, and recognition of inconsequential minutiae that might conceal a clue. Neither he nor Rawlings bothered to volunteer any information about Cruickshank's actions and what might have been his intentions at the end. The debriefing team had been sangfroid. "Yes. We understand he shot the Lebanese guide, Habib. Yeah. Somebody sure as shit nailed Cruickshank, too. But—hey—neither one of them were our people." They would ask the CIA for a theory. (Cruickshank was CIA. That was news to Grainger.) As to the other shots . . . a shrug and a dismissal: "Like horns honking in New York City!"

It was all speculation. The DIA knew Cruickshank was a strange one who didn't like Arabs in the first place. So, who knew? It was no use alienating the CIA or pointing the finger and making baseless accusations. Cruickshank killed Habib. Someone killed Cruickshank. Period. There was no need to remind either of them that this was a matter of national security beyond top secret.

Grainger and Rawlings had been, since 1994, ostensible independent contractors, with the government being their actual employer. They had been "released," erased from the rolls of SFOD-Delta—Delta Force—in order to pursue deniability beyond deniability. Officially, they no longer existed. Uncle Sugar remained their principal employer; however, when he wasn't actually employing, he was acting as their agent and broker, farming them out to various friendly interests. Their services were richly rewarded far beyond their E-7 pay rates as Delta boys.

Six months after the Root, they were tasked with an assignment to hit Mufti Sa'ad Al-Din Al-Alami, head of the Takfir wal Hijra*—Excommunication and Flight—the most violent and prolific of the Egyptian terrorist organizations. The target was intercepted at a conference of international terrorists in Kenya. Grainger's eight hundred meter shot missed the intended and instead killed the man standing next to him, Mustafa bin Nidal, who was actually an Israeli agent from the Shayettet, on loan to AMAN. Now, a year later, they hadn't worked since. The burn notices had gone out. They were unemployable and without pensions. It was limply intimated that maybe Grainger should hang it up. At thirty-eight years old, well, maybe the eyes were going. Grainger knew it wasn't his eyes.*

Rawlings had followed him into this self-imposed exile. He had stuck by him with perseverance and dogged loyalty. But, semper fi wasn't paying the rent, and Grainger was still incapacitated, haunted—if not tormented—by the shot he had made and also by the nagging questions about that day that remained unanswered; questions that denied him quietus.

GRAINGER looked over at the Colt Mark IV Government Model .45 ACP that lay on the linoleum counter. He hoped he was only contemplating going to the shooting range. Inside the motel it was dark. Outside, there was nothing but double-parked fifteen-year-old cars and defeated people living out their lives of quiet desperation in working-class apartments where the only thing to look forward to was the possibility of a good citizenship–promoting orgasm on Saturday night and a nod from the boss on Monday morning. Grainger didn't even have those prospects.

The telephone rang. Grainger didn't look up. It rang again and once more; then the answering machine's integral electromechanical voice responded and told the caller to leave a message.

It was Rawlings. His voice sounded gravelly, distant. "Hey, Lon. It's me, amigo. You there? Pick up. Come on, man, I gotta talk to you."

Grainger focused on the noise of traffic as it blended with the sound of a Boeing 737 on final approach into the Long Beach Airport.

"Well, shit then, just listen. I got this call back yesterday from . . ." The voice paused, coughed, remembering old precautions. "Hell, you know what I'm talking about. Got the offer. It's a hard contract . . ."

Grainger stared with unfocused eyes.

"Listen. I got to do something. Even the fucking rats and the *cucarachas* are complaining there isn't enough chow here. If I don't go to work soon, I'll be going on tour with the Salvation Army. You hear me, Lon? Sorry, buddy. I can't hold on any longer." The telephone disconnected. The call light on the answering machine blinked red, arhythmically pulsing like a fading heartbeat.

Grainger heard the plea but had retreated somewhere deep down inside, where he couldn't be reached.

The mail chute on the front door clattered open with a metallic authority that jerked him erect. A piece of mail sailed through the opening and hit the floor; a final notice. A second envelope leaped through the mail slot and lofted forward, doing summersaults until it crashed on the orange shag carpet; a computer dating service flyer. A third piece burst through and fell heavily to the floor, a throwaway newspaper. *Mail carrier must be practicing or killing time.* There was a pause, a cease-fire. The brass gate slammed shut. Grainger turned his eyes slowly toward the countertop. The mail door quietly opened, but Grainger caught the movement. He turned back. A single envelope poked through the slot. Then, with the flick of a hidden wrist, the container was airborne and on a glide path headed directly for him. It floated on the currents. It had wings. Radar. It landed at his feet, one edge balanced on his bare foot. Grainger looked down at the smudged, handwritten script and the single stamp. He picked up the envelope and saw it was from P and J, somewhere in Texas. He didn't know any P and J from Texas or anywhere else. He was momentarily tempted to throw it out with the rest of the mail. Something changed his mind. He held the envelope in his hand for a moment and then opened it, the way girls do opening a Christmas gift when they want to save the paper and ribbon. He read:

Dear Mister or Misters, you are guys I hope. My name is Joey and my best friend is Ponce but his real name is Enrique. We live in Zapata with father Paul, father Leon, Brother Lemuel, Sister Felicia, Uncle Humberto and the other kids. Ponce and I were wondering and thinking that if you weren't doing anything you might come down here and help out with things. Father Paul fights all the time and gets hurt and Father Leon tries to help but we have no money to pay you right away but we are saving some promise. You said in the magazine you were looking for any wet work. It don't rain here much, but the river is real close and we wash clothes and play with the hose on Sunday sometimes. The magazine also said you deliver messages long distance or personal and that you straightened out messes. I think that is what we are looking for. I wrote this letter but Ponce says to ask you to send your financial requirements which he says are important to you.

Joey and Ponce I am 10

Grainger read the letter again and sat up in the chair. He remained motionless for a while, then edged up to his unsteady feet. He stumbled to the telephone and dialed. When it was answered, he said two words. "Let's go."

THREE

THE left-hook, right-cross combination landed hard, flinging a spray of sweat and blood into the first two rows of spectators. A woman in a black cocktail dress sprang up from her first-row seat, wiped the glistening drops from her forehead, and thrust her index finger into a black-ringed, crimson mouth, sucking and lapping her digit like it was a cherry Popsicle. The fighter was hit again and spun to his right, going down hard. He impacted the canvas like a butchered cow falling off the hook at the slaughtering yard. The woman screamed in orgasmic delight and grabbed the crotch of her companion, squeezing until he winced.

Julius "Jules" Moore looked away from the ring. He couldn't take much more of this. *I can't take much more of this? Hell, it's The Disciple, my man, that's taking it, not me!* Moore was The Disciple's manager, trainer, corner man, cut man, counselor, and confidant; everything but priest. He didn't need a priest. The crowd roared its blood lust. They were getting their money's worth tonight. The Disciple was back on his feet. Moore still couldn't look and instead stared with disgust at the fucking vampire in the black dress in the first row licking blood and sweat. *Bitch probably don't never see the light of day.* Jules turned back to the action. "Jab. Stick and move!" he exhorted. *Jab. Stick and move. Shit.*

El Tormento was written in gold letters on his black satin trunks. He had thirty-four smoker and semiprofessional fights and won a lot of them. Lost some, too. No matter. He would win tonight. His barrage of body shots thudded into The Disciple, and his opponent sagged to the floor. The referee moved in to push him to a neutral corner, but not before he got a shot in to the temple. The crowd was on its feet again and the *puta* in the front row was showing him her tits.

The Disciple pushed himself off the canvas, on all fours, weight on his gloves. His head was a kaleidoscope, a volcano of pain, a bass drum with a madman beating it with a baseball bat. He was hurt. *Three* . . . The Disciple watched the sweat drop from his forehead and pool in front of his eyes. A glob of semicoagulated blood fell free from his nose and burst on the canvas. He seemed to be able to breathe better now. *Five* . . . He saw the dancing feet of *El Tormento* bouncing up and down in front of him. True to his name. *Seven* . . . His left arm sagged a bit. *Lie down, yes. Lie down.* He raised his head and saw two sets of large eyes looking at him from what must have been the aisle. *Nine* . . . The Disciple pushed himself to his feet, staggered against the ropes, and steadied himself. The referee jogged over and held up two fingers, moving them across his face, testing for nystagmus and brain damage. He banged leather. He was okay. *You want to throw hands? We'll throw some hands.*

The referee waved the fighters on, and *El Tormento* rushed confidently toward him from the neutral corner; too confidently. A straight counter off the jab caught The Tormentor flush on the jaw, and he reeled off balance. Jules was on his feet, yelling from the corner. "Press the bastard!" A right and left cross found their mark. "Hook! Jab! Jab," Jules cried out, almost hysterical. "Pound 'im. Don't lose the initiative." An uppercut was followed by two thudding body shots.

The Tormentor's mouthpiece dislodged, flying away from a

thundering hook. He was hurt, wildly looking for the bell to save him.

No mercy. Nothing can save you.

The Tormentor's hands dropped lower, and a double jab–right cross put him on his knees. *El Tormento* gazed out at the audience. The *mujer* in black was no longer smiling at him. He slumped to the canvas and rolled to his back, watching the lights above him orbit in sync to the noises in his head while the man in stripes waved and pointed at him. Then the lights went out.

"GREAT fucking fight." An excited fight fan shouted into the locker room at The Disciple, who sat on the edge of an ancient wooden table with his fighter's factotum, Jules, at his side.

An immense hand pulled the fight fan unceremoniously back from the door, and a low voice told him to *vamanos*. A middle-aged Caucasian in a white suit and a matching fedora pushed through the door. A Latin bodyguard who resembled the WWE's Undertaker shadowed him. The man in white lit a cigar. "They had you at ten to three to go down hard before the third round. You kicked some major ass out there. You're a real crowd pleaser. I can book you again in two weeks to fight Johnny Manteca, *El Peleador del Toro.*"

Jules cut the wraps from his fighter's hands. "Maybe later, Clarence. We'll think about it. Get back to you mañana."

Clarence removed a thick, flash wad from his pocket and peeled off ten one hundred dollar bills. He slapped them down on the table. "Easy money."

Jules looked at the cash. He kept cutting the tape. "It's money, but it ain't easy."

"Yeah. Well, you two put your heads together and let me know real soon. Gotta book this thing pronto." Clarence wheeled to leave, then looked back. He took his cigar out of his mouth and pointed it at The Disciple. "Yeah, one hell of a fight." He jerked his head at The Undertaker. "Rodrigo. Say good-bye to *El Cura*."

Rodrigo dipped his head briefly toward The Disciple. *"Adios, Padre."* The locker room door swung shut behind him.

Julius threw the last of the adhesive tape into a trash can and looked at the battered face of his main man, *El Cura,* "The one who heals." He almost forgot. *El hombre con manos de piedras* was a priest.

"OH, Lordy, Lordy. We have been summoned once again to free the oppressed and stomp the shit out of the grapes of wrath." Rawlings leaned back in his seat. The wind blew noisily through the Dodge Coronet convertible. It made the same whistling racket with the top up or down and, since it was one hundred degrees in Tucson and the air conditioner didn't work, the top was down. They had purchased the car from Cal Worthington off his lot in Long Beach "as is," with their rapidly dwindling cash, but got it at what it was really worth when Rawlings pointed out to the salesman that the speedometer had been set back. Not that Cal had anything to do with it.

Grainger was driving but not much else. Rawlings punched him lightly in the arm. "Tell me one more time, buddy. One hundred thousand dollars for a couple weeks' work, and all from a forty-dollar ad in a merc magazine? Now, *that's* value." Rawlings tilted his head out the window and shouted a long, warbling "Whoooooeeeee" that was drowned out by the rush of oncoming air.

Grainger didn't respond. He couldn't. The truth was coming, and it wasn't going to set anybody free. He didn't think his partner really expected an answer. Rawlings thought he knew what the story was, and he just liked savoring it. Grainger pushed the wing vent wide open and let the hot air ripple his army-brown cotton T-shirt. *The fabric of our lives: Kevlar. Ballistic nylon. Spun ceramic.* Those were the fabrics of life.

He realized he would have to pay the piper soon, but he would deal with that when the time came. He settled back and watched the poles of the endless barbed wire fences flash by in hypnotic monotony. He was back. But there was always a beginning. . . .

For Lonnie Delbert Grainger, that beginning came in Miles City, Montana, where his dad raised Poland China hogs for a living and supplemented his income as an antelope hunting guide during the season to help feed the family. Lonnie remem-

bered his dad being interviewed once by a female reporter from a television station in Laramie. She was doing a serial piece on the American farm family. She had asked his dad what he would do—"hypothetically"—if someone gave him a million dollars. His dad excused himself and spat his chew behind him and answered, "Jest keep on farming till the money ran out." That pretty well summed it up for Lonnie, who saw no future in hogs.

After high school, the family agreed that his brother Jeff showed a lot more potential yelling "Sue-e, sue-e" after the hogs than he. The farm was going to be his brother's. No problem. Lonnie preferred antelope hunting. He accompanied his dad whenever allowed and soon became uncannily adept at concealment and stalking the wary beasts. More. He discovered a latent—perhaps inherent—skill. He could shoot a rifle. Not just shoot. Any fool could pull a trigger. His skill was consummate. Young Lonnie could hit a target with a 250–3000 Savage Model 99 lever action mounting full buckhorn sights farther out than most men could with a .270 glassed with six-power optics; better than the hunters guided by his father who were armed with exotic pieces chambered for belted magnum calibers like the 7 mm Remington, the .257 Weatherby, or the .264 Winchester Mag. He collected many a trophy buck for city-bred hunters who paid him to make that shot on a wise old trophy animal who wouldn't allow you to get within seven hundred yards of him. By the time he was seventeen, his blood pressure was measured in feet per second, and his trigger finger tingled within fifty feet of an accurized rifle. He even sweated Hoppes Number 9. Lonnie was a rifleman. He was a hunter.

His father was not a hunter. Not that he had anything against killing game animals. But one thing he wouldn't tolerate was a lack of respect for the game. Lonnie remembered how one time a New York stockbroker and his pal came out wanting to shoot a trophy buck. Opening day they were sound asleep in their motel when Harold and Lonnie came to get them. It was seven-thirty before they even left the room and nine o'clock before leaving the restaurant. Well, they were paying. Harold Grainger transported them west of town to the plains hunting area. The stock-

brokers groused about having to walk. They opened a case of beer, loaded their rifles, and had an accidental discharge before they left the Jeep. It was going to be a long day.

Near three o'clock, Harold spotted a herd of animals grazing along a slope across the expanses from their grassy hillock. There was a big, double-pronged buck leading the herd. Too far to shoot, his dad had told them. They laughed at him and told him to quit worrying; Dominick was a regular deadeye dick. Over Harold's protestations, Dom laid down on his Banana Republic safari jacket and cranked off a round. The distance was later paced at 615 yards. The .308 Norma Magnum round managed to hit the antelope in the flank and cripple it. Dom got up from the prone, took another gulp of beer, and said, "Told ya."

They walked to the fallen animal. It was dragging its haunches around, leaving a bloody circle of meat and blood. Dom and his pal stood around and laughed. Dom poked the dying animal with the muzzle of his rifle. Harold Grainger dispatched the buck with a single bullet to the brain. He then put the barrel of his Colt Python .357 against Dom's head and told him and his friend to drop their rifles and strip off their clothes. They thought he was kidding until he blew a hole in the ground at Dom's feet. After stripping them, he made them paint each other with the blood of the animal. He then smashed their inlaid-stock rifles against each other, bending the barrels, twisting the receivers, and pitching the machine-turned, jeweled bolts out onto the prairie. Dom said he was going to pay for this, but Harold calmly told him he had already paid.

Sitting naked in the waning October sun, Dom and Phil received the word. They were vermin, maggots intruding upon a noble world. The antelope existed and could be hunted and killed but deserved respect. They had no comprehension of respect, or of what life meant or death entailed. They were never to return, he told them. If they did, he would kill them. Lonnie believed he was serious. It was a six-mile walk to the road and then another two to the country store where they could telephone the sheriff if they wanted. He tore up their antelope tags. "You don't deserve to tag him." He also broke the horns off the animal. It was no longer a trophy. And that was it. Lonnie fol-

lowed his father out, leaving the stockbroker and his pal sitting in the dirt beside the antelope.

They never heard from the dudes again. A month later, Lonnie hiked back out to the site. The carcass was still there. A lone crow stood vigil over it and pecked at the worms that gathered to feast. There was nothing else. Three months later, while setting some irrigation pipe, his dad died of a heart attack, short of his three score and ten biblical allowance. Jeff took over running the farm. Lonnie's mother said it was just fate, and that he shouldn't feel bad about leaving her and the farm. "We're all just playing out God's destiny," she said. Things were preordained. He left for the army the following summer, never to hunt antelope again.

Lonnie enlisted for the U.S. Army Airborne. He completed basic training at Fort Leonard Wood ("Lost in the Woods"), Missouri. After advanced individual training at Fort Polk, Louisiana, he was sent to the three-week airborne course at Fort Benning, Georgia. Completing jump school, he was assigned to "America's Guard of Honor," the Eighty-Second Airborne Division, as a fledgling paratrooper, derisively referred to as a five-jump chump. *A year later he was initiated into the combat fraternity in Panama and later the Mideast, battling Saddam Hussein's Republican Guard. Returning from the Gulf War, he volunteered for the Rangers. After acceptance, he reported to Fort Stewart, Georgia, home of the Second Ranger Battalion. After being vetted and completing RIP, he was assigned to the Ranger Course at Fort Benning's Infantry School—with its adjunct field trials in the Blue Ridge Mountains around Delonega, the swamps and glades in and around Eglin AFB, Florida, and the deserts surrounding Fort Bliss, Texas. Upon the completion of Ranger School, he was meritoriously promoted to Sergeant E-5.*

Grainger's range scores caught the eye of his company commander, and he was selected to attend the Army Sniper School at Fort Benning. He graduated first in his class with a range record and field techniques scores that most said would never be equaled, let alone broken. A year later he volunteered for Special Forces and was accepted for training. Assigned to the basic Q-Course at Fort Bragg, North Carolina, he met Myles Rawlings, who had come directly to SF from the 101st Air Assault

Division, from that unit's Pathfinder Detachment. Rawlings, a streetwise tough kid from San Pedro, California, and Grainger, the hog farmer's son from Miles City, Montana, had come together in symbiosis.

"**FUCKING** A. Look at that will you? Old Burma Shave signs. You can only see these things in Arizona and Texas."

Rawlings's voice brought him to the moment as the last of the faded red-and-white signs whipped by them. He slowed down and pulled over to the side of the road. It was Rawlings's turn to drive.

THE campesino was up and running now for the large boulder that afforded some protection. He dove for the boulder and rolled to his side, coming up with his back against the blistering hot rock. He wore no shirt. It was part of the rules: *Pantalones. Zapatos. No çamisa.* Pedro Martin Morales's breath came labored as he peered over the top of the rock. He saw the numbered red stake one hundred meters across the open expanse to the gully. He looked at the sun. The first bullet had come close, but they had not gotten him. *Only one more stake to go.* It was time. He kissed the crucifix that dangled around his neck on a shoelace. Then he was up and sprinting, bent low, dodging over basketball-sized rocks with sharp edges. *Fifty meters to go.* Sweat poured into his eyes. *Thirty meters. La estaca.* He kicked hard for the stake. Ten meters from the marker, Pedro turned sideways and looked back at something unseen. His chest evacuated, and his backbone blew out as the 180-grain Nosler H-Partition projectile fired from a 7.82 mm Warbird Magnum chambered rifle passed through his sinewy body. An angry, rumbling growl crawled across the broken field. Pedro Morales had made it to the red stake.

THE man at the bench on the elevated shooting platform worked the bolt on the Lazzeroni-Sako TRG-S rifle and slowly ejected the empty cartridge from the smoking chamber. He caught the brass case in his hand and examined it methodically, turning it over, kneading it, feeling the heat generated by the fifty thousand PSI ignition.

The atmosphere on the hill was part carnival, part funereal. Not blended. Bifurcated. Eleven human beings occupied the hilltop from where the killing shot was made. The king of the hill was Estaban Rios, but even he stood respectfully behind *el tirador*—the shooter—who, ostensibly, was his. With Estaban was his brother, Raoul, a man with porcelain skin, pouty lips, and manicured hands. The snap judgment was that he was effusively feminine. But a second look mocked that impression and insured he would never convincingly be described as effete. His eyes burned like coal on fire. Zapata's police chief, a frequent guest of The Game, as it was called, also looked on. To Buck's right, three men stood together: Tong Nguyen, Nero Ramirez, and Bando Allcott. They were known collectively as the NRA. *Tiradores.* They were the trigger fingers of the king, eternal winter, and poster boys for men behaving badly. The last was bored, the first was fascinated, and Ramirez thought they were both *muy loco.*

The two women stood off—separately—watching nothing and seeing everything. One was Rosa Fuentes, Estaban's old serving woman, who never spoke. The other was Sonja Ochoa, a Santeria priestess, known as a santera. She was a Creole Druidess. And each man on that hill knew for certain she could see the dark side of the moon, the other half of a one-eyed jack, and inside every one of their tarnished souls and blackened hearts.

After a decent interval, Estaban came forward and placed his hand on the shooter's shoulder. "Well done, my friend. Well done indeed. Such precision at such range, deflection, wind, motion . . . magnificent."

Another man wearing thousand dollar Tony Lama crocodile boots and a white Stetson wasn't as impressed. "Horseshit."

Estaban eased around. *"Perdón?"*

Big John Hill, a Texas millionaire auto dealer from Houston, snorted. "You heard me plain enough. I said horseshit. H-O-R-S-E-S-H-I-T. Regular American English, *sabe?*"

Estaban Rios placed his hands together, fingertips touching in an imperial pyramid. "There is a problem, señor?"

No one fucked with Big John. Big John was *big*. Maybe not six foot six, but most definitely 245. He practically owned Corpus Christi and employed half the wetbacks in town washing cars at his ten statewide used car lots and two Caribbean export locations. He had invested big buckaroos in his shooter, J.R. "Junior" Carter, a recently discharged lance coolie from Uncle Sam's misguided children. The lad sported a whitewall haircut and had flashed his credentials, a DD-214 discharge form with an entry noting duty with a STA platoon, surveillance and target acquisition. That was then. Hill looked over at his investment. *He's supposed to be the best around, and the fucking kid blows a shot that couldn't have been more than seven hundred fucking yards. So the greaser was moving. BFD. Son of a a bitch if there isn't fifty big ones on the line.* Big John looked over at a grim, dejected kid in a camouflage uniform, holding his Remington in one hand and his Johnson in the other. *Fuck.* "You're Goddamn straight there's a problem . . . *sen-yoooor.*"

"And what might that be?"

Big John's finger jerked to a stop at the end of his thrusting arm that pointed down across the range. "That slippery punk of a runner never showed himself whole to my boy, forcing him to take a shot at a partial torso only."

"Yeah. Less than an E silhouette," muttered a dejected Junior Carter.

Estaban fronted a smile while suppressing a mirthless laugh. "That is most unfortunate. The fortunes of—shall we say—gaming? It is difficult to predict with any—"

"Fuck a bunch of prediction, hombre. I want my money back."

Rios raised an eyebrow. "Señor, if you insist, but I must warn you—"

"Yeah, well I fucking insist."

"My refunds are never in silver . . ."

The shooter's name was Montezuma, and he fired the 7.82 mm Warbird Magnum casually from his lap. The round took off the upper part of Big John Hill's left ear and creased his temple. The severed portion of the ear fell at his feet. Big John's eyes were Biafra big.

Rios looked at the ear. ". . . only in lead."

Big John Hill's teeth rattled against each other, and urine seeped down his leg into his croc boots. *Where are the police? Christ, there's a cop right there looking at me, grinning.* Big John backed away, clasping his bleeding, cropped ear. He didn't really want a refund. He was just joshing and goofing a little.

Junior Carter trotted after Hill. *What the fuck did he want from me, anyway, a guarantee?*

A man with slits for eyes and sideburns that melted into a mustache covering most of his mouth strolled to the savaged ear and picked it up. Nero Ramirez waved it at the retreating pair. "Señor. You forgot your ear."

Estaban Rios mounted the elevated shooting platform next to Montezuma and looked out across the shooting range. He breathed deeply several times and swung his arms. Caesar turned to the Senate. "A man who cannot lose with dignity and humility should not play. No?" He turned to his brother. "Raoul. Have the runner buried by the red stake. Let it be his headstone. See to it that his widow receives the forty thousand pesos, as agreed, and remove his daughter from the brothel." Estaban smiled. He could afford to be magnanimous. With the devalued peso, it was still a bargain. Estaban knew that, if nothing else, he was a fair man, a man who controlled the entire known world. Then Rios became aware of the priestess looking at him, and he was again reminded that all power has its source and sustenance. And its limitations.

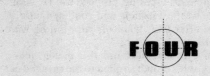

FOUR

ZAPATA. Even Larry McMurtry didn't know it existed. The main drag was paved, not that you'd notice. A layer of dirt covered Verdugo Street. The city limits sign slumped sideways on its corroded pole, held by only one rivet.

Grainger stopped the car in front of the sign. His watch indicated high noon.

Rawlings had to turn his head sideways to read the faded lettering on the rusted metal. He leaned over and looked at the odometer. *One thousand five hundred and seventy point one miles from Long Beach to this? And "this" doesn't look like much.*

Grainger eased out the worn clutch and the Coronet lurched forward. The town seemed deserted. The population appeared to have fled, leaving behind a few parked cars, a mongrel dog lying in the shade, and a battered wheelbarrow standing forlornly against a broken, sun-bleached wood fence. Except for the dog, it was a ghost town.

Rawlings's head and eyes rotated like a gun turret. "This? This is it? What is this, Lon, Sleepy Hollow? Somebody has action in this burg?"

The Dodge moved slowly past Garcia's drugstore. Grainger noted it served as the Greyhound depot. The town post office was also inside. He would remember to send a general delivery address to Stoneman. The police office was across the street. A black officer watched from the steps as they drove by, his eyes interrogating them. Somebody was moving down the sidewalk. Grainger stopped the car.

Rawlings leaned out and waved. "Hey, partner. Where can a man get some fire water around here; something to cut the trail dust?"

The man in overalls and denim shirt appeared comfortable in the ninety-five-degree heat. He stopped and slid his gnarled hands into his pockets. "No place in Zapata, mister. It's a dry town. Real dry. Nearest watering hole is El Boondocks, out of town a piece, in the county. Maybe try the small carnival set up on the edge of town, straight ahead. They serve beer, I hear." He moved on without waiting for any follow-up inquiry. He said his piece, exhausted his word allocation for the day.

Rawlings called after him. "Yeah, thanks, Pops." The man was probably not much older than his thirty-six years. He *seemed* older.

They found the hotel—the Casita Zapata—more a ramshackle boardinghouse. The weather-beaten, two-story building shared tenancy with a general store below. Its four rooms rated a half-star on the Triple-A scale. The stairs were in the back, and the desk register was above the feed scale. Credit cards were not accepted, and cash was in advance. *Perfect. Viva Zapata, 78076.*

They unloaded the car and carried everything up to the room, passing a man and two giggling women, who were coming down the stairs. It was the only sign of life around. There appeared to be no other guests. The room had two dingy windows facing the street. Grainger saw potential.

Rawlings saw nothing. "You sure you got the right intel on this place, partner? It looks bankrupt; unless it's like that town in that Bruce Willis flick, *Last Man Standing*." He sat down on one of the twin beds. Dust rose and settled. "I'm going to take a shower and then lather up a second time at that Boondocks slop chute. You wanna go?"

Grainger turned from his surveillance of the street. "No, you go ahead and knock yourself out. Check it out for us. Take the car. I'm going to walk around and recon a bit."

Rawlings bounded up from the bed. "I guess we'll make contact with the employer tomorrow, huh?"

Grainger nodded. "I guess we will."

Rawlings stretched and headed for the door.

"I thought you were going to shower first?"

Rawlings looked back. "I am, but first I'm going down to scold the concierge. I asked for a room with twin kings and a bidet."

IT was a small carnival with small rides, except for the Ferris wheel, which dominated what passed for a midway. Sawdust had been scattered to hold down the dust and dirt. The dust and dirt were winning. The place smelled of diesel, hot engine oil, and burning grease from the hamburger stand, all mixed with the acrid fumes of popcorn left too long in the hopper. The barkers and ride operators were bored. They beckoned listlessly to the few people who walked up and down the single walkway, mostly the curious with no money to spend on entertainment.

Grainger sipped on a flat beer in a Coke cup. At least it was cold. He heard the shots and for a split second he was somewhere else. He crouched down instinctually, before realizing the shots were coming from the shooting gallery, a little arcade. The sounds weren't suppressed .30 caliber weapons, but .22 Rimfires shooting CB caps, also known as gallery shorts. He drifted in that direction, compelled to investigate, but unsure why.

SLOANE Nadine McKenzie said no again, but this time she added, "I'm sorry." It killed her to say no to these kids. There were six of them who looked at her, all with large eyes that seemed to say it was okay, they really understood. *Maybe I'll go home and watch* Ordinary People *and then slit my wrists.* She looked across the counter to the overhead rack where the teddy bears, bunnies, and dinosaur Barneys looked down on them. She had watched four would-be sharpshooters plunk down their money into the grimy hands of the grinning carny. All had come up empty. Nada. Zip. She knew there was just no way.

The greasy, massive hulk behind the counter blew a ring of smoke from his green cigar and leaned over the counter, inclining toward her, tugging at his crotch. "Hey there, pretty woman. How 'bout pulling the trigger on one of my guns?"

Sloane looked straight through him, ignoring the innuendo. "No. Not today."

The kids lined up behind her, staring at the stuffed animals. They didn't have to speak for her to know what they were thinking. Sloane searched her purse and found the remaining twelve carnival tickets. Enough for the carousel and maybe a snow cone.

"Come on sweetheart, I'll spot you a buck." The carny rubbed the stubble on his grizzled chin.

A child took Sloane's hand. She looked down at the angelic face, filled with hope and expectation. *Still not destroyed by reality.* She breathed out and reopened her purse, looking for some money. She had to do something; make an effort.

"Mind if I try?"

Sloane turned around and stared at the stranger in the jeans and the khaki cotton-canvas shirt. *Dirty-blond hair, kind of messy, six feet, clean fingernails, small scar on his cheek. No farmer, no auto mechanic, and definitely not from around here.* "It's a free country, mister."

Grainger stepped up to the counter where the rifles were laid out, chained to pedestals.

The carny's name was Firpo, and he was irritable over being interrupted during his seduction. *This guy thinks he's some kind of knight on a rescue mission. Fuck him. I'll drain this asshole's wallet dry.* "So, what's it gonna be, hotshot?"

Grainger turned around and leaned against the counter. He counted six children. He took a twenty-dollar bill from his shirt pocket and laid it down in front of the arcade operator and raised six fingers.

"Six times, with a couple bucks' change. You got it, sport." The carny loaded the first rifle, whistling off key and grinning stupidly to himself. He dropped the rifle on the counter in front of Grainger. "Show the lady what you don't got." He sucked in some phlegm and swallowed.

Grainger ran his hand down the length of the rifle, touching the front sight. There, he applied hard sideways pressure with his thumb.

The carny's eyes narrowed as he blew a cloud of smoke toward Grainger.

Sloan stared. The kids watched, fascinated.

"For the big pink teddy bear?" said Grainger.

The carny snorted, flashing yellowed, nineteenth-century dental work. "The last row of ducks, Sergeant York."

Grainger eased the rifle into his shoulder and leaned lightly into the wood: stock weld, breath control, and trigger squeeze. *Crack. Crack. Crack.*

Down range, the row of ducks disappeared, one by one, to the accompaniment of the rhythmic single shots that rang out. The carny spat out his cigar and unfolded his arms.

"For the large blue rabbit?"

"The lollipop sticks."

Grainger fired the next loaded rifle until there were no more lollipop sticks. One shot. One stick. "The jolly green frog?"

The carny jettisoned his arrogance and passed so quickly through apprehension he didn't realize he was now greeting desperation. "Now, wait a fucking minute . . ." He threw Grainger's twenty-dollar bill on the counter.

Grainger raised his head, his eyes lasering the carny. "I said, 'The jolly green frog?' "

The carny swallowed hard and blinked. He had never seen a look like that before. He was used to intimidating people. Now this stranger was making his knees wobble. "The sailboats," he managed to croak.

The sailboats were torpedoed, one by one. Then there were no survivors among the pinstriped suits with tommy guns, and the steel pop bottles all in a row fared no better, nor did the little tanks.

Grainger laid the last rifle down and brushed the empty brass from the counter.

The carny used a pole to bring down the animals from their perch. Then he closed up shop before Grainger could tell him his rifles needed maintenance. The front sight blades were slightly bent.

Grainger handed each kid a bear or bunny. One got Barney. There were no arguments. The kids hugged the animals as he faced the woman on the midway.

"That was some shooting. Who taught you?" she asked.

"No one, I guess. Just one day you discover yourself."

She considered the cryptic response for a moment. "Some discovery. Look . . . the kids all thank you." She turned to the children. "Don't you, kids?"

There was a chorus of thank yous and a couple *gracias.*

Sloane turned back. "And I thank you. They're from a church orphanage. I'm the nurse there." She studied the stranger and then asked what she already knew. "You're not from around here, are you?"

"No," he said.

"Passing through?"

"Maybe. I don't know yet."

"You don't know what it meant to these kids, but—"

"Could be you don't know what it meant to me. Maybe I'll see you again."

Sloane gathered the six little ones around her like a shepherdess. "No. I don't think so."

He watched them disappear, turning a corner at the end of the sawdust.

THE current of the river washed the sand away from his bare feet, burying them deeper in the water. Father Paul Teasdale stood in the middle of the great river, on an alluvial fan of sand formed by a curve of the land upriver. His body agonized. He had to kneel down to splash water onto his face. One eye was closed, and he had a gash on his forehead that burned when the water washed across it. He could have taken the pedestrian bridge, but he preferred to wade across. The Rio Grande didn't part for him, but it accepted him. Paul got up, his clothing dripping. The fresh breeze cooled him and had a baptismal effect. Paul moved one foot in front of the other, sloshing the shallow water, heading back to Zapata.

Ponce and Joey followed the priest at a respectful distance. They had waded across the river and crept into the warehouse where the fights took place every three to four weeks. Father Paul had forbidden them to watch, but they always went. Father Paul never mentioned it until the next time when he'd just say again he didn't want to see them across the river.

ON the American side, the border patrolman sat on an overturned bucket studying the river. He had surveilled *el Rio Grande* forever. He was a passive, distant observer, watching the priest wade across to the Mexican side to only wade back again, broken. He knew about the fights, held practically every month, and of the man called The Disciple. He was going to write a book someday about what he had seen while watching on the river. But the border patrolman wondered; maybe it was the river doing the watching.

THE woman's voice was silky and sultry with a slight accent. Her breathing was just right, and he could sense whenever she licked her lips, took a breath, or touched her hair. He imagined she looked like Catherine Zeta-Jones.

"I just can't say no. I hope you understand. You're a man and can appreciate my dilemma."

Yes, I am a man. He closed his eyes in the dark. "Of course I understand, my child; go on please."

The woman uncrossed her legs and leaned forward. Her face came partially out of the shadows. "I just want to give myself to any man who shows interest in me. Do you think it's because my father wouldn't hold me on his lap when I was a baby?"

"That is always a possibility, but do go on."

"I bought a pink peignoir which, by the way, I'm wearing under my dress right now; but you don't want to hear about that." The voice was now a purr.

"Yes I do. I mean, of course. It is all part of the sordidness you must release, the demons that must be exorcised."

"I am a lustful slut and so ashamed about feeling so good. I have freshly sinned, coming directly to you from the Casita Zapata, where not an hour ago Monica Williams, Harvey Sparks, and me were locked—all together—in the most unspeakable sexual embraces you couldn't possibly ever imagine. Such bizarre and wicked variety, and there I was. You probably can still smell the froth of our frolic on me even as I speak to you, Father."

Father Leon Arnulfo Ortega inhaled deeply. She was absolutely right about the smell but wrong about his inability to imagine. He stopped himself. *He* was starting to feel ashamed.

Her cooing voice brought him back. He leaned against the confessional partition, eyes crossed, black hair glistening with sweat at the tips.

"Do you want me to continue, Father? There's a lot more. Or I can save it for next week."

Father Leon bit his lip and looked down at his lap.

"Father? Is there to be penance?"

"Penance? Yes, of course, penance. Say a couple Our Fathers—that would be the Lord's Prayer—and remember not to recite it the Protestant way. Add three Hail Marys, and light a candle with an offering. Then go home and take a shower." He heard her reciting her exit lines in a low murmur like she was auditioning for *Lolita* instead of asking for forgiveness. He leaned back again and heard the penitent's curtain open and then close. He would have let her continue, but the recorder on his lap said he was out of tape. The scent of her recent engagement lingered. *Madre Dios*. He was bathed in sweat.

Father Leon Ortega needed to stretch and check to see if there were any more confessors waiting for absolution. He exited the rear of the confessional and peered around the corner. The "on-deck circle," as he liked to refer to it, was empty. He breathed a sigh of relief and clutched his latest addition to his collection. Then he heard voices, and one of them was Father

Paul's. He also recognized the other. Leon ducked back into the safety of his cave.

"Your face looks horrible, Father Paul. I find it incomprehensible that you failed to catch a baseball and it hit your face. It must have bounced back and hit you four times." Bishop Cornell Pike was head prelate of the archdiocese.

Father Paul Teasdale hated all lies, whether of commission or omission, even those in service of a worthy cause. Compromise with the truth was the root of all evil.

Bishop Pike lit a cigar and inhaled deeply, followed by a billowing dissipation. "I think it's very important for you to keep in mind that whatever the current sermon, the Church will always be the vicar." He regarded his cigar with great affection. "Cuban, not Cuban seed. These are imported for me. They are one of my weaknesses."

"Yes, Excellency, one of your weaknesses."

Bishop Pike stopped in the aisle, opposite the confessional. He ran his pudgy fingers through his thinning hair. "I detect your disapproval in every word and gesture, Father, and your sarcasm is noted. But allow me to be brutally honest. The Council of Bishops is extremely disappointed with you and Leon. You generate no revenue for Houston or Rome. Your church looks like a war zone. The worst part is you are about to lose the parish to foreclosure—"

"I know, Excellency. We are trying. The children—"

Leon shrank deeper into the recesses of the confessional.

Bishop Pike waved off the continuation of response from Father Paul Teasdale. "Of course, Father Paul, the children. *Toujours les enfants;* but think of your career. The Holy Mother Church is eternal, but no-load mutual funds and municipal bonds are now yielding seven percent, according to Solomon-Smith-Barney. It's a business, my son. Think of it that way; it will give you some perspective. We must stay on top. We must grow; publish or perish, so to speak. And you're not helping." He punctuated each word with a jab of his cigar aimed at Father Paul. Pike took another long drag on his cigar. He released the smoke. "A Cohiba Robusto. Quite indulgent, no?"

Father Paul's jaw tightened. "We are oriented toward fighting injustice as well as saving souls, Excellency."

"Yes, yes, of course. But I am here to—let's be generous—counsel you. Take this not as a warning but rather as a word to the wise. Get back to doctrinaire redemption theology; but do it with style, Father. Whatever you do, abandon—or at least deemphasize—this revolutionary, secular involvement with politics and class. These are subversive notions that cry out for inquisition. My God man, you aren't a Marxist, are you?"

"No. Nor are we Liberationists. We only want to change the local status quo. We only wish to promote justice, preserve dignity, independence, and peace; but there are monsters loose here."

Bishop Pike leaned against a pew. "I see no monsters. I see only a new medical clinic."

"Sometimes monsters tithe to conceal themselves. They can be invisible or in other shapes."

"No matter, Father Paul. If monsters wish to tithe or be otherwise charitable, why shouldn't you be gracious and accept? For the children, of course."

Paul focused on the silver crucifix dangling from the bishop's neck. " 'A little that a righteous man hath is better than the riches—' "

" ' . . . Of the wicked.' Matthew 7:12. Father, we all learned that passage. Riddles, scripture, allegory . . . We must not be so . . . literal. Perhaps you are right, but no matter. Change is mandated. Since Vatican II, the Catholic liturgy is different; think of it more like a Wal-Mart employee's rally, a Marriage Encounter, the Oprah show. Have you seen it?" He fingered the dust on a pew. "No, of course not. No matter. People must be made to feel good about contributing to the Church, made to realize they are insuring their ultimate salvation. Stop talking about Hell and demons incarnate and rather emphasize separateness. It might go a long way toward preserving your parish." He paused, and his tongue flicked a piece of tobacco from his lip. "And it would stifle all this talk in Houston about recall." Bishop Pike stopped and looked around. "Where is Leon? I have missed him again."

In his shrouded cubicle, Father Leon Ortega cringed. He did not wish to see Bishop Pike. *Let Father Paul fence with him.*

Pike refocused on Teasdale, fixing him with a solemn face. "These are trying times for the Holy Mother Church. The pedophilia scandals have drained our coffers. It is incumbent upon all of us to fill the void." He touched his face lightly with his fingertips. "From the pulpit, or as you raise the chalice, tell your congregation that industry is their salvation, the answer to their earthly melancholy. Work shall set them free."

"I believe Hitler was the one who said that, Excellency," said Father Paul.

Bishop Pike looked at the ceiling and at the cobwebs clinging there. "No matter, Father. Respond to wisdom from any source."

"When the peon and campesino, the ranchero and *jimadores* ask how much to give from all their increased industry, what shall I tell them, Excellency?"

Bishop Pike pushed off the pew and came back to full posture. He took Father Paul by the upper arm firmly and squeezed him affectionately. "Ah, yes. What to tell the canaille . . ." Pike released the pressure and smiled beatifically. He wheeled around and strolled toward the exit. At the double doors he paused and looked back. " 'More,' Father Paul. Tell them, 'More.' " The doors of the church closed behind him.

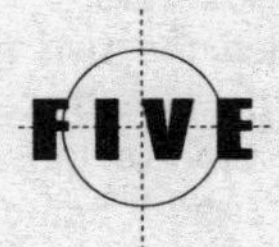

FIVE

RAWLINGS watched from the foot of the church steps as the balding man in the scarlet robe descended regally. The regal one passed without acknowledgment, placing a tasseled hat squarely on his head as he entered a chauffeured black Imperial parked at the curb. *Got the car right.*

Lon Grainger knew the moment of reckoning was drawing nigh. Soon—very soon—his partner would know that it had all been a deception . . . *perpetrated for what?* Grainger was at a loss to explain why he had chosen to involve Rawlings in something that was nothing but his feeble, grasping-at-straws attempt at salvation. He understood his own operative psychology, but it was selfish and unconscionable to drag Rawlings into this charade when the man believed this was going to result in a hard contract.

"Great cover. Jesus, I mean a church! It looks real, too. Total James Bond; class with a touch of pure, absolute genius. Who would ever think?" He turned and slapped Grainger on the back. "I owe you, buddy."

Yeah, you owe me, buddy, but not in the way you think now.

The two men mounted the steps and entered the church.

There was the faint smell of some kind of incense in the air. They walked past the foyer and peered into the vestibule. Two parishioners knelt in prayer.

Rawlings put his fingers into the holy water receptacle and tasted the water. "Potable," he said.

Father Leon approached the two men with apprehension. They did not appear to be the type that attended church. Neither did they appear to be the kind of individual who might be repentant. Leon hated this. Then it came to him. They had to be here answering the note he had pinned up on the bulletin board at Garcia's, offering food and pocket money in exchange for help around the church. *Of course, that's it. Relax.*

Grainger watched the priest approach. He appeared to be getting progressively slower the closer he came.

Rawlings nudged Grainger. "Don't this beat all. Security in priest fatigues. Look at that bulge under his left arm. I can spot an Uzi in a shoulder rig a mile away."

Leon was near now. The tape recorder under his vestment was getting slippery, pinned to his side by the pressure of his arm. *I should have removed it.* He cleared his throat. "May I help you, gentlemen? You're here about the job?"

Right out in the open and to the point. Rawlings liked that. "You bet we are."

Father Leon gestured behind him. "Please wait in the pews. Father Paul and I will be with you in a moment. No need to genuflect, unless you are Catholic."

Rawlings looked at Grainger and shrugged. Then both men sat in the last pew.

Rawlings nudged his partner. "Laying it on a bit melodramatic, isn't he?"

Grainger wanted to tell him. He wanted to say, "Let's just get back into the car and head . . ." He realized they had nowhere to head. So he remained silent.

A nun walked by and smiled at them. A man in the brown cloth robe of a brother walked beside her. He nodded to them as they passed. Across the church a Hispanic man in his fifties swept the floor, never looking up. The priest who had greeted them returned.

Leon beckoned to them. "Please come with me."

They entered the rectory to see a man in priest's garb lighting a candle with a pole lighter. He turned around. "I am so pleased you could come . . . that you had the courage to come. I have not seen you around here before. You are new . . . ?"

Rawlings looked at the man's face. It looked like he had the mumps and a poltergeist did a tap dance on his forehead. *Either they were training hard or were playing some major Rugby.* He stepped forward and extended his hand. "Yeah. We came as soon as we—Lon actually—got the letter."

Father Paul hesitantly took Rawlings's hand and let his be shaken by the other. "The letter . . . ?"

"Yeah. You know, from *New Breed.*"

"Well, actually we *are* seeking the employment you are offering," said Grainger.

Rawlings took a step closer. "Can we inquire what the op is about? You know, in general terms, what it entails. Details can come later at the brief, but we'd like to get a glimpse . . . you know."

Father Leon understood there were strange people about, and here was an example. "Well, there's sweeping the floor. The roof needs repair. The desks in the children's rooms all require maintenance."

Rawlings scratched the side of his face. "Look. Mr. Grainger and myself haven't been briefed on these operational codes and mission whiteouts. All we want—"

"Padre, may I confer with my colleague for a moment?"

Paul and Leon looked at each other, one befuddled, the other puzzled.

Paul clasped his hands together. "Of course. Use this room." He and Leon left and closed the door behind them.

Rawlings paced around the room. "What the hell is going on here, partner?"

Grainger stared right at him, his eyes boring in. "Sit down, Myles. Let me tell you a story."

RAWLINGS sat slumped in the chair for a full ten minutes without saying a word or looking up. His muscles twitched a bit; otherwise there was no movement save for the sideways gnashing of his jaw grinding his teeth.

"You can kill me if you want."

Rawlings looked up. "Kill you? No way, buddy. But, I would like to crush your fucking nuts with a sledgehammer and spread your guts out for the buzzards, you son of a bitch."

The door to the rectory pushed open. "Who are you guys?" Then Sloane McKenzie saw Grainger.

Grainger faced the woman from the fair. "Just a couple day laborers—"

"Who drove from California just to answer a notice pinned on the bulletin board at our local pharmacy, to help a church which can't even afford to pay full wages . . . My ass."

Two sets of eyes appeared behind Sloane, and one said, "We asked them to come." Joey and Ponce pushed to either side of the nurse. Joey held up *New Breed.*

Ponce stared at the incarnations. He shuffled forward. "You came. You really came."

Grainger nodded. "We got your message."

Joey stepped in front of Ponce. "I told you they would come."

There was a tentative knock on the door of the rectory. Father Paul peered around the edge. "Is everything all right?"

"Yes, Father. Please, let me handle this," said Sloane.

Paul looked quizzically about and then backed out of the room.

Sloane knelt down in front of Ponce and Joey. "Scoot. You boys wait outside. I need to talk to these . . . gentlemen."

The two boys shuffled out of the rectory, casting rearward glances. Nurse Sloane McKenzie stepped over to Rawlings and grabbed his hand. She turned it over, inspected it, and threw it down. Then she looked at both of them. "You responded to a letter from Joey and Ponce? You had an ad in a mercenary magazine? If you're day laborers, I'm Mother Teresa. You're contract hitters."

Rawlings got up from his chair and said to Grainger, "That's all right, I was just leaving." Rawlings brushed by Sloane. "I'll see you in the car."

Grainger looked at her in silence.

"Who are you?"

"Does it matter?"

"Maybe not. But what you do, does. You work for Rios?"

"Who?"

Sloane was unmoved by this display of innocent ignorance. "Look. If you work for Rios, you're busted. If not, then none of this is any of your business. So go back to where you came from. There is no money here."

RAWLINGS leaned against the Dodge convertible and stared numbly at the bleached blue sky. His mind was a vacuum. Then he became aware of the kid standing in front of him.

Ponce followed the big man outside and saw him by the car. He was the one who came to help. "I'm Ponce."

Rawlings peered down without smiling. "Never heard of you, kid."

Grainger descended the steps of the church and got into the passenger seat.

Rawlings spun around and got behind the wheel. "Like you said, let's go. Maybe the Honduras contract hasn't been filled."

Ponce leaned in, looking at Rawlings. "You came."

Rawlings started the car and looked back at the gangly boy. "Yeah, kid; I came, I saw, I left. What did you say your name was?"

"Enrique," he said in a hushed voice. "They call me Ponce."

Rawlings turned out into the street. "Yeah, well, you take care, Potts." The car rumbled down the street with a muffler sounding like it was burning out.

THE man in the old Chevy pickup drove by the Casita Zapata and saw the Dodge. He slowed but didn't stop. Seeing the California plates was enough. Everything was on schedule and just about as planned.

ROSA Fuentes, serving woman to Estaban Rios, held her tray of *bebidas, botanas,* and *antojitos.* She waited to be called. She was invisible.

Warden Refugio Joaquin Ybarra Duran caressed the money he had received for "referring" Pedro Martin Morales to The Game. His facility held many men like him: debtors and drunks and even a few murderers. Morales was just a ranchero, a peon debtor, but they were all cash cows to him. "I can continue to furnish a virtually limitless supply of 'volunteers' who see participation as a road to the commutation of their sentence. Plus, there is the money dangling like a carrot. Do not worry."

Estaban Rios turned on Duran and said evenly, "I do not worry, Señor Duran. Others worry at the hint that I might. *Comprendes?*"

Duran tried to swallow discreetly, but his pulsing Adam's apple betrayed him. "Of course, jefe. What I meant . . ."

Estaban hardly heard him. Duran was a sycophant who erroneously considered himself almost an equal. He thought that being able to provide very expendable and unaccountable human targets for the very profitable Game made him indispensable. There were plenty of other available resources. But Duran had other assets of interest and usefulness. His riot suppression unit made up of cutthroats and sadists was always good to have available should he ever need reinforcements. Not that he ever would. Even the Colombians knew better. He possessed plenty of local muscle, in varying grades and quality. He was an equal opportunity employer. But ultimately, he had the NRA: Nguyen, Ramirez, and Allcott. And of course, Montezuma, *El Silencio. My very own Four Horsemen of the Apocalypse: Famine, Pestilence, Plague, Death. Maybe only Death, times four.* To be sure, Duran was a cretin, but a useful cretin.

"Patron? I was saying, what I meant—"

"I know what you meant, Refugio, and I appreciate what you do, believe me. You have your money, no?"

Duran patted his pocket. "Ah, *sí, sí.*"

The flower garden of Estaban's hacienda was his personal sanctuary and retreat. The place was as serene as a Buddhist temple; an exotic monastery of flora and fauna growing in neatly manicured patches. Multicolored roses and deep purple lilacs provided aromatherapy. There were African violets circumscribed by snapdragons and red tulips segueing imaginatively to marigolds and sun-yellow lilies. Oleanders the color of mauve frost competed with pink petunias in orderly plots. Geraniums in crazy-quilt patterns were contrasted boldly with black orchids and white magnolias, which were Sonja's. He rarely shared the serpentine paths of his garden with the likes of Refugio Duran, but there were exceptions.

Estaban smoothed his pencil-thin mustache and smiled to himself. Women said he looked like Ricardo Montalban. Personally, he thought it was closer to Julio Iglesias. The truth was more Lee Van Cleef. No matter, because at fifty-three, his skin was still smooth and resilient; but a face-lift was not inconceivable for the future. Estaban was no preening peacock or foppish dandy. But he was obsessively neat. He was self-educated and self-made. He outwardly eschewed the passions of the mob, and the greed of a money-mad, meretricious world, while nevertheless employing those vices whenever convenient. Paternalistic and patriarchal, he ruled by the force of personality, and sometimes by force alone. He was el jefe supremo. There is a word in Spanish that has no single English translation: *caudillo.* Rios was an apotheosis of *caudillo.* His power was unshared and absolute.

Estaban watched a fly investigate a flower. Cautiously the insect wiggled closer to the velvet petals. *Yes, my garden is my retreat from a venal world.* The leaves of the Venus's-flytrap snapped shut, entombing the fly. The plant's digestive juices began their inexorable work. The garden was his only retreat.

Jackbootlike footsteps crunched on the gravel walkway. Bando Allcott advanced like a robot. His face belonged carved on a totem pole. It was superimposed upon a body that—if not moving—might be mistaken for a granite pillar; Stonehenge with legs. He stopped in front of Estaban Rios and bared his vampire teeth. "Two men came into Zapata in an old Dodge convertible with California plates. They're staying at the hotel. The maid said she thought they was checking out tomorrow."

"They were at the church this morning," said the santera, her dark eyes burning like black light, the white oleander in her hair a perfect silent allegory.

A smirking laugh burst from Raoul Rios. "Maybe they were praying, eh?"

Sonja Ochoa, the priestess, fixed him with her stare, her indigo eyes boring into him, riveting Raoul motionless. "These men do not pray on their knees." She released him so he might answer.

With one finger, Raoul removed the single bead of perspiration that bisected his nose. "Then, how do they pray?"

"They *prey,* Raoul. Like the lion."

Estaban Rios coughed to subside tension and regain control. "So, my seer, advise me."

The santera emptied the contents of a leather pouch, which hung suspended from her neck. She squatted down on the pathway and scattered the predictors of fortune and doom of Santeria on the ground: chicken bones, the dried blood of a cat, the leg of a frog, the intestines of a pig, a section of horn of a goat. There was also the beak of a rooster and the fangs of a water moccasin. She gathered everything in her hands and shook them while mumbling some incantation in no understandable language, the Santeria equivalent of talking in tongues. She then threw the pieces like she was rolling dice and peered over them. Sonja closed her eyes and stirred the arrangement with the feather of a crow and gazed again. She arose slowly. Her expressionless face turned to Estaban. "It is well to be rid of these men. Their capacity for violence and chaos matches yours, my most generous sponsor."

Allcott spat into the garden. "You want us to fucking take care of the problem, Mr. Rios?"

Rios's eyes turned to fire. "Do not ever again spit or curse while in my garden. Do you understand?" He waited for no response. "The answer is no, but monitor them until they leave."

Allcott swallowed and nodded. He knew better than to spit and cuss in the garden. He had better redeem himself. "One other thing. One of them shut down the shooting gallery at the carnival across the river." He glanced tentatively at a shadow on the veranda. "I heard he never missed a shot."

Montezuma stood under a large banana tree, barely visible, listening. Most women found him attractive. Slender, evidencing distinctly Nordic-European features with Latin highlights, with light brown, sun-streaked hair, cut halfway between Caesar and George Clooney. His most striking features were his eyes, which were iridescent blue and gleaming with the intensity of industrial lasers. The eyes were also marked with a slash of yellow, like that found among predatory cats. No one ever stared him down. Men crossed the street to avoid walking past him. Women often daydreamed about what he might be like as a lover. He remained motionless, considering. *Never missed a shot.* It was very interesting.

Estaban dismissed Allcott and regarded Sonja, his light and his darkness, she who remained ever present, even in his sleep, be it dream or nightmare. Everything else was his possession, but by *La Alma Negra* he was possessed. This was Estaban's only hint of fear. Black Soul provided him a scintilla of the chilling sense of vulnerability. Not that he loved her. Love corrupted, and he couldn't remember loving anybody, not even his mother.

Estaban looked down and saw a small mound of dirt just off the path, among the henbane that he personally cultivated sometimes. The mound was teeming with ants, and they were in his henbane. He addressed Duran. "You see, my dear Refugio, I am at the top of the food chain." He raised his custom vaquero boot over the mound. The heel impacted the mound, pulverizing the dome, grinding the dirt underfoot, and crushing all visible movement. "I do not worry."

DUSK fell complacently, arranging itself into moody layers of light and darkness. The ubiquitous border wind blew dust devils and tumbleweeds across the highway along with periodic walls of gritty dirt. A miniature twister played hide-and-seek, a whirling plume of dark sand darting among the giant saguaro cacti. The sun hung low in the sky, precariously suspended, casting angled rays of gold that made the motes of dust in the air radiate.

A Gila monster lay on the warm asphalt, feeling the vibration of the approaching car. It was only the second one to come north this date, not that the Gila monster was counting. Instinct compelled the prehistoric minilizard to move. It wiggled off the road into the brush. It was time to hunt.

"**I'M** sorry," was all he could think to say.

"That you came?" Rawlings said.

"That I involved you."

"Forget it. If you can't get fucked over by a friend, why bother."

An old gas station loomed ahead. It had looked abandoned

when they passed it on the way into Zapata. This time they saw movement. Grainger pulled in and stopped in front of the two cylindrical pumps. A leathery relic in Big Ben Coveralls, a Houston Oilers T-shirt, and rubber thongs rocked back and forth on a dilapidated chair. He looked at them for a while, then removed the headset from around his ears. "Deborah Harry's making a comeback. She's a hottie."

Grainger regarded the man's gnarled hands.

"If you're too damn lazy to pump your own gas, I suppose I can, but I'm a-gonna charge you extra."

Rawlings pointed to a hand-painted sign. "The sign says Full Service, old man."

The man rolled to his feet as the momentum of the chair rocked him forward. "Who y'all calling old man? You ain't that far behind me, you know. You two might even catch up. Getting old comes on quick. You ever listen to "Turn Around" by the Kingston Trio? Well, ya oughta. Anyway, if you believe everything you read in advertising, you're gonna be in a world of hurt. Full Service is a manageable deception, according to our Supreme Court."

"Hey, we don't want no musical lectures on aging, legal opinions, or other geriatric bullshit. We just want gas," said Rawlings.

The old man remained unbowed. "I don't take plastic, checks, or promises to pay. Cash only and on the barrelhead."

Grainger raised a hand in surrender. "Okay, sir; whatever you say. Fill 'er up. Ethyl."

The old man grumbled as he descended the steps and grabbed a fill hose. He cranked the lever and jammed the nozzle into the tank. "Ain't heard nobody call premium petrol, ethyl since. . . . Hmmm. Let's see . . . 1999. Hell no; it was 1998 when that fella come through here in a Corvette." The old codger looked out across the desert. When gas started pouring out the fill vent, he removed the hose.

Rawlings looked at the pooled-up and spreading gas spill. "We're not paying for the overflow, Pops. The EPA would have your ass for that, old man."

The man ignored Rawlings and said to Grainger. "I suppose you want me to wash your windows, huh sonny?"

Grainger smiled. "Naw, that's okay."

The old man laughed out loud. "Too bad. If you said you did, I was going to tell you to use your window washer." He cackled to himself.

"Yeah, you're funnier than a pay toilet in a diarrhea ward. How much farther to the Boondocks?" said Rawlings.

"That, sir, is a freebie. Just up the road a piece. Turn right off the main road, onto the dirt cut just past the cattle guard and drive about a quarter mile in. Can't recommend it, though. It's no place for strangers."

Grainger paid and started the car.

The old man wiped his hands on his Big Bens. "Just so you never say I cheated y'all dishonestly . . . I only have one grade of gas. Charge different prices, though; so people feel better. Gave you the cheap price. I kinda like you two, for no reason that I can figure. Your friend's a prick. Thought you ought to know."

Rawlings suppressed a smile despite himself. The Dodge wheeled out onto the highway.

ZZZZZZAAAAPP.

The electric chair for airborne bugs was working overtime. A large moth managed to squirm and wiggle its way through the double layer of grates to find the electrocutioner waiting. The 125-volt, 2500-watt device fried the moth, incinerating the wings instantaneously, and then igniting the body, finally exploding the head, which remained alive long enough to witness its own immolation. Mosquitoes . . . *ZZZZZZaaaapp*. No contest; nothing but a brief burst of matter changing form. Flies . . . *ZZZZZZZaaaapp*, and a minor light show that didn't even dim the lights. The machine showed no mercy. Ever since Texas switched from the electric chair to lethal injection as the state's ultimate sanction, the bug zapper had risen in popularity and here, tonight, it was the main attraction at El Boondocks; the allergy test that all bugs fail.

The smoky bar was crowded. Sitting at a small table inside the Boondocks, Grainger faced Rawlings in silence; lost in private thoughts about the past, where they had been, where they were now, and the future. *There's always a future. It just doesn't always include me*. He raised the glass of beer to his lips.

Rawlings hadn't made it to the Boondocks the night before. After Grainger walked down to the carnival, he had fallen asleep. No matter, he could make up for it tonight. This was going to be his last night in this inferno of heat and dust and nothing else. He looked around. *Asshole to elbow. Everybody and his uncle within a fifty-mile radius must be here*. He looked out at the bug zapper on the porch. It was frying chitinous insects five at a time. He swirled the last of his beer in the mug and grunted to get Grainger's attention. "Did I ever tell you I met my old lady in a place like this? In New Mexico."

Grainger stared at him over his beer. "I'm staying."

"Sort of thought you would." Rawlings swiveled around, searching for a waitress, and saw one that looked like she was designed specially for bowling alleys and redneck saloons. He raised his empty mug toward her and waved. "Hey honey, can we get a table near a waitress who's breathing?" He turned back to Grainger. "I guess I always figured we'd see it through to the bitter end; dust off our last gunsel and retire. I figured maybe we'd open up a watering hole near Bragg and call it the Sniper Bar and Grill. I even considered hanging a neon sign out front saying, All You Need Is One Shot. Something like that."

Grainger nodded and ran his index finger around the rim of the glass. "Something happened in Beirut."

Rawlings leaned back in his chair. "Shit, Lon. Something happened in Belgrade, Mogadishu, Tegucigalpa . . ."

"You forgot Kenya."

"It wasn't your fault. If you want to wear a hair suit for the rest of your life, be a Tibetan monk." He shrugged. "We're just kind of like paper plates after the picnic is over; or bum wad after somebody's wiped their ass. It's just the way things are."

Grainger stared, fixated on the yellow liquid at the bottom of his beer mug. "Maybe so. But I still took the shot. It was my decision."

Rawlings came back quickly with his rescue line. "Draw your third T.S. slip and see the chaplain. The shot was on. It was the time-to-target fucked things up. No way to account for it."

"Your damn pants on fire, sweetheart?" The bowling alley cocktail waitress was wearing chaps and pasties, and not much more. She was snapping her gum like an old mechanical typewriter.

Nice tits, but a row of teeth that look like tombstones on Boot Hill. Rawlings disengaged from Grainger and studied the eye-level belly button of the trailer park refugee. "My Lord, this makes me wish I was a cowboy. *Dos mas cervezas para yo y mi amigo*. Make that Coors Light *por moi* and another Dos Equis for my sidekick here."

The waitress masticated her chewing gum and it showed itself as a glob of pink distorting her lips, before disappearing back inside the fluorescent-red, minicave of a mouth. "Coming right up, Billy-Bob." *Good looking, but another one of those why-don't-we-get-drunk-and-screw types*. She shook her tits and headed off to see the other animals.

Grainger swung his eyes around the saloon. It was the seminal country bar as imagined by any homesick cowboy, real or Midnight. This was hard-core country. There were no props of barbed wire and gold mining pans on the wall or pictures of Gene Autry; but there were bullet holes. This was shit-kicker paradise. It was a powder keg with an unknown length of fuse that was always lit and would absolutely periodically explode. El Boondocks was not the place to take a date. He came back. "Where will you be going from here?"

"South, I guess. Like I said, maybe the Honduras offer is still open." He gave it a beat. "What was it Lon? The kids? The woman?"

Grainger swiped at a persistent fly. "I don't know, Myles. Maybe just the echo."

The waitress dropped two beers on the table and walked away.

Rawlings called after her, "Yeah, we'll mail you the tip."

"Time's up. We need your table."

The voice belonged to Godzilla in a Stetson. Rawlings cocked his head and studied the fur under the cowboy hat. Godzilla had a friend of lesser stature, with prominent piglike eyes. He sported a bandanna and a pool cue that was slapping time like a windshield wiper against his leg. Rawlings considered the bigger one's hairy face. It probably still made his mother wish she had watched television that night. "I didn't know we were on a timer."

"Well, y'all know now," said Pig Eyes.

Grainger sipped his beer, saying nothing.

Godzilla leaned on the table in front of Grainger. "That your piece of shit car out front with the Californicate plates?"

Pig Eyes slammed the butt of his pool cue down on the floor. "Only pansies and pussies come from California." He leaned closer. "Now, which one are y'all?"

"We were just having a quiet beer. Let's leave it at that," replied Grainger.

Godzilla growled. "I get it now, Josie; they're pussies *and* pansies."

"You boys are looking at a lot of undignified entertainment," said Rawlings.

Pig Eyes snarled. "Is that so?"

Rawlings looked at Grainger and shrugged. "We tried." His foot swung out from under the table, catching Pig Eyes with a foot drag. The cowboy went parallel to the ground and slammed down hard. But it wasn't the floor his back impacted. It was Rawlings's bent knee, in a spine-snapping maneuver right out of the Delta martial arts textbook, borrowed from the WWE's death drop. The sound was like a two-by-four snapping in half.

Grainger smashed his boot into Godzilla's instep. The cowpoke folded ninety degrees. Grainger's knee slammed into the hirsute face, sending him crashing over another table. Both cowboys lay like rag dolls on the floor, making small groaning sounds, which meant they were still alive; not that it mattered.

Rawlings had been taught—and fully believed—in total war. "No mercy" was a factor of survival, not indicia of a brutish nature. There was no "measured response," no "escalation of force," no "only that amount of force necessary to overcome resistance used against you." It was all or nothing, on or off, either/or. As the shrink had said at a Fort Bragg class on the psychology of killing, "For those of you who may think there is no such a thing as an innate killer instinct in humans, I might suggest that the next time you brush your teeth, take a closer look at your incisors."

Grainger stood at the table and watched the silent crowd for reaction while Rawlings finished his beer.

The cocktail waitress tiptoed to them hesitantly, like she was Kal-Kan and they were Velociraptors.

Grainger held out his open hands. "We didn't want any trouble."

The waitress glanced at the motionless cowboys. "That's trouble on the floor. Those gents both work for Estaban Rios." She focused on the broken pair. "Damned all mighty if they didn't buy the whole whup-ass . . . took a run at the wrong people tonight."

Grainger threw ten dollars on the table. Rios. That was the second time somebody had referred to that name, and both times unfavorably. He headed for the door and the way parted for him.

Over in the corner of the bar, a man sipped his tequila and watched. Nero Ramirez took everything in, logging copious mental footage of what he had just witnessed. He also had an ambient light photograph.

As the swinging double doors closed behind them, the singer on the jukebox was saying he was going back to a better class of losers.

ZZZZZAAAAAP! The electrocutioner got a couple more.

SEVEN

AT seven A.M. they drove from the hotel to the church without an exchange of words. Rawlings stopped the Dodge at the steps and swung out into the street. Even at this hour it was already prickly hot. A farmer eyed them from the feed store and a couple pickup trucks with hounds in the back crawled past. Several wary parishioners tentatively climbed the steps, looking around like they were committing treason, or suicide.

Rawlings opened the trunk and placed his hands on the two duffel bags inside. "You'll need this stuff. Take it."

Grainger shook his head. "You keep it. I'll scrounge something." He looked at the other man. There was no use denying the inevitability. "Been a long time, partner. Lot of water over the dam."

"Under the bridge, too. I guess there just comes a time when we all move on," Rawlings said. He walked to the driver's door. "See you around, sometime."

Grainger climbed three church steps and looked back as Rawlings swung the Dodge into the street, lowered his aviator sunglasses over his eyes, and drove off without looking back. He watched until the car dematerialized in the glare of the sun.

Nero Ramirez nudged Allcott as the Dodge approached.

Tong Nguyen clasped his hands together and placed his fingers under his chin as the dirty convertible motored slowly by. His eyes followed the lone driver as he reached the end of *Calle Verdugo* and made the left onto Perimeter Circle, headed for the highway. *One down, one to go.*

Rawlings kept the automatic transmission in low gear as he drove on the circle. The small carnival was being torn down. He turned on the radio. Kris Kristofferson. Man couldn't sing worth a lick, but he sure could write a song. He felt the sun hot on the vinyl seat as the turnout to Highway 83 approached. ". . . And Lord, it took me back to something that I'd lost somehow, somewhere along the way . . ." The Dodge didn't seem to respond. Of its own volition it kept on driving around the circle. He stopped for a mutt in the street who thanked him by pissing on his tire. He maneuvered around a Frisbee in the street and watched a man on his knees pulling weeds in his front yard. ". . . And there's nothing short of dying that's half as lonesome as the sound . . ." A woman walked two dogs on a leash, and someone had his car up on a jack. An ancient Hispanic man stacked mesquite logs alongside a shed. Firewood in ninety-degree heat. Then he was at the opposite end of Verdugo Street. He kept driving, around the other half of the circle. The river. The sun glistened off its muddy flats, making it look like liquid gold. Across the narrows, he could see Mexico. It looked just like more of Texas. He idled the car down while paralleling the river. Two fishermen in a small boat appeared motionless on the grand river. A cat crossed his path. It was black as midnight and not a ladder in sight. Two kids in diapers stood in the muddy flats of the river watching him. A young girl carried two buckets of water, but set them down to wave. He drove a little faster. The north end of *Calle Verdugo* appeared. He drove on.

Rawlings missed the turnout once more and the same mutt was there, looking at him curiously as he passed. The old guy pulling weeds was there, too. The woman with the two dogs was gone, but the Frisbee was still in the street. The hoary Hispanic *ranchero* looked like he was going to pass out, and he still had a pile of wood to stack. He stepped on the accelerator a little and the Dodge seemed more responsive. He shifted into drive. Past the south end of Verdugo, the river loomed again. This was like an amusement park ride. The continual left circle provided a welcome pressure against his seat belt. The fisherman had a fish on the line, or maybe it was just a snag. The kids in diapers had a mother, and the girl with the water turned into a yard as he went by. He accelerated and took the north stretch of Verdugo Street at thirty-five miles per hour. *Just one more time. See if the guy got all the weeds; if there was really a fish. Find out if the two sets of diapers made it home. Check out the antique Hispanic gent stacking wood.*

Forty-five miles per hour now. The Frisbee was gone. The dog had his tail toward him. The fishermen had pulled anchor, and the girl with the water was standing with a guy old enough to be her father. He probably was. *The Hispanic man? Missed the Hispanic guy stacking wood. Musta been looking someplace else.* Rawlings leaned forward and grasped the wheel with two hands. He thought he heard the peals of the church bell summoning the faithful. At fifty miles per hour, the centrifugal force threw him into the turnout and he skidded out onto Highway 83, scattering gravel, headed for some better place.

GRAINGER climbed the steps slowly and entered the darkened church. He let his eyes adjust to the low light level. The church appeared empty. *No*. One person sat in the back row, where they had sat yesterday. It was the nurse. Grainger realized the interior of the church had been vandalized. There were overturned tables and paint splashed on the walls. The altar appeared slightly off kilter. He moved forward until he stood opposite Sloane.

Sloane McKenzie looked up at him and unfolded her hands. She hadn't been praying. Her knuckles were white. "We had visitors last night." Her eyes became shadows. "What are you doing here?"

"I heard the roof still needs fixing."

STRAIGHT into eternity, the highway led away. Mirage waves rose from the burning asphalt in undulating patterns, obscuring the horizon. Visibility was limitless only if you moved off the pavement and looked across the desert or out over the river.

Down the road, shimmers of heat made it look like you were driving into a tunnel on fire.

Rawlings stopped the car in the middle of the roadway. His shirt stuck to his back against the vinyl seat. He had come a long way to be going back to nowhere. Myles Rawlings was never one to be hesitant about jumping in with both feet. He was never equivocal or precatory. He never qualified his positions or hedged his bets. It always was that way, far as he could remember. . . .

Myles Rawlings attended high school in San Pedro, California, where he was born. San Pete was part of the mother city of Los Angeles, but LA acted like Pee-dro didn't exist. It was an unsophisticated little embarrassment; a dock with a town attached. Its lifeline was the 110 (Harbor) Freeway that connected it with downtown, some twenty miles north. The city had a pall of gloom around it: fog and smog, a sunless melancholy caused by an eternal marine layer. It seemed to affect everybody eventually. San Pedro had a disproportionately high suicide rate. People attributed it to the phenomenon of environmentally initiated depression. His dad drove a cross-country eighteen-wheeler, and his mother watched soaps and ate bonbons. She blamed it on the weather. They weren't exactly what you might call a close family.

Myles made All-State on the wrestling team his junior year. He was a natural athlete with gladiator pectorals and coconut deltoids, as well as a good-looking kid with a dimpled smile and a face made up of right angles. Women loved him. Down at the 49er Tavern on PCH in Long Beach, he made Cal State virgins shudder with the flick of his pool cue. After high school, he stuck around town and attended CSULB while working on the dive and fishing charter boats sailing out of the Twenty-second Street Landing and the Cabrillo Marina. He was only a deckhand, but it was good, outdoor work. One day he was swabbing down the deck of a fishing charter boat called The Happy Hooker *after returning from a trip to the Cortes Banks. One of the drunken customers threw a pile of fish guts onto the clean deck. Myles asked him to clean it up. The drunk laughed at him, saying that sure he'd clean it up, using Myles's head as a mop. Myles tied him up like a pretzel and broke his arm. He then stuffed the fish entrails into his pockets and pitched the drunk headfirst off the vessel. The man sued the boat, and Myles was fired. He was told he had a problem with anger management.*

The following day the first television feeds came in from the Panama Invasion. Myles thought that the Army was a perfect place to exercise his aggressions. He told his parents, and they were both glad to see that their son had made a life choice—and that they had gained another room for storage.

After basic, Infantry AIT, and parachute training, Rawlings reported to the 101st Airborne Division as a novitiate infantryman. After a year, he became bored. He volunteered for Special Forces, the Green Berets. It was at Fort Bragg that he met Grainger. Together they completed the Special Forces "Q" course at Camp Mckall, North Carolina. After the qualification course, they were tabbed with the Special Forces arc, worn proudly on the left shoulder. Rawlings opted for specialty training in Light Weapons and Demolitions. Grainger completed Light Weapons and then went on to Fort Sam Houston for six months of medical training, where he practiced gunshot and other trauma surgery, anesthetizing and operating on goats and pigs shot with nine millimeters.

Having completed their specialist's training, they both attended the Jungle Warfare School at Fort Sherman, Canal Zone, Panama. From there both men were assigned to the Tenth Special Forces Group in Bad Tolz, Germany, in an advisory capacity. Later they were transferred to the Seventh at Fort Bragg in a training billet. Both lived the life: a sports car and a Rolex watch. Rawlings even had the divorce and the rest of the symbols of caste. A year positioned with an A detachment on active deployment, and they were again looking around. They found what they were looking for on a post bulletin board at Bragg while there on TDY for HALO training. First Special Forces Operational Detachment—Delta had "assignment opportunities." They signed on for the long haul.

Delta held its selection process in two cycles: fall and spring. After once again taking and passing what the Army called the SCUBA/HALO physical, they were assigned to the fall selection cycle. After they got the nod of approval from the "chancre mechanics" (as Rawlings referred to all medical personnel), they were subjected to a week of psychological testing designed to eliminate the Rambos and other unfits. The Army was looking for a working blend of contradictions: self-reliant team players, dispassionate berserkers, noncerebral geniuses, culturally sensitive assassins, those capable of being molded into warrior priests. As could be expected, there were few men like that. But, when the last inkblot was dry, Grainger and Rawlings were among the chosen few who were determined to be the kind of men who would not be found wanting when the time came.

After psychological vetting, the one hundred candidates for Delta entered the selection processing stage that lasted one month. The initial PT test was grueling and designed to weed out all but the fittest. The ninety-one survivors moved incrementally to the Uwharrie National Forest, North Carolina; Camp Dawson, West Virginia; and Nellis AFB, Nevada; for field evaluations. Forced marches of eighteen miles with an eighty-pound rucksack were excruciating. And the successful time to complete? Unstated, but, "Ten-minute miles don't cut it, gentlemen."

There was the forty-mile land navigation problem, also with no successful completion time given. Just get from point A to point B ASAP. Easily stated, except the contour lines, symbolic of elevation on a topographic map representing the terrain, were so close together it looked like one big, brown barrier. It wasn't just steep terrain. It was a precipitous mountain, a near-vertical escarpment, five thousand feet to the top. There was no wonder that even outstanding soldiers started to look for excuses to give it up. Then there were the survival treks, and Escape and Evasion exercises, aka SERE: Survival, Escape, Resistance to interrogation, and Evasion. A whole OPFOR army was positioned between you and your goal; a warren of sadists who would, with shameless glee, strip you naked in forty-degree temperatures and put you in a steel fifty-five gallon oil drum sunk into the frozen ground. Most of these ordeals were run alone, being designed to test self-reliance, capacity to endure extremes, the ability to improvise, the stones to persist, and the guts to drive on, no matter what the excess or no matter how far beyond the previously experienced or imagined limits of pain and suffering.

Having survived field evaluation, they returned to Bragg to face the final obstacle, the last impediment to joining Delta, a four-hour interrogation by five Delta veterans. Their decision was final—not subject to appeal—and determined whether you went on or not, no matter how well you had done in the previous phases of the selection process. "We don't care that you're some Airborne-Ranger hotshot stud. We don't give a shit whether you're a born soldier. We're up to our ass in heroes. You think Vietnam was a mistake? No? Yes? Why? You were assigned to read The Prince. *How did it strike you? What do you dream about at night? What are you afraid of? Really afraid of? Don't give me that no-fear bullshit. What do you think of the Waffen SS? What are you really good at?" Even, "How many angels can dance on the head of a pin?" Serious question; serious answer. Ten skinny ones or five fat ones. And . . . "How long is a rope?" Twice as long as half its length. Then, "What do you have to offer us?" and, "What makes you think we need you, Sergeant?" To that interrogatory, Rawlings had leaned on the board's table and answered, "Because you can't make me quit. And because I know where you all live." They didn't think he was joking. He wasn't. They gave him the nod.*

The last question they asked Grainger before they let him go was a hypothetical: "You've been inserted on a mission of the highest priorities when you are accidentally discovered by a little girl playing in a stream you're crossing. She's ten years old, a cute kid with dark eyes and a wide smile. She's seen your team. You're in enemy territory. Are you going to kill her, Sergeant? Are you going to take her along for the ride, Sergeant? Or, do you give her a pack of MREs and a Tootsie Roll and ask her not to tell, Sergeant?" The five-man panel of hardened Delta veterans waited for an answer. Grainger stared straight ahead and forced his eyeballs not to blink. Without hesitation, he answered. "I'll do whatever is necessary."

Barry Sadler's Top Ten song from the sixties, "The Ballad of the Green Berets," proclaimed, "One hundred men would test today, but only three win the Green Beret." Delta held true and faithful to that not-very-exaggerated reputation. The spring class before them, it was rumored, vaporized, i.e., there were no survivors. No one made it through the selection process. It was a wash. In their fall (fiscal year) class II selection program, Grainger, Rawlings, and five others received orders to report to the Special Operations Training Facility at Fort Bragg—the Sorbonne of killing schools—where they would learn to become the world's best looters and shooters, terrorist terminators without peer, and masters of military-engineered disaster. Officially never acknowledged as existing, nor ever commented upon by the Army, Delta was the absolute cutting edge of the green machine.

It was said—only half tongue in cheek—that "if you killed for money, you were a mercenary, and if you killed for pleasure, you were a sadist. But if you killed for both you were Delta." Yet, a Delta warrior, if asked in a tavern who he worked for, would look you straight in the eye and tell you blandly that he was a cashier for Piggly Wiggly or an operator for Ma Bell. It was an inside joke. Uncle Sam became "Ma Bell." They were definitely operators. So, it was only a little deception. It was all guts, glory, and gun smoke, but invisible.

Politicians loved them. Delta took out the garbage so they could pretend the Civics 101 model of U.S. government was fully functional and that culturally sensitive diplomacy was working marvelously. And, if a Delta trooper happened to get killed, there was no need to publicly mourn on CNN. Or any requirement to explain to grieving wives or inquiring minds anywhere. Killed in a training accident. Case closed. To be sure, there would never be a ticker-tape parade and not a single yellow ribbon on an old oak tree. But they liked it like that. They were their own chroniclers. Theirs was an oral history transmitted in drunken camaraderie at pubs they kept open after hours. Only they knew the truth. It wasn't just a job. It was an adventure. They had become all they could be.

Delta was held in awe by a limited public who had but a

hint of the total reality and only an inkling of the true nature of their operations. Delta warriors were the Army's magicians and the envy of the also-elite Rangers and Airborne. They had business cards that announced their specialties: Bars cleared. Revolutions started. Assassinations plotted. Tigers tamed. Virgins converted. Alligator's castrated. . . . They were killers in blue jeans and baseball caps, with civilian haircuts and non-regulation mustaches, employing garrotes and light sabers. The steely glance and the stiff upper lip were government issue. They were the Ph.D.s of applied violence. They were the military's X-File. They were what every combat trooper wanted to be. They were what every warrior dreamed of being: a Delta boy, the dreaded D. They were the ultimate practitioners in the ultimate trade.

RAWLINGS pushed open the door and stepped out. The temperature was now over one hundred degrees. He smoothed his mustache and ran his fingers through his sweat-matted hair. His shoes treaded on sticky taffy. He swiveled in a complete circle and leaned against the furnace-hot hood. The radiator trembled, cycling boiling water that sounded volcanic. He looked at the yellow stripe that bisected his legs and ran down the middle of the road. It pierced the mirage, where it disappeared. One hundred feet ahead of him, a dead armadillo lay flattened on the road, probably hit by the only car to pass this way today or yesterday. Two patient vultures waited, perched on a cactus, biding their time. The stripe and the armadillo: that's all there was in the middle of the road. Rawlings got back into the Dodge. He had made his decision.

When he was gone, the vultures descended on the armadillo and began shredding its flesh.

Sunday mornings were a bitch.

THE ball arched high into the air, causing Ponce to shield his eyes from the sun. He ran backward, trying to maintain contact with the ball, when he collided hard with Bando Allcott. It was an unmovable object. Ponce bounced off and collapsed onto the street. His head spun, and he could actually see stars.

"You got no eyes? Run into me without watching where yer going?"

Ponce tentatively picked himself from the ground. "I'm really sorry, sir. I wasn't watching where I was going. I'm sorry."

Joey walked slowly up to Ponce. He had thrown the wild pitch. "He didn't mean anything, sir. It was my fault."

Allcott rubbed his face. "Shut up, kid. If I want something from you, I'll squeeze it out of you." He turned back to Ponce. "You're one of those punks from the orphanage, aren't you?" Allcott picked up the ball Ponce had been chasing. "I'll just keep this and maybe teach you some manners." Allcott backhanded Ponce. He went down, blood spurting from his broken lip.

"What did you say your name was again, son?" The voice came from across the street; a man sitting in a dusty, 1990 Dodge convertible.

Ponce looked up from the street. Bando Allcott's eyes narrowed.

Rawlings got out of the car. The door slammed shut behind him with a sprung-hinge sound as he walked toward Allcott. "You were saying something about manners. I didn't quite catch the whole conversation. Was there a lesson in progress I could join in on?"

Bando Allcott rustled his shoulders, dug his heels into the street, and pushed his hat back on his head. "You happen to know who I am, mister?" His mouth twisted in smiling menace.

Rawlings moved one finger, which traced a path around his ear. "I can't say for sure, but you look like a pair of boots and a hat sandwiching a six-foot piece of horseshit."

Allcott's smirk disappeared, and a flat, expressionless veil dropped over him. If the remark was intended to enrage him, to make his adrenaline pump, to make his hands tremble and shake, it failed. It only made him mad and determined. He dropped his right hand, and it found the grip of the big, custom .454 Casull hand cannon he kept holstered on his hip.

Rawlings saw the big cowboy lower his hand, watched his eyes betray what his instincts intended to do even before his mind had made the final decision. He had the edge of a schooled and practiced gunfighter.

Allcott began his draw but found himself staring into the muzzle of Rawlings's SIG Sauer P226, and it was leveled right at his head. Like a batter caught in a balk, he froze. He heard the words, "Drop it or die." It was his option. The Casull fell to the pavement. Allcott's eyes were aflame. His reputation depended on his ability to intimidate, and there were people watching who were seeing him fold and drop his $1,100 custom Casull. "You should've kept going. You're a walking dead man."

"Maybe that's true, but right now you only get to live because I hate bloodshed on an empty stomach. And you're about to become an exception. You got ten seconds to get invisible."

Allcott backed away, hands half raised, his nod at offering defiance.

"One more thing, tough guy. Leave the ball."

Allcott stared at the stranger for a moment, and realized he was still holding the rubber ball in his left hand. He dropped it and resumed backing up until he disappeared around a corner of a building.

Rawlings motioned to Ponce. "Pick yourself up and get off the street, Potts. Pronto. Move." He eyed the other boy. "You, too, son." He picked up Allcott's revolver and checked it and then moved thirty feet laterally down the street. He stepped up onto the sidewalk, telling two people who had stopped to gawk to go home. There, he waited, both guns hanging loosely at his side in the 105-degree sun. He didn't have long to wait.

Bando Allcott burst around the corner with a sawed-off Savage pump shotgun. He fired two buckshot rounds into the street where Rawlings had previously stood before realizing the target was no longer there. He whirled, looking for his enemy. Then he saw him. He raised the shotgun.

The two handguns fired sequentially; a single 9 mm Parabellum 115 grain Silvertip hollow-point from the SIG followed by a 255 grain .454 inverted base wadcutter from the Casull spat from the muzzles. Rawlings discarded the Casull and switched from the isosceles position into the Weaver combat stance he favored. The sights of the P226 aligned, and he pulled the trigger twice. The SIG was now in single-action mode. He saw the rounds impact, the entry points marked by dust that flew from Allcott's shirt. Blood from the first two impacts was already spreading into a red spiderweb stain.

The initial rounds caught Allcott high in the chest cavity and penetrated without exiting. Allcott staggered backward from hydraulic shock and the organ rupture caused by the two bullets. He was still on his feet despite the effect of the sledgehammer blow from the Casull, which now—as he had often joked over many a *cerveza*—was letting in a hell of a lot of air and letting out a mess of blood. Only problem, it was happening to him, and he couldn't believe it. Then the next five bullets hit him in a hailstorm of semijacketed lead. The projectiles walked their way up from his belt buckle to his throat. Allcott was sure he had hit the son of a bitch. Then his mouth was in the dirt. He thought somebody was trying to blind him with bright lights. Now they hog-tied him, and he couldn't move anymore. Finally, somebody turned off the lights, and he was able to rest.

The gunfire still echoed as Grainger burst out through the main door of the church and scanned the street, searching for the source of the war. Two blocks north on Verdugo the first thing he saw was a man lying in the street. Then he saw the Dodge. He vaulted down the steps and sprinted up the middle of the street, dodging the small crowd of people that had gathered, halting in front of the perforated body of Bando Allcott.

Rawlings pointed the SIG at the deceased from where he stood on the elevated sidewalk. "Retroactive birth control." Ponce and Joey stood behind him.

Grainger looked at him. "Myles?"

Buck Downs stalked up from behind and struck Rawlings on the back of the head with a beavertail sap. Twice. Rawlings went to his knees, and Buck slammed the handcuffs over his wrists. He kicked his prisoner into the prone. Downs prodded Rawlings with his foot like he was a trophy black bear, wounded but still dangerous. When Rawlings groaned, Buck jumped back involuntarily, like he had stuck his finger in a light socket.

Grainger advanced on Downs, his steps a predatory stalk, his face a death mask.

Buck drew his Ruger and cocked it. "Stay back. You are 'bout to interfere with a duly constituted peace officer in the course of his duties. Your penalty is instant death."

Sloane ran up and grabbed Grainger's arm on the outside chance he was going to take Downs up on the challenge. "Don't be stupid," she said.

Downs grinned, turned, and press-ganged two men into helping him carry Rawlings to jail. Buck gave his authority to the reluctant help as something he called *posse comitatus,* although he pronounced it *pussy-come-and-get-us.*

Officer Levon Butler pushed his way through the small, curious crowd.

Buck pulled Rawlings to his feet. "Go on Levon. Make yourself useful by getting that deceased citizen outa the middle of the street."

When Downs had gone and the street cleared, Sloane found she was still holding on to Grainger. She self-consciously released his arm. "Ignorance is nine-tenths of the law. Welcome to Zapata, Mr. Grainger."

AFTER almost eighteen months, his only success was the uncovering of the probable name of the operation: Tantrum. He had managed to cross-reference it to the DIAIAPPR of OPLAN Tilt. Thereafter it was a stonewall. Anyway, the name probably didn't mean a thing. For the most part, a computer selected the code names for Black Bag and other classified, clandestine operations, so semantics didn't inadvertently betray the mission. The Panama incursion was called Operation Just Cause, and the Saddam ouster, the Iraqi War, was termed Operation Iraqi Freedom, but those were political and named in that light.

Richard Arturo Stoneman sat at his desk at the Central Intelligence Agency, George Bush Center for Intelligence, as the McLean, Virginia, headquarters was now known. Recently promoted, he was now the senior security officer, under the assistant director of the Office of Security, within the Directorate of Administration. He had been transferred from the Directorate of Operations in 1993, upon his return from Africa. It was his job to ferret out traitors and turncoats from within the Agency, and when summoned, from without. His liaison staff was still assisting the Frat Boys Incorporated in determining the extent of al-Qaida penetration of sleeper cells into the country post 9-11. Cooperation between the Agency and the Bureau was something new.

The search for Operation Tantrum was different, unofficial, and obtaining the answers to this one could cost him his job, if not get him prosecuted for violation of the recently enacted National Secrets and Security Law under the Patriot Act, as well as his omerta, his sworn, eternal vow and oath of silence. Or worse. But he owed a debt of life—his own—and he was a man who paid his dues and debts. Stoneman's security clearance was Yankee White, i.e., he was cleared beyond top secret, into the rarified aerie where classifications were classified. He was deemed an individual of "unquestioned loyalty to the United States." Stoneman's absolute loyalty was his honor.

Security clearances notwithstanding, he knew he had to be circumspect in his quest, or he might raise more than a few eyebrows. The almighty Agency rubric was "need to know." He didn't. He had made discreet inquiries with some close associates at the Defense Intelligence Agency about Beirut, but drew a blank. By all logic and reason, the DIA and the boys in the Pentagon's E-Ring should be the ones with the answers. After all, Operation Tilt—the DIA's code name—was their gig, not the CIA's. But the DIA was at a loss to explain the events of that day, other than that they considered the mission at least a qualified success. The wild-goose shooters had targeted—and taken out—Saleem, their target. Sure, there was some "minor" (that always sponsored a cynical laugh) collateral damage, but nothing serious. There was a little fallout, and some blowback from the Israelis, who were peeved at being tagged as the fall guys, but things basically had evolved as planned. The spooks at DIA said there was no telling about the fireman who tagged Cruickshank and the indig. Nor did they have an answer as to what the other shots were about. "Hell, man. It's Beirut!" They chalked it up to what Baron von Clausewitz called "the fog of war" and "the friction." Modern translation: "Shit happens." *Anything to avoid the leprosy effect of a failed mission.* Stoneman understood Cruickshank was a Company man, but his presence was strictly as an observer and liaison, the man on home turf in interagency support. He was merely an incidental. The file on Operation Tantrum was most likely the Agency's slant on the joint project, probably the Company's disavowal of a three-humped camel. The report undoubtedly politically pointed the finger at the DIA and the Pentagon while lauding the CIA's contributions. It was just a preliminary estimate, but his SWAG was that it had something to do with the liaison concept of the operation and Cruickshank's salting the scene in the false-flag finale.

Stoneman realized the absolute imperative to couch his inquiries as casual curiosity, something in itself taboo in the community. He had no mandate or authority, but it was his only alternative. He rationalized that what he was now planning did not compromise the security of the country he loved. Tomorrow he would interrogate the Cyber 220 Mainframe and IBM-Cray supercomputers.

THE black leather sap glove thudded heavily into Rawlings's chest, sending him and the chair he was tied to over backward. He managed to raise his head before the impact with the concrete floor.

"Looks to me like cold-blooded, premeditated capital murder under the Revised Statutes of the Great State of Texas." Buck Downs mopped his brow. This interrogation business was tough work.

Officer Levon Butler picked up the chair with Rawlings stilled secured. "That's not what the independent witnesses say, Buck. I've obtained five percipient statements, and they are unequivocal that it was self-defense."

Buck wiped his mouth with the back of his gloved hand. "Now, you just shut your mouth, Levon, and get set to book this fella for murder one, after you print him."

Levon Butler placed himself between Downs and the bound man. "I won't tolerate you abusing the prisoner anymore. I'll book him, but just leave him be."

Buck pulled his powdered-lead sap gloves from his hands and massaged his fingers. "Yeah, sure, Officer Butler."

Rawlings coughed. "If you're done using me as an Everlast bag, I'll make my telephone call now."

Buck grinned broadly. "Sure nuff, killer. Who you want to call?"

"Special Agents Sturgis and Weir, FBI office in Houston."

Buck Downs blanched. He gnawed convulsively on his lower lip and rubbed his bulbous nose while scratching his head. "Watch him for a minute, Butler." He left the room and made his way to the telephone in the front office where he made a call. He hung up and strolled back. "Ah-hum." Buck fidgeted around. "This investigation is still being conducted, and I have concluded it would be, ah, premature to incarcerate your ass at this time. But don't fucking leave town without checking with me first." He walked out of the cell room into his office and out the front door. If murder won't stick, there was always aggravated hooliganism.

Levon Butler untied Rawlings and removed the handcuffs. "Sorry, mister. There was only so much I could do."

Rawlings massaged his wrists and touched his chest tentatively. "That's okay officer; we all have to live with our limitations." He headed for the door.

"Hey. You were bluffing old Buck, weren't you? 'Bout the FBI and all?"

Rawlings managed to find a cryptic smile from somewhere among the hurt. He took a painful breath and walked out into the sun.

Grainger was waiting for him.

Rawlings grinned. "Had to see if the mesquite got stacked."

Grainger had no idea what he was talking about. It was okay. He was back.

RAMIREZ hated the music, but he stood patiently dissimulate and impassive. Estaban had some strange tastes. There was a pause in the noise. He guessed the song was over, so he spoke. "Let me, Tong, and *los otros* kill these *vatos locos, patron.* We must avenge Señor Allcott before the Punta Roja peons and gringo peasants, the *Zapatistas,* and the rest of those *putos Americanos* feel we are without *cajones.*"

Estaban waited until the last stirring strains of "The Ride of the Valkyries" drifted off before turning off the CD player. He clasped his hands behind his back as he leaned forward, over the wrought-iron partition, and looked out at the river from the vantage point of the veranda of his hacienda. The shacks and slums of *el pueblo de* Punta Roja were in the other direction. His "zoning" prohibitions forbade tampering with the ecology or any construction obstructing his view of the river. He turned to Ramirez and, beyond him, his brother Raoul, who was cursing at a girl giving him a manicure. "It is beautiful from here, no Ramirez?"

Ramirez glanced across the land toward the Rio Grande. All he saw was cactus, tumbleweed, and dirt. *"Sí, Jefe, muy lindo."*

Estaban touched the glistening tips of his hair. "You see but you are blind, Ramirez. You comprehend nothing. We cannot afford the chance that this gringo has connections with the FBI. I cannot take that risk until we have verified some things. Especially now." He put his arm across Ramirez's shoulder. "But, I assure you, *mi amigo,* we will deal with the problem to your satisfaction."

Nero Ramirez knew now that the santera was right. These were devils, and they should have been killed before they killed. "As you wish, Jefe, but I have personally witnessed them fight at El Boondocks. These two are not drifters."

"Then, what are they, *compadre?*" Montezuma stood at the sliding glass door to the veranda.

Estaban turned toward Montezuma and considered his unannounced intrusion. *Yes, he is an impertinent, presumptuous, arrogant man, but a very dangerous one. Plus, he has proven profitable.* "Ah, *El Silencio.* It doesn't matter. Once we receive the shipment from Colombia, then we finish business. Principally, it is still the church that bothers me. We cannot co-opt them. I cannot buy them. I loathe waiting for foreclosure to remove them."

Raoul looked up from his indulgence with his hands. He stretched his legs and stroked his monogrammed, black silk Oscar de la Renta jacket. "Then they must die, *mi general.*"

The young manicurist was trembling. Raoul was agitated, animated, waving his arms demonstratively. She peeled a cuticle with the scissors, and a spot of blood formed on Raoul's finger.

Raoul Rios jerked his hand back. He looked at the minute smear of blood on his index finger.

Tears welled up in the woman's eyes, eyes that were as large as black checkers.

Raoul backhanded the woman, knocking her off her chair. "Nero. Send this one to *la casa de las putas*."

Montezuma regarded Raoul with contempt. There was a time, back in Cuba, when he would have killed Raoul for abusing a woman like that. *Maybe I will kill Raoul anyway, someday.* It was possible. But Montezuma, whose real name was Federico Christo Mendez Lorca, had other thoughts now. *These two men . . . Who are they, and why are they here?* Not even Rios seemed concerned with the greater questions. He knew that one of them was named Rawlings, from the hotel registration, if that indeed was his name. It didn't mean anything to him. But he would find out. He would determine who they were. He looked at the picture Ramirez had given him, taken at the bar. *Two men. Strange.* It gave him an odd sensation. *Very odd, indeed.*

Rosa Fuentes returned to the kitchen.

THE church was empty except for Leon, Brother Lemuel, and the two men Paul wished he had never met.

"I cannot condone killing. It is anathema. No matter what the supposed justification. Ponce is one of our wards, and we of course are grateful; but this death I cannot condone." Father Paul paced in circles. He paused and looked at the filtered light streaming through the stained glass window, giving a kaleidoscopic effect to the inner church.

"Myles didn't have any choice."

"Rubbish. Are we to blame it on pagan fate or the position of the stars? Or on circumstances beyond our control? No. I will not suffer any pleas offering deterministic excuses. We are each responsible for our actions." All the old wounds on Paul's face reasserted themselves.

"It wasn't his intention—"

Paul waved Grainger off. "You know what they say about the road to Hell?"

Grainger nodded.

"Nor," Paul continued, "will I allow our church and orphanage to be turned into Fort Apache."

Father Leon forced a cough. "What Father Paul means is that now Estaban Rios has the excuse he needs to destroy us."

"I didn't know this had anything to do with you," said Rawlings.

Paul retreated, a bit subdued. "Unfortunately, it does."

"How so?"

"You want to know what's going on?" said Paul. "Perhaps we owe you that. Please sit."

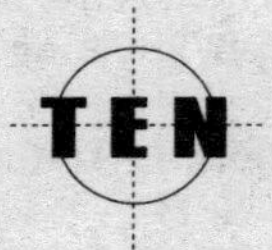

TEN

THE pervasive hum of the supercomputer turned the open elevator into an echo chamber and his body into a tuning fork as he stepped out into the gray basement. The electronic whine of the unseen beast made him shiver.

Stoneman had his electronic badge read by the laser identifier. The green light illuminated.

The two guards at the vaultlike door to the subterranean computer room went through the formalities. "I recognize you, Mr. Stoneman. Your mission statement authorizes accompanied access to the computer. Your assignment parameters have been authenticated. Please be advised that all documents examined, computerized or hard copy, are accountable crypto material and must be logged as accessed." The guard stepped aside, and Stoneman entered with his two shadows from Technical Services who would verify that he didn't overstep his authority, although palpably they were there to facilitate the verifications.

Officially, Dick Stoneman was here on business. His job was to conduct a psycho-cybernetic inspection for intrusions and evidence of hacking. He was to run select software programs, which would be loaded by Tech Services, who would in turn assist in passing judgment on the integrity of the scanned material. If there'd been a compromise, he would know. The identity of every viewer of computerized data was logged. Every inquiry was discoverable, and electronic fingerprints indelible. If you were there, they knew. There was always a trail; so the surcharge of his exploratory authority was risky.

Stoneman sat and watched as the technicians went on-line with the software package. When they were ready, he punched in the codes to run and scan various preplanned inspections.

Thirty minutes later, another program scanned through, and data showed clear. One of the baby-sitters yawned. The two Tech Services operators were talking quietly to each other. Sweat oozed from every pore of Stoneman's body. He typed in "Tantrum" and hit Search.

GRAINGER spoke for the first time. "So, this guy—Rios—controls the police chief and politicians in Zapata as well as law enforcement and government across the river? He operates with impunity, running a drug operation with distribution over the whole Southwest?"

Paul bowed his head. "Who he cannot buy, he murders."

"He has a small army at his disposal and unlimited financial resources," said Leon.

Paul darkened. "He wants us out or dead. We are the last bastion of opposition to his terror."

"Sounds like you need Batman and Superman both," said Rawlings.

"FILE deleted . . . File deleted . . . File deleted . . ."

Stoneman typed in "Tantrum" again and hit Enter.

"File deleted . . . File deleted . . . File deleted . . ."

One of his shadows appeared at his shoulder, looking at the screen. "What's up, Dick? How'd that come up?"

Stoneman iced over, struggling to control his racing heart. "I don't know. I must have hit the wrong key or something."

The man chuckled and slapped Stoneman on the back. "Strange. Anyway, no other computerized aberrant behavior seems apparent, and it doesn't look like the Martians have penetrated Big Brother. The DCI and America can sleep secure, at least for tonight. What do you say we pack it in?"

"Yeah, sure. Why not." Dick Stoneman withdrew his access key, and the techs recovered the software.

He was out of luck. They were all out of luck. Then it came to him. *Unless . . .*

THEY left Rawlings talking to the priests.

Sloane and Grainger made their way down the sidewalk of *Calle Verdugo.* The late afternoon sun perched precariously on the rooftops and was slowly sliding off the back sides. They walked without talking for a while. She stopped and looked at him. "Estaban Rios controls the local bank."

Grainger followed her eyes to the peeling stucco and faded exterior of the Zapata Merchants Bank. It looked like the kind of place that, if you were planning to rob it, you'd first have to make a deposit.

She read his thoughts. "It doesn't look like much, but they cash all checks on Fridays, and practically everyone owes the bank. Rios funnels his business laundry through there and on to Laredo and McAllen." She stroked her cheek absently. "He bought the first and second trust deeds to the church and the orphanage properties and is waiting around like a vulture. We're two months in arrears while Rios waits, sitting across the river in imperial splendor, like *Il Duce.*"

"He makes a good Disney villain," Grainger offered lightly.

She whirled around. "Closer to Beelzebub. You have no idea."

Grainger stared at Jennifer Anniston hair in need of some help. She was slender, with runner's calves and hands that needed a manicure and some polish but looked comfortable without. Her mouth eschewed lipstick and revealed even teeth when she smiled. And that was only once, at the shooting gallery. There was something about her . . . "How is it you know where he launders his money?"

"I just know. Leave it at that. The problem is, now Rios isn't going to wait. He's going to take you down and us with you." She stepped in closer. "For some reason, I have a feeling that might be something easier said than done." She started walking again without looking to see if he was following. "Rios controls this town with a carrot and a stick." She stopped and pointed. "You see that building over there?"

Grainger looked at a modern, one-story building with a Spanish roof. He nodded.

"It's a medical clinic, built with drug money and blood; but the people on both sides of the river treat there for free."

They walked on to the end of the street. An old warehouse building spanned the block. On the front wall, a message was splashed in white paint: *Vivimos Felices Gracias a Rios.*

Sloane pointed at the warehouse wall. "See that? Know what it says?"

"Not exactly."

She translated. "We live in happiness thanks to Rios." She turned away, motioning with her head in the direction of a building with an adjacent playground. "That school was built entirely by a grant from Rios."

"So, there's a moral dilemma. Is that it?"

She ignored the question. "Rios is waiting for a big shipment coming in from his Colombian suppliers, which is another reason he's reacting uncharacteristically slowly to your presence. But narcotics aren't the worst of it. Rios runs a shooting game with human beings as targets."

He didn't bother to inquire how she knew about Rios's drug shipment. "And no one says a word? How does he obtain his targets?"

"Fear, money, and the promise of freedom. Most of the runners are convicts from the Mexican State Prison across the river, outside of Punta Roja. The warden is on the payroll, just like everybody else who has any power. *Mordida* rules." She grabbed his arm. "Once in a while Rios will get some poor campesino who thinks he can accomplish what no one has ever done."

"What's that?"

She released the arm. "Survive." She turned away. "Rios has some sort of medicine woman, a practitioner of something called Santeria. Ever heard of it?"

"Can't say as I have."

"It's a Latin take on some African witch doctor hocus-pocus. Plus a mix of Catholicism and voodoo mutated into some kind of mystic cross between faith healing and Satanism. She's Rios's *mano de recho.* She's got all the locals spooked. The bitch is a regular sorcerer's apprentice." When Grainger remained silent, she continued. "Rios also has a shooter. A killer named Montezuma; some kind of sniper." She looked sideways at Grainger.

Grainger dropped his eyes and then looked at hers. "What about the Border Patrol?"

"*La Migra?* Forget it. There's one resident agent assigned to this whole area, and he doesn't have jurisdiction. He doesn't even chase anybody anymore. He just sits and watches the sieve. Can't say as I blame him none."

"Why don't you call in the FBI?"

She laughed. "Murder isn't federal jurisdiction."

"Corruption is."

"Prove it."

"**WHAT** kind of handymen are you? Exactly what is it you—you and your companion—do, Mr. Rawlings?" Leon had both eyebrows raised.

Rawlings gave him the standard Delta response with a shrug. "We kill for peace."

"God have mercy on us." Father Paul buried his face in his hands and ran his fingers back through his black hair. "Leon . . . Leon. These are not handymen. They are killers; professional assassins." He made the sign of the cross.

Leon cocked his head, and his expression went flat. But a trace of a smile curled up at the edges of his mouth.

Rawlings snorted. "It seems that you have a particular problem, which narrows the appropriate solutions; otherwise, I guess you're right. That's probably what we are. Now, I personally don't care if we stay or go, but my friend out there wants to stay. So I guess you'll just have to make up your minds."

"Very well. If you would be so kind as to wait outside, I wish to discuss this matter with Father Leon."

Rawlings made his way to the front door and exited the church.

* * *

MONTEZUMA sent the information via e-mail to Havana. It went to a Web site advertising low-cost vacation excursions to Cuba and promised information and details on ways and means to circumvent State Department prohibitions against travel to that country. Arranged and prepaid through an operation in Canada, you could visit Cuba with impunity, it was advertised. The site was also a front for the DGI, the Cuban Directorate of Intelligence. His transmission requested travel information for "Myles Rawlings and an unknown-at-this-time companion." He also transmitted a form filled out with pertinent data germane to his inquiry. He scanned the photo given to him by Ramirez, which was taken at El Boondocks and sent that, too. Montezuma had many lasting connections, not only with the DGI but also the DGIC, Counterintelligence, and the DGPNR, the General Directorate of National Revolutionary Police. He would find out who these men were. He looked again at the picture Ramirez had given him of the two outsiders, taken at the bar. It was not the best picture, but for some inexplicable reason, it still gave him an odd, off-balance feeling.

He left the Cuban Travel Agency site and logged on to do a little day trading. No need to consult the S & P index, conduct any P/E research, or calculate the short-term volatility. He planned his buys with a little help from his business associates and their satellite feeds. He always possessed an insider's knowledge. His benefactors were all beyond reach of the SEC. He checked his options and marked those that caught his fancy. He loaded his worksheets. He was a patient man. And would soon be a rich one.

"**THE** end never justifies the means." Paul pointed a long finger at Leon. "I am aware that you create capital for the church by selling your confessional tapes. Not only is it sacrilege, it is a betrayal, and mortal sin. And your silver hip flask is forever half-full." He sagged, fury ebbing.

Leon bolted up. "*You,* so self-righteous and oh so holy. What would you have me do? Become a pugilist?"

Father Paul took the remark like a punch to the stomach. He collapsed heavily into a pew.

"Is it not," said Leon, in a softer voice, "really a choice we both make between competing evils—the lesser and the greater—in order that good may survive?"

"When, Father," said Paul, "did you become so pragmatic?"

"When the first fist found its mark on your face, Father."

Paul supported his face in his hands. "Compromise has always been the root of all evil for me."

Leon stepped over to Paul and put his hand on his friend's shoulder. "Then let them etch it on your gravestone tomorrow so we may get on with feeding the children today."

Paul looked at the front door. "Compromise does not include recruiting killers to aid us in our fight for justice. Killing to end killing? Destroying to preserve—"

"Nehemiah built the walls of Jericho high. He armed his flock. He trusted in the Lord, but he believed in the sword."

"That is 'eye for an eye' of the Old Testament." Paul extended his arms toward Leon. " 'Thou shalt not kill.' Have we forgotten?"

"Father. Father. The Protestants corrupted God's word; took it out of context in their King James translation. The Holy Church has correctly interpreted that as, 'Thou shalt not *murder.*' You know that."

" 'He that lives by the sword, shall die by the sword.' " Paul recoiled, searching for ammunition in this dialectical exchange.

"Father. In Romans, Paul clearly interpreted that passage to mean that if the sword is your law, then you *should* die by the sword. Christ's greatest disciples were soldiers: the Roman centurion Cornelius. King David was a man after God's own heart, and David slew thousands. Sol. Gideon. Joshua . . . Warriors all, and beloved of Christ."

Paul slumped in resignation.

"Father. Recall also Genesis 9:6. 'Whosoever sheddeth man's blood by man shall his own blood be shed.' "

"Must we rely on the old books?"

Leon was on fire. "Minutes before they came to arrest our Lord, remember, he said to his disciples, 'He that hath no sword, let him sell his garment, and buy one.' " He smiled triumphantly. "Luke 22:36. The *New* Testament."

Paul stared at the floor. "Are we to delight in death? These are not converts to Christ or disciples of the Word, but only killers. You are proposing nothing less than an orchestration of violence. What justifications can you possibly offer for recruiting death makers for this proposed bloodletting?"

"If you have a problem with the toilet, you call a plumber. Who better to shed blood than death makers?" Leon scratched his cheek. "Consider this," he said. " 'He sayeth then, let me embrace the death makers to my bosom that I may ward off the wicked and the depraved and those who would prey on my flock.' "

Paul regarded Leon as he contemplated the words. They were vaguely familiar. "Thessalonians?"

Father Leon smiled triumphantly. "No, Father. Leon Arnulfo Ortega."

GRAINGER and Sloane approached the church, their arms brushing each other now and then. She seemed to be unaware of the contact, but the touching made the hairs on his arm stand erect.

"Ponce's mother was a whore across the river. Father unknown."

"Was?"

"She died; throat cut with a broken bottle of Corona because she was unable to go one more. Joey's old man was one of Duran's prisoners. He was just a simple debtor who was killed in one of the shooting death matches a year, year and a half ago." She bit her lip. "And that . . . thing . . . your partner killed today? His name is—was—Bando Allcott. A real piece of work."

Grainger grabbed her arm, pulling her toward him. "Yeah?"

She swung around. "Yeah. He and one named Ramirez and another, an Asian—Vietnamese, I think—named Nguyen work for Rios in a special capacity. They're known as the NRA, but I don't think Charlton Heston would approve. The trio form Rios's own special little squad of enforcers, his very own Rainbow Coalition; minus one color as of today."

"What makes them different from any other hired guns?"

"To get their job, they had to prove their absolute loyalty to Rios."

"How?"

She turned away. "By killing a blood relative."

ELEVEN

THEY found Rawlings sitting on the front steps of the church. Sloane went inside the church, leaving Grainger behind.

"We leave, they die," said Grainger.

Rawlings traced a meandering pattern with his index finger in the dust of the top step. "We stay, maybe we all die."

"My name's Runyan," said a gravelly voice. "I think we may have some mutual interests. Maybe some common denominators." The man leaned on a walking stick, an Irish shillelagh, gnarled and weather-beaten, like his face. He appeared to be in his late forties. His piercing eyes were clear and ice-blue. They emitted a focused glow.

Rawlings considered the stranger. "We breathe the same air and walk upright. That's probably where it starts and stops. Do we know you?"

The man smiled. "Not directly." He looked over his shoulder and took off his cowboy hat. "Hotter than Hades. And getting hotter, it looks like. It feels like a storm could be brewing." He wrinkled his face a little and shrugged his shoulders. "You can feel it in your bones. Weather like this . . . once you experience it, you never forget it. Mogadishu. Belgrade. Guatemala City; I heard they have weather like this."

Grainger stole a glance at Rawlings, who was staring back.

"You know . . . if you get the time, come on up and see me. My place is—as they say around here—up the road a piece, ten miles north on 16. You cross a wadi and take the first dirt road to the right, all the way to the end. You can't miss it." He turned and hobbled off, only to stop and turn. "I'll be expecting you."

When the man was gone, Rawlings said, "Ever hear a Texan call a dry wash a wadi?"

SLOANE held out her hand. "Father Paul. Reconsider your position. These men are what we need to fight back."

Paul seized her by both arms. He wanted to shake her and make her understand. "You are a nurse for the children of this parish's orphanage. What do you know of fighting such monumental evil?" He stepped back. *The irony . . .*

She loosened her tensed muscles, and he let her go. "I know right from wrong and good from evil." *I left out "truth from lies."* "I know how the mothers of these children have become whores in Rios's brothels and their fathers slaves to his drugs and victims of his . . . Game."

Leon touched Paul's arm. "I agree. Who is to say these two are evil? They are merely men who appear to be possessed of unholy talent. I believe God intended for them to be delivered to us."

"Father Leon is right. I know you have objections concerning these men, but consider . . . When drowning, one doesn't question the morality and ethics of the hand that reaches out to save you. Think of the children and what will happen if we don't do something."

Paul was adrift in a current taking him downstream and powerless to redirect himself. "You both invoke a moral presumption of knowing God's will as well as a damnable pragmatism. I think that what we are considering is tantamount to entering into a pact with Satan, who in the end will damn us all to perdition."

"Men like those two home in on heat," said Leon. "They seek fire. Rios has created a Hell here for the people. And what fire is hotter? Others flee the flames. These two embrace the flames. For everything there is a season, Father . . . if you believe Ecclesiastes."

Paul held his head to keep it from spinning off. *Why have I become so inarticulate? Why have I no intellectual counterpoise?* He had to concede the battle, but not the war.

THE Black Vault.

The vault was where all written documents of the CIA were warehoused. These were the hard copies. Dating back to the days of the OSS and its founder, William J. "Wild Bill" Donovan, the Black Vault contained the Agency's history and its darkest secrets.

Stoneman watched as sesame was opened and the event logged. He was there demonstrably to check a file coded Tarantula, a recent operation against the *Islamique Armee,* the principal and most violent of the Algerian terrorist groups. The mission had failed. It had "gone white," been compromised. Stoneman had this unexpected windfall, this gratuitous opportunity: Tarantula. Tantrum. The file juxtaposition was perfect. He had quickly suggested a possible counterpenetration, an internal infiltration that resulted in the Tarantula caper disintegrating. The clues were in the file, he stated. No one else thought so. They were already calling him Daffy Dick Stoneman. But he had authority to enter the Black Vault for evidence to support his theory. His deceit had worked. So far.

Stoneman walked down the long, dank aisle, the faint hum of the air conditioner audible somewhere in the background. The vault was environmentally controlled with a constant temperature of sixty-eight degrees Fahrenheit. Surveillance cameras positioned at the end of all rows silently watched and recorded. He moved to the *T* row. The Black Vault could pass for a mausoleum. Files were contained in tomblike enclosures, some two stories high. Stoneman found the section he was looking for. He slid the movable ladder down its rail and climbed to the top. Bradley, his security monitor, sat down on one of the many chairs that were evident throughout the vault. He folded his arms and watched Stoneman with a bored expression.

Stoneman pulled out the drawer and found the Tarantula file. He thumbed through the papers and took a few notes. Then he slid his hand up past the red divider tab to the next folder. He saw the word Tantrum. Underneath, it said, "Sensitive Compartmented Information." Then . . . "Special Access Program." He moved his right eyeball as far as it would stretch without turning his head. The surveillance camera seemed to be staring right at him.

GRAINGER watched the stranger disappear, receding like a shadow. He looked at Rawlings.

"Don't look at me. This place is the fucking twilight zone."

Grainger entered the church, leaving the questions temporarily behind him.

Sloane looked up.

Grainger noticed that the brother and the novitiate nun named Sister Felicia were sitting in the pews along with the unnamed Hispanic custodian.

"They have decided—and I have reluctantly agreed—that we will enlist your help. But I want to make it perfectly clear we are not sanctioning any violence or mayhem. You are to consider your tasks defensive in nature. Furthermore, we have nothing to pay you with," said Paul.

Grainger nodded. "Everything is not about money." He noted Rawlings's grimace.

TANTRUM. Stoneman parted the file and looked at the material. His memory wasn't exactly photographic, but he was a speedreader, thanks to the Agency. He held his breath. A loud scraping noise made him jump. Bradley had pushed his chair away from the wall. Stoneman's mouth was dry, his throat parched. He tried to swallow, but couldn't. The words flashed by, small pieces in a large jigsaw puzzle: "Beirut. Cross-reference DIA OPLAN Tilt. Operational objective: 1) Final target resolution. 2) State Department security. Defense posture perspectives. State Department casualty—mortal. Subsections: Pre-Op Risk assessment reconsidered. Target identity: Unknown. Political unit linkage—indeterminate. NFI. Order of battle. Center of gravity. Command and control nodes." A vulnerability paragraph. "Post-Op Political implications. Foreseeable consequences. Protocol. Contingencies. Assets. Liaisons. Best—Probable—Worst case damage assessments."

All standard intelligence report stuff.

"Known and Unknown factors resulting in death of assignee and mission compromise of Terminex Team Ying-Yang. KIA/WIA. Zen Man." His hands vibrated more than trembled. "Historical factors: Mogadishu. Brand-X. Nexus." *Jesus!* "Bayes' Subjective Probabilities: Inconclusive. Opinions and Evaluation of survivor's statements: Reliability and truth cannot be judged. Failure Analysis. Conclusion: Marginal note: Murphy was working overtime. Recommendations: Need for revamping interagency coordination systems."

Stoneman closed the file, pushing it back into place. In his profession, truth was a relative thing. He understood that. Nonetheless, once you sorted through all the boilerplate and floss, it became crystal clear. The Agency wasn't a passive observer, and Cruickshank wasn't providing casual liaison. The CIA had a separate agenda from the DIA's revenge plot. The Company was using Grainger and Rawlings as bait in an attempt to lure and neutralize some unidentified terminator with "most wanted" status on their hit parade, and this someone had a connection with Mogadishu and something that happened there. "Brand-X." That was Grainger and Rawlings's Mogadishu call sign, and that put him square in the middle. His sweat turned to ice.

"Hey Dick! You about ready? Why don't you check out the damn thing? Have 'em put it on microfiche. Maybe they'll authorize it so you can study the thing at your leisure, sitting in a chair in a secure room." Bradley fidgeted below him.

Stoneman hardly heard him. *Mogadishu. Brand-X.*

GRAINGER moved to the pulpit, onto the elevated Mass service platform.

Paul cleared his throat. "You haven't formally met Brother

Lemuel Sotelo, Sister Felicia, and her father, Humberto Anaya. They are with us. They are family." He sat down next to Sloane.

Grainger held the pulpit firmly with both hands. "Temporarily, we're probably secure. It's important that you allow Myles—Mr. Rawlings—and myself to handle this without assistance or interference. Should things deteriorate, you won't be held responsible."

Leon snorted.

Grainger looked at Leon, then continued. "Does everybody understand?"

There was a murmur from Leon and Paul, who then translated into Spanish for Humberto.

"We're moving back to the hotel. When things start, we'll be in the bush. Before that, we need to make some arrangements. Do some reconnaissance. We should have some time before the balloon goes up," said Rawlings.

Father Paul sprang up. "I cannot give my blessing to this. You seem to be planning a war."

Grainger came out from behind the pulpit. "We are anticipating neutralizing the enemy. When we figure out an operations plan, we'll discuss it."

"Render unto Caesar, Father Paul," said Leon.

Grainger and Rawlings passed Father Paul, headed for the door.

Sloane gripped Father Paul's hand. "War has already found us, Father. We just never had an army." She turned her head and watched them leave. "Until now."

Paul watched the door of the church close behind the two men. *"Vaya con Dios."* It was a reflexive blessing, given in a hoarse whisper. With more conviction he mumbled, "God save us."

STONEMAN sat in his office with the lights off. Sweat dripped from his armpits and ran in rivulets down the sides of his body. He had accomplished what he had set out to do and had—hopefully—escaped detection. He was almost physically ill. He couldn't help thinking about one of the foreign agents in his stable when he was a DO case officer working under NOC—nonofficial cover—in Prague. The Office of Security had responded to his "grave concerns" about the loyalty of one of his operatives. They ran a polygraph on Karmin, his Czech indigenous agent. He was determined "deceptive" on questions of loyalty. The security officer put it to Karmin plainly. "You evinced negative physiological reactions." Then he gave Karmin the final admonishment; a nine-millimeter. *One round. Through the head.* The official report later said only, "The matter was resolved in the interest of National Security." Another caravan of drops queued up under his arm. Stoneman took a deep breath. All he had to do was communicate with Brand-X, and he was free.

THE Dodge pulled up in front of the church. Sloane stood on the steps with Ponce and Joey. Grainger got out of the car and approached her. Ponce jumped to the bottom step and headed for Rawlings.

"I think it's time we had a talk," she said.

"Here?" Grainger said.

"Look . . . I . . . Can we take a ride?"

Rawlings laid his hand on the kid's arm as the boy stood silently at the side of the car. "Hey, Potts, don't you ever go to school?"

"My name is Ponce . . . P-o-n-c-e. And it's summer vacation."

"Oh, yeah, I forgot."

Ponce leaned into the car.

"Look, kid. Is there something I can do for you? I mean, quit staring at me, will you?"

Ponce put a hand on the steering wheel. "I just never met anyone like you. I guess I like you, too."

"That's nice, son, but I'm not going to be around long enough to make it worth your while. Know what I'm saying? Now, go on."

Ponce backed up, the edges of his eyes wet.

Sloane walked to the car. She started to get in the back, but Rawlings stopped her with his hand. He crawled into the backseat.

"Good tactical principle. Never let an unknown subject sit behind you," she said.

Grainger got in and turned to Rawlings. "Ms. McKenzie wants to take a ride."

Rawlings opened his hands, palms out, and shrugged.

Grainger backed out into the street and drove off. *"Good tactical principle . . ." Launders his money . . . Has knowledge about drug movements . . . "Murder's not federal jurisdiction . . ." Referring to us as hitters . . . What kind of nurse has that kind of vocabulary and insight?* He let those questions ride.

He pulled into a stall outside Garcia's drugstore and got out. "Be back in a flash." He returned a minute later and winked at Sloane. "Letter to Santa."

A few miles out on Highway 83, Sloane pointed out a dirt road. "Turn here," she said.

They drove to the end of the road, to a small stream that cut through a grove of cottonwood trees. Scattered boulders and prickly pear cactus grew among the sage, catclaw, ironwood, and crucifix thorn bushes. A nest of meadowlarks scattered upon their approach, and a covey of plumed desert quail flushed from the briars and brambles.

Grainger turned off the engine and waited.

Sloane opened her door and held it open with her foot. "I used to come here sometimes, once in a while, to think." She took a deep breath. "Smells good, too; it's the eucalyptus trees, I think." She slid out of the car and took a few steps.

What is she doing? Grainger stepped out of the car and moved toward her.

Rawlings looked at his big Seiko wrist chronometer. He put his feet up on the backrest of the front seat.

Sloane picked up a stone and flung it into the staid creek. "I want to help," she said.

"You already have. Listen. Myles and I have work to do." Grainger took her by the arm and started to pull her toward the car. He saw the sky unbalance and the trees go sideways. He was airborne for a brief moment and then flat on his back, still somehow holding on to her arm. Sloane was straddling him. It was a jujitsu hip throw, and he never saw it coming.

Rawlings leaned forward and clapped lethargically from the backseat.

"No, you listen to me, you arrogant, egotistical, chauvinistic son of a bitch." She whirled around to confront Rawlings, who had stopped clapping. "Goes for you, too, asshole—double." She turned back to Grainger, who was rubbing his head. "I don't know why you're in Zapata, but I've been here for two Goddamn years watching and recording and eating my guts out . . ." She released Grainger and moved away.

Rawlings stood up in the backseat, staring hard.

Grainger got up off the ground. "Who are you?"

"Sloane Nadine McKenzie. I think." She brushed some of the dirt from his shirt. "Two years, deep cover assignment. I'm DEA."

A rooster tail of dust followed them, even though he wasn't driving that fast. Unasked questions hung heavily in the air.

"Investigate. Document. File reports. What was ever done? Nada. 'Keep up the good work, Agent McKenzie . . . ' " She could have been talking to herself; the words carried back into thin air.

Grainger stole a glance at her. "The nurse bit? A cover?"

"No. That's for real. I'm an LVN. Was working on my RN at Bronx General in the ER for a couple years. I used to throw my guts on a daily basis, seeing ten-year-old kids addicted to crack, pregnant women overdosed, and three-month-old babies going through heroin withdrawals and fetal alcohol addiction. I wanted to do something positive to impact that. So I joined the Drug Enforcement Administration. I thought I'd seen it all. I was wrong."

Rawlings leaned over the seat. "So, here you are."

She nodded. "So, here I am."

THE mail came early on Saturday. Stoneman was waiting for the postal carrier as he came up the walk to his condo. The letter was sandwiched between the Texaco bill and a local merchant's coupon book. He went inside and made sure the door was locked. He looked out the window to see if there were any Acme Plumbing vans outside with parabolic mikes or Patty's Pizza trucks with microwave receivers zooming in on his Fourth Amendment rights. *Just because you are paranoid doesn't mean it isn't true.* He crossed the living room and sat in the beige leather chair. He opened the letter and found what he knew he would find.

SLOANE McKenzie was alone in her spartan room located off the connecting hallway between the church and the orphanage. She had revealed herself to these two men without really knowing why. She knew nothing about them. Their pasts didn't seem to be open to review or their histories to discussion. They were a different sort of human being, for sure; not the sort you'd see at Club Med, enamored of the channel changer, or spending their week's pay buying lottery tickets. She could only guess what they had done and where they had been. It didn't matter now. It probably was for the best. She was committed to seeing this through, and they were the best things in sight. Here she was, in Texas. When she left DEA headquarters in Washington, D.C., for this assignment, the joke was that she had been given a choice: Hell or Texas. And Sloane, not wanting to appear a coward, selected Texas. It was a joke. Then. Now she was here, a Bryn Mawr graduate with a degree in Comparative Religions with proud parents telling everybody that their daughter was on a sabbatical, working on her graduate degree at Cambridge University in merry old London town. Yes. It was definitely a graduate degree she was working on. Only it was from Zapata U. And she'd never be able to explain why there wasn't any diploma.

She sat on the bed and considered that in her thirty years of life she had accomplished little of any note. She hadn't read a book in six months and only watched an occasional video of a film that was probably at least a year old. She was out of touch with life. She hadn't had a relationship since Derek, the intern at Bronx General. They dissolved their unwedded union when he took an offer at Johns Hopkins. She managed a slight smile. If it weren't for BOB—her battery operated boyfriend—she most likely would have hung herself. This town had nothing to offer her by way of male companionship. She couldn't afford to get involved, even if it did. But then again, she wasn't really looking. A sperm donor was the last thing on her wish list. She allowed her thoughts to drift to the vaguely erotic, although denying it to herself. The one called Rawlings was better looking, but the other one seemed to have a little more depth and passion. *What the hell, I'm not a contestant on* The Dating Game. *They're just convenient tools, not heroes out of a romance novel.* Someday she would connect with her soul mate, if there was such an animal. She stared at the ceiling. The most important thing was to be able to believe in something. She once had, and maybe it was time for some of that old-time religion. She fell into a fitful sleep.

THERE was a pounding somewhere in the distance. Drums? Heartbeats? Thunderclaps? She opened her eyes for a moment, forgetting where she was. It was the door. She rubbed her eyes and wiped the sleep from them. She threw on a robe and answered the knock. It was Brother Lemuel.

"Those two men are in the church."

Sloane dressed and ran a brush through her hair. She thought momentarily that she might do her face, and then realized she wasn't going to condemn herself to that role. She walked down the hall to the church. They were waiting for her.

"You said yesterday that Rios was expecting something big?" Grainger said.

Sloane nodded, still a little groggy. She looked at her watch. It was only 6:30 A.M.

"If you can find out from your people some intel, it'll help."

She couldn't suppress a yawn. "I'll see what I can do." She looked around the church. It was empty. "Look. You understand this is all between you two and me. The priests don't know anything about me other than I'm a nurse, a good Catholic girl from New York."

"Sure."

"Do you need any equipment? Weapons? I have an MP-5 and a Beretta 92F that I've kept hidden."

"You have a submachine gun? That's good. We may need it—or you may need it," said Rawlings.

They started for the door. Grainger stopped and looked back at her. "Sorry we had to get you up to ask."

She waved her hands and shook her head. "No problem."

Grainger glanced at his watch. "I'm expecting a phone call in . . . ten minutes."

She brushed back a fallen strand of hair. "And then?"

"And then," he said, "I have to pay a visit to an old friend who I don't even know."

THE burnished bronze of the Marine Corps Memorial gleamed in the early morning light.

He could see Private First Class Ira Hamilton Hayes from the telephone booth. Hayes was the Pima Indian, the one on the far left, reaching over Franklin Sousley's shoulders for the staff of the flag that was being raised on Mount Suribachi, Iwo Jima, in April 1945. Richard Stoneman looked at his watch. It was 0800—8 A.M. in civilian parlance—in Arlington. That would be 0700 in Po-Dunk, Texas, or wherever Grainger was. He turned a full 360 degrees looking for anything out of place. *Ten more minutes. Maybe I should take a walk, feed the pigeons.*

THE drive from Falls Church to where he would make the call was a short one. But he doubled back, made U-turns, and ran a couple red lights to see if there was a tail on him. He even sped to the parallels to determine whether there was a max-effort, multiple-car mobile surveillance operation working him.

He had time to think about what he had seen and learned. *Mogadishu.* The Dish seemed to hold the answer, or at least was a major clue for an answer to the question of what happened later in Beirut. He waited, and he remembered. . . .

The Stone Man. His mother was Ecuadorian and his father American of Scotch descent. Thus, he had adopted the hide-in-plain-sight operational code name of Stone Hombre. Stoneman had, in the jargon of the Company, an "exceptional operational mind," i.e., he was a particularly effective spy. He was a man with a plan, and the future was bright in the DO, the Directorate of Operations. He was one of their stars, a man who made things happen, even when they didn't want to happen. In September 1993, he had been ordered to Mogadishu, Somalia, to coordinate military action with the Darod clan of Mohamed iad Barre, against their principal political rival, Mohamad Farah Aidid and his Habr Gidr clan. Reportedly, this was in order to balance the equities, stabilize the balance of power, and level the playing field in favor of democracy. Such proffered-for-public-consumption pabulum notwithstanding, Stone Hombre knew the reality was strictly pragmatic, the need to influence manageable forces friendly to our way of thinking.

Operation Restore Hope, as the administration's global robocop Somali mission was euphemistically titled, had taken a dump. The Marines, who had been deployed like the Salvation Army Meals-On-Wheels, handing out Red Cross goodie baskets to the Somalis, had saddled up and gone home and had been replaced by the Rangers and Delta operators, now tasked with taking down Aidid. His name in Somali meant, "He who suffers no insult." It was a fair assessment. Aidid was UN public enemy number one ever since the slaughter and mutilation of twenty-four Pakistani peacekeepers in Mogadishu a month before. Stoneman remembered it all clearly now, like it was happening again. The afternoon of 3 October . . .

The gunmen from the Habr Gidr burst into the room where he was meeting with the Darods. In the hail of gunfire and exploding grenades that followed, his security team was killed. He managed to make it out a window but found himself trapped in a hostile, black, Islamic city, running for his life among the alleys of that portion of Mogadishu called by task force personnel, "the Black Sea." In and among the booths and stalls he ran, panicked and bleeding slightly from a shrapnel wound. He shot dead a Somali man who confronted him, or maybe just got in his way. He remembered bursting into the back of a burned-out, looted hotel. He activated his locator beacon and worked his way through the old kitchen, up the flights of stairs, to the top of the hotel. He hoped he hadn't been followed. He hoped he hadn't been seen entering the building. He hoped someone would monitor his distress signal and locator. He hoped they would send a helicopter and rescue force. He hoped.

He could hear gunfire and explosions erupting, seemingly

everywhere. It sounded like World War III had broken out in Mogadishu. He collapsed on the floor and leaned against a wall. He looked at his rib cage. He hoped he wouldn't bleed to death. Hope in one hand and shit in the other, and see which fills up faster. He probably would bleed to death. . . .

DETECTING nothing, Stoneman dialed the number. There was a midring pickup. There was no need for conversation. It was going to be omnidirectional communication, an intelligence briefing, albeit an abbreviated one, filled with gaps. He could only remember so much, and all the answers weren't available, anyway. "There was an overlay operation. The Center for Intercourse and the Arts had a contingency op in place, a couple of them. There was a Terminex team—code name Ying-Yang—monitoring your show. There was some kind of co-op deal being negotiated on site with the mark with the CIA and State collaborating. Saleem was being turned west. The Agency was coaxing him into being their inside man in the Middle Eastern terror network and al-Qaida links. The face value op was the NMCC's and DIA's objective to kill Saleem as payback for the Colonel Higgins assassination and the Beirut Marine barracks massacre. There are some holes in this review, but I only had the vision for five, six minutes max. I'm doing the best I can. I don't have a photographic memory, for Christ's sake. The CIA/State deal was struck with Saleem, but you executed your man before they could make notification to the Agency liaison—Cruickshank—to have you halt the proceedings. The report said OPCON called him, but it was too late. Conclusion was that Cruickshank dumped the Arab guide on his own authority, but here's the zinger. There was another act out that day, a regular three-ring circus. The Saleem/State deal was apparently also a sideshow. The real CIA mission was a setup. The Company sniper team was supposed to take out a shooter who had you as the bull's eye, nothing personal, and business as usual. It seems this ghost shooter was a top opposition pro assassin identified by code name only. Freelance or national origin is indeterminate, but he'd been linked to the assassination of a few first-tier agency operatives. They were using you to get to this extremely high value target. Apparently they had intel that he would be there to do the deed. He had some personal hard-on for you, but no one knows why. That's because no one knows who. The problem probably was he spotted the Terminex team right after he dusted off our guy Cruickshank, whether by design or mistaken identity is unknown. The bogey turned on them. This boy was good; bagged and tagged his limit that day. Three of our people. He did unto others before they did unto him. That's the probable case scenario. Info only: The State Department salesman making deals with Saleem took a sky dive off the balcony after you clipped the target. The Arab's security department was pissed. This information comes from a report called Tantrum, an after-action assessment of the OPLAN promulgated in-house, eyes-only, by the director's board."

He paused and scanned his surroundings while he listened. "No. No identities on the Terminex team. The shooter was code-named The Zen Man. That's all I got. Top-of-the-line talent, but triple-layer backstopped. There *is* a connection though, a fucking bizarre one. Mogadishu. This triangle had something to do with Mogadishu. There was some after-action intel developed—rumors, innuendos, supposition, D-rated reliability stuff—that the mystery shooter had some connection with you and something that happened in Mog. You and Rawlings . . . I saw your code designator—Brand-X—mentioned a couple times. The phantom optical man out there in Beirut was putting his personal PS on things for something that happened in Mog. Even the Bayes' estimates couldn't put the finger on why you were the bull's-eye. You need to think back to yesteryear and debrief yourself about your ops in Somalia." He paused once again and turned full circle. "Look. This is all I got and all I'm going to do. Whatever the answer is, it has something to do with the Heart of Darkness, but I don't know what. It's weird. I've thought about it myself. If you figure it out, don't bother to call. I don't want to know. Listen. This squares us. I owed you for what you two did. But, Sergeant Rock . . . We're even up."

He hung up the telephone in slow motion. *So, Grainger was in a phone booth in Zapata, Texas, with an emergency contact at the local Catholic church?* He didn't care if it was on the planet Mars. Contacts were terminated. *Fini.* He swung open the folding door and stepped outside. *A man never forgets. A man pays his debts.* Richard Stoneman had just retired his obligation. *Paid in full. With interest.* He was a free man. He went to feed the pigeons.

YESTERDAY'S enemy.

There were so many of them it didn't pay to hold a grudge, develop any passion, or patronize some conviction that you were serving a greater good. National interest was a shifting sand. A man condemned as the devil's own today could be sleeping in the Lincoln Bedroom tomorrow. He was an executioner, much like the shogun's decapitator of feudal Japan. He had accepted his executory role in government. He had followed orders and—for the most part—had accomplished the mission. He rarely took it personally or reveled in the accomplishment; not that he shrank from the responsibility or the consequences. Yes, in many ways it was like an antelope hunt. Mostly, it was only business. He had been trained. He had been taught. He had been schooled. He even had received an education; but that had come later. Education was what remained after most things he had been taught had been forgotten. Now, it was no longer business. It was something far more important. He thought about what Stoneman had said about Mogadishu, and he would think on it. Soon. Right now, he had other things on his mind. Lon Grainger drove north on County Road 16, looking for the wadi.

YOU *can't go home again.* Myles Rawlings was not Eugene Gant. He did not howl at the moon—anymore at least—or run madly in circles, going nowhere. However, a roaring drunk was still well within the realm of possibility. But you never could go back. What you were hoping or looking for was never there waiting. He never went to a high school reunion. The chicks would all be fat and his old friends bald or dead, sometimes both. It was also the reason he had hunkered down in east LA instead of San Pedro.

His father had made a long haul to Biloxi, met a woman, and never came home. His mother took up with the manager of a hotel on Gaffey Street. Everything about San Pedro seemed different. Only the Grand Theater on Sixth Street remained unchanged. It still had *Fail-Safe*, with Henry Fonda, on the marquee, the last film shown there. It had always been there as far as Rawlings could remember. He had wandered around San Pedro, and it might as well have been Katmandu. *You can't go home again, not even for a visit.* There was a knock on the door.

Rawlings drew his Walther PPKS and moved to the side of the door. The mirror he had removed from the bathroom was placed opposite the door so what the person entering the room saw was only a reflection of the reality with the gun. He quietly unlatched the door and stepped back. "It's open."

The door creaked open slowly, and a hand appeared. Rawlings grabbed the attached arm and pulled. Ponce staggered through the door. Rawlings looked into the hallway and saw nothing. He closed the door. "What the hell, kid?"

GRAINGER found the dry streambed and the dirt road just past it and turned off the highway. A mile in, he saw the cabin. It was situated on a bluff overlooking a canyon. A few desolate trees were bent in various twisted postures, leaning at various angles—but all in one direction—victims of a near-constant wind that blew. Grainger stopped the car one hundred meters from the cabin. He turned off the engine and listened while he press-checked the Colt Government Model .45 pistol on his lap. A dog barked somewhere. *So much for surprise.* He started the car and rolled forward.

He parked in front and got out. He could taste the dust on his teeth, a thin film of grit. He mounted the three pine-plank steps and stood on the rickety porch. It was a wooden cabin with an oak front door reinforced by steel ribs like gargoyle talons. *Whoever he is, he's a cautious man.* The barrel of his Colt nudged his hip.

"Don't step on the welcome mat; it's booby-trapped." The voice came from his right flank; a man with a dog—a liver-and-tick German shorthaired pointer—at his side. The man wiped his hands on an oily red rag and held Grainger's stare, unblinking. He leaned lightly on his gnarled shillelagh. "I'm working on the generator out back. It's my only source of power."

Grainger rapidly calculated the man's visible assets: *He's no accountant. Tough, except for the reliance on the stick. Favors his right side. Right-handed. No visible weapons.* "Is there anything else I should know, Mr. Runyan?"

Runyan's lips peeled back. "One bit of information at a time, Mr. Grainger."

"First bit. I need information about the weather and how you know so much about it."

"Please come inside. I never talk about the weather in the sun."

Grainger followed Runyan into the cabin. The spring-loaded front door clenched shut behind him, like an iron claw.

"**WHAT** is with you, kid? You stalking me or something?"

"I like you and just want you to like me."

"Look, Potts—"

"Pon—"

"Yeah, Ponce. That's right, I forgot. Look. I'm no baby-sitter, and I don't have time for this right now. Go do some kid things, why don't you. Get your boom box and listen to Puff Daddy."

"That's ghetto. You don't know everything, mister. I can tell."

"How's that, son? And what's ghetto?"

"Puff Daddy is now P. Diddy. And ghetto is no place. It means, sort of like, bad. Or good. Depending."

Rawlings sat on the bed. "No kidding? You learn something every day."

Ponce grinned. "I know lots of stuff, and we could share with each other. I mean, you tell me something that I don't know, or a story, and I'll tell you. It'll be pro."

Rawlings looked at his watch and then the kid. "Pro. Right. Okay, Junior, just this time. I've got a while to kill. But if a grenade comes through the window, I'm throwing you on top of it. Understand?"

Ponce understood. It was a great deal. A real bargain. "Da *bomb.* Okay. Deal. You first."

THE inside smelled musty but was otherwise orderly in a male sort of way. There was a pile of dirty clothes in the corner and unwashed dishes in the sink. The trash cans were full, but not overflowing. There was a place for everything, and everything seemed more or less in place. *Feng shui* it wasn't, and Martha Stewart would have had a heart attack, but Grainger didn't give it much of a second thought. One thing for sure, there was no womanly influence.

Runyan read his thoughts. "I live alone, so there's not much need for compulsive neatness, I suppose."

Grainger's eyes rotated around the room. "How do you know my name?"

"Lonny Delbert Grainger, aka the Long Ranger; also as the Widow Maker, post the Cairo operation. You were tagged with the Distant Death for the Belgrade caper, and, after Colombia, *El Dedo del Diablo.* You were hung with that one after that fourteen hundred meter shot you made in Bogota in—"

"I know when it was."

Runyan smiled. "Of course you do. A remarkable legend, really, starting in Delta and carrying right over into the private—well, semiprivate—sector. My favorite showstopper was the shutdown you did on that Panamanian, the head of *Vendetta, S.A de C.V.,* on his honeymoon in the Poconos. Fifteen hundred meters away; you potted him from the next zip code."

"How do you know that? That's classified beyond—"

"Not beyond me, my boy. You used a prototype M40A2 rifle based on the Remington 40XB action in a wildcat caliber, eight-millimeter-.338. It had custom double-set triggers, a Unertle twenty power glass with a . . ." He rubbed his head. "Tapered-post reticle, mill scale and ranging stadia. I was glass bedding the actions back then."

"You built that rifle?"

"The Gale McMillan Company supplied the counter-sunk crowned barrel. The rest was my contribution to history."

"**ONE** time when I was in Bolivia with Indiana Jones—"

Ponce held up his hand. "No way, Mr. Rawlings. Indiana Jones is a movie character."

Rawlings eyed the kid curiously. "Can't fool you, huh? Okay. I was there on deployment with Mr. Grainger when we were in Special Forces." In response to Ponce's furled eyebrows, he added, "You know, Green Berets. American superheroes."

Ponce's head bobbed up and down in recognition.

"Okay. Here's something I'll bet you don't know. The Qurungas tribe down there in Bolivia never speaks."

"The women, too?" said Ponce. "That's phat."

"Fat?" Rawlings shrugged. *Kid talk.* "Hard to fuc . . . hard to believe, huh? Now, I read about this guy in a book about saving the elephants in Africa, called *The Roots of Heaven*. This character in the story swears to never speak again until the locals stop poaching the elephants, and they were free to roam, or something like that. But I never would have believed it unless I saw it with my own eyes; a bunch of people looking like mimes because they lost their vocal cords as a result of some genetic defect."

"I'm going to tell that story in Brother Lemuel's summer school class tomorrow. It's totally tight."

"Totally true, too . . . ah, dude," Rawlings said. "Your turn."

"Okay. I know wrestling is fixed. When Vince McMahon gets beat up on TV by Stone Cold, it's just fake. Nobody ever gets hurt. Father Paul . . . Now, he gets hurt when he fights."

Rawlings shifted on the bed. " 'Father Paul?' "

Ponce leaned forward and began.

* * *

"SO, which agency of our exalted government did—do—you work for, Mr. Runyan?" asked Grainger.

"Call me Pappy," he said. "Does income tax evasion qualify as federal employment?" He chuckled self-consciously over his attempt at humor. His mouth tightened. "You're thinking that making rifles doesn't access the kind of info I have. You're right. I was an intelligence analyst geek with the DIA. The rifles were a little profitable sideline."

Grainger rustled in his seat. "I'd like to trip on down memory lane and explore your résumé with you, but let's get to the bottom line. What's this got to do with me?"

Runyan centered his backside on a large wicker chair. He lowered himself precariously, then collapsed the last two feet into the chair.

Grainger noticed for the first time that he was wearing some kind of back brace.

Runyan leaned forward on his walking stick. "On a bad day I need two of these to get around, but it beats a walker. I hate being a fucking cripple."

"Tell me all about it; after you tell me what this has to do with me and my partner."

Runyan moved his back in a slow circle, searching for a neutral zone. "Let me tell you a story."

"WE were in Ethiopia once—this is top secret, son—fighting injustice and looking to pave the whole damn place and make it a parking lot when I found out that the letter *A* is the thirteenth letter of the alphabet for those people. Now, there's some cultural diversity for you, huh?"

"Did you kill anyone when you were there?" asked Ponce.

"What is this, an interrogation or an information exchange? I plead the Fifth Amendment."

"Are you a criminal?"

Rawlings leaned over and looked Ponce in the eye. "Depends on who you ask."

"You've been everywhere. Done everything. Tell me more stuff about places and people."

Rawlings stroked his chin. "Okay. Here's a real *Mondo Cane* one for you. We were in a country called Mauritania once, doing God's work . . ." He looked at Ponce for a frown or a smirk. There was none, so he went on. "The Bedouins . . ." Ponce's look said he hadn't got that far in school. "Nomadic tribesmen," explained Rawlings. "They have a system of law and order called *Haj El Orfi*—The Law of Knowledge. They have a ceremony called *Bisha*, a real simple test for truth. The suspect charged licks a white-hot iron pan with his tongue. If it scorches, it shows he's lying. If not, it proves he's innocent." He caught Ponce's wince. "I gather you prefer the lie detector and a jury of your peers, huh?"

"They're never going to believe me when I tell this in Brother Lemuel's class." Then he wanted to know all about Rawlings, what he did when he was a boy Ponce's age.

Rawlings told him about sports and his family, making up some of it as he went along, whenever the reality didn't quite fit. He also told how he would take the bus to Culver City and spend the day in Arvo Ojala's leather shop. "Arvo Ojala, kid, the greatest gunfighter that ever lived. Better than Wild Bill Hickock and Doc Holiday. Ojala made the holster rig for Richard Boone for the old *Have Gun, Will Travel* series. Arvo was the guy who faced—and was gunned down by—James Arness as Marshall Matt Dillon every week for twelve years in a row on *Gunsmoke*. Catch it on cable, son. I also hung out with Thell Reed, National Fast Draw Champion."

"What did you do there all day?"

"Became a secret gunslinger. They said I was the fastest they'd ever seen. They called me *El Rapido*."

"You were faster than Señor Ojala?"

"I don't know about that, but I was faster than greased lightning and could slap the opposition in the face twice after I drew and then catch the twirling gun in midair. But . . . maybe not as fast as Arvo."

"Wow."

"Now, you tell me a story. Okay?"

"Sure," said Ponce. "Zapata used to be called Hard Luck.

The name got changed back during *La Revolución*. Emiliano Zapata crossed the Rio Grande to escape the forces of the dictator Huerta. He stayed for a night. Before he went back across the river, he made a speech on his horse down at the square. He said it was better to die on your feet than live on your knees. There's a plaque down by the park that has his words on it, if you want to see it. After that, people just started calling Hard Luck, Zapata."

"Yeah. I saw Marlon Brando get ambushed on his white horse in the movie." He slapped his knee. "That's a nice slice of history, Ponce. Now I need one more. How is it you came up with a copy of *New Breed* and knew to write us?"

Ponce opened his mouth. "Oh, that."

"I moved here four years ago after I retired. I was married then. My wife, Annie, died soon after we got here. She was killed. After that I swore a self-imposed celibacy upon myself and took to reading the Stoics, taking solace in them telling me that 'the door is always open.' I also have put my remaining energies into rifle construction. Special rifles; the kind that only a very few men can appreciate, become part of." He pointed his stick at Grainger. "You, Lon, are one of those men."

Grainger realized the man wasn't answering any questions to his satisfaction, but he felt he was drawing nearer to something.

With a struggle, Runyan pulled himself from the chair. "Let me show you some things." He led the way to another small room off the main one. It was filled with benches and cartridge reloading presses, primer punches, deburring tools, tumblers, powder scales, and micrometers. He moved to a bench and picked up a single round of ammunition. The brass gleamed. "Recognize this?"

Grainger shook his head.

"I didn't figure you would. It's a .338 Lapua Magnum. Some ballistic purists refer to it as the 8.6 × 70 mm. It's developed from the .416 Rigby cartridge. The case is shortened a bit and the neck diameter reduced to seat the .338 bullet. It's slightly over bore capacity. The ballistically efficient nickel-copra core bullet of 250 grains coupled with high velocity, means you can reach out and touch somebody as far as your limitations will allow. The muzzle velocity chronographs a hair in excess of 3250 feet per second and doesn't drop below the speed of sound until almost fifteen hundred meters out. The remaining energy at two thousand meters is over six hundred joules—four hundred fifty foot-pounds. The trade-off is a bone-jarring recoil."

Grainger couldn't help but be impressed with the external ballistic performance. But he still wasn't any closer to an answer.

Runyan was still talking. "The rounds are all formed individually utilizing only virgin brass; but I still mike each case. Then I tamp one hundred twenty-four grains of Alliant RL25 powder. Each charge is scaled; no powder measure. Federal 215 magnum primers provide ignition and, voilà." He set the cartridge down on the table and opened a door to a closet. He removed a large canvas case, which he placed on the floor. "Go ahead and open it. I can't bend down very good and can hardly tie my shoes. If it wasn't for Velcro, I'd be barefoot forever."

Grainger pulled the rifle from the case. He knew immediately this was a very special weapon. It looked like the current issue U.S. Army M-24 sniper rifle, but a little different.

"Looks a little like the M-24, doesn't it? There are some important differences. This one sports a Timney adjustable single-set trigger that can be disconnected in a target-rich environment. The lock time is under .0020. It has the same basic Remington 700 action you're familiar with although mated to a Shileen Super Match grade barrel that is fully free-floated. That's the way I do 'em now."

Grainger found the words escaping involuntarily. "It's beautiful."

"Eye of the beholder, I guess. The synthetic, laminated stock is adjustable for pull and drop. It might not be everybody's idea of a showpiece, but its zero is unaffected by climatic conditions. Notice the scope?"

Grainger did.

"I don't know whether you're familiar with this one. It's built by U.S. Optics Technologies in California. Outclasses the Leupold Mk IV, which you undoubtedly know is the supposed gold standard. That's the SN-2, Ultra-High Resolution: thirty-millimeter titanium tube, 5.6-28 variable power, mil-dot illuminated reticle, and ranging stadia calibrated at ten X, and the ERGO parallax adjusting system. It has an extra-long eye-relief for the heavy recoil of the .338 Lapua. It's drop-tested from six feet on concrete and waterproof to thirty feet, for the SEALs. Lever-lock mount on the NATO Picatinney rail makes the scope easily removable if need be. Returns to absolute zero every time."

Grainger ran his hand along the length of the weapon, then handed it to Runyan. "I came to talk to you about—"

"I know what you came to talk to me about."

"Then tell me what I need to know."

Runyan laid the rifle down on the bench, studying the man before him. "Do you believe in destiny, Lon?"

Grainger shifted his weight to the opposite foot. "I don't know. Maybe."

"You. This rifle. Even me. We're like Jung's theory of synergistic energies, all coming together at a moment in complementary time. But, it's choice, not chance that determines destiny."

"Is it for sale?"

"Money is not the value of things; you of all people know that." He went to the front door and opened it, looking out. The pointer stood guard on the porch. He turned back. "Ever think about dying, Lon, about your legacy? What will it be?"

Grainger moved toward him. "I try not to think."

Runyan pointed an accusatory finger. "No; you do, Lon. Or else you wouldn't be here. This is more than simple curiosity."

"How's that?"

"I know about more than Belgrade and the Poconos. I also know about Beirut. I've made it my business to know all about you." Runyan stood lopsided in the doorway. "Like I said, my wife was killed a couple years ago. A big, black limousine ran her over and never stopped to see what the bump was. The owner of that automobile had what you might say was total immunity. He was untouchable. I buried her and waited. For you."

"THIS older guy came up to us one day while Joey and I were playing stickball and asked us if we wanted a root beer float at the drugstore. I thought he was a molester or something like they told us about; but I never had a float—"

"So he bought you one. And then what?"

"He talked to us about all the troubles the orphanage was having and showed us this magazine he had with a circle around a part he wanted us to see. It was about you. He told us that if we would write, you might come. I didn't believe him. Joey did."

Rawlings got up off the bed and looked out the dirty window. "He look about forty-eight or fifty, walk with a limp and a cane?"

"I don't know how old he was, but he was limping. No cane. It was a crooked stick."

The walls seemed to be closing in. There was a fifth dimension to everything.

"I kept tabs on you and Rawlings right from the beginning. I have a few contacts in The Community, as you might suspect. I knew you'd never come down here for any reason I could concoct or sustain once you got here. I couldn't figure out an angle. Then one day God gave me what I needed: the ad in *New Breed*. The day you placed the classified, I knew. Jon Clement at *New Breed* advised the DIA as a routine merc notification. I got a call that night. I slapped a little drugstore psychology together, and it came to me that the one way to get you down here was the kid angle. Under the circumstances, I didn't figure you could resist. Truth is, I never considered that Rawlings would make the trip. Just the same, it's even better, maybe." He drifted off.

"If you know about Beirut, why don't you tell me what happened."

Runyan found a wall to lean on. "The shooter who drilled Cruickshank was on the Agency's top-priority target list. Most wanted. Intel was that he'd be there. Seems he wanted to kill you for some reason. His employer, reason, or cause . . . unknown. There was a State Department/CIA deal with Saleem going down, but it was strictly incidental."

Grainger nodded. *That fits with what Stoneman said.*

"Lucky for you he nailed Cruickshank when he did."

Grainger registered the words but pushed them away. "I guess I could use that rifle."

"You know how a man achieves immortality, Lon?"

"Can't say that I do."

"By his deeds, Lon, by his deeds. Estaban Rios has a shooter named Montezuma. His real name's Lorca. *Cubano,* not Mex. One hundred twenty-nine confirmed kills at last count, in Angola, Zimbabwe, South Africa, Yugoslavia; a couple in Portugal and more than a few locally. Might even be more by now. You'll meet him."

"What do you want from me?"

Runyan hobbled past Grainger to the bench where the rifle lay. He picked it up and moved slowly back to stand in front of Grainger. He handed over the rifle. "There might have been a time when I may have considered my own payback. I guess that was my intention when I moved here. Now, you're going to be my surrogate."

Who is using whom? Or does it matter? Revenge was a basic human motivation. *Any enemy of my enemy is my friend.* "What happened to your legs?"

Runyan felt his left leg. "It's a personal problem. Spinal injury. Industrial accident. workers' compensation matter. Don't mean nothing anymore. I'm still a rock."

Grainger reached for the rifle.

IT was dusk, growing dark rapidly when they finally left the cabin. Grainger inhaled deeply and smelled a fresh scent in the air he had not noticed before. Cicadas flew in circles and buzzed noisily, oblivious to the fact they would never see the sun rise. Fireflies blinked on and off and danced like tiny lanterns among the desert flowers that grew wild against the walls of the cabin.

While Runyan and the dog watched, Grainger made three trips to load the trunk with rifle, ammunition, spotting scope, binoculars, and other items that were provided. When the last article was loaded, he shut the trunk and turned around. Runyan was standing on the top step.

Runyan watched his sniper load the gear, considering the

irony of his selection of executioners. The reality was that circumstances had selected. Fate had determined the cast; he was just a facilitator, a player in The Game. He looked back at Grainger. "One thing, Lon. Remember . . . You always miss the shot you don't take."

Grainger nodded, got into the Dodge, and started the engine. He put it into gear.

"Lon!" Runyan hobbled down the stairs and limped toward the car. "I didn't tell you everything." He struggled to stand unsupported. "I'm going to give you another reason to be here. Beirut. Montezuma . . . He was the third shooter."

THIRTEEN

THERE was a rapid knocking on the door. Rawlings pushed Ponce down behind the bed and assumed his defensive position. "Cancel the pâté de foie gras," he said, the Walther pointing at the door.

"That's goose liver, and I know you only eat fried food."

He opened the door and let in Sloane McKenzie.

Sloane looked at Ponce. "So this is where you've been. It's almost dark. You run on back and help Joey with his chores. And take the backstreets. Stay off Verdugo."

Ponce came over to Rawlings and said, "Phat." He slapped Rawlings's hand and ran out the door.

Rawlings moved to the open door and looked up and down the hall. *Still a morgue.* He closed the door. "Lon's doing some checking. He'll be back in a while."

She hung her head for an instant. "I'm sorry I missed him." She forced a smile. "I should have some word soon on that shipment Rios is expecting."

"Well, that's good. I hate this sitting around. It makes me nervous. And I'll be sure to tell him." Rawlings shifted uncomfortably. "Should I emphasize the shipment or missing him?"

Sloane hesitated for a moment. "Both." She quickly added, "We're having a little fiesta for the kids at the church tomorrow night. If you and Mr. Grainger haven't started World War III by then, you're welcome to join us. It's no orgiastic bacchanal, so don't be getting any ideas." She hoped she didn't sound too eager.

"I guess I better write down some of this so I don't forget," he said.

Sloane folded her hands in front of her. "You seem to like Ponce. I would have bet it all that you were one of those kind of guys who classified all kids as curtain climbers."

"Rug rats," he added.

"Snot lickers, for sure," she said with a smile.

"They are," he said, "but this one is almost an adult. He knows stuff."

"Yes, you're right. He's twelve going on thirty." She smiled again. "And here I thought you were insensitive."

"I'm not insensitive. I just don't give a damn."

She didn't know whether he was serious or not. It almost didn't matter. "I guess I'll be going." She moved to the door and put her hand on the knob. She looked back at him. "Don't forget the party. Ponce will be disappointed." She studied him for a moment. "Do you really think you can save them?"

Rawlings walked to the door and opened it for her. "If you're willing to pay the price, no one can stop you."

Sloane managed a wry smile. "Thanks," she said. "Keep your Glock cocked." She closed the door behind her and faced the empty hall. *If you're willing to pay the price . . .*

Rawlings leaned against the door. *She was right about one thing. The kid got to me.* For him, it had always been "the cat's in the cradle and the silver spoon" syndrome, although the spoon was just plastic. He realized he was a mirror psychological image of his father, who had been physically and emotionally an absentee. He had overheard his high school shrink refer to it as, "an occultly broken family." This kid Ponce had managed to chip away at that inheritance. He drifted in thought to the pending salvage operation. They always had stiff price tags.

One hundred percent mortality was the probable case. *Well, if you want to live forever, life is bound to disappoint you.*

"**BUENAS** *días, Padre.*" Raoul Sergio Rios dipped at the waist, his gyroscopic eyes fixing the priest who stood so forlorn in the center of the little enclosed playground of the orphanage. The morning sun was already a scorcher.

Nero Ramirez cast a glance around at Sister Felicia and Brother Lemuel as they kicked a can with the children. He scowled at that old man, Alberto, Humberto, or something; always bent double doing stoop labor, sweeping or raking a few leaves. Ramirez wiped the corners of his mouth as he focused on Felicia. *One night with me, and she would abandon the nunnery.*

Father Paul closed the physical gap between them.

Raoul grinned broadly and held out his arms. "*El Cura.* Why do you not greet me with open arms and a courtesy *'Bienvenido?'* "

"All who come in peace are welcome, Señor Rios. What do you want?"

"Why, Padre . . . I, who take my confession with Leon, am always interested in 'piece.' " He turned to a leering Nero. "No, Ramirez?"

Ramirez belched a mirthless grunt. He was still thinking about that nun.

When the priest remained undemonstrative, Raoul yawned. "A pity you find my wordplay lacks humor. To the point . . . Estaban wishes to speak to you. Now."

Humberto stopped raking, and Felicia and Lemuel halted playing soccer with the Pepsi can.

Father Paul remembered there was a fighter under the cloth. "I will not suffer your brother's intimidation. I will not—"

Raoul raised his hand like a conductor and spread his fingers while bowing his head. "*Por favor, Padre.* Think of your children."

Nero Ramirez shook himself free of his carnal thoughts in time to scan the yard with a glare of menace.

Paul realized he had just awakened to the nightmare after the nap.

FEDERICO Christo Mendez Lorca received his Internet message from the travel agency. It stated that his request was being processed and was too lengthy to be provided on-line. It would be delivered "by other means." Montezuma knew that meant a courier would contact him, and what he had to say would be of the highest importance. He understood these two men were not what they seemed. *Nothing ever was. Yes, soon the truth would come out.*

The silent presence interrupted him. He closed the Toshiba laptop and turned around to face Estaban, who was flanked by that witch who played on the superstitions of all these idiots.

Estaban watched Montezuma quietly, but he knew that, even with his back turned, the man was totally aware of his presence. What he really wondered was whether Montezuma was also cognizant of Sonja. "I do not pay you enough, Señor Lorca? You wish to trade on-line and be a self-made capitalist?"

"No, Señor Rios. I am just insuring none of us is overtaken by events, as they say, that there are no unintended consequences. It is the age of total information dominance and network-centric, cyber warfare. The universe extends beyond Zapata and the influences you exert upon your empire."

Estaban opened his mouth to say something but found only a benign smile. Montezuma was most likely mad. At a minimum, he was surely beyond comprehension. That didn't bother Estaban. It was only things beyond his control that troubled him. Sonja touched his arm. *Yes. The priest.* He remembered something else. He turned back to Montezuma. "One more thing. You remember the man who took his refund in lead . . . at the cost of his ear? Well, he has issued us a special challenge. He has a *tirardor nuevo,* a new shooter. It is to be *hombre contra hombre.* Your compensation will include your usual fee and bonus. I took the liberty to speak for you."

"THE kid told me essentially the same thing," said Rawlings when Grainger related that Runyan had "dropped his pants" about the *New Breed* connection. He collapsed into a chair when Grainger told him that a shooter for Rios was the X-factor in Beirut. "Then what are we still doing sitting around on our asses here? This is some kind of setup. Everything is too pat. This is taking coincidence to new heights. You know what they say . . . 'Coincidence and happenstance are enemy action in disguise.' I say we bail before the Grim Reaper gets the distance."

Grainger stretched out on the bed while Rawlings paced furiously around the room, pausing occasionally to look out the window. The midmorning sun promised to deliver another unmerciful beating. After a period of pacing, Rawlings stopped. "Okay. If you buy it, I'm still in. I guess you had to be there to hear it from the horse's mouth, huh?"

"Yeah, I guess so," said Grainger.

Rawlings told him about Sloane's visit.

Grainger nodded absently in response to the information about the drug shipment. He was more interested in her "missing him."

Rawlings noticed the interest. "It's a double entendre, partner, with a single meaning. It means she's sorry she missed you, like UPS leaving a note when you're not there to accept a delivery. I wouldn't count on it being more."

It could be just that. He admitted as much to himself.

HE had studied art and architecture once and knew the differences and textures of the Spanish Revival and the Beaux Arts; he appreciated Art Deco as well as the Gothic Renaissance. Thus, he could not help but admire the hacienda. Its architecture was Mediterranean, perhaps with a touch of Moorish influence. It's art, however, was a bit too Baroque. *Not enough Monet*, Paul thought. He was escorted through the courtyard into the reception room. From there he was taken—after an interval, which he understood as intending to impress upon him his subservience—to the conference room. It was empty. Ramirez and Raoul left him alone, standing among the mahogany and oak, brass and chrome textures of the room. Paul hated himself. The wages of sin were indeed sumptuous.

Estaban entered with a flourish. He held a brandy snifter in his hand and swirled the amber liquor with a fluid motion. "Father Paul. What a pleasant surprise. So good to see you." He waved his free arm around the room. "Be it ever so humble, no . . . ?" He noticed that Sonja and Paul had made eye contact, and she held him—as she did all men—paralyzed like a boa constrictor about to engulf its prey. "Ah . . . very good. You should get to know her better, Father. She, too, is a religious representative."

Paul broke away from her with some difficulty and confronted Rios. "What is it you want, Señor Rios?"

Estaban put both hands on the conference table. "Do they not teach the social graces at the seminary any longer?"

"They teach to be wary of *el Diablo.*"

"*Bien, bien,* Father Paul. *Touché.* And to the point . . . One of my men is dead. Two more have been critically injured in a barroom brawl. All this perpetrated by the godless men you allow to pollute your church."

Father Paul's face reddened. " 'Godless?' You dare pronounce judgment? You have the audacity to speak of godlessness in others?"

Estaban's knuckles turned white as he leaned fiercely into the table. "You wish to moralize with me? I, Estaban Zamora Elfego Rios, am more of a holy man than you. The peon and the poor refer to me as *El Salvador.* I have built the clinics, the schools, the playgrounds."

Paul clenched his fists. "And the bordellos. You proliferate *las drogas* that kill our people. You sponsor your murderous Game. You buy people with money and spill the blood of those who would resist you."

Estaban sipped from his glass. "A fair summary, Father. Yet, I am still like *el rio.* My bounty flows to the people."

Paul pointed a finger at him. "You delude yourself. You are not the river. You are a sewer. You are a vulture feeding on the liver of Prometheus. But you have built your dens on quicksand."

Estaban pushed away from the table, a grin spreading across his face. "Your metaphors are destined to become fable, *Cura.*" His grin disappeared. "But, be advised and warned for the last time, you are a thorn in my side. I cannot—will not—allow your seed of discontent to flower into revolution. My control is absolute. I am offering you your church, your life, and the life of those who surround you. There are two choices: Pax Rios or annihilation."

Paul struck his wrath but not his colors. "I must have the freedom of my faith, and the liberty to confront evil."

"Your faith is yours, Father Paul. Your license to take it public is revoked," Estaban hissed.

Paul wheeled and headed for the door. The priestess blocked his way. Her gaze again held him, the spider and the fly. She moved close to him. He could smell her scent; not a perfume but a musk odor of woman essence, the likes of which had sometimes awakened him at night to a sweat. Her voice was without edge, unctuous, a sensuous purr. "Have you ever had a woman, Priest?"

Father Paul trembled inwardly as he fought to remain externally unperturbed. Fluid built up in his throat. He wanted to swallow, but resisted. *She must not see.*

"You know, I have seen you fight," she said, her black-ice eyes changing color in the reflected light. "With some practice, you could be a champion."

With Herculean effort, he disconnected from her stare. He broke for the door in slow motion.

"One more thing, holy man," said Rios.

Paul stopped at the door, which was held open for him by Ramirez.

"I, too, was raised in that orphanage which you now call yours. But I cannot allow you to destroy me for the sake of my fond memories and self-assumed obligations. I have paid those debts by my deeds, not empty words like you offer."

Paul remained transfixed at the door.

"You are familiar with the Mexican saying, 'Raise crows, and they will peck out your eyes'?"

Father Paul looked past the heathen priestess. "Yes," he said. "Unless you kill the crow first." *God forgive me.*

"**NAW,** this is Jules. I'm calling for The Disciple. No. Get someone else for next Friday. He can't make it. He says he's getting ready for some other fight."

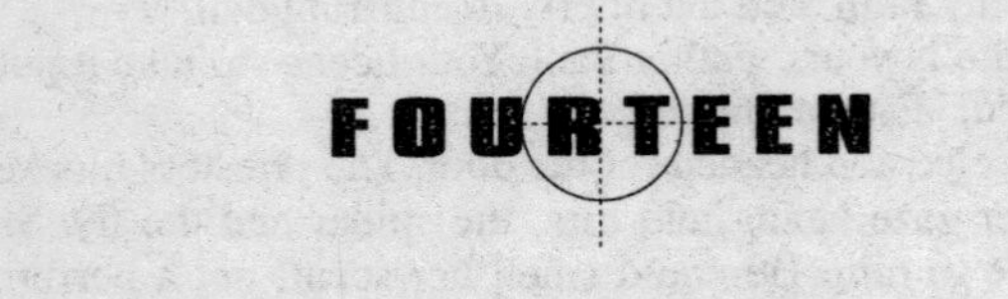

FOURTEEN

"**ADMINISTRATIVE** arrangements and details first, Señor Hill." Estaban patted his forehead with his handkerchief. "Allow me to compliment you on your . . . shall we say perseverance, after the last unfortunate misunderstanding."

Big John Hill remained silent but eyed his antagonist balefully. His hand moved unconsciously to his half-ear. "What goes round comes round, sen-yooor. Living well and taking your *dinero* is going to be the best revenge."

Estaban looked at his watch. *Nine o'clock. Another day, another quarter million.* He turned his head, looking at the playing field before swiveling back, the gracious host once more. "Fair enough. We have each deposited two hundred fifty thousand dollars into a mutually agreed escrow account in the Zapata Merchants Bank for distribution based upon the result of today's event. Correct?"

"Yeah, that's right, amigo." Big John had a bandage that ran around his head, covering his ear. "You're going to pay big time. I got my plastic surgeon to pay."

The priestess sat on a chair in the shadow of the only tree on the hill, looking out over the range. Nero Ramirez stood in the sun, next to Estaban, his thumbs tucked into his two-inch-wide leather belt that bore his name in bas relief at the back. Montezuma remained aloof, ignoring the group. He had an emery board and appeared to be filing his nails.

Rios touched his nose and cradled his chin with his cupped hands. "Shall we make it an even five hundred thousand? Just in case your cosmetic surgery bill is larger than anticipated."

"I don't have that kind of cash on me, but I like the sound of one half million good old Yankee dollars." Big John slapped the man standing next to him on the back. The unsmiling Dolph Lungren clone remained unexpressive.

"I have no problem, Señor Hill. Your word is your bond, no? I will take your promissory note." Rios snapped his fingers. Rosa Fuentes bowed and produced a notebook and pen.

Big John Hill grinned. He scribbled out a note and signed it.

"Señor Remudios, from the bank, will witness and hold all financial instruments." Estaban motioned to Nero Ramirez, who brought over a briefcase. "I anticipated you might be tempted. Here is my share." He opened the leather case, revealing paper-wrapped bundles of one hundred dollar bills.

Remudios, a thin weasel of a man, took control of the briefcase and the handwritten note.

Estaban turned to Hill and his man. "A review of the simple rules: The playing field is five thousand meters long by forty-one hundred meters wide. Your man enters on the east and . . . mine . . ." He looked at Montezuma. "My representative enters on the west. As Montezuma is more familiar with the terrain, he will have the disadvantage of looking into the sun. Each man moves toward the other, each at their own pace. They fire when they wish. Each may quit by raising the white flag we have provided them. Both men have only two cartridges. There is a ten-hour duration limit, at which time the game is called. Or goes into . . . sudden death. Does everyone understand the rules? Are there any questions?" Rios raised his eyebrows.

Hill's man plied his prefight psych-out, staring at Montezuma, who continued to ply the emery across his right hand.

Montezuma ignored the *ojos de pistola.*

Hill pointed at Montezuma. "What? Is he some kind of faggot, filing his fucking nails? It's going to be the last things he files. That son of a bitch is going to pay for taking off my ear."

"It was I who took your ear, señor. Montezuma was merely the instrument," said Estaban with a smile.

"And it's going to be you who pays also, sen-yooor," replied Hill. "And we have no questions except maybe, where do we bury your boy?" He laughed alone.

"Bien. Bien," Estaban said with a smile. So be it. May the best man win. Let the game begin."

Hill's shooter tore the white cloth flag he had been given from under his shirt. He wiped his sweaty face and wadded it up into a tight ball. He threw it against Montezuma's chest, the whiteness unfolding and falling onto the dirt.

Montezuma remained undemonstrative. He had his own white flag draped over his arm like a sommelier. He folded it in half and then again. He then draped it around his neck with a flourish.

Hill's shooter watched his opponent closely. His mouth twisted, expelling an indecipherable oath.

Montezuma turned and made his way to his starting point.

Romulus, Hill's shooter, laughed heartily. He had the weasel on the run. A man approached him and said, *"Buena suerte."* Romulus thought it was odd that his foe's apprentice or assistant would wish him good luck. He shrugged. *Mexicans.* He headed for his jump-off point.

Servando Chavez smiled and watched the arrogant one move down the hill. He wondered if the *tirador* knew that life was very short.

Rios turned to Hill. "What was the name of your man, again?"

Hill opened his mouth, showing more gold than teeth. "Romulus," he said. "And say good-bye to your faggot."

Romulus. Estaban thought it a strange name for a Russian.

ROMULUS Anatoly Volchkov was a sniper, a Russian sniper, formerly of the reconnaissance battalion of the 123rd Airborne Division. He was a *desantnik,* a paratrooper, a rear area raider trained as a marksman. He had also been assigned for a time to the Interior Ministry OMON, the security troops. Now, with Russia an impotent ghost, an emasculated transmutation of its prior robust self, he had been out of work, but no longer. Having immigrated to Canada, he was recruited by an individual who said he had just the employer for a man with his talents. He crossed into the United States easily and made his way to this forsaken territory. But Romulus liked lost lands and causes. It brought out the best in a man. He missed Afghanistan, where his long rifle had accounted for thirty-five of those Mujahedeen fanatics. He had the Order of Lenin, which today in Sevastopol, his hometown, would get him a two-ruble beer—if you had two rubles. Today, he fancied to make twenty-five thousand American dollars. This wasn't even going to be a challenge. He had only to pop this local deer hunter or squirrel shooter, and he would be rich. Romulus Volchkov pissed on the ground and stirred the mud with his boot. He smeared the concoction on his face and buttoned his camouflage smock.

Romulus watched as a starting flare soared into the air over the observation hill. He removed his rifle from its hard case and threw the bolt open. He removed a single round from his pocket and inserted the cartridge on top of the magazine follower, pressing down gently. The round seated with a satisfying metallic *clack*. Romulus's rifle was an Armalon Model BGR in 7.62 × 51 mm. He knew it well and had made several kills with this very model. Big John had presented it to him as a gift. He had zeroed the Schmidt and Bender 4-16 × 50 police marksman scope himself and was satisfied with the three-quarter MOA accuracy. He then thought for a moment about throwing away the second round. He would only need one. He smiled to himself. He would keep it as a souvenir. Romulus stepped across the imaginary line of demarcation onto the killing ground.

MONTEZUMA watched the signal flare arc across the white sky and burn out before it reached its zenith. He had already crossed the flaccid stream that marked the west boundary of the field a half hour before the start time. He had made his way in a circle, getting off line with the sun. He loped along easily, knowing full well his presence was undetectable from the east position. He carried his Lazzeroni-Sako TRG-S with the two rounds taped to the composite stock rifle. He made his way north toward the only high ground, the rolling, sagebrush-covered hills that dominated that end of the designated field. He looked at his watch. He would have time. A thunderclap announced the presence of a coming summer storm. He drank from his canteen on the move and passed through the vines and briar thickets unimpeded, like a ghost. . . .

Montezuma was Cuban, born in the port city of Cienfuegos; exactly one year—to the day—after Batista had abdicated. His given name was Federico Christo Mendez Lorca, and he remembered being born. It was more than biologic memory. It was something he could feel. He remembered emerging from the warmth into the cold. Since then he'd been warm and he'd been cold. And warm was definitely better.

His father was a soldier, a colonel in Fidel's Army of the Revolution. Previous to that, he had been a major for Fulgencio Batista. He had seen the light early on. Joining Castro, he helped in ousting Batista, thus thwarting the Yanquis' *plan to colonize Cuba while assuring himself—and his son—a place in the new Cuba. At age twelve, young Federico was taken to an Army firing range and allowed to shoot an SKS rifle. His sense of aim was phenomenal and instantly noted. At sixteen, he won the Cuban Military National Rifle Marksmanship Competition against his country's best military marksman. At eighteen he became a cause célèbre for Raul Castro, Fidel's brother and defense minister. He also came to the attention of the Russians.*

The Soviet Union sent its best sniper instructor, a senior sergeant named Mikhail Zharkowski Volushon, to Cuba to convert the boy from a lad with a great eye for the bull's-eye into something much more deadly: a sniper. Volushon was Spetsnaz, the Special Forces of the Soviet Union and their killer elite. He was himself a master rifleman who had fought for the motherland and against imperialism since he was fifteen. Volushon's father had battled in Stalingrad as a child and had met Vasily

Ivanovich Zaitsev of the 284th Rifle Division, the greatest of all Soviet snipers, credited with killing 240 Nazis. It was Zaitsev who killed Major Erwin Konings, Kommandant *of the Reich's sniper school at Zossen and finest of all German snipers. Konings had been airlifted into the Kessel of Stalingrad specifically to kill Zaitsev. Stalingrad became his burial ground. The "Nobel Sniper," as Zaitsev was officially called, outsmarted Konings, killing him in the ruins of the great city. His father had told him all the stories when he was a boy. Yet, Volushon considered that the Cuban might be the equivalent of Zaitsev, if not surpass him in skill.*

Volushon taught young Lorca all that he knew. He nurtured his abilities until the day when the student paid the ultimate compliment to the teacher and vice versa. He bested him in his ability to camouflage, in target detection, observation of details, fieldcraft, and shooting. Volushon departed after four months, returning to his Spetsnaz until then engaged in Afghanistan. He left behind a master sniper whom Volushon considered without peer. Federico Lorca was a shooter without remorse, conscience, regret, or sympathy. He was the epitome of the hunter. He was the actualization of the killer instinct. He was the personification of Death. He took to his art with an unparalleled enthusiasm. In honor of the great Aztec ruler, he adopted the nom de guerre, Montezuma.

Completing his sniper training with the Russians, he was offered an opportunity—sponsored by Cuban Intelligence—to attend the University of Havana. After two years studying English, politics, and literature, he was tasked by the DGI. He was to continue his education in Miami. Lorca "escaped" from Cuba and made his way to the exile community. He enrolled in the University of Miami and majored in philosophy. He also infiltrated the CCC, the Cruzada Cubana Constitucional, *the principal anti-Communist, anti-Castro Cuban paramilitary group in south Florida. The entire time he continued to shoot and hone his survival skills in the trackless swamps. His English became polished and almost accent-free. He became a learned man of letters who passed intelligence information on to the DGI at every opportunity and dead drop.*

After graduating, he longed for a return to Cuba and the thing he loved best. He volunteered to join a CCC "Grey" team infiltrating back into Cuba by boat. After training for a month in the Everglades, they went operational, landing on a deserted beach in the black of night, near Caibarien, on the north-central coast of Cuba. Later, when he was on guard, he slit the throats of his sleeping companions and made his way back to Havana with the agent list that doomed the virulently anti-Castro 30th of November Group.

Once back in Cuba, he made his desires known. His future was assured. He became the king's own special emissary. He went where he was needed, executing the will of his government until the time came when he could no longer be contained. After years of faithful service, he obtained the extraordinary consent of Castro to become a free agent, subject to recall, if needed. All totaled, 135 men and woman had fallen to his rifle. And he was still a young man; even though now forty, his face was unlined. And the optical sight guaranteed him mastery of his art and science for some time to come.

He was *El Silencio.* The Silence. You never hear the bullet that kills you. The shadow moved on.

GRAINGER heard the sound of thunder, and the sky darkened. A thunderstorm was coming. He looked out the window at the deserted evening street below. Rawlings had gone back to the orphanage to make an appearance at the party for the kids. *Maybe I should have gone.* But he had things to do and more to ponder. He stared out the window, watching a black cloud skirt the town and move downriver. It appeared to be over Mexico, that fecund, primeval place. Mexico was smoky and pungent, where civilization touched but never seemed to settle. Mexico was a place where a man could straighten things out in his life without interfering encumbrances. It was a place for working things out. If it didn't exist, someone would have had to invent it. He stared out the window. He remembered the last tango in Mogadishu, and he knew that if what Stoneman had said was true and the answer to Beirut lay somewhere hidden in the ruins of Mog, then it had to do with blood. The memory flooded back in color, sound and smell. . . .

"I thought it was Miller time," Rawlings said. The day wasn't over. They were being tasked with another "operational priority." The staccato, high-speed blender *whop* of the MH-6 "Little Bird" chopper drowned out all other sound as it flitted over Mogadishu, the capitol of Somalia. Somalia—shaped like a sea horse trying to look inconspicuous—lay along the northeastern edge of Africa, anchored in the south on Kenya and clinging desperately to Ethiopia at its head. In October 1993, the drums of war were beating fiercely. An operation had been mounted to seize a cabal of Aidid's top lieutenants. Initially, the plan had gone well; then, everything disintegrated. The Rangers and Delta's "C" Squadron had secured their targets but had walked into a hornet's nest. All of Mog—it seemed—had turned out to stop them. And gun control in this town—where Kalashnikov AK-47s and RPGs were sold in the Bakara Market for a half million Somali shillings, the approximate equivalent of $100 U.S.—meant only having a steady hand.

Grainger and Rawlings had been operational on a select targeting mission and were returning to the airport where they were billeted with the Rangers and the rest of Delta's "C" Squadron when the call came out. A SPECCAT, code-named Stone Hombre, was trapped out in the city. Two Black Hawk choppers were also down. The natives had gone from restless to savage in a heartbeat. Every man who could ride or walk was part of a rescue op being mounted to save the task force now pinned down in the city and close to being overrun. There was nobody else available to pull the CIA's ass out of the fire.

They landed briefly at Mogadishu airport, headquarters of the American Task Force Ranger. There, a lieutenant colonel and a man in civilian clothes who might as well have had Spook tattooed on his forehead met them. They resupplied with mission-specific equipment and reboarded the MH-6. It was going to be hairy, a rescue operation to save the Christians In Action. Grainger figured it was a kamikaze mission. The body bags were already being stacked up on the strip.

They rode on externally mounted benches, secured on stanchions that were jury-rigged on the two-pilot MH-6, as they vectored toward the Olympic Hotel. The best estimate was that was where Stone Hombre had gone to the ground. His radio was acting as a transponder beacon and transmitting intermittently on the guard frequencies at 40.5 on the FM band and at 243 megahertz on UHF. If the SPECCAT was still alive, they would make voice contact on a push of 121.5 MHz on the FM band—the survival/rescue frequency—if he was monitoring his AN/PRC-112 short-range radio. Their radio call sign and operational code designator was Brand-X.

As they rolled in toward the Olympic Hotel, Grainger could see a mass of black humanity below, running and firing. Some of them turned toward the threat from the sky. An RPG flashed by them, narrowly missing the chopper. The RPG was an anti–tank and personnel weapon, but no one had apparently told the "Sammies" or "Skinnies," as the Americans called the Somalis. Another rocket propelled grenade sizzled past, the Chinese writing plainly visible on the forest-green missile as it flashed by them, trailing a thin line of smoke. The aircraft crew was firing up the area with the ship's Gatling gun, chewing up real estate and humanity with equal affinity. The pilots took them in fast and at a steep angle to the roof of the Olympic Hotel. The swinging, cranelike arm deployed with the attached two-and-a-half-inch ropes. The lines spiraled down until they titillated the open roof of the hotel. *Fast rope.* Grainger and Rawlings swung onto the ropes and dropped.

Fast roping had largely replaced aerial rappelling in the military by 1990. It provided a faster access to the ground, was less complicated, and didn't require carabiners, harnesses, and special tie-downs. You didn't have to unsnap from the rope or run out the free end. You just put on your heavy-duty gloves and slid down like a flying fireman. You were free to shoot, loot, and scoot.

They hit the roof hard, and the heavy ropes came spiraling down upon them like huge, angry snakes. The Little Bird went vertical and soared away. For a second there was silence. Then the war reclaimed them.

"BIENVENIDO." Brother Lemuel greeted Rawlings at the gate of the orphanage and let him in. They passed through the yard into the small building that was contiguous with the church and that served as the home for the thirty children cared for by Paul, Leon, Lemuel, Sister Felicia, her father, and Sloane McKenzie. Inside in the dining area, tables had been decorated with pictures hand-drawn by the children. A small cake was on the table, and a rendering of Jesus Christ blessing the children hung on the wall.

Rawlings edged forward, the proverbial whore in church. This was not his typical haunt, but he was curious, and the woman was intriguing.

"So, you made it?" she said.

He turned around. "Yeah. I never miss a party."

Sloane's lips parted in a smile. "Hope we don't disappoint you. No Jack Daniel's or dancing girls; just some nonalcoholic punch and cake." She looked past him, craning her neck in an exaggerated gesture. "Your partner . . . ?"

"He sends his regrets. He's deep in thought planning and plotting. It's dirty work, but someone has to do it. So I volunteered for the party."

She laughed, but Rawlings sensed disappointment. She was still intriguing.

THEY dropped down, back-to-back, squatting on the sandpaper-textured roof. Grainger swung the M-21 rifle from his shoulder and inspected the Leupold 10 × 40 Mark 4 M3 telescopic sight. It was a Superb B optical system, rugged, reliable, and ballistically cammed for the 147 grain M-118 7.62 millimeter round. He flipped the attached scope lens covers up and quickly examined the lenses.

Rawlings motioned toward a small superstructure on the other side of the roof. They moved at a crouch to a rusted access door. It was open, bent and broken at one hinge. Three bullet holes cut a diagonal across the tin face.

Grainger pushed the creaky door open and peered inside.

Seeing nothing, he entered. When his eyes adjusted to the dimness, he motioned to Rawlings. Once inside, they sat in silence, listening to the ambient sounds, distinguishing what was benign and what was a threat. Grainger resnapped the lens caps into place and slung the M-21. He gripped the Heckler and Koch MP-5 PDW submachine gun hanging from his neck and across his chest on an assault sling and moved down the stairwell. Rawlings followed, carrying a "Minimi," a M-249 Squad Automatic Weapon (SAW) which fired the standard U.S. 5.56 × 45 mm M-855 or SS-109 ball rounds. It took belted ammunition or M-16 magazines. He also carried a Spec-Ops Phobis International (enclosed slide) M-9, mounted diagonally in a Bianchi UM-84 holster.

At the top-floor landing Grainger halted. The stench was overpowering. Human offal littered the stairwell, and flies raised off the feast like biblical locusts. He removed a hand radio from his Eagle Industries Tac III assault vest and mashed the Push-to-Talk button. "Stone Hombre . . . Stone Hombre, this is Brand-X. Do you copy?"

A rush of static answered, followed by a shaky voice. "Ah, Brand-X . . . Where the hell are you guys? Come and get me, I'm wounded. And Jesus Christ, hurry."

CIA Officer Richard Stoneman huddled against the wall of a corner room on the top floor of the hotel, bleeding and pale, fighting shock and wide-eyed terror. Blood seeped from his wound and pooled up beneath him. He held a Beretta pistol, and he almost shot the man coming through the door. He dropped the weapon in relief when he saw their faces. "Thank God, you're here. Where are the rest of the troops?"

Grainger looked at the wounded CIA man. "The cavalry had a previous engagement. What you see is what you get."

Rawlings moved to a window. "Don't worry. All our rescue work comes with a money-back guarantee."

Grainger patched up Stoneman's wounds using curlex and a combat dressing and told him he would live, at least until someone killed him.

"How come they only sent you two?" groaned Stoneman.

They heard the first voices coming up the stairs.

* * *

MONTEZUMA did not attempt to take the high ground, but he knew that his opponent would. He considered all factors, realizing his foe was not an amateur and should not be underestimated. To do so was folly and led only to one very undesirable result. The man would logically make for the tactically appropriate high ground and take up a position, hoping to catch a glimpse of his opponent. He would not beat the brush trying to flush the quail. Montezuma understood that any sniper worthy of the name would know that movement was the number one target detection indicator. No, he himself would provoke this action his own way.

Montezuma looked at his watch and understood he did not have much time to spare. The opposition would be along soon. He regarded the dominating heights above him and visualized his position from that perspective. He had the right spot. He moved into a patch of brush bisected by a fallen log. He found what he had hoped for and went to work. When he had finished, he exited the location and dropped down into the gully to its rear, leaving no trace of his presence. He moved to a location two hundred feet away from the fallen log and constructed an expedient hide. He finished and burrowed into the earth to wait. From his lair, he had a full view of the highest elevation point all the way to the tree line at its base. He could also see his fallen log, two hundred feet from where he lay. He knew he would never see his opponent silhouetted against the skyline or walking upright in the open like some village idiot. He took it as gospel the man was a professional, and he would treat him as such; and kill him as such.

ROMULUS was bathed in a continuous sweat from the heat of the early afternoon sun. *Texas is like . . . No. Nothing is like this place.* He saw the high ground and knew he had made it before that fool they found to face him. Romulus knew he was in better shape. He had run and jogged part of the way. Now stealth was required. He would command the peaks. It would be he who would find the enemy, he who would destroy. Romulus circumnavigated the high ground's thickly vegetated base in order to secure the heights from the rear, to the reverse slope. He would leave no visible evidence of his presence to the front. He began to climb inexorably toward the top.

The briars cut him, and his sweat ran down in rivulets, burning the superficial wounds he sustained. It was of no consequence. He would cure them in a spa with three harlots to attend him. Romulus attained the military crest of the reverse slope and peered over the top for a moment to consider the view. He could see the river from here and the distant knoll from where the pampered enjoyed the show. Well, he would give them their show. Romulus settled into a slight depression and cleared away a field of fire for himself. He carefully ensured that none of the vegetation or earth was disturbed, which might reveal a different texture or tone to any eyes below him. He laid his rifle out in front of him and peered through the lens. He was ready. *Let him come.*

"**SO**," said Father Paul, "your parents were Catholic? Where did you have your First Communion?"

Rawlings watched the orphan kids eat their cake and drink their punch. They seemed happy, yet strangely subdued for a bunch of kids at a party. He saw the waiflike Sister Felicia and Brother Lemuel chatting with Sloane. The other priest, Leon, was talking to the old man, Humberto, over in the corner. He took a sip of his lemonade. "In the back of a '67 Merc I borrowed from a friend."

Father Paul dropped his eyes momentarily and was at a loss of words to reply. He understood the irreverent response, in more ways than one. "I sense you are not a religious individual."

"Do I call you Father? I mean, I hardly called mine that," Rawlings said. "But, in answer to your question, sure, I'm religious. I've got my gods: Smith, Wesson, and Colt, the Father, Son, and the Holy Ghost. I even wear a KISS T-shirt so Bibles will bounce off me."

Paul cocked his head. "I would think a man in your line of work would have been drawn closer to his maker. What about death? You have a choice, you know, before you transcend to the hereafter."

Rawlings finished his drink and brought his eyes back to

bear on Paul. "I heard a story told once. Death comes to this guy and offers him two pills, one white and one black. Death says to him, 'Choose white for life or black for death.' So, naturally the guy picks the white pill. Then he dies. Now, as he's dying he looks up at Death and says, 'But, I chose the white pill. Why?' And Death slaps him on the back and says, 'Yeah, I know. But the game's rigged.'"

Paul inclined forward. "I think that parable misses the point." He wanted desperately to understand these two men but was getting nowhere. "I just want you to know you are not alone and that with God anything is possible. I also believe we should keep all our options open and not resort to violence to reconcile matters. I counsel patience."

"'Let us run with patience,'" said Rawlings. "Hebrews, 12:1."

"You know scripture?"

"Only those passages that have military significance, Father," Rawlings drawled. He watched as Sloane placed some tomatoes, onions, chilies, and cilantro by a large bowl. "Father, with an assault rifle and a bunch of grenades, anything is possible." He handed Paul his empty lemonade glass and turned toward Sloane.

"At least you must take solace in believing that God's love is forever," offered Paul.

Rawlings shook his head. "Love is not forever. Only death is forever."

As Rawlings took his first step in retreat, Paul entreated, "Then, what is it you believe in, Mr. Rawlings?"

"High-resolution optics, high-velocity rifles . . . overwhelming firepower." Rawlings headed toward Sloane with a secret to share.

THE M-26 grenade exploded in the stairwell, spewing shrapnel and splinters in all directions. It killed the first four Somalis bounding up the stairs and wounded three others. The rest retreated down the stairwell. But the enemy now knew they were here. The high-pitched chatter of many alien voices could be heard floors below.

"What do we do now?" said Stoneman. "How do we get out of here?"

Rawlings peered down the stairwell at the bodies strewn about. "One thing for sure; not that way."

Grainger tried to raise somebody on the radio, but the traffic was so heavy he couldn't get through. He looked out the window and saw smoke rising in several locations. Hundreds of Sammies were visible, running in the street, yelling and screaming; half of them appeared high on khat, a local narcotic extracted from the plant of the same name. Most of them were recognizable as clansmen; "technicals" as the warlord's militiamen were called; but there were also the *mooryan,* local bandits, known in the Somali vernacular as *dai-dai,* meaning "quick-quick." It was an eclectic crowd. There were also mothers with babies on their backs carrying RPGs and teenage girls scrambling to bring an RPD machine gun to bear. There were old men with grenades wearing the traditional garb of the Somali male called the *ma-awis,* a multi–colored and hued wraparound skirt. Every male also seemed to be wearing a loose-fitting, long-sleeved, off-white shirt, making them indistinguishable from one another. Everyone was armed. It made them easier to kill.

Grainger could see that the Somali focus was principally on the Rangers and Delta who were barricaded farther down Hawlwadig Road, but some of the fulminating throng was turning their attention to them. He killed his first Skinny with a head shot, the man's skull exploding like a ripe pumpkin dropped from six feet onto concrete.

Grainger yelled at Rawlings, "Cover those two windows. I got these." From their position in the corner suite of the top floor, he had a panoramic view of the action below. He threw the radio to Stoneman. "Cover the hall and stairwell with my sub gun. And keep trying to raise somebody. Our call sign is Brand-X. The Charley-Charley bird is Night Rider." He turned back to the window and sighted in on a man waving his arms about and shouting orders. *A leader.* It doomed him. He killed him with a torso shot.

Grainger's M-21 was the accurized version of the M-14 rifle. It had a National Match barrel, which meant it was among the first ten barrels to be swaged with a button rifler. Being semiautomatic, he did not have to manipulate a bolt handle for each shot, and, with its twenty-round magazine, it gave him an enormous amount of highly accurate firepower. He swung easily to another target. The crosshairs centered, and he squeezed the trigger. He was firing now in rapid succession, felling targets as fast as they appeared. At first, most of the crowd was confused and ran from cover to cover, fearing that the Rangers were killing them in unprecedented numbers. None of their measures were effective against the plunging fire falling on them from above. It was not until Grainger had killed twenty-one that most realized the source of the murderous fire. *Only targets.*

"When the going gets tough, the tough go full-fucking-auto!" Rawlings screamed out the window and let off another burst of fire from the M-249 "Minimi." Two Somalis dropped in the street. An old woman ran out and retrieved the weapons. He was going to hold his fire, then said, "Fuck it," and slew her as she ran back toward cover, an SKS and an AK in her arms. The killing fever was up. Everything was fair game.

A large Somali emerged from hiding behind a wall on the roof of a building opposite his position, two hundred meters out. The wall ran at an angle away from Rawlings's position. The end of the edifice was not visible, being blocked by the corner of a building and by rubble and smoke from burning tires. The man fired and ducked back behind the invisible portion of the wall. Rawlings waited. The next time the Somali fired and retreated, he fired a burst against the smooth stone wall. He knew what the result would be. There was no return fire from that sector. Rounds impacting a hard, relatively smooth surface at more than fifteen degrees and less than forty degrees will invariably travel down the plane approximately six inches out. It was an immutable law of physics. He didn't need to see the man to kill him. It was in the killer's handbook. He changed the assault pack on the SAW and fed the hundred-round belt into the feed tray as a bullet tore out a portion of the windowsill. The Skinnies were getting the range, but so was he. He dropped two more. *Dazzle 'em with style. Riddle 'em with bullets.*

Grainger had to search for targets now. The Somalis had abandoned the open street and were now firing from doorways and windows, from behind garbage piles and burned-out cars. Fire from the Rangers and Delta kept them looking in two directions. He found a target. He sighted and fired. The figure recoiled and disappeared. *Man? Woman?* They were only targets, and he was only a machine. Spent rounds accumulated at his feet.

Stoneman stumbled into the room, desperately trying to suppress the panic welling up inside of him. "Christ! We came to help these people, to win their hearts and minds. Can't we talk to them?"

Rawlings let loose another burst and dropped down onto his haunches beneath the window. "Sure. Let me try." He stood up and yelled out the window. "Hey! You out there. Stop shooting. We're from the American government, and we're here to help."

Rawlings dove for the floor as the window exploded from a fusillade of shots. An RPG round ricocheted off the exterior wall but failed to detonate. He looked up at Stoneman. "They said they don't want any help. Now, get back to watching the stairs and keep on that radio. Try to raise the White House. Tell 'em we're sorry, but we have to bury these hearts and minds."

ROMULUS watched the sun descend from its zenith, a red, irregular ball, jagged at the edges, distorted as it lost intensity and fury. The day was still fiery hot, but the first breeze from the river was detectable. He held his position, motionless and emotion-free, the extension of himself pointing out in front of him like another appendage. He saw movement, almost imperceptible, except to the trained eye. *Yes. He is there, by the fallen log, seven hundred meters to the front. A hint of white. The fool with his "surrender" towel. You are about to surrender your life.* Romulus noticed a small gleam, a reflection caused by the sinking sun reflecting off of glass. *His rifle scope. He's there.* The sniper moved slowly, adjusting his position with excruciatingly slow movements that betrayed nothing. He brought the rifle to bear and looked through the ocular lens. *There! A speck of the towel.* He could even make out its texture. *He does not realize* *his lair has been discovered. He will never know.* Romulus Anatoly Volchkov counted his American dollars in his mind as he brought the scope's post reticle with the open circle superimposed on the crosshair to the aim point, just above the glint of glass and the speck of whiteness. *Where his head will be.* He squeezed the trigger slowly, like he was caressing a nipple on the breast of some other man's wife.

THE sound of the shot reverberated. Its echo seemed to bounce off the distant mountains and ricochet back and forth, reluctant to fade.

"Well, it's about fucking time," said Big John Hill. He crushed the aluminum can of Lone Star beer in his paw. "I think you'd better send out the retrievers to bring back the corpse, sen-yoor."

Estaban flicked his tongue into his Tequila and touched the edges of his mouth with his handkerchief. He turned to Sonja. "What is your vision, my fey priestess?"

"Priestess, my ass, hombre. She's just a half-breed bitch with some tarot cards, and she has all you fucking Mexicans bamboozled." Big John thrust out his jaw. "Why don't you send her off to exorcise one of them chupacabras that's always biting one of you greasers in the ass."

"Your insight, Sonja," Estaban repeated, more deliberately.

She looked out at the range and held her hand out, then brought it back in front of her face. "He is premature. But he will soon be correct."

A second shot punched a hole in the shroud of silence.

MONTEZUMA sensed the time was near. His calculations were approximate but reasoned and based on experience. He watched the hilltop. He heard and saw the indicators of a rifle discharge. His own weapon was positioned for an uphill shot, and he needed little maneuver to come on-line with the target. He knew where his enemy was but waited for the man to expose himself. To make sure he was not himself about to become a victim of some perfect design. The head appeared, looking down range, toward the fallen log. He felt nothing as he brought the profile into focus, the crosshairs centering on the ear canal. He felt nothing as he teased the trigger until it obligingly released the firing pin, seemingly of its own volition. He felt nothing when the man's head erupted in a froth of vapor and disappeared from sight.

Lorca, the master sniper, emerged from his hide and walked easily over to the fallen log. He bent down and examined what he had left, an hour before. He picked up his white towel and flung it back onto his shoulder. Sprinkles of shattered glass decorated the vegetation, the remnants of the shot glass he had suspended in the brush. His opponent's bullet had been unerring. He looked at the termites that swirled around the piece of wood he had baited with a packet of sugar. His estimate of their industry was good. The termites had found the stick that supported the cradle he had built for the towel. The voracious insects had chewed their way through the base of the stick until it collapsed. Unsupported, the cradle fell, creating just the subtle movement he needed. The shot glass, which had hung suspended from a bent branch, became exposed by the fall of the towel. The deception had been complete, and fatal. *Primitive genius.* Federico Christo Mendez Lorca, aka Montezuma, congratulated himself. *Cunning is everything.*

He strode up the hill, taking his time now. There was no hurry. He would collect the man's rifle and perhaps keep it. Maybe he would donate it to Señor Rios's collection. At the top of the hillock, he found the man where he knew he'd be, already becoming a feast for the fire ants. Montezuma regarded his victim dispassionately. He had no emotion one way or another about this man or his killing. Had his opponent known what he was up against, he would have fled. But that was fate and not for him to say. Montezuma took the towel off his arm and wiped his face of sweat and dirt. He threw the rag on top of the dead man. He picked up the rifle and hefted it. Nice, but he would donate it to Rios. He was about to go back down the hill and make the long hike back to the observation hill when he hesitated. He regarded the dead man again. He removed his knife and cut off his foe's trigger finger at the first joint. He searched the man's pockets, finding a single round of ammunition. He rolled the cartridge between his thumb and forefinger and felt its steely point. He put it in his pocket. It would make a good souvenir. He began the trek back. The late afternoon sun was still hot. That was good. Warm was always better than cold. Lorca felt nothing. But he remembered everything. And he longed to return to his secret place.

FIFTEEN

"MY secret salsa recipe," he said. "I'm going to share it with you."

"Really?" said Sloane. "Where did you learn to make salsa?"

"A little old Mexican woman who lived across the street from us in San Pedro gave it to me on her deathbed 'cause I mowed her grass for free for all those years." He grinned at her.

"And now you're going to share that top secret with us, huh?"

"Correct," he said. "Just to soften the image a bit. I want to show you it's not all blood, guts, glory, and gun smoke."

Sloane backed up a step and swept her arm toward the wooden chopping block on the counter. "Have at it, Chef Pierre . . . or Pedro."

Rawlings found a large wooden bowl and slid it into position. He tested the edge of a kitchen knife with his thumb. "This will do." He took a large tomato and quartered it. "Since we do not have a Veg-O-Matic, I will reduce this vegetable by the old method." He sliced and diced like a crazed *teppan-yaki* cook. "You can supplement the tomatoes with a small can of sauce late in the season when they aren't so juicy. If you don't use tomato sauce, you have *pico de gallo,* which translates—"

"Rooster's beak. I know," she said.

"Sounds bad but tastes good." When finished, he threw the tomato pieces into the bowl. "Next, the onion. Always use a red onion if you have one." He carved up the onion and it joined the tomatoes. "Then the cilantro. Always use fresh. Use only the leaves. Discard the stems." He proceeded to hack and hew until the cilantro was minced. "Next is the celery, which adds a crunchy texture to the mix." He banged away with the knife, cutting the celery into bite-sized morsels and scraping them into the bowl. He flipped the knife into his other hand. "Next, the piece de résistance, señorita. *Los chilies.* Ah, I see you have the right varieties: Anaheim for flavor, serranos for the burning sensation of hellfire. Jalapeños for bite with mercy, and yellow wax chilies for ambiance. Never, under any circumstances, insert bell peppers. The result is instant ruination." He cut the peppers up into tiny pieces. "Always wash your hands after handling peppers, children, and especially before going to the bathroom." He scooped up the pieces of chilies and tossed them into the bowl with a flourish. "Next is the tomatillo, which you know is half pepper, half tomato; a must in any salsa fresca worthy of the name." He peeled the bark from two tomatillos and cut up the green vegetables that joined the growing soup.

Sloane watched with unabashed amazement. He was a reminder to her that you could never fully predict a person. If the moon had a dark surface, it also had a side where the sun shone. The other side of a one-eyed jack might even be smiling.

"Next is the seasoning. Here it's largely a matter of taste. I personally prefer a dash of lemon and a squirt of lime." He paused a moment and faked a look of bemusement. "Or, was it a squirt of lemon? No matter. Then, add in seasoned salt and pepper, some garlic or garlic powder, and any other seasoning that strikes your fancy. Stir . . ." He whirled a wooden spoon in the mix. "And, voilà. Salsa." He pushed the bowl toward her. *"Bien provecho, señorita."*

Sloane timidly inserted a tortilla chip into the mix, half expecting it to burst into flames. Instead, her palate was treated to the best salsa she had ever experienced. She stepped back and looked at him. "Amazing," was all she could think of to say.

He was looking intently at her, and she didn't know what to do. Under other circumstances, she would have been flattered that a good-looking man like him had taken an interest in her. But her thoughts were on another.

He put the wooden spoon down and knew intuitively she had made her choice. It was okay. *It's a fiction that you can seduce women. They merely select you. It was only a thought, anyway.* He smiled warmly at her. "He's at the hotel."

Her eyes widened. She didn't know she was that obvious. Sloane punched him lightly in the arm. "I love your salsa."

"**THEY'RE** coming up the stairs!" Stoneman was near hysteria.

Rawlings hurled through the door onto the landing of the stairwell and dropped two M-67 fragmentation grenades onto the next floor. He rolled a third primed hand grenade down the steps. A Somali picked it up just as it exploded. Pieces of bone and flesh speckled the wall as the figure obliterated. Rawlings fired his SAW into the stampede beneath him and ducked the returning hail of bullets that caromed off the steel railings and buzzed by his head like angry hornets.

Stoneman fired his M-9 until the slide locked back. "I'm out," he screamed.

Rawlings pitched the CIA man a spare magazine from his assault vest. "Get Grainger's Skinny Popper like he told you," he said, referring to the H & K MP-5 PDW. Stoneman scrambled into the room and emerged with the weapon.

"Do you know how to use that piece?" shouted Rawlings.

Stoneman answered by firing down at two Somalis who had crawled over the mounds of dead in an attempt to retrieve weapons. One of them jerked like a palsied puppet and slumped over the heap of dead and dying.

Rawlings gave him a thumbs-up. "That's it. Some more effective diplomacy." He tossed Stoneman a hand grenade. "Now remember, boys and girls; once you've pulled the pin on Mr. Grenade, he is no longer your friend."

Stoneman caught the equal opportunity destructive device,

frantically checking the cotter-key pin. "Who are you guys?" he shouted in the din.

"The Dreaded D," Rawlings yelled back. "Big D, little E, L-T-A. Who else would be stupid enough to come all this way to pull somebody from Crybabies, Intellectuals, and Assholes out of the fire?" He looked down the stairwell again. *Yeah. Killing is our business, and business is good. The Sammies are shit. But they have quantity. And quantity is its own kind of quality.*

Grainger made his forty-third kill of the day. Forty-five spent 7.62 × 51 mm cartridge cases lay scattered about the floor. He kicked the empty brass out of the way to keep from slipping on them. Rawlings was yelling at another window, a primal scream of delight and defiance of death. Myles was in his element. He saw the Caucasian.

The man was wearing a tan beret and an odd, not-immediately-identifiable camouflage pattern uniform with muted reds and light, sandy browns in shadowy, wavy patterns. He was carrying an AKS-74U "Krinkov," the shortened version of the Russian 5.45 × 39.5 millimeter assault rifle that replaced the AK-47. There weren't many of them around. That probably meant the guy was important. He was about seven hundred meters away, by reference to the mil scale, and very aware that there were active snipers around. The man was pointing a swagger stick at a Somali, who was waving an AK and shaking his head. *An adviser. Probably merc, but maybe Russian or . . .* A burst of machine gun fire caused Grainger to duck. He heard Rawlings's shout of "Fire burst of six," and the rattle of fire from his SAW in response.

Grainger yelled at Rawlings, who hollered back, "I see him." He got back up and obtained a visual on the man. He was organizing the locals for maneuver on them. The focus of the Ranger/Delta battle seemed to have shifted. More and more Skinnies seemed to be massing. Somali organization was not a good thing at this point. He moved to the opposite edge of the window for a slightly better angle but could still only pick up the man intermittently. He marked the position as the man ducked down with three Somalis behind a wall. Grainger zeroed in on the wall, but then took the time to fire up a Somali armed with an RPG who stepped out into the street, aiming at them.

Grainger returned to the wall. He focused on his best estimate of where the target might reappear, concentrating on the end of the wall. A moment later a beret slowly rose up into the sight picture; then a pair of sunglasses, and finally a full head. Grainger let his breath out slowly and deliberately. The rifle fired, its sound almost indistinguishable among the cacophony that was engulfing them.

Grainger could see only a hand that lay exposed leading to a body that was concealed behind the wall. Some unseen hands dragged the arm behind cover. He could see the beret lying in the street. It held the scalp and half the brains of whoever had been wearing the thing.

Rawlings stopped firing for a moment. "Seven-point-six-two holes make invisible souls. Long distance is the next best thing to being there. Nice shot." He went back to his window.

"I got somebody on the radio," yelled Stoneman. Grainger dropped down onto the floor beneath the window. Rounds zipped and cracked through the opening and thudded into exterior and interior walls. Bits of plaster showered down and dust floated thick in the hot air. "Throw a grenade down the stairs and crawl over to me." Grainger projected his voice over the tumult.

The grenade exploded, and Stoneman crawled over on all fours, bringing the radio. Grainger made contact with the orbiting Command and Control bird. He was promised a Black Hawk on station in ten minutes for the extract. They had to stay alive awhile longer. Grainger chanced a peek out the shattered window and saw that hundreds of maddened Somalis with blood lust and vengeance were moving like a wave toward them. "We gotta get to the roof."

They bolted for the stairwell and shot the vanguard of two Somalis who had crawled over the pyramid of bodies on the lower landing in an attempt to get to them. Exiting out onto the roof structure, Rawlings covered the access door. "I'm out of grenades," he said, wiping the sweat from his face. "And I've only got two '16' mags left, and my Eickhorn," referencing his German *Fallschirmjaeger* spring-blade fighting knife.

Grainger peeked over the wall. A sea of black humanity chanting for their blood and firing from all four sides surrounded them. Concrete chunks, wood splinters, and stone chips flew in an uninterrupted fountain of debris. Rawlings fired into the stairwell from his position at the door. He fired again, then discarded the empty magazine. "These guys won't quit. I've got enough for one more rush."

Stoneman ran to the door. "I'm out of ammo."

Rawlings handed him his Phobis M-9 with its last fourteen cartridges. "You know what they said at the Little Big Horn?"

Stoneman shook his head.

" 'Save the last bullet for yourself." Rawlings fired six rounds semiautomatic and dropped four technicals. The last fell against the door. He was now operating in the zombie zone, that state of exhaustion and near mental collapse where everything not dummy-corded to you with "550" line was lost, and where only your noncerebral responses separated you from the dead. But that was where the Dreaded D did its best work. Being able to operate in the zone was one of the elements that placed the "D" apart from common soldiery. The zone was where the wheat got separated from the chaff. The zone was a good place, because there they were able to operate and survive while others lay down and died.

"We're dead," screamed Stoneman, almost incoherently. "We're not going to make it."

Rawlings pointed his SAW at Stoneman. "Shut up. Don't make me kill you and waste a bullet waiting for a Skinny. You're not dead until I tell you you're dead." A Somali burst through the door, and Rawlings cut his throat with a slash of his paratrooper knife. "*That's* dead," he said pointing at the bloody Somali. "You ain't."

He heard the choppers coming.

RIOS ran his finger hypnotically around the rim of his brandy snifter and watched the figure approach. The lengthening shadows made the man only an unidentified stick figure looming in the distance.

"Get ready to be a half-mil poorer, Rios." Big John Hill spat the words. He wasn't letting it ride. He was supercharged. "Yeah. I heard one of those *'curendera,'* something like this one you got here . . ." His jaw jutted toward Sonja. "Found Jesus's face on a tortilla she made. Encased it in plastic. She had Mexicans flocking to the fucking thing. Then, another bitch sees some saint on the side of a Chevy and calls it 'The Shrine of the Camaro.' She charges twenty pesos for a look-see. Making a Goddamn killing. No wonder you fucking spics are washing cars and picking tomatoes."

Estaban remained outwardly serene. His mien was Mahatma Gandhi, his hands folded in a pyramid in front of his chest. He slowly unfolded them and took the decanter from the tray held by the unobtrusive old woman standing nearby and refilled his glass. "You really must try some of this tequila, Señor Hill. It is my private stock. It comes all the way from Pueblo Tequila, just west of Guadalajara, in Jalisco. True tequila can only come from the volcanic soil. You know, it is a primitive-looking plant, savage in appearance, but pure of soul, as only a Mexican can be. Guillermo Romo, *el presidente* of Herradura brought me this selection, pure blue agave. *Anejo*—"

"Keep your liquor," said Hill. "You can embalm your man . . . with—"

Montezuma crested the slope of the hill.

Estaban took another sip of his special stock. "Are you sure you won't change your mind?"

Montezuma handed the dead man's bloody rifle to Rios, who accepted it with a nod, a smile, and a raise of his glass. Montezuma strolled over to Big John. "I have something for you also, señor." He held out the severed finger.

Hill staggered back, his mouth convulsing.

Montezuma turned away, then turned back. "Ah yes. One more thing." He reached into his pocket and removed his emery board. "It sensitizes the finger to the trigger. It does not make a man a *maricon.* Señor."

Big John stared catatonically, his head reeling and his stomach in revolt. He turned and stumbled down the hill. *It's impossible.*

Estaban called after him, "I will call your bank in the morning. See to it I am not disappointed." Before Hill disappeared, he added, "Look at the positive. You now have two body parts for your collection. Sen-yoor." Estaban forgot the gringo the minute he was out of sight. He had more important things on the agenda. His shipment was coming. Plus, it was time to lean on the priests.

Servando Chavez raised his clenched fist in front of his face as Montezuma approached him. He tightened his muscles and set his face into a victory scowl. His fist shot into the air. Chavez had cast his lot with Montezuma. He knew life was very short.

THE AH-6 made a gun run over them, its General Electric minigun spewing destruction at 6000 rpm. An MH-60 Black Hawk descended directly over them, its prop-wash winds at hurricane force. Pieces of tin, rocks, rubble, and miscellaneous debris became projectiles. They shielded their eyes as the uncoiling rope—which featured nylon appendages, straps, and buckles at regular intervals—plunged toward the roof.

Rawlings poked Stoneman. "When you see me running, you better catch up."

The device hanging from the Black Hawk was a special purpose insertion-extraction apparatus. The SPIE rig was developed by the Marines for their reconnaissance units, but pirated by Delta, who used anything that worked. The Army normally utilized the STABO rig for spec ops extracts, but nobody was wearing the required extraction harness.

When the SPIE rig hit the roof, Grainger shouted, "Now!" and they ran for the lifeline. Three Somalis burst through the roof door but were machine gunned by the crew chief manning an M-60. Grainger secured Stoneman, and then both he and Rawlings strapped in. The helicopter rose, the three of them dangling like soap on a rope. Another escorting AH-6 made a rocket run, destroying the roof. A piece of the disintegrating building grazed Grainger's cheek. A flesh wound, it was just another caste mark.

They cut through the sky at 130 miles per hour on the ultimate E-coupon ride, headed for the safety of the Ranger and Delta compound at the airport, scornful of the torrent of bullets that split the sky around them.

Over the roar of the wind, Stoneman reached up and grabbed Grainger's hand. "I don't know what to say. You saved my life."

"Forget it," Grainger shouted down at him.

"No. I can never do that," said Stoneman. "If there ever comes a time . . . If there is ever anything I can do for you . . . I'll pay you back. I swear."

Grainger waved him off with an unheard laugh. *Yeah. We'll have to get together sometime.* He tugged at Rawlings's boot. "Hey! *Now* it's Miller time."

They flew on, dangling from a rope high over Mogadishu, Somalia, East Africa. Stoneman was sure at that moment he would live forever.

SIXTEEN

A soft knock at the door. Grainger turned away from the window and drew his Swenson customized .45 from his shoulder holster. He moved off line. "Who is it?"

"Sloane. Sloane McKenzie."

He uncocked the weapon and stepped to the door. He opened it, first looking down the hallway and then at her. "Thanks for letting me know it was Sloane *McKenzie.* That eliminated the possibility it was Sloane Smith or Sloane Degorski."

"Can I come in?" she asked.

Grainger stepped back, and she entered the room.

"I always wondered what these places looked like from the inside." She sniffed. "It smells musty, sort of." She hesitated. "Well . . . here. I brought you something to eat." She held out a paper plate covered in tinfoil. "It's probably cold." She brushed back her hair. "Your partner is down at the church making scorned-woman salsa and fencing with the staff."

He took the plate. "Fencing?"

"Dialectic. You know. Verbal jousting. A riposte here, a bon mot there . . ." *My sentences all seem to drop off into dangling participles.* She noticed the rifle lying on the bed. "That's some shootin' iron you got there, Cisco. Can I look at it?" It gave her something to do with her hands.

Grainger put the plate down on the peeling veneer desk and went to the bed. He picked up the rifle and handed it to her.

She hefted the piece. "*Whew.* Is this the Ted Nugent autograph model, or what?" She shifted the balance of the rifle in her hands. "This is definitely some weapon."

"It's only a tool. The weapon is the man behind it," he said.

"Like . . . 'Guns don't kill people. People kill people'?"

Was that sincerity or sarcasm? He couldn't tell. "You could put it that way."

"Well, it's a bit heavy for a winsome lass like myself, but I'm sure you handle it just fine. She was doing her best to keep it light, but she knew she was failing. *Why am I drawn to this darkness and danger? What am I doing here?*

Grainger reached over and took the rifle from her and stacked it in a corner.

"I have the feeling," she said, "that at some time in the past you were more of a fun person."

Grainger thrust his hands into his pockets. "Funny thing. I had the exact same feeling about you."

Sloane shivered slightly. She found her eyes holding his in an embrace. This was crazy, but she was going to say it anyway. "I have a confession to make." She rocked slightly, heel to toe. "I didn't walk all the way over here just to . . . well, I mean I *did* want to feed you . . . I mean—"

"What *do* you mean?" he said.

Her mouth parted slightly, searching for more air than seemed available. "I came to try to seduce you." She dropped her head. " 'Man's heart is through his stomach' and all that . . ." She stared at the floor. The frayed carpet needed cleaning. *I've made a fool of myself.* She raised her eyes and stepped back toward the door. "Look. I'm sorry. It was stupid and presumptuous of me."

He felt anesthetized. "You can quit trying."

She raised her head.

"You already have."

She tried to swallow but couldn't. This wasn't the Sloane McKenzie she once knew: aloof and distant, cool and breezy, tantalizing but unavailable. He hadn't even taken her out for a date, not even coffee or small talk after a movie. *I'm acting like some trollop.* She had not moved and was aware of him looking at her eyes, not ogling her breasts. "I want you to know I haven't been with a man for . . . well, a long time."

Grainger found himself smiling again for a second time in the hour, a recent record. "That's okay," he offered, "I haven't either."

They laughed simultaneously. Each took a step, closing the gap. Their hands reached toward each other, fingertips touching lightly. Then he took her forearms and pulled her to him.

Blood drained from the rational side of his brain, making him dizzy and slightly deranged. Her head tilted up, and her mouth searched for his. She seized his lower lip between her teeth and pulled him to her until he sealed her lips with his. He picked her up, and she kicked off her sandals as he carried her to the bed.

He laid her down and unbuttoned her blouse. She wiggled out of it for him. He gazed down at her heaving breasts and watched her heart beat fiercely, matched by her breathing. She pulled up his shirt and placed the palm of her hand on his flat stomach. When she took his hand to the hook on the front of her bra, he slid the two pieces apart and her breasts sprang free, her nipples pouty and erect.

She pulled his face onto her breasts and held him there for a moment. Sloane loved being a woman. She gloried in the fact that ultimately she was in control.

"You're very beautiful," he said, raising his head from her body.

She lifted his shirt from him and replied, the words slipping through a coy smile, "I'll bet you say that to all the girls you make love to."

"No," he returned, as he uncoupled her skirt and slid it down her legs. He then stood up and undid his trousers as she lay on the bed with her hands behind her head. She saw his erection tease his underwear. He shuffled out of his underwear and stood naked before her, lean and taut, scarred and marked. If he died young, he'd have a beautiful corpse.

Totally male and magnificent, she thought as he descended

onto her. She struggled to remove her panties as she felt his passion intensify.

Grainger concentrated on not blowing this one. He could never recall the peaks of sheer lust he was experiencing now. He was soaring high and wild. Her wet mouth was on his chest, and she was uttering wicked, abandoned things. As he grabbed her hair and forced her head back—mouth agape, teeth flashing, forehead moist with sweat—she shifted her body to receive him.

Sloane felt him enter her effortlessly, and she obligingly slowed her movements to accommodate his need to relax and survive this sublime torture. Every time she moved, he responded with a slight groan and an excruciating look of pleasure on his face. It could have been pain. The expressions were the same; but she didn't think so. She could feel him whole and rigid within her, and the tumult of her ecstasy came on recklessly and shamelessly. She released herself to her own exploding sexuality.

His mind spun in a psychedelic vortex, discharging its unbridled energy along with his spend. Sloane collapsed under him. They both lay suspended in the firmament of an erotic stillness, having passed from fire into cradling warmth.

FATHER Leon was not drunk but rather just slightly inebriated, as he preferred to think. He leaned against the wall in the corner of the church recreation hall, talking to Rawlings while Father Paul looked on disapprovingly from the other side of the room. The kids had all gone to bed.

Rawlings looked at his watch. *Twenty-two hundred. Ten o'clock.* She hadn't returned, so he couldn't go back. He turned again to Leon. "Well, Father Leon—"

"Lay-Own, Señor Rawlings," said Leon Ortega, wagging a drooping finger. "It is pronounced Lay-Own." Leon poured wine into a glass he was holding in one hand from a bottle he maintained in the other.

"No problem. Hey, can I just call you Leon and you call me Myles instead of son?"

"Yes. Yes, of course. My son." Leon giggled hysterically. He pointed his glass. "So, tell me; what is the plan?"

"The plan is to scatter the enemy before us, burn his villages, lay waste to his lands, and take his daughters."

"Is that our plan? Really?"

Rawlings grinned. "No, Leon. That actually was Ghengis Khan's plan."

Leon made the sign of the cross. "Paul told me your parents were Catholic. Yes? Then you are indeed of the faith."

"No, Leon. You have my respect but not my faith. I told your cohort what I believed in. And it wasn't Catholicism."

"Ah, it is not normal to be without faith."

"You know, Leon, I once woke up from a nightmare dreaming I was leading a normal life. No. I think I'm about as far away from normal as you can get. Like they say, 'Just do it.' "

Leon propped himself up. "So, you are an animal of stimulus-response, pleasure-pain?"

Rawlings liked old Leon, who probably wasn't even forty yet. He wasn't priestlike at all. Maybe if more were like him, he would still be Catholic. "You know, I was in Thailand where the Buddhists believe that in order to get past suffering and pain, you have to get by pleasure. I tried it. Seriously. I lasted until noon and then broke my vows in a Bangkok whorehouse."

Leon tittered again. *Even the eunuch at the orgy has an imagination. You can't castrate that.* He held up his glass. "Fine drinking whiskey is the Catholic answer to Buddhism." He took a swig. "Distilled spirits are better, but Burgundy will have to suffice for tonight." He put his arm around Rawlings. "I am glad you are among us. Stay. You have a home."

Rawlings slapped the top of Leon's shoulder and squeezed it. "You're all right, Leon. I've always wanted someplace to come home to."

Leon looked at him through bleary eyes. He swayed a bit, and his words were starting to have smooth edges. "Killing for peace. Does it work, my son?"

Rawlings still held on to Leon's shoulder. He slid his hand up to the priest's neck and clasped it affectionately. "Father . . . I'd have to say about like fucking for virginity."

Leon raised one finger into the air, and his mouth opened as if he had something further to say. Then he collapsed his finger and his face brightened. "Yes. I see the problem."

Rawlings released his grip. "Gotta go." He waved to Paul and shook off intellectual reengagement with Leon. He walked to the door and opened it. Lightning split the black sky. A summer storm was brewing. He shut the door behind him and headed for the river.

Rawlings made his way to the river and dropped down an eroded wall of dirt. He walked out onto a sandbar and found a high spot. He sat down and felt the storm build in power. Thunder boomed like artillery in the distance. Lightning zigzagged through the darkness, heralding the coming of another thunder drum. A follow-up bolt illuminated the darkness. He counted the seconds from the lightning until Thor's hammer reverberated. Three. That meant the strike was approximately 3300 meters away; light visualization being virtually instantaneous and sound traveling at 1100 meters per second.

The water glistened as if it were ice. Tiny luminescence made it sparkle and glow. Across the Rio Grande, the pale lights of Punta Roja flickered. The warm breeze began to pick up. Then the rain came. He looked up and let the drops impact his face. He wasn't sure if faith and belief in the ineffable was a blessing or a curse, weakness or strength. Whatever it was, it wasn't for him. He had invested in today. The immediate. He never gave a thought about the hereafter. A warrior couldn't afford to think about tomorrow. But someday he wanted to go home.

IS *that a body floating downstream?* From his position overlooking the river, the border patrolman focused his NVD on the shapeless object that bumped along the shallows of the Rio Grande. *Naw. It's just a log.* He sat on his worn, green canvas folding chair and shifted his attention to the man sitting on a mound down on the sandbar. Through the ANPVS-4 night vision device—an obsolescent, second-generation starlight scope donated to the Patrol by the Army at Fort Hood—he could clearly make him out; a stranger, although he had heard there were two of them in town. It was a town without anything, including secrets. He shifted in his seat. It would soon rain—and probably rain hard—and then he'd have to retreat to the safety of the cab of his gas chamber–green Chevrolet Suburban. He was *la migra,* an arm of the Department of Homeland Security, and represented the majesty of the federal government in these parts; but he didn't take his job all that seriously anymore. Catching wets and throwing them back across the border was fun—pointless, but fun—when he was in his twenties and thirties, and maybe even into his fourth decade, but now that he was fifty-four and facing mandatory retirement next year, well, things just weren't the same.

From his location on the bluff he could watch the river in two directions. This was his favorite spot. It gave him a feeling of omniscience. He could see boats coming from both ways, but, because of the bluff and the bend in the river, they couldn't see each other. It was sort of like being able to see the future. He could see what lay ahead for each boater. It was a secret thing. He never told anybody.

He had been the resident agent in Zapata now going on eleven years, and he expected to retire next summer and live out his life in a trailer park for seniors, next to his grandkids in a nearby Detroit suburb where his son-in-law spun the heads of hex-head bolts with an air impact wrench on the assembly line for FOMOCO while complaining to the union reps that his job "ain't got no dignity." Wayne was a whiner, but his kids were angels. He would put them on his knee and tell stories. *Truth or fiction, made no never mind.* His wife had left him six years ago for a literary agent she met at a writer's convention and moved to New York. She had been trying to sell that collection of poetry and short stories on the Southwest for a long time. He wondered if she ever did.

Here, he was his own boss. He religiously sent in reports of his activities, but mostly just changed the dates on the old reports and recycled them. No one said a word. In fact, he had a string of commendations for keeping a tight rein on illegal immigration in his sector. *Few arrests? No activity? Excellent suppression and deterrent effort.* It was typical bureaucratic semiotics; the flip side of the body count syndrome in Viet Nam. Sure; every once in a while an ad hoc Patrol task force would descend on the area and make an illegal-immigrant sweep. A week later they'd leave, mostly empty-handed. *Damn fine job you're doing down here in Zapata. Keep up the good work.* The raids had become more infrequent. He hardly saw them anymore. Not that he didn't do his job and bust the occasional felon or other lowlife that came to his attention. He had of course quit dealing with Buck Downs years before. *The corrupt son of a bitch. Heard his officer, the colored boy, is all right . . .*

The border patrolman shifted in his seat again. His bleeding hemorrhoids were giving him a problem more nowadays, but so was his paunch of a belly, his cheeky jowls, halitosis, acid stomach, flat feet, and the heartbreak of psoriasis. *Didn't have no acne, though.* Pretty soon he was going to have more hair on his nose than on his head. *I'll need a squeegee instead of a comb by the time I pull the pin.* At least the badge wasn't as heavy as it once was.

A lifetime before, he had been in Viet Nam, stationed with The Big Red One at Di An, north of Saigon. He hadn't been in the bloody infantry or anything. He hadn't been a grunt, a mud roller, but he had done his part. He got drafted and went east instead of north like a lot of pukes did. He had been one of the "Mamas and the Papas," an MP. It wasn't glamorous work or anything, nor particularly dangerous, but he wasn't ashamed either. But still, just once, he wished he could get his licks in against the bad guys. He was aware of what was going on in and around Zapata and Punta Roja. He listened to the rumors, heard the shots, and witnessed the *Dia de los Muertos*—normally observed in November—"celebrated" every month; sometimes twice. Who wasn't aware or hadn't seen the *ofrendas* erected by the bereaved? He had quit advising his superiors via memo. They had admonished him: "It's a Mexican National problem. Mind your own business and focus on your job description."

The border patrolman returned the scope to his eyes and looked back at the crazy bastard just sitting, staring at the river. He hoped the guy wasn't planning on committing suicide, 'cause if he was, he was going to be successful. He thought about things again. *Just once. Just fuckin' once.* Then the rains came.

SEVENTEEN

HIS heartbeat kept rhythm with hers, both accompanied by the whirring concerto conducted by airborne and land-based creatures outside the window. The wispy white curtains rustled and swayed, blowing in and out of the open window as the wind commanded. A thunderclap announced the coming of the rain. It all smelled so fresh.

"The fountain at the Bellagio in Las Vegas. From now on, any time I see it, I'm going to think of you." She was laughing and happy. She lay on the bed next to him. "Tell me about you. I want to hear it, warts and all."

He held her head, cradled in the pit of his shoulder, as he idly stroked her hair and ear. "You don't want to know."

She rolled over and rose up on her elbows, her mouth pursed a bit. "Try me."

"There's no polite word for it."

"So, give me the impolite."

He put one arm under his head and shifted his weight to one side. The glory of her nakedness was still distracting. "How about mercenary?"

"How come I'm not shocked? What kind are you?"

He reached out and touched her arm and stroked it absently. "How many kinds are there? I've killed almost two hundred men; killed them, and most of them never knew I was there." He snapped his fingers.

She looked right at him without blinking. " 'Cry havoc! And let slip the dogs of war'?"

"Something like that, except at some point I took control of my own leash."

"Then you were almost like God."

"God was never around."

She stopped the movement of his hand. "You only killed the bad guys. It was your job." She wouldn't let him condemn himself.

"An assassin I knew for a while . . . before he died . . . an operator for the DGSE—*Direction Generale de la Securite Exterieure,* the French intelligence service—told me once what the difference was between a freedom fighter and a terrorist." He touched her arm. "Do you know what it is?"

She shook her head.

"A freedom fighter is anyone who kills for France. Anyone who kills a Frenchman or a non-Communist is a terrorist. I guess it all depends on the perspective." He squeezed her hand. "I don't feel guilty for what I've done; it's just that—"

"You're trying to walk in another man's shoes?"

He laughed softly. "You know, when I used that exact expression with Rawlings, he said if I wanted to walk in another man's shoes, I should go bowling."

She worked her hand over his, intertwined their fingers. "Who'd you work for?"

"Serve all. Love none. Sam, mostly. The Company. DIA. Pentagon wet work ops that needed deniable proprietaries unconnected to the military or any intelligence agency. An occasional sanctioned government export detail. Some U.K. reciprocal deals in Northern Ireland and terrorist neutralizations in Bolivia, even for the DEA once down in . . . *That* I know you don't need to know. And, in case of any inquiries, my DA 201 file shows me as deceased, killed in a night training, water landing parachute jump in Panama. 'Shark-infested waters at the mouth of the Chagris River. Body Not Recovered.' "

"Rawlings?"

"Same basic effect," he responded. "Killed in an explosion of an artillery ammunition dump. Closed casket. He's buried at Arlington; caisson ceremony, rifle volleys, Taps, and all. We don't officially exist."

"What happened to you?"

He let go of her hand and let his arm slip out from under her head. He lay flat, with his hands clasped behind his head, staring at the dirty ceiling. "What happened? What happened . . . ?"

She leaned over him and brushed his cheek. "Yes. Tell me the story. Please."

"Some stories are for others. Some are just for yourself." He resisted. These were top secret operations he had sworn never to reveal. There were vows of silence. But, there had to be exceptions. *That's probably what every traitor tells himself.* He looked at her citronella eyes. Grainger was partially hypnotized by her. Her eyes were like magnets, nexorably turning his dark side inside out. He needed to talk to her. "Long time ago and far away, I took a shot at a high-value priority target that was even farther away."

"Did you—"

"Hit the target? Yes. I managed to hit the target, but, a millisecond before that bullet took out the intended mark, it blew out the chest of a ten-year-old boy."

She found her clenched hand moving involuntarily to her mouth. "Oh, Jesus . . ."

"Now, most every night I see his face in a twenty-four-power rifle scope with the crosshairs over his heart."

She laid her hand on his chest. "It was an accident. A mistake."

He turned his head and captured her eyes. "Tell that kid it was a mistake." He turned his eyes back to the ceiling. "At the shooting gallery . . . It was the first time I had a rifle in my hands for some time. I haven't been at my best."

"You fooled me along with six kids. Anyway, the way I heard it, only the mediocre are always at their best."

"I hope you're right. In any case, thanks for trying." He

propped himself up against the headboard and covered his nakedness. "What about you?"

"First day of the rest of my life. I'll be honest. I'm sick of waiting for justice to happen and expecting the law to do it. For the last two years I've sat around here like some dopeless hope fiend, thinking I was doing something positive by taking notes and gathering intelligence, waiting for the deliverance from evil. I love those kids, but I'm tired of being Clara Barton and Mother Teresa, caring for the survivors of terrorism, ignoring the underlying problem, and begging to live another day. I don't care about luxury, fame, or having a pied-à-terre in the *Dixieme*. None of that means a thing."

"What do you want?" he said.

"I want to be *La Femme Nikita*. You know, like the one buzzard said to the other, 'Patience hell; I'm going out and kill something.' " She used both her hands to grab his. "Don't think I'm crazy or some closet sickle slayer; but I've seen enough around—"

He put his finger over her mouth.

She slowly took his finger away. "I don't exactly know why this happened between you and me, but I'm glad it did. I don't expect flowers, courtship, or a follow-up. It's probably best if we just pretend it didn't happen, at least for a little while. I want you to be able to concentrate."

"If that's what you want . . ."

"If I can hold out . . ." She leered in jest and slid closer to him. "You've got just two jobs left."

"Two jobs?"

"Love a good woman." She kissed him hard on the mouth. "And kill some bad men."

She got up, tawny and glistening, her nakedness like an art object. "I almost forgot."

He concentrated on her face.

"Rios's big shipment? I had to dig for this one. The word is it's coming in three days." She bent over. "I'd love to stay for an encore, but I better get back." When she was dressed, she kissed him on the cheek. "I'll be back." It was not bad Schwarzenegger. She turned and slipped out the door. It was going to be a wet run back.

Grainger looked out the window to try to catch a glimpse of her. There was only darkness. He thought of Mogadishu again and knew what the link to Beirut had to be.

At Midnight, Rawlings knocked on the door. Grainger let him in. "You look like a drowned rat."

Rawlings shook himself like a terrier. "Yeah, you know when it rains and you're out in it, you get wet. Got something to do with hydrogen and oxygen molecules." He mopped his head with a towel and threw it at Grainger. He went to the bathroom, looking for another one. "I could have been a contender." He looked at Grainger's rumpled bed. "Thought I'd give you a break." When Grainger didn't say anything, he added, "Hey, don't thank me or anything; for not interfering and staying out in the cold."

Grainger dropped the wet towel on the floor. "You remember the white guy I took down in Mogadishu?"

Rawlings stopped looking for a dry towel and came to full mental attention. "Yeah. Sure."

"What kind of cammies did he have on? Do you remember?"

"What kind of *cammies* did he have on? Now, that's what I call real nice postcoital conversation." When Grainger showed no signs of appreciation, he added, "Hey, okay. I was only kidding." Rawlings sat down on his bed. "They were those zigzag pattern ones, I think, with the reddish hues and shadows in sand color." A soldier remembered details like this. Like a girl remembers the dress she was wearing when she parted with her virginity.

Grainger nodded. "Yeah. That's how I remember it, too." He folded his hands. "What country?"

Rawlings stroked his chin. "Jesus, Lon. How the fuck should I know? Next thing you'll want me to guess his hat size. What's so Goddamn important—?"

"Think."

Rawlings hung his head. He *had* seen those camouflage uniforms before. *Where was it?* He looked up. "Angola. They're

Angolan. I'd bet my ass on it. Remember those butchers who ambushed the UN caravan? We later hit them in the Sudan at the oasis. They were wearing the type. Same-same."

Grainger remembered. He also knew Rawlings was right. *Next question.* "Angola. Who had an interest in the adversarial proceedings there?"

"Well, shit Lon, you know. It was us incognito, clandestine as hell, and surreptitious to the max advising the good guys, versus . . . the fucking—"

"Cubans." *It was the Cubes.* And the dots got connected.

"IN the name of the Father, and of the Son, and of the Holy Spirit . . ." Father Paul glanced at Joey and Ponce, his altar boys beside him, as he celebrated Mass for the few people who still braved attendance. He made the sign of the cross as he turned to the six people who constituted his congregation. His anointing hand froze.

"No. No. Please continue . . . Father." Raoul Rios stood in the middle of the aisle. Tong Nguyen and Ramirez flanked him, standing just to his rear.

The santera stood in front, wearing a black robe with a short train. The deep, flowing sleeves made her look like a lethal vampire bat; a prom queen crossed with a dominatrix mated to a particle-beam weapon. The Devil had sold his soul to her. Sonja strode forward toward the altar, slowly shaking a rattle made of rattlesnake tails. She stared at each parishioner with burning eyes. The rattle's sinister hissing pulsed like a pit viper's warning. She stopped beside a stubborn woman who continued to wield her rosary furiously between her fingers. "The spirits of the dead speak to me. And I to you. Go from this place and its false idols and idolatry." She pointed toward the open door.

The woman bolted from her pew. She covered her face with a veil and ran from the church, holding her hand over her mouth. A man quickly followed.

Sister Felicia and her father, Humberto Anaya, sat alone, isolated in a front pew. She cast nervous glances at the priestess, but Humberto continued to concentrate on his hymnbook.

"Get out. This is the house of the Lord," said Paul.

Raoul opened his arms to embrace the church. " 'Get out?' Do you not believe that we are all God's creatures; that He would grant us sanctuary?"

Ramirez laughed.

"To the pious, not the profane," said Paul.

Sonja worked her way to the pulpit.

Paul turned to Joey. "Go on now. Take Ponce and find Brother Lemuel and Father Leon and tell them I will be along soon."

Joey and Ponce backed away and disappeared.

Sonja stared at Paul, who stared back. He would not let her intimidate him.

"You are a handsome man. Your features are distinct, not delicate. Your scars give you character. You are full of denied sensuality and suppressed erotic need."

"I am a man of the cloth; of the faith. I am a priest."

"You are certainly many things; but beneath that robe and your pretensions you are just a man."

"And you," Paul said, "are a harlot disguised as some soothsayer; a fraudulent fortune-teller offering false gods. Your prophecies are all delphic; meaningless."

She turned to face an empty church. Only Humberto and Felicia remained and in cowered silence. She shook her rattle hypnotically and turned back to face Paul. "A man is not a man without having had carnal knowledge of a woman."

Paul trembled with what he hoped was rage but knew was not wholly. "Leave this place. You have desecrated the house of our Savior."

Raoul spat the gum he was chewing into his hand and stuck it to the top of a pew. "We understand you experienced some vandalism from nonbelievers several nights ago. A shame. Perhaps the police could help. On the other hand, it may have only been a righteous protest over you harboring those two criminals." Raoul came abreast with Felicia. He looked over at her and whistled, a long, low sound; more like a hiss.

Paul stepped down from the elevated platform. "In the name of God, leave her alone."

Raoul moved his eyes, and Tong Nguyen caught the gesture. He swaggered over to Felicia and took her by the arm. Humberto rose in protest, but Tong pushed him back into the seat. Tong brought the woman over to Raoul. Felicia hung her head, her eyes downcast.

Raoul put his fist under her chin and forced her face up close to his. "You are quite beautiful I am sure, under your habit. Perhaps sometime I will verify my assumptions." He ran his hands down her neck and manipulated her breasts roughly. "I love the curvature of a woman's body." He placed both his hands on her hips and pulled her into him.

Felicia shook uncontrollably, riveted with an all-consuming fear and trembling.

Humberto wrung the tears of impotent rage from his eyes with the backs of his fists.

Paul was seized with a fury he could not control. He was back in the ring. He moved toward Raoul.

Ramirez sprang to block his path, a double-barreled, sawed-off shotgun that he had pulled from an across-the-back holster in his hands and pointing squarely at Paul.

Paul lurched to a stop. His breath came in tortured gasps, and his heart beat against his chest as if to free itself. "An eternity in Hell will not repay you enough for today."

"Today is its own reward, priest." Raoul pushed Felicia away from him and wiped his mouth as he regarded her with lust-dulled eyes. He turned to Paul. "I almost forgot why we came. The distraction was substantial. Yes, I remember now. You will preach to those who still dare come to this place that my brother is *El Salvador,* that he is like their father, and they should come to him. He will provide for all their needs." He turned to Ramirez. "Just like Don Corleone, eh Ramirez?" Ramirez responded with a vacuous stare of noncomprehension. Raoul returned to Paul. "You will no longer rave against him. I will not ask if I am understood."

Rios motioned to Nguyen and Ramirez with his head. "I will take it on faith that you have comprehended." He looked once more at Felicia. "I will also take her charms on faith until they can be taken otherwise." He backed out of the church, waving his hand hypnotically back and forth, like Miss America on a float in the Rose Parade.

On his way out of the church, Ramirez stopped at the poor box. He ripped off the cover and threw it on the floor. He removed the three coins inside. He turned back to the altar and flipped a coin into the air. He caught it and slapped it down on his forearm. Uncovering the coin, he looked up. "Ah, too bad. Tails. You lose." He wheeled around and was gone.

Sonja Ochoa, the Santeria priestess, followed him out. She seemed not so much to walk but to flow as she moved backwards. Her eyes never left Paul. She was *La Alma Negra,* the black soul.

FATHER Leon sat in the dark of the confessional again. No tape recorder ran. He leaned against the wall of the booth and considered what he must do. He had just listened to a man's last confession, a man who this afternoon would run the gauntlet of The Game, a game he had no delusions of beating. He ran for the pesos so his wife and child might be spared the strife and toil of their current existence. There was no other way. He had come to make his peace with God.

Leon remained in the dark, at war with himself as he struggled with the competing virtues of the inviolate veil of the confessional versus the sanctity of life. It was his vow as a priest to preserve the relationship of penitent and absolutionist. *A life now or a soul later?* Leon pulled the curtain open and stepped out into the light.

UPSTAIRS, in his room, Father Paul stood in the bathroom and looked at his face in the mirror. The doppelgänger mocked him. *I am a flea among elephants.* The face darkened, and the lips curled up into a snarl that metamorphosed into a mocking leer. He smashed the mirror with his fist. He struck out again, and with the other hand until blood dripped down between the fingers of his clenched hands. *Damn her. I am a man.*

THE hill.

The sun was the color of magenta, casting dandelion-yellow bolts in the late afternoon. Estaban stood on his hill from which he could observe his playground. Sonja stood with him, now in a simple peasant dress. Estaban looked at her. She made the prosaic look exotic. He wheeled on his heel to face the Japanese shipping magnate, Toshiro Okasuna, and his shooter, an ex-sergeant in the Arab Legion named Muzammil Siddiqi, who was supposed to have accounted for scores of Israeli soldiers during the battles around the Golan Heights in the last great Israeli/Arab conflagration. "In accordance with the ground rules, you will have the first shot once the target passes Stake One at six hundred meters."

Okasuna dropped his binoculars onto the strap around his neck. "*Hai.*" He grunted some guttural words that sounded like something Estaban had heard in the ninja and samurai films he favored.

The tall Arab said nothing.

Estaban continued. "As agreed, Okasuna San, the stakes today are somewhat higher than normal. We must make absolutely sure we are both in concurrence with the protocol."

"Yes. Yes," said Okasuna with a desperate urgency to his voice.

Montezuma looked at the Japanese with undisguised contempt. *He probably pays others to have sex for him. He is nothing but a voyeur of life.* He wished the man were the target.

"If your man's first shot misses or merely wounds the target runner, you forfeit $100,000 of the million in escrow. You of course understand?" remarked Estaban.

"Yes. I understand completely, Mr. Rios," said Okasuna. "And naturally the same applies to your man." He bowed slightly and smiled. "Should we get that far."

The eternal, inscrutable East. Estaban bowed back. "Most assuredly, Okasuna San. If the runner lives to face my representative, we assume all consequences."

A Mexican peasant walked past them, led by another man. He stopped in front of Estaban and reached out to clasp his hand. He then removed his *sombrero* and bent at the waist.

"Homage to the sovereign, Mr. Rios?" inquired Okasuna.

"No, Okasuna San. *Morituri te salutamus.*"

Okasuna bowed deeply toward the runner. " 'We who are about to die, salute you.' The salutation of the gladiator before the emperor in ancient Rome." He watched the diminutive figure disappear down the slope of the hill before turning to Rios. "You thought it was 'pearls before swine,' did you not?"

"Not at all. I never underestimate the cultural grasp of my friends or the capacities of my enemies, Okasuna San. You are a tutored man. And perceptive. Perhaps the day shall be yours after all." He motioned for Siddiqi to take his place on the executioner's bench.

Javier Gonzales Cardenas waited in the shallow depression before the starting stake. He crossed himself and looked out at the second numbered *estaca roja,* 100 meters away, across broken but essentially open ground. He looked back and saw the flare rise into the sky and he knew he was seeing the last things he would ever see. With God as his *testigo,* he prayed for the last time for his family. Then he was up and running.

Siddiqi marked the runner's scramble from cover and was tracking the dodging target. His finger tightened on the trigger. He looked up. The man had tripped, or . . .

The sound of the rifle shot rumbled like a distant kettledrum, a booming and authoritative, all-encompassing signature.

Okasuna put the binoculars back to his eyes and scanned down range. The runner was writhing on the ground. He turned to Rios. "What is going on here, Mr. Rios? Is this your idea of a poorly conceived but well-executed joke?"

Estaban stared down range with an insentient look crawling up his face. "I am not sure, señor. But, I will find out."

"I could have been playing golf in Hawaii. I came here for what is unavailable elsewhere," said Okasuna.

Montezuma looked across the field with his eyes. He needed no binoculars. "The man has a bullet hole in his left leg. He is crippled."

"What of our arrangement?" said Okasuna. "I must pay my man."

Rios held out his hand. "I will indemnify you. But this game is over for the day."

Siddiqi stepped down from the platform. He shrugged. He would be paid. It didn't matter.

Okasuna walked off the hill. He had a satellite telephone in his helicopter. He would phone ahead to the pilot of his private jet for tickets to the islands. Honolulu was still a possibility. Tomorrow was not completely lost.

Ramirez thrust his hands into his pockets. "Do you wish me to eliminate the campesino, patron?"

Rios eyed Ramirez balefully. He was beyond admonishment or lecture on honor or integrity. "No, Ramirez San," he snorted, "You will *pay* him."

Montezuma's eyes swept the range, speaking to no one in particular. "That shot. It was made—I would estimate—from over eight hundred meters, from that low ridge by the tree line." His head turned to Estaban, eyes dancing. "It was truly masterful. Angling. The target was moving diagonally. Absolutely exquisite." He laughed uproariously.

His shadow laughed with him.

Estaban ran his fingers through his coal-black hair. "I am glad you are enjoying yourself so much. At least one of us has experienced a profit today." He joined Montezuma in looking down the slope. "But you are overly indulgent, no? The spoiler missed. He hit only the leg."

Sonja laughed. "No. He did not miss."

Estaban turned to her, his brow furrowed. *An intention to wound the man? To what end? And who? Who indeed?*

A servant from the hacienda came up the trail leading to the hill. He approached Montezuma, who stood at the edge of the slope, still looking across the field. "Excuse me, Señor Lorca. There is a man at the hacienda. He says he is your travel agent."

NINETEEN

LAWRENCE Dakes was drunk. But he was among friends, so he was at ease.

From the veranda of the château—and that's the only word to describe it—the Potomac could be seen meandering in its perennial flow to the sea. You could also see the Washington Monument, cracks and all, thrusting into the sky like a giant phallus. The smell of lilacs wafted, and the acres of rolling green grass looked like a gardener's nightmare.

Stoneman had a lot on his mind. His girlfriend said she missed her period, and the Director of Security wanted to see him in the morning. And Dakes was drunk and hanging onto him like a cheap suit.

"We lie to each other, cheat our friends, and cover our own shit in white linen and invite others to feast. Isn't that right, Stony?"

"Yes, I guess we do all that, Larry."

"But doncha just love it?" Dakes leaned in, arm draped across Stoneman's shoulders, spilling half his martini onto Stoneman's dinner jacket.

Stoneman gritted his teeth. He had saved for a year to buy

the Armani dinner jacket in order to have something elegant for events like these ambassador balls. It had set him back seven hundred bucks. "Don't worry about it," he muttered.

"Sorry, old boy. I'll catch the cleaning (hic) bill." Dakes rotated wobbly, cloaked in a stage-worthy conspiratorial mien, clutching Stoneman's arm. "Keep this under your trench coat, but I gotta share the gore with someone. I'm working on the draft of a linkage coordination for a proposed Tantrum . . ."

Stoneman's head turned slowly toward Dakes. His brain scrambled to clear away all extraneous personal problems. His fingers tingled, and his heartbeat increased exponentially. " 'Tantrum?' " *Jesus, they're on to me. They found out. Dakes is on duty investigating me.*

"Yeah brainiac, Tantrum. You haven't been in the Directorate long enough, I guess. You'll find out. Internal false flag gig. Big time CYA. Magic paper trail leading nowhere. An entire literary fiction. Truth's very own vanishing act, replete with clues, red herrings, and dead ends, all intermingled among facts and reality, for the curious . . . I create masterpieces. I'm working on this one now, and it's a fucking beaut. You remember the Osama bin Laden neutralization mission that went south. I know you heard the consumer version. I start with the first vision—"

"Tantrum?"

"Jesus, Stoneman. Get ahold of yourself. Did I pronounce it wrong? *Tantrum*—the cover-up. No film at eleven. Get the whole story here."

"There's more than one?" Stoneman needed a drink of water.

Dakes tried to focus. It was difficult. "Damn straight. Far as I know, there've been probably ten or twelve since 1964, when the precursor instrument—Feint—was renamed and replaced by the present apparat. The reports aren't issued numbers except for internal control. There's no computer record. Tantrums go directly into the dead pool in the Black Vault." His drink sloshed over his glass from both sides. "The Tantrum operates like those *Matrix* flicks. Seen any of them? Creates an entire new reality. It *is* the new reality when we're trying to forget the old reality, the *real* reality." Dakes's blood-alcohol level was rising. "And persuade the skeptical and convert the unbeliever to our truth via our vaporous creations." He licked his lips, savoring his own genius. "Am I making this clear?" He slumped into Stoneman.

"So," Stoneman said, pushing Dakes away, "Tantrum is not a single operation but the *maskirovka* after the fact?" He used the Russian word for camouflage and deception.

"Exactly so, Comrade."

"What's the criteria, old boy?" said Stoneman, as casually as his chaotic psyche permitted. "What triggers the implementation?"

Dakes threw down his drink in one dramatic gulp and brushed back his unruly-by-design George Stephanopoulos hair. "In the history of this noble organization, from the Great Khan Donovan to our now pale shadow of *The Prince*, there has been only one seminal event thought worthy of the effort." He leaned closer. His upper lip twitched, and his tongue slipped over his lips. "Total closure." He tried to wink, but both eyes shut, and his face twisted into a grimace. Then he said it again, this time speaking into his tie tack like it was a hidden microphone. His other finger sliced across his sallow neck. "Total closure."

LORCA dropped the buff-colored file on the polished cherrywood table. The conference room of the hacienda was magnificent. Montezuma appreciated the rich, neoclassical ambience but remained aloof and untouched by the decadence it represented. He only worked here. "The Distant Death. I should have realized. He has been known by other names also. In Latin countries he has been called *El Dedo del Diablo.*" Montezuma leaned on the table over the file that had been given him by the emissary from Cuban intelligence. It was complete: dates, places, analyses, profiles, pictures.

"The Devil's Finger?" Estaban rubbed his jaw reflectively. He motioned for the old woman holding his glass of purified water. He took the glass from Rosa Fuentes and waved her off. "You know him?"

"Let us just say that I have knowledge of him. We share a professional reputation. The man is a living myth. There are those who say he is not one man but the composite of twenty *Yanqui* assassins."

Raoul chuckled mirthlessly with a mocking intonation. "Does this man have statues in parks commemorating his prowess, Señor Lorca?"

Lorca fixed Raoul with a scornful look that transcended the neutrality of his words. "I should say, Señor Rios, that it is more significant that he does not. He is a legend that still lives."

Estaban slammed his fist into the file. "Your legend has today cost me perhaps a million American dollars." *A million lost here, a million lost there. Pretty soon you're talking real money.* Estaban shook it off. "The day after tomorrow . . . the shipment."

"Then what, Brother?" said Raoul.

Estaban shifted his eyes to Lorca. *El Silencio. La resolución de los problemas.* He put his arm around Raoul and stretched his lips thin across his teeth. "Then, dear Brother, the legend dies."

MONTEZUMA left the group and walked outside the hacienda, out onto the open desert, toward the river. *Grainger. It was truly he.* There were few nights that he did not think about him. About Beirut. About that day when he had come to kill and instead was thwarted by circumstance or fate. Perhaps Fate was now rewarding him for his patience. He also thought about Joaquin "Tico" Lorca, his older brother, a lieutenant in the People's Revolutionary Liberation Army of Cuba. In 1993 he had been an adviser to local progressive revolutionaries in Somalia. He was killed by a sniper's bullet, fired by this man Grainger, in a place called Mogadishu. It had taken him some time to identify his brother's killer. It had cost him much in time, money, and favors. He was, after all, no longer in the direct employ of the Castro regime. He was a freelance assassin, at the service of the man or institution offering the greatest incentive. Thus, he had to rely on influence and his own indulgences, his own barter system. He offered blood for information; that and the legendary status he enjoyed with the Cuban military and intelligence service. Although he had not forgotten his quest, he had resigned himself to the fact that it might be some time before he could again pick up the scent and finish what he had started out to do. Now the man had been delivered to him, fortuitously, it appeared. But he would have to be careful. Appearances could be deceptive, and deadly. However, he believed Fate had decreed. This verdict would be final.

Federico Christo Mendez Lorca—known as Montezuma—unbuttoned his shirt and scratched his chest. His tattoo of *La angel de la muerte* dominated. Her wing tips stretched from nipple to nipple and fluttered as his fingers ran over the skin. The magnificent tattoo was the work of an artist in Miami. The angel moved with his every breath and was still with him. The pulse of his heart gave the angel life. Montezuma absently rebuttoned his shirt. *Yes*. From his verdicts there was no appeal.

"**YOU** missed," said Joey as the rifle fired, and no hit on the metal plate target across the arroyo could be detected. Then the distinct sound of the impact of a high-speed projectile upon steel sang back across the expanses.

Lon Grainger looked up from behind the rifle and into Joey's eyes. "When the target is far away . . ." He motioned with his head across the divide. "The bullet takes time to get there. Then the sound takes time to get back. That steel plate is nine hundred meters away. It takes about two seconds to get there. Understand?"

Joey nodded and took his fingers out of his ears.

Ponce kept chewing gum and looking at the rifle.

Joey touched the rifle. "Can I try?"

Grainger laid his hands on the sandbagged weapon. "Maybe someday. But I'll let you look through the scope." He moved over as Joey rolled behind the rifle. "Close one eye. Move the other eye back and forth until you see the whole picture."

"Wow! I can see a far way away. And this thing has a neat pointer!"

Grainger lay on one elbow watching Joey. *Neat pointer. Yeah, son. A neat pointer.* He then felt the subtle ground tremor even before he made the visual. He watched as the feather of dust approached down the dirt road that led to the impromptu range he had set up to recheck the zero on the rifle. Runyan was right on a couple scores. The recoil was substantial, especially in the prone position. But he already knew that. He had made the shot on the runner from eight hundred meters. The scope also maintained its zero, despite being removed and replaced onto the lock rings.

A pickup appeared out of the swirling dust. Sloane got out of the truck and brushed herself off. The boys ran to the vehicle. She grabbed them and whirled them around. "You boys learning anything?"

"Yes, ma'am," said Joey.

"Why don't you check the back of the truck? There's a soda for each of you in the ice chest."

Ponce climbed into the bed of the old Ford F-100.

Sloane put her hands on her hips and looked at him, holding the rifle over his shoulder and resembling a white hunter on the Serengeti looking for King Solomon's mine. "Rios is taking delivery of a year's supply of wholesale Bolivian marching powder, Colombian labeled. The transfer takes place at an old abandoned airstrip across the river, about twenty miles from here. My desk-bound homies in Houston have been fed disinformation. They think it's been canceled."

"Think?"

"They're victims of an organized deception. A source closer to home tells me differently. It's going down tomorrow morning."

"Mind if I ask how you know so much about what the enemy is doing?"

"No, I don't mind," she said, "you *asking*."

The boys came back, slurping root beer.

"I haven't just been sitting around on my butt waiting for miracles to happen."

Grainger let it slide. "What happens after they get the dope?"

"Then," Sloane said, pointing at him, "they're coming for you."

"WE now have what we've been waiting for." Grainger leaned against the communion rail and spoke to Leon and Paul.

Brother Lemuel stood solemnly by, his hands folded on his faded brown robe. Rawlings sat in a pew next to Sloane. Her eyes never left Grainger.

As he had promised, he didn't reveal the source of his information. "Tomorrow morning is delivery day."

Leon stood up. "Not to interrupt, but I learned that Javier Cardenas will live. The bullet missed a bone and passed through his leg. He is at the clinic. I cannot thank you enough."

"It was a tungsten bullet; armor-piercing, so there was no expansion," said Grainger. "It was the best I could do."

Paul sat in silence. He concluded that Leon must have obtained the information on Cardenas's intention in the confessional. He had saved a life at the expense of breaking the most sacred of commitments. Paul alternately rejoiced and celebrated life and recoiled in horror over the ecumenical treason upon each revolution of the matter in his mind.

"In addition," Grainger said, "our strategy has been altered a bit in reliance upon information from Father Leon—"

"Lay-Own. Please."

"Sorry," said Grainger. "But, you are sure about this? Absolutely sure?"

"As predictable as the rising and setting of the sun. I hear his confession every month. Tomorrow morning. He will be here," said Leon.

"All right then. The successful completion of this part of the SIOP will insure a margin of safety and prevent the unrestrained retaliation normally to be expected as a result of the implementation of our interdiction mission." Grainger looked at the uncomprehending faces sitting and standing around him. He had inadvertently slipped into another milieu. He was delivering an operation concept overview, a prologue to a five-paragraph operations order to a Delta team. "I'm sorry," he said.

"No. No. Do not apologize." Leon was again up and aroused. "An alien voice is appropriate here. I think we all understand the essence without the necessity of comprehending the text precisely."

Grainger nodded. "Then, as agreed, Myles will operate here with the internal matter, and Father Paul, Brother—"

"Lay-mew-L."

"Lemuel, Paul, and myself will handle the delivery site."

Grainger looked over at Paul. "You know, there is no real reason you or Lemuel have to go. I can handle this myself."

"I speak for myself," said Paul. "This is not your fight. I must go to do whatever I can and must."

"He speaks for me also," said Lemuel.

"Okay," said Grainger. "We just didn't want to involve you unnecessarily."

"We are involved," said Sloane. "Everybody's involved."

Leon's voice cracked slightly. "I am sorry I cannot do more than be a shepherd to the children."

"It's just as important as the other assignments," said Rawlings.

"Remember. From here on there is no turning back. Once we execute tomorrow's actions, we will have burned our bridges. There will no longer be any options, no refuge, no negotiations," said Grainger.

There was a uniform murmur of assent. Except from Paul.

"What will be the end of this? We seize persons and property, and then what?" Paul looked to each face.

"Number one. We finance the buy-back of your church mortgages. Two. We hire security personnel to protect you and your people pre and post the disruption and stabilization stages. Three. We bleed off Rios's operational funds, interrupt his cash flow. Fourth—and just as important—we shatter the status quo, challenge his supremacy, rupture his myth of invincibility and dominance, and finally we expose his vulnerability. Then we can—"

"But how can we anticipate Rios's reaction to all of this? What if we cannot negotiate?"

"I don't think Lon was talking about negotiating," said Rawlings.

"What if none of that works?" said Leon.

Rawlings looked at Grainger, who nodded.

"Then," said Rawlings, "we decapitate the beast."

Decapitation does not sound anywhere near negotiation! But surely they mean to bargain. Paul steadied himself against the communion rail.

"Consider, Padre. We have to have a certain amount of flexibility to improvise," said Grainger.

"It appears to me that nothing is more improvised than the plan." Paul was lost. He didn't understand the strategy of violence, at least outside the ring, but he let it drop. "I will be with Mr. Grainger, but I must make one singular demand upon you, Mr. Rawlings."

Rawlings nodded. "Go ahead."

"There must not be any sacrileges in our church; nothing that profanes the holiness of the temple of God. Swear to me."

Rawlings looked the priest in the eye. "Okay. I swear." He turned to Paul. "Up until now, this guy Rios has made all the rules around here. Now we're going to start breaking them. We find a way or we make a way."

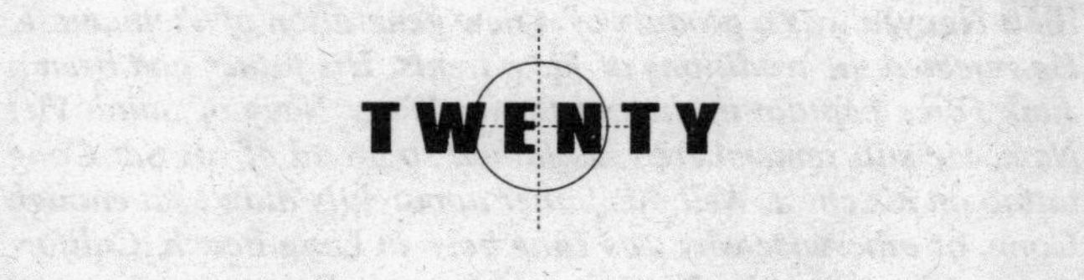

TWENTY

THE Butterfly Knife *click-clacked* again, its polished steel blade alternately disappearing and reappearing from the black handles. The supple wrist of Tong Pham Nguyen flipped the blade out once again, and he slashed at the air, severing an imaginary brachial artery. *Click-clack.* The knife folded, and he tucked it away into the pocket of his size-28-waist DKNY jeans. He welcomed the coarse desert wind that blew across the dirt strip and hurled particles of sand and dust into the air. He liked the primitive feel of it. *So long as it does not interfere with the landing of the plane.* He was in charge of this operation. And he loved that, too. Mr. Rios had chosen him instead of Ramirez to meet the delivery and insure its safe passage into their hands. That also was a good sign. He had nothing to worry about from the Federales or local police. They were all paid. He had only to accept delivery and make payment. His only concern was that the Colombians might try to take the money and keep the cocaine. But his crew of six would insure they made no such ill-advised move. Nguyen looked around at the six armed men he had brought to the old strip. He waved to Zaldiver and DeSoto, moving them farther apart from Barrera. Yucca plants lined the runway. They looked like a shaggy guard force of a hundred Yosemite Sams, each armed with daggers and bayonets. *Yes. I like the primitive feel. . . .*

TONG *Nguyen was a product of a new generation of Vietnamese. He rejected the traditions of his parents. His father had been a Junk Force captain in the old Brown Water Navy of South Viet Nam. He still remembered his father, so proud of his Sat Cong tattoo on his chest. Well, his father apparently didn't sat enough Cong, or otherwise why was Tong born in Long Beach, California, and raised in Westminster, along Bolsa Avenue and Brookhurst Street in Orange County's Little Saigon?*

Tong had been a gang member since eighth grade. His specialty was home intrusion robberies and debt collection for the cartel that lent money to Asian gamblers. The usual vigorish was 10 percent per week. In the business, he was known as The Executor. He counted on the insular nature of the Vietnamese cultural community to shield him from police detection. It wasn't entirely successful. As a result of his first strike, he spent two years in the county jail as a condition of a suspended sentence to state prison. He was seventeen at the time but was found unsuitable for the jurisdiction of the juvenile justice system. He was tried as an adult. A year after his release, he was arrested again and convicted once more. This time he was sentenced to Soledad, where he spent three years of a seven-year sentence. While there, they tried to punk him, make him into a bitch; in prison patois, "turn him out." The screws told him that a frail, smooth-skinned young boy like him could only survive by getting hooked up with one of the gladiators, for protection. It was the only way he could avoid the wolves—the pack rapists—or the other gorillas that preyed on the weak. That was what he was told.

Tong earned his stripes—killed his first man—in the prison latrine. He shanked a big African, a member of the Black Guerilla Family, who used to pump heavy iron in the yard. He emasculated the man with a homemade knife, manufactured out of a Campbell's soup can. Tong remembered the man had his eyes closed and thought that Nguyen was going to bring him off while he sat on the commode in the recreation room toilet. His eyes had opened wide when Nguyen severed his penis, and then even wider when he drove the former navy bean soup container straight into his throat. Tong then gave him his own version of the Colombian necktie. He stuck the shriveled cock into the gaping hole in the dead man's throat and left him there, draining blood all over the floor.

Tong walked back into the recreation room and smiled at all the BGF playing pool. He continued to smile affably as he ran his bloody index finger along his throat. He bounced out with a jaunty gait. After that, Tong was hung with the moniker Mad Dog. It wasn't an exaggeration. Thereinafter, he was left alone. The BGF. The Aryan Brotherhood. The Mexican Mafia. La Nuestra Familia. *None of them wanted anything to do with him. Three years later, when his behaviorally modified sentence ran to term, he was released.*

Nguyen couldn't afford California's strike three. He migrated to Corpus Christi, where the Vietnamese were in constant battle with local Hispanic and white fishermen over fishing rights and territories. For a while it was a shooting war. He hired out as a soldier, but nuoc mam, a vile smelling fish sauce, and pho, Vietnamese noodle soup, were not in his diet anymore. Nor was their battle any crusade to him. So he drifted down to Ciudad Juarez and Nuevo Laredo, where he worked for Joaquin "El Chapo" Guzman and the cartel and then the Zetas, the Zs, for a while. Unfulfilled, he heard about Estaban Rios and made his way to Punta Roja. The offer of employment was more than adequate. But it was conditional. There was the relative thing, which Tong felt was no problem. He said he would, but Rios wanted proof.

Tong returned to Westminster and found the Nguyen he was looking for, a bully he remembered from high school. He killed him in the parking lot of a club in Garden Grove using a baseball bat. He waited around until the Orange County Register *ran the story in Local News. Phong Van Nguyen murdered in a parking lot. A particularly grisly death. GGPD and Orange County Gang Task Force investigating. He invested a quarter in a newspaper and took three extra copies out of the rack for good measure. He took the next scheduled Greyhound back to*

Zapata and Punta Roja, proof in hand. Rios was satisfied. Tong was on the lucrative payroll.

TONG Nguyen looked up at the empty sky and the merciless sun that baked this land. He still laughed, remembering the story. There were only about forty surnames in the Vietnamese cultural lexicon. Finding another Nguyen was easy. It was Brown, Smith, and Jones, all put together, ten times over. He bowed in a mocking gesture. It was funny as hell.

The sound of the approaching aircraft was faint at first. Nguyen heard it before the others and shouted to them to get ready. The throbbing motors sounded like an unbalanced washing machine. The sound increased in a crescendo as a C-47 aircraft winged in, low on the horizon, under radar surveillance. It barnstormed over the field, and Nguyen could see the pilot looking down at them at not much of an angle. The aircraft circled in the distance and made another pass. Nguyen didn't bother to look up. After the plane passed the second time, he pulled his Ruger P-85 automatic and checked one more time to make sure a round was seated in the chamber. *"Listos, muchachos?"* he said, his Spanish accent slightly tainted with English and a dash of residual Vietnamese.

The old surplus military transport plane came in upwind and set down smoothly at the head of the runway. It taxied to the end and maneuvered toward where Nguyen and his crew waited in the sun. The pilot locked one brake and accelerated the port engine, driving the C-47 around until the cargo door was opposite Nguyen. The engines shut off and whined down, shuddering a bit. Then, with a cough and a kickback, they were silent. The cargo door slid open, and a man in a dirty white tropical suit sauntered out, framing the doorway, eyes squinting against the sun. He slipped on a pair of wraparound sunglasses and thrust his arms forward. *"Ai. Mucho calor."*

Tong's command of Spanish was limited, although his crew was mostly fluent if not particularly articulate. *"Bienvenido, amigo,"* he managed, with an exaggerated sweep of his arms.

Panama Jack surveyed the scene for a minute and then jumped down. *"Donde esta Nero y Raoul?"*

Tong approached the milkman. *"Hablas Ingles?"* The man nodded. "Ramirez has another assignment, and Raoul had to attend to his spiritual needs, I was told. My name is Tong, and I will handle today's transaction." He held out his hand. "You have the merchandise?"

"You have the dinero?" said the sweating man, taking the offered hand tentatively. He motioned with his free arm, and three men jumped down from the airplane. They were armed with an AK-47, a shotgun, and a MAC-10. They quickly spread out.

Tong chewed on his cheek. "I suggest you tell your scum to chill. Señor."

Panama Jack unbuttoned his silk shirt and worked the fabric in and out like a bellows, fanning himself. "A mere precaution. But, tell your gutter trash likewise. There is more than thirty million in nosegay in this plane, and my unforgiving employer holds me responsible to see to it that we are properly . . . compensated. Peacefully. *Entiendes? Verdad?"*

Tong smiled through even teeth. *"Du ma nhieu,"* he said bowing politely. *That's 'Go fuck yourself,' in Vietnamese, greaseball.* He needed an amicable solution. At this range, he would be sawdust. He waved to his men. *"Todo esta bien, muchachos."*

The milkman's florid face was encased in a thin sheen of sweat. *Fucking slant-eyed Chink. Doom on you, too, pendejo. Or whatever it was you said.* Gook talk all sounded like tin cans and rubber bands to Ramos Medina Guzman of Medellin. "The money. Just a peek, uh?"

Tong raised his hand and snapped his fingers. Two of his men unloaded a metal chest from the van where they had maintained watch. They trudged down the hill, carrying the chest between them, finally placing it between Tong and the dirty snowman. They stepped back, hands on their holstered guns.

Tong squatted down and opened the chest. Stacks of one hundred dollar bills in treasury wrappers filled the trunk.

"Por favor?"

Tong stepped back.

The man knelt down and ran his hands over the money. His face broke into an irrepressible grin. *"Bien. Bien."* He removed a penlike object, which he ran over a selective sampling of the bills. Top. Middle. Bottom. Packets of hundreds overflowed and fell onto the ground. Three minutes later, he stood up. "*Perfecto.*"

Guzman signaled to unseen eyes in the aircraft. Two men appeared. One jumped down and took a large valise handed down from the man remaining in the aircraft. Then came another and another. Finally there were six large leather suitcases lined up.

"*Por favor?*" said Tong.

Guzman bowed. "But of course, hombre. Help yourself to a sample."

Tong opened each of the six containers, exposing their contents of white powder in large plastic Ziploc bags. He chose one arbitrarily. He dropped a bit of the powder into a vial he had been provided previously. The clear liquid turned purple as he was told it should. If it had not, Tong would have killed the man in front of him when he stood up. He slowly arose. "As you said, señor . . . *Bien.*"

Guzman clapped his hands. "Then I will take what is mine, and you shall have what is yours." He turned and raised his hand to motion to his three guards. His head exploded. The top of his scalp flew off and slapped against the skin of the aircraft, where it momentarily stuck before slowly sliding down into the dirt. Bits of skin decorated with sesame seed–size pieces of brain draped obscenely over what was left of Guzman's head. He sank to the ground, looking like Flat Top from an old *Dick Tracy* comic strip.

A loud *boom* echoed across the strip. Tong knew it wasn't thunder.

The man standing in the open door of the C-47 jerked loose of his momentary paralysis. "You double-crossing motherfucker," he screamed, reaching for a revolver he had tucked under his Hawaiian shirt.

Tong felt like he was moving in slow motion, but he managed to reach the Ruger a second before the *vato* in the door leveled his gun. Tong shot him four times in the chest. The man staggered back under the force of the impacts, disappearing into the interior of the plane. Tong was wondering what was happening when the burst from the MAC-10 caught him on his right side. Twelve rounds hit him, spinning him around, dizzy, but not really feeling any pain, just a little vertigo. *Someone is going to pay for this.* Tong felt the darkness closing in on him. And he knew for one instant that it was in fact he who had paid.

Gunfire erupted from all quarters. Guzman's three men stood their ground and slugged it out with Tong's six men, Latin style; *mano o mano, hombre a hombre,* toe to toe. Never give and inch. A shotgun blast excavated one chest. A .44 Magnum round took out a heart. Eviscerated stomachs fell next to punctured lungs. Lacerated livers countered a face missing all features. Bullets hit the plane as the pilot tried to start the engines. A bullet through the side window put a dime-sized hole just above his ear, straight through his intercom set.

Smoke, dust, debris, and gun smoke choked the air. A single intermittent groan came from somewhere among the fallen. A face emerged from the gloom and shadows of the C-47. A bent-double figure eased around the corner, peering out at the grisly carnage that surrounded the aircraft. His hand trembled as he jumped down, his Makarov pistol swinging wildly to and fro, cutting the fetid air. His body slammed violently into the side of the aircraft. Frothy blood spewed from his mouth, and he tried in vain to hold himself erect, using the aircraft as support. He only succeeded in arresting his fall by sliding down the skin. A red smear marked his passage to the dirt.

"**MY** God. My God. What have we done here? What have I allowed? My God . . ." Paul Teascale's voice drifted off as he watched the aftermath of the carnage, eight hundred meters down the gentle slope from where he, Lemuel, and the killer Grainger had set up their position. He had witnessed the arrival of the airplane. He had seen the nature of the transaction through the binoculars provided him by Grainger. He had been a witness—most unwillingly—as this killer beside him calmly shot the person in white. Yes, he was transfixed, pinned, like a rabbit being stared down by a cobra maneuvering for the kill. It was morbid and unnatural, but he could not tear his eyes away from the slaughter.

Grainger focused down slope. He had only killed two men: the delivery boy in the Good Humor suit and the gutless piece of dung who let his buddies die before he crawled out of his hole. He felt some of the old surge return.

Lemuel had never seen anything like this except in the John Woo films he would sometimes watch when Leon and Paul weren't around: *Hard Boiled. The Killer. A Better Tomorrow.* He loved Chow Yun-Fat. Those Chinese gangster films gave him an odd feeling of revulsion mixed inextricably with raw delight; leavened, of course, with a touch of guilt. But this was something else. This was real. *Narcotraficantes. Paramilitares. Guerrilleras.* This was God striking dead the unbelievers. This was Nehemiah destroying the Ammonites and the Ashdodites, the Samaria and the Sanballat. And, like Nehemiah, Lemuel trusted in the Lord. But now he also trusted in the sword. He looked over at Grainger, who lay behind his weapon. He was Lemuel's new Chow Yun-Fat.

Grainger got up from the prone. He looked down at the two men. "Let's go."

They walked together down the bare slope, stepping around the occasional sagebrush and rock pile. The buzz of the desert began to return, a buzz that had been silenced by the rupturing sound of gunfire. They passed a giant cactus and were within a hundred yards of the plane when Paul stopped. He swayed unsteadily, his head circling his shoulders.

"Are you all right?" said Grainger. "Sit here for a while. Come down when you feel better."

"No. You will need my help." Paul staggered on.

Grainger stepped gingerly among the dead, checking the bodies, rolling each face over with his boot.

Paul was an observer to a bad film. He was not a participant. The last man he looked at had no chest. He was about to be sick when he heard the groan. He ran to the rear of the aircraft, where its tail touched the ground, and found the man. He was still alive. "This one is still alive."

Grainger looked up from inspecting a corpse. He walked over to Paul.

"Yes. Yes. He is still alive. Quick. Help me!"

Grainger squatted down next to the priest and gave the sprawled man a quick once-over. "Later, Padre. Right now I need you and Lemuel to load their van. We're going to requisition that as a bonus. We'll pick up our car on the way out."

Paul stared, transfixed.

"Padre! Now. Pronto."

Paul was cataleptic, but obeyed. He ran back up the hill to where the van was parked. Halfway up the slope, he called back, "Please help that wounded man."

Grainger and Lemuel gathered the money and cocaine and brought them out to the runway where the van could maneuver. Grainger inspected the interior of the plane. He checked the dead pilot. He was sterile. So was the plane. There were no flight plans or other documents, not that he expected any. The interior was stripped out; not even a nylon jump seat. He picked up a gray cowboy duster. He stepped over the dead body by the cargo door and leaped down. He yelled at Lemuel to help him secure all the weapons. Lemuel came over at a trot. He inventoried a Steyr AUG SA, two M-16A1 rifles, a Mini-14, three AKs, a Remington 870 twelve-gauge short-barreled shotgun with extension magazine and folding stock, a MAC-10, an M-1 Garand, and an M-2 Carbine, along with ammunition and numerous handguns.

Paul slid sideways down slope in the van, looking for passage to the strip down the old, overgrown trail. He drove out onto the strip and stopped by the stacked material. He opened the door and jumped out and ran to the wounded man. "What about this man? We must take him to the clinic. We must. I cannot let him die."

Grainger grabbed Paul's arm. "I'll take care of him. Help load the van with the chest, suitcases, and weapons."

Paul staggered back, synapses short-circuiting and eyes alternately teared in disbelief and teared in horror. He ran to help Lemuel.

Grainger nudged the dying man with his boot, Then he heard the rattler. A desert diamondback lay coiled fifteen feet away in a clump of sagebrush, its large, triangular head swayed back and forth. He dragged the body to the waiting snake. The reptile warned him away. The death rattle became a loud, vibrating hiss. He gathered the man's torso in his arms. He heard him moan as he pitched the form onto the reptile. The diamondback met the form halfway.

Grainger walked back to the van where Paul and Lemuel waited inside the loaded vehicle.

Paul lurched back toward where the man lay.

Grainger grabbed his arm. "He got an injection."

"Morphine?"

Grainger swung into the van. "Something like that."

Lemuel climbed into the van through the sliding door. Paul remained outside, staring off at nothing.

Grainger started the engine. "Get in, Padre. Mount up. We have to go."

Paul slumped, pulled himself into the van, and shut the door. "The man . . ." It was neither question nor statement.

Grainger half-turned toward Paul. "Don't worry about him. His own kind will take care of him." He put the van into gear and left the runway for the old road heading for the ravine where they had left the car.

Paul stared blankly out the window. "This place is so far from God."

"God left this part of Texas a long time ago," said Grainger.

Paul rested his arm on the door frame. "I am so far from God." He put his head in his hands. *"Deus absconditus."*

Brother Lemuel Sotelo looked back one more time at the dead. He remembered Nahum: 2:13. ". . . And the sword shall devour thy young lions; and I will cut off thy prey from the earth, and the voice of thy messengers shall no longer be heard." For a fleeting moment, Lemuel considered whether he had responded to the wrong calling.

TWENTY-ONE

THE old woman's hands shook as she tried to light the candle in the third terraced row. Her hands trembled uncontrollably, partially from the palsy that had struck her on her seventieth birthday, five years prior. But she trembled mostly because Raoul Rios and his two bodyguards were watching her with malevolent eyes from the doorway of the church. She tried once more.

Raoul regarded the old hag trying to light a candle. *A perfect example of why euthanasia should be universally practiced. The test should be when you can't light a Goddamn candle on the third try. The consequence would be you were instantly carried away to purgatory.* Raoul made a mental note to remember to add taking His name in vain to his list of confessional items. He walked over to the woman and grabbed her shaking hand. He moved the match to the candlewick as the terrified woman closed her eyes. He kissed her on the forehead. She ran from the church, pursued by demons.

Raoul laughed to himself. *I must get some dispensation for that good deed.* He motioned with his head, and his two bodyguards advanced into the church, looking up and down each row of pews. Reaching the altar, they turned back and nodded to Raoul.

Raoul looked at his watch. It was the appointed time. He entered the confessional and knelt in the darkness. Raoul felt good about confessing. He could literally feel the weight of his sins being lifted from him. Unburdened, he was free to assume another load until his next scheduled shedding of guilt. "Bless me Father for I have sinned, as you well know."

The lattice partition slid open.

"It has been one month to the day and hour since my last confession." Raoul saw the gun. A dart from the gun hit him in the neck as a hand reached through the opening and clamped his mouth. Raoul struggled feebly for a moment and then went limp. The partition between compartments opened, and Raoul Rios was pulled through to the rear.

Sergio Calderon looked at the pictures in a *People* magazine as he leaned up against the back of the last row of pews. He faced the front door, half dozing in the warmth of the late morning sun. Jesus Lopez Moreno, his partner, paced incessantly. Calderon looked at his watch. Raoul was certainly giving the priest his money's worth; of that, Sergio was sure. He looked up from his magazine toward Moreno. "Will you stop pacing? You are driving me loco."

Sergio had finished his magazine thirty minutes ago and now he, too, was looking at his watch. It had been nearly an hour since Raoul had entered what Sergio heard him call "the tollbooth." Moreno wrinkled his features at him. Calderon shrugged but walked quietly over to the confessional and listened. He heard the sounds of conversation. He turned to Moreno and raised his palms to the ceiling.

Fifteen minutes later, Jesus Moreno could take no more. "Something is wrong. This thing has never taken this long. We must do something."

Calderon shivered. *If I interrupt Raoul in the middle of his release . . .* But Moreno was right. He walked to the confessional, wringing his hands and speaking softly. "Raoul? Forgive me, but it has been over an hour." He listened to the voices, and there now seemed to be a pattern, a certain monotony to the prattle. Calderon stroked his nose and considered his options. His heart raced. "Raoul?" He was greeted by the same pattern of sound. "Raoul," he bellowed, as he tore open the curtain.

Calderon picked up a tape recorder. Intermittent voices from the small machine mocked him. "Moreno," he managed to croak.

Moreno ran to the confessional and pushed past Calderon. He kicked in the partition and plunged through to the other side, his weapon drawn. *"Pinche cabrón."* He saw the note on the vinyl seat. He picked it up. His English comprehension did not include reading. He handed the message to Sergio.

Calderon grabbed the paper and read, "BACK OFF OR HE DIES." He translated for Jesus.

Moreno knew he was a dead man. He could not report back to Estaban that they had failed to protect Raoul. It was understood that if Raoul should ever die, they had better find their two cold bodies nearby. Frantically, he tore through the church. It was deserted. The echo of his barren footsteps mimicked the pounding of his heart.

Calderon felt the ice freezing around him. He rushed to the front door and stood on the landing. Shaking, he searched up and down the quiet street. Moreno bumped into him as he fell through the door and bounded down the steps to the bottom. Calderon ran into the middle of the street. He scanned desperately in all directions, hoping for a miracle.

"Hey."

Moreno looked at Calderon before turning toward the source of the voice at the top of the church steps.

"Get off of that step. Hombre."

Moreno staggered back, although he only vaguely understood the words. He found common ground on the street, standing shoulder to shoulder with Calderon. He drew with Calderon, to kill this *puto,* to fill his body with so much lead he would sink in *el rio* without additional weight.

Rawlings caught Moreno with the first 9 mm Mag-Safe round. It hit him in the forehead with the effect of a Barry Bonds home run swing. *No need for a follow-up*. He shifted smoothly to the second target, who had his Colt Trooper revolver coming to bear. *Triple tap.* The rounds came fast. Rounds one and two impacted the chest. The third slammed into his throat. Rawlings regarded his foes clinically. *The Strasbourg tests were right. Mag-Safe pills tear 'em up.* The time from his first shot to the last was three-quarters of a second. *El Rapido.* Rawlings stepped down the stairs, his Smith & Wesson Sigma dangling at his side. No "dead man's five seconds" would come from either. He picked up their firearms. "There will be no sacrileges in this church. I gave my word."

BAR glasses and whiskey bottles shattered against the wall, airborne for twenty feet, propelled by an arm itself controlled by the enraged psyche of Estaban Rios. "Find them. Kill them. All of them." Estaban pounded the top of the bar in impotent rage, a psychotic frenzy. His arms and legs felt numb, as if all the blood in his body was contained in his skull.

Estaban's eyes flashed wildly as he leaned back against the bar of his *casa de putas.* The whorehouse was called El Paraiso. The brothel was opulent by local standards. Tijuana chic, it featured red velvet drapes, gold-braided curtains, and pictures of naked women reclining on fields of black velvet. The spiral staircase led upstairs, where business was transacted. The six rooms were always occupied. The staff roomed in the back. The bar served watered-down drinks at fair prices. Entertainment was also reasonable. Estaban liked to pass on the savings. But today, he would not be consoled.

Warden Duran chanced a glance at Buck Downs. This was one storm to hunker down and weather until it blew itself out.

Ramirez swore this was exactly what he had warned them about. And that made him just about smarter than all of them. "I knew we should have killed them, Jefe."

Jaime Escalante, the *cantinero* and head bouncer of El Paraiso, stood patiently behind his bar, wondering if he should pick up the broken bottles and glass. Escalante had a broken nose and a face that was principally made up of scar tissue from burns sustained when he was sixteen. Someone dropped a match after lighting a cigarette while he was siphoning gas from a car. When he smiled, his fanglike teeth made him look like a vampire with a goatee.

Estaban steadied himself on the corner of the bar. He pulled the fingers of both hands through his hair. "I would request that you keep your hindsight to yourself, Ramirez. I pay you to shoot, not think."

Ramirez considered it a compliment. He nodded, in compliance with the suggestion.

Estaban massaged his temples. "I also pay for and expect results, Ramirez. Like you, Tong was paid to succeed."

"Well, at least he died trying," Buck said.

"He failed," shouted Estaban. "His incidental death is of no solace nor concern to me."

Buck Downs shrugged and changed the subject. "Not a trace of anything at the strip, except a lot of dead bodies. My first conclusion was that the Colombians pulled a rip-off, tried to burn us for the money."

"And your considered opinion now, *Comandante*?" Estaban sniffed.

"The way I figure it, there was some kind of what we in law enforcement call a *catalyst.* Something set shit off, in other words. I wandered all over that place, gathering clues. My opinion is they was bushwhacked. Somebody shot one of them from top of the rise, and that was the spark that started the war. I found where they laid up. And it looks to me like another vehicle was driven out of a ravine, quarter mile from the strip. Tire tracks—"

"Thank you, Chief Downs, for solving this mystery for us. I'll see to it you get mention in tomorrow's paper." Rios exploded again. "You idiot! We know who is behind this. You should have spent your time considering how we are going to exterminate these, these . . ."

"I had the strip cleaned up and the plane flown out to Nogales to the dismantlers. It's a cube about three feet across by now," said Buck glumly.

"My money, you *pinche* fucking gringo. What about my thirty million dollars?" He rubbed his forehead roughly. "And what about my brother?"

Buck Downs wasn't that intimidated. Twelve fingers of tequila had emboldened him. "Run 'em to ground, and you'll find your cash. And, as to your Raoul, it wasn't my day to babysit. But, I am gonna arrest them soon as I locate them. I've got enough evidence to—"

Estaban's face flushed, veins pulsing madly on his neck. "No, you imbecile. There will be no arrests. You were anticipating a jury trial perhaps? Justice is mine. Nor will I wait any longer for our bank to foreclose on the church. We will burn it down." He turned around, and then spun back to Buck. "If you find them, kill them." The idea enthused him. "Yes. Kill them. Torch them. The fires of Hell will not be so hot."

Refugio Duran saw his chance. "Shall I ready *Capitain* Vargas and our riot suppression unit?"

"None of that will get your money back, Estaban. Or your brother," said Sonja.

Estaban forced himself to decelerate. "What will?"

"Consider, Estaban. You do not confront the tiger when he is facing you."

"No?" said Estaban. "Then what do you do?"

The santera reached out and snatched the air. "You steal the cubs."

Estaban felt the blood that had been boiling his brain subside and flow outward to the extremities of his body. He turned to Escalante, who had just finished cleaning up the glass and alcohol. "Jaime. My finest tequila. Serve my one hundred percent Agave Azule for everyone. *Reposado. Solomente anejo.* Nothing but the best."

Jaime Escalante found Estaban's private stock under the bar, behind the cosh and twelve-gauge double-barreled "Coach Gun" he kept for when the moon was full. He set up the drinks.

Estaban raised his glass. "For Sonja, *aqua miel.*"

"If I were you, I would be thinking about my reply to the Colombians. They may be curious as to what happened to their merchandise and your money," said Montezuma.

"Fuck the Colombians," spat Rios. "Let the *putos* come."

"And they shall. But I understand that Raoul's 'protectors'—Calderon and Moreno—are dead. Shot down in the street."

Rios exhaled. "The only good news. It saves me the cost of two bullets." He wadded up the warning note and flung it across the room. "And I do not back off." He wheeled on Ramirez. "Nero. *Por favor.* The cubs."

FELIPE Aguirre was one. The other two were named Rafael Alarcon and Ramon Zamudio. Alarcon was a Chilean killer and escapee from the federal prison in Valparaiso and Zamudio, a *Chilango* street tough from the slums of Mexico City. They were led by Nero Ramirez. The four men circled the church and approached the orphanage from the rear.

Sloane turned around at the sound of the side gate to the playground area opening. She saw Ramirez with one she knew only as Aguirre and two others she recognized but couldn't identify by name. "Get out," she said as Ramirez approached.

Ramirez laughed. As he drew abreast, he aimed a looping, openhanded blow at her head. Sloane managed to slip the paw and maneuvered Ramirez to throw him. Aguirre grabbed her from behind. Ramirez recovered. His loss of face was tangible. He hit her in the stomach and backhanded her hard across the mouth.

"Pinche gringa. Puta. Next time you defy me, you will feel my true anger." He hit her once more in the face.

"Say, Nero. Perhaps it is not your anger she wishes to feel." Aguirre pursed his lips and made kissing noises toward her.

A dozen children stood still, watching. Among them were Joey and Ponce. "If I was a man, I would stand up to them all," said Ponce.

Joey remained motionless. "I would be happy if I could just do something about that Ramirez."

Ramirez brushed past the bent-over Sloane and strolled by the children. "In a year or so, *muchacha,*" he said to a budding girl of twelve.

Alarcon grinned lewdly. "Old enough to bleed, old enough to butcher."

Ramirez looked over his shoulder at Aguirre. "Which one is it?"

Aguirre shrugged his shoulders. "It was one of those two." He pointed to Ponce and Joey.

Ramirez pushed aside a small girl holding a bright purple

Barney dinosaur on his way to the boys. He considered for a moment, then reached down and grabbed Joey's arm. "You. You're coming with me." He pulled Joey by the arm toward the gate.

Sloane managed to catch her breath as Ramirez passed. She seized his arm, but he flung her down and kept on moving.

At the gate Ramirez stopped and looked back at the woman. "Zamudio. Take this *niño.*" He returned to where the *gringa* female knelt on the ground. He threw down a folded note. "I almost forgot. That is for the *Norte Americano* that they say is called *El Dedo del Diablo.*" He returned to the gate. Before exiting, he looked once more at her. "Don't worry. Maybe I'll adopt him."

TWENTY-TWO

STONEMAN wasn't nervous anymore. Most likely it was going to be the end of his career. Maybe he might even wind up on a metal slab at the Rue Morgue as a result of the matter being "resolved in the interests of national security." At this point, he was fatalistic, which was saying he didn't give a flying fuck. He had walked into Director of Security T. S. Castagna's office unannounced and shut the door. He stood at semiattention in front of the director's desk and told him he wanted to see the real file covered by Tantrum VII. He advised the director he knew there was another black-classified folder and that he was fully aware that the file constituted special compartmented intelligence. But a man's life was on the line, and if he didn't get the file, he was going to Seymour Hirsch, Bob Bernstein, or Bill O'Reilly with the whole story. *Show me the file or fire me; promote me or shoot me.* If the latter appeared the probable case, he was prepared to say that there was an envelope addressed to the *Post* waiting to be mailed in the event of his untimely demise.

Tony "Tough Shit" Castagna was Buddha tranquil. He sat down at his desk and asked who the proposed recipient of this information was going to be. Stoneman told him it was someone named Lon Grainger. Castagna picked up the telephone and authorized immediate access to the file. "I know who he is," he said, hanging up.

Stoneman stopped at the door and asked what Grainger was to his boss.

"He beat me for the Wimbledon Cup at Camp Perry in . . . never mind when. It was by one ten ring. Damn gust of quartering wind."

Stoneman closed the door behind him. *Maybe Castagna has a heart and soul after all.*

THE original Beirut CIA operation code name was Condor, and he had the file in his hand. This was the reality, not the ass cover provided by Tantrum VII. The best lies were those that contained 90 percent truth. A casual perusal and comparison of the two files, a perfunctory perusal, might even have given the impression the two reported the same information. Upon closer examination of the referrals and addendums, it conclusively proved otherwise. He found here what he knew he would. *Total closure.*

Stoneman took his time reading Condor. Castagna had given him the ground rules: No copying. No notes. No tape recorders. No photos. No removal from the vault. No second chances. Transmit only vis-à-vis. Reveal a minimum. Exercise judgment consistent with the interests of national security. The great God. Stoneman turned another page and read. He now understood absolutely that they were all sacrificial, expendable on behalf of the "interests of national security."

When satisfied that he had what he needed, he left the vault. He exited the complex and booked the first flight he could get out to Houston with a commuter connection to Corpus Christi. He recently believed he had discharged his debt. He was wrong. The job wasn't finished. The obligation remained. Whatever Grainger and Rawlings were involved with out in Texas was their business. They would probably be killed anyway. But if they were, it damn sure wasn't going to be because Stone Hombre failed to deliver.

* * *

"LA *ciudad de los muertos,"* said Paul. " 'The city of the dead.' It was to be a retirement community for Americans, but the builder absconded with the investors' funds halfway through the project."

Grainger drove slowly, skirting the perimeter of the dead village. Tumbleweed circled aimlessly. The frames and gutted interiors of a ghost town stood bleaching in the sun. There were many tall structures for such an insignificant, desolate place: A forlorn church with a bell tower. A water tower. A lengthy construction that was to be an apartment building and a small complex of what appeared to be shops. Everything was now one color: desert. This was a scorned town bathed in eerie shadows, attended by a constant, mourning wind. Now it was home only to snakes, gophers, the ubiquitous carrion crow, and an occasional marauding coyote looking to make an easy meal of a house cat dumped in the desert.

Grainger took it all in as he drove by the skeleton of the town that was supposed to be called El Vista Grande. He motored on, guided by Lemuel, who drove their Dodge Coronet ahead of them. Lemuel appeared to be testing the shock absorbers at every opportunity. "And what do they call those mountains?" he said, pointing to two jagged peaks that rose from the desert floor, another fifteen or twenty miles out.

"Las Calderas del Diablo," said Paul. "The Devil's Boilers." He stared at the twin monoliths. "Everything here belongs to the Devil."

Grainger studied the mountains and scanned the desert. Together, they looked like a Mesolithic diorama at the Museum of Natural History. The colors were military desert mocha camouflage in a mottled blend of bittersweet hues, blends, and textures. The mountains were huge chunks of charbroiled beef in a primordial brownout thrusting up, eclipsing a curtain of pale blue sky.

They stopped at a nameless crossroads, an intersection of two uncharted dirt tracks etched on the hardpan surface of the desert. The trails appeared to meander purposelessly, crossing each other more by accident than design, a Winchester House of paths leading nowhere. The inhospitable terrain seemed to stretch forever. From their location, only sand, dirt, and cactus could be seen. The spindly spines from the ocotillos branches littered the sand. Pillars of fuzzy-tipped munz's cholla cacti soared fifteen feet upwards. The huge, domineering saguaro cactus, with limbs larger than telephone poles, rose over fifty feet into the air. Joshua trees with their hairy, twisted arms looked like gigantic brown lilies. They had taken those unmapped dirt roads that Lemuel remembered from his boyhood, where he had played and frolicked, before he heard the clarion call. The color of both vehicles was now indistinguishable from their surroundings, their earthen tones acquired from passage through and blending with the progenitor desert.

THE gasoline came from two five-gallon jerricans that were mounted on a rack on the rear of the van. They had been taken down and now sat on the ground. The dope lay pyramided in a mound of whiteness. Grainger cleared a ring of all combustibles from the desert floor and emptied a five-gallon can, spreading the gasoline evenly over the bags. Then the second red can splashed out its contents, in lurching gulps and surges, until the plastic-covered powder was soaked.

"Step back," said Grainger. Lemuel and Paul jumped back. The flaming match arced toward the pile, which seemed to explode into flames almost in anticipation. The stack was an inferno.

The funeral pyre of cocaine burned furiously as the three men walked away upwind, back toward the two vehicles. At the van Lemuel helped Grainger transfer the money from the chest to the six suitcases, each containing five million dollars. The guns from the airstrip were placed in the trunk of the Dodge convertible.

Grainger turned to Lemuel. "You sure you want to do this?"

Lemuel nodded, his eyes concentrating still on the fire; his mind still at the airstrip.

"All right. Take the van straight to Brownsville. Park it at the Trailways depot and take the bus back to Zapata." He took the single kilo bag of coke remaining and tossed it into the back. "Make sure that's inside when you park it. And don't get stopped by the Department of Public Safety."

Lemuel got in behind the wheel and started the engine.

Grainger came to the driver's window. "Remember. No stops."

Paul's face cracked into a facsimile of a smile. He gripped Lemuel's arm. *"Vuelve, amigo. Vaya con Dios."* He watched the van disappear behind a cloud of dust and cactus.

Grainger watched thirty million in cocaine change into a slag pile that resembled a huge burnt marshmallow. Then he sat down to wait.

THE sun was resting on the top of a cactus when the dust from a vehicle approached. Two hundred yards out he saw Sloane's pickup truck.

She pulled alongside. "Some directions. Right at the saguaro. Left at the streambed. Follow the desert wren." She was wearing sunglasses, which did a poor job of concealing the swelling and bruising on her face.

Grainger stood at her door and touched her hair. It was an intimacy that did not escape Paul. "What happened? Who did this to you?"

"Rios's men took Joey."

"Who did this to you?"

She looked away. "It doesn't matter."

"Who?"

She turned back and touched her face. "Ramirez and a thug named Aguirre, with two others along for a cheering section. I've got their names in my little black book of people to see, things to do." She tried to smile, but her swollen lips made her look like she just had all her teeth removed and the dentist had pumped in novocaine with a turkey baster.

"I'm sorry," said Grainger.

"Don't be sorry. Just put it in your own little black book of IOUs." She took a breath and tried to grin. "Besides. We got Raoul."

Grainger nodded.

Paul came to the door and looked at her. He wiped his eyes.

Sloane took his hand. "Now you know what you look like after eight rounds."

Paul turned away.

Grainger walked to his car. He got in and drove it up alongside Sloane's pickup. "We'll get Joey back. I promise."

She slipped off her sunglasses, revealing her black eyes. "One more thing." She handed him the note. "I took the liberty of reading it." She watched Grainger read the message. "Don't do it. It's a trap. They want to kill you. I already told you so. And after the hijack at the airstrip . . ."

Grainger folded the note. If this super-shooter named Montezuma wanted to talk to him, he was going. There were still some unanswered questions. He turned to Paul seated next to him. "Padre. Please go with Sloane."

"You're going, aren't you? I should have just trashed that note. You're crazy. They're going to kill you. And then what will we do?" In a smaller voice she said, "What will I do?"

Paul got out and entered Sloane's pickup. The rumblings of exhaust passed through old mufflers and bounced like sonar echoes off each vehicle.

"El Dedo del Diablo? The Devil's Finger? Is that you?" she said.

His head snapped around. "Only a nickname. Just something that got repeated once too often."

"With no rational basis in fact, I suppose? Unless you're a proctologist, I'd say the reference probably has something to do with those skills demonstrated at the carnival. No?"

"Could be. Gotta go. I'll see you tonight at the church. After dark."

She tried to purse her lips to throw him a kiss. It didn't work. Instead, she put her hand to her mouth and sent it his way with a flick of her wrist.

Grainger drove off, following the tire tracks that were already beginning to disappear in the face of the rising afternoon wind. The opposition's intel was efficient. *They know who I am.*

Sloane and Paul sat together without saying anything, watching his car dematerialize.

"You have been with us for almost two years of appreciated service. I want to thank you," said Paul.

She turned halfway in her seat to look at him. "You don't have to thank me."

"You have ministered to our sick and kept the rest of us well. You have done this for practically nothing. Plus, I have noted, whenever we have managed to pay you something, that same amount appeared in the poor box."

She gripped the steering wheel.

"However, I thought, perhaps at some time you would have come to me, to talk to me, to tell me the truth."

Her heartbeat paused. Her palms got clammy.

"I believe in my heart that you have done your best to serve two masters and have tried to reconcile yourself to that conflict. When these two men came, I saw that drama intensify. I witnessed the turmoil surface. And I wondered . . ."

She tried to swallow, but couldn't. "Wondered? What?"

"I have wondered, which of your dilemmas is addressed by these men? Is it our communal predicament, our crisis defined by reference to the children? Or—"

"Or—"

"Or is it your other life, the professional one, the one that was the original impetus and motivation for *infiltrating*—that is a harsh word—our parish?"

She dropped her eyes and hands. "How long have you known?"

"Three months after you came here, I was chasing a squirrel that had entered the church and made its way to your room. Under the bed I found a black machine gun. It was marked Property of the DEA."

She sipped a breath through her teeth. "I didn't intend to deceive you. I was under orders. It was my job. It wasn't much different than yours. We both fought what we perceived as evil. I did what I could to help. I couldn't tell you. It would have involved you."

"What now of your personal, emotional involvement with this man?" Paul motioned in the direction of Grainger's vanished car.

"That's between him and me. It won't interfere with what we have agreed to do."

He gazed for a while at nothing in particular. "So tell me," he said, "does the coming of these two men solve both our problems, or only yours? Do they kill and leave, or kill and die? Is the victory they offer Pyrrhic?"

"I can't answer those questions for you. I don't know what the end will be to this or what the aftermath will be, or for that matter what the hereafter offers. All I know is now we have done something. We have challenged this abomination; and isn't that what we both want?"

"We have sowed the wind and can only hope now we do not reap the whirlwind."

Sloane felt like she was in the confessional. "Forgive me, Father Paul. I haven't been truthful. I know." She started the car.

"Where are we going?" Paul said.

"To the town square."

"To what end and purpose?"

"To see if you agree with Emiliano Zapata."

THE old man reluctantly slid the earphones from around his ears as the dirty, desert-yellow van pulled in and parked, too far from the pumps to want gas. "You need gas, or are you just comparison shopping?" He hollered down from the top steps of the shack that served as his home and business.

Lemuel waved him off as he got out of the van. "No need to bother. I just want a soda."

"That'll be fine. I got Orange Crush and Dad's Root Beer. Got Texas Red and Red Man chew. Lone Star and Mexican *cerveza,* too, I'll sell if you ain't John Law."

"Just a cold soda," he said slapping dust from his trousers.

The old man jerked a thumb. "Inside the garage bay. Big cooler. Leave a dollar on the workbench."

Lemuel raised his hand in acknowledgment and headed for the open bay. His mouth felt like a sun-bleached steer skull. He hadn't slaked his thirst with an Orange Crush for ten years.

At the opposite end of the station a man hung up the telephone and watched Lemuel walk to the garage. He swung open the folding door and made his way toward the pumps, where he could get a better look at the van. He noted the license plate and returned to the booth.

Lemuel ambled back toward the van, an Orange Crush in both hands.

"That was one dollar *each,*" the old man exhorted from his perch.

"Yes. I know. I left two dollars," said Lemuel. "And thank you."

The old man grunted to himself and replaced his earphones. *"Muskrat Love." Captain and Tennille. Now, there was a song. They don't write 'em like that anymore.*

The stranger at the phone booth watched Lemuel drive away, heading southeast, toward McAllen and Harlingen. He lifted the phone off the hook and dialed a number. Collect.

The van was air-conditioned. Lemuel had it on Max Cool. He luxuriated in the igloolike temperature inside as he watched heat mirages the size of tidal waves boil outside, rolling over the landscape. He finished the last of his second bottle of Nesbitts and threw the empty container onto the floorboard of the passenger's side. He turned on the radio and pushed the preselect buttons to see what the former occupants listened to. The Astros were playing at home. He hit Scan and found a country station from Laredo and three Mexican stations. He settled for Vincente Fernando crooning something about *"Tengo miedo que me rompas el corazón."* He loved the feeling of isolation and freedom provided by the emptiness of the highway and his command of the vehicle.

Lemuel drove, as he was instructed, at five miles per hour under the posted speed limit. Between Zapata and Lapeno, the next outpost on the way to Brownsville, there was just more of nothing. This stretch of Highway 83 ran through the International Falcon Reservation. It was where all the locals came to hunt falcons. The terrain was desolate, almost postapocalyptic. The van picked up speed on the down side of hills and slowed a bit climbing back up the modestly hilly terrain. It was like a gentle roller-coaster ride.

At one time he had considered becoming a priest. It had been his aspiration, his vision of life's highest attainment. Becoming a brother was a stepping-stone to the priesthood. After school, he returned home to Bustamante, where he had been born. He had eagerly volunteered for the Zapata assignment. He would apprentice under Paul and Leon and then attend the seminary. That was then. Now, he was not so sure. Life seemed to have other offerings. He still felt the pulls of the spirit, but . . .

Lemuel accelerated as he climbed a steeper-than-average slope. He eased back as he crested the summit. The white line ran for miles ahead until it disappeared in a bend that skirted an outcropping of rugged bluffs. From one mile away he saw the body lying in the roadway. He took his foot off the pedal and allowed the van to coast. *No stops.* He remembered the admonition. But he didn't recall an *under no circumstances.* There was a body lying in the road. Somebody was hurt and probably dehydrated. He could have been lost in the desert. Lemuel still responded to the call. The van slowed.

Lemuel turned out into the opposing lanes of traffic as he slowly passed the body. The man was facedown on the near-molten asphalt. *Surely he must be dead or near death.* The van continued to move. One hundred yards past the body, he stopped in the roadway and looked back through the side view mirrors. The body remained inanimate. Lemuel gripped the gearshift lever and thrust the transmission into reverse. The van moved backward in precipitous fashion, zigzagging across the whole breadth of the highway. Pulling abreast of the figure, he skidded to a stop.

Lemuel got out of the van and ran to the man. "Mister. Señor. Are you all right?" He knelt down next to the man and rolled him over. A .38 Special revolver was pointed right between his eyes. Two other men emerged from a culvert beneath the level of the road just as the man on the ground said, "I had no faith, *Hermano.* I bet you wouldn't stop."

GRAINGER passed the three matching black Honda Super Hawks on his way to the rendezvous with . . . He hoped it wasn't death. The three motorcyclists screamed by him going in the opposite direction at over one hundred miles per hour. The combined high-speed passage rocked the car. He had other things to think about.

The sun was at its zenith, white hot and blinding, as he pulled into the parking lot of El Boondocks. The lot was empty except for a lone gray Porsche parked by the door. Grainger got out of the vehicle and stood for a minute assessing the situation. There was not much to assess. You either walked in or you turned around and left. He felt his Colt nudge him reassuringly in the small of his back. He moved to the door on an oblique, the gravel crunching like broken glass under his boots.

He pushed the door open and slipped inside, letting the semidarkness flood over him. The fetid air was thick and humid, victor over the rusted swamp cooler on the far wall. The odor of stale cigarettes assailed him. He placed his back to the wall, every sense on full alert. Every sight, sound, and smell was rapidly processed, diagnosed, and categorized. After a minute his eyes adjusted to the cavelike interior. He eased the door shut. The darkened barroom enveloped him completely. His spine vibrated, and the back of his neck tingled in anticipation. *Of what?* The unknown was enough to trigger the response, especially this much of it. The chairs were all stacked on the tables. The soles of his boots lifted with a cracking sound, sticking to the glue formed by last night's spilled beer. The pungently bitter, merged aromas of stale *cerveza,* whiskey, and sweat greeted him as he eased forward another step.

He saw him standing at the far end of the bar, almost invisible in the shadows cast by the overhanging ceiling. The man's back was toward him, but there was no doubt he was absolutely aware of his exact position. Grainger moved slowly, closing the gap, sensing every nuance of his environment, measuring the man he faced, gauging his risk with every step. Now he was ten feet from the figure, who still had his back exposed. He waited, taking the opportunity to inspect him. The man was of average height and build but appeared lithe and agile. The man set down a drink he held and turned around.

"It is not often one gets to meet a legend face-to-face," Montezuma said, fixing his adversary with an eye that looked like it was drawing a bead.

Grainger let his breath out slowly. "Are you talking about you or me having the privilege?"

Montezuma laughed heartily. "I would have thought you would be an arrogant man. There are those who say I am." He pushed away from the bar. "You may not know me now, but you soon will. If only momentarily."

"I already know you and don't like you."

Montezuma smiled thinly and leaned back against the bar. "That was a splendid spoiling shot you made a few days ago . . . on the peasant. However, it was very expensive for my current employer. You upset a lot of people."

"I'm heartbroken."

"I don't think you are. But, in any case, it was not your best work. Now, that was a truly remarkable shot you made in Budapest in—what was it?—ah, yes, 1995, a busy year for you. You are an artisan, señor."

"No. You got it wrong. Amigo. I just shoot people."

"Of course you do," said Montezuma. "I have personal knowledge of that."

"Let me guess. Like in Beirut?"

"Excellent 'guess,' Mr. Grainger. I had—how do you *Yanquis* say—a box office seat to a wonderful execution under the most trying of circumstances; a triumph of skill over obstacle. It was a shame about the boy, but *ces't la guerre.* I understood you reacted most unprofessionally to the killing. Remarkable, really, considering your history."

Grainger edged sideways, working an angle, just in case. "The information that I have is that you did more than sit on your ass. You racked up three scores that day."

Lorca touched his cheek. "Three?"

"I don't know whether to thank you or kill you. The one you shot next to me was about to kill us. Or at least it looked like he was." Grainger raised an eyebrow. "So, Mr. . . . ? What do I call you?"

"Names are important for the victor only. But, in the interim, my name is Federico Christo Mendez Lorca. I am also known as Montezuma by friend and foe alike."

"So, I say again, Mr. Lorca, do I thank you or kill you?"

"Thanking me would be so much easier, Mr. Grainger. But there is no need. It wasn't I who killed the CIA man named Cruickshank."

Grainger unbalanced. "What are you talking about?"

Montezuma cradled his chin. "I mean simply, I did not pull the trigger on that man. I would surely take credit for what would have at that time been my one hundred and seventeenth kill. No, the two that I killed immediately after made the shot. Now *they* were most assuredly trying to kill you."

Grainger looked for something to hold on to. Outside, he remained an iceberg. "You expect me to believe that?"

Montezuma dropped his cradling hand and came erect. "Believe whatever you will, Mr. Grainger. When I engaged your saviors, the shooter was preparing for his second shot."

"How was he going to do that? We were down beneath the level of the windows after Cruickshank got tapped."

"I'm sure you were. He was using a supplementary thermal imaging sight and what I would suspect were some kind of tungsten or armor-defeating rounds to penetrate the plaster walls. Oh, they would have had you. They were on an open roof. I was positioned on the minaret of a mosque, thirty feet higher in elevation."

Grainger's feelings were on his face.

"Yes. It is terrible, is it not? To be betrayed? To think you are the hunter when in reality you are the hunted? To owe your life to a man who will certainly end up killing you? The ironies are exquisite. I saved your life. I shot those two. Killed them, I believe. The spotter for sure with a head shot. The other appeared mortally wounded, but I cannot be sure."

"How do I know you're not lying to me about all of this?"

"Mr. Grainger. Why would I lie to another professional about something so inconsequential as this? What benefit to me? It is the simple truth. Accept it."

Grainger knew he was telling the truth. There was no purpose in the lie. He was there. He saw what happened.

Montezuma waited, but there was no response from Grainger. "However, the answer that has continued to elude me is who? Who were those men trying to kill you? And why? Whoever they were, it is a closely held secret. No one in my services was ever able to determine. Even the Russians had no information, unless of course it was they in some reciprocal vendetta. I thought perhaps you would be able to shed some light."

Grainger disliked sharing shoptalk with this man. "I can't help you sleep at nights there either. But maybe you can help me."

"Perhaps."

"What can you tell me about the secret opposition?"

"There were, as I said, two men; both Caucasian, as far as I could tell. The weapon was French, a Model F2. They were equipped with a spotting scope and sophisticated communications equipment. The shooter was wearing a bandanna on his head and a camouflage T-shirt. The spotter had amber-lens shooting glasses."

Grainger looked down at Lorca's shoes. *Bandanna. T-shirt. Amber-lens shooting glasses. How about a hat with a propeller on it?*

"One other thing I noted through my rifle scope . . . The shooter had a mark on his left shoulder. I think it was a tattoo. It looked like a circle with one side dark and the other side light. A circle divided by a meandering line."

"Like the yin-yang symbol?"

Montezuma clapped. "Yes. Like that. Something very much like that. Light and darkness." He touched his face gently with the tips of his fingers. "But of course, you are aware that they were not my principal target. You, señor, had that privilege."

"How did you know I would be there?"

"His name was Habib, I believe. A venal little man who would sell his soul if the price was right. He vended information freely. I was informed that an American assassination attempt would be made in Beirut. This Habib knew only that there was a target and the general location. I knew who the target had to be. It was relatively simple to conclude that the Americans would send their very best to make a shot that had to be attempted at extreme range. I positioned myself accordingly. I knew it would be you. As you see, I am well connected."

"Which brings us to the reason you targeted me in Beirut. The man I killed in Mogadishu. Who was he?"

"The quality of your Intelligence is checkered, but your powers of deduction are good. Motive refined to its pure essence. He was my brother. An adviser to one or the other of the warring clans."

"So, it was revenge that brought you to Beirut?"

Montezuma slowly rotated his head. "The obvious answer is not the correct one. I said the 'pure essence' of motivation. Reputation; of course, couched in the guise of a vengeance quest. I really wasn't that upset. We weren't that close. Tico was a *pendejo;* an insufferable socialist and Castro dupe. He was a true believer, all for *La Revolución.* My mother probably mourns him, but I have six other brothers. I came to kill you pro forma, just for the record and to seize your karma. I wanted to take your reputation, like an Old West gunfighter in your cinema."

"Well, then I guess you were just crushed that day. Have you recovered yet?"

"No, Mr. Grainger. As a matter of fact, I have grown ever more disconsolate as time has passed. But things are looking up. My only worry—now that God has delivered you to me—is that Rios will kill you before I get the proper chance."

"Yeah. I hear he's pretty upset about the drugs, his money, and his brother."

"Yes. In that order." He leaned back against the bar. "I do not care about his money or his simpering sadist of a brother. I only care about the enhancement of my professional reputation and the value of my services in the worldwide marketplace. And, of course, the exalt of my ego. You understand, no?"

"I understand that you're fucking nuts."

Montezuma's eyes narrowed. "You may not have heard of me before recently, but perhaps for just one fleeting second you will come to acknowledge me. Actually, you and I are quite alike."

"No, Mr. Lorca. There is one significant difference."

Montezuma's lidded eyes slid open. "And that being?"

"I'm a little bit better."

Montezuma smiled affably. "Then it is settled. The gauntlet is down. The die has been cast. Fate shall be the hunter."

Grainger backed up two steps. *Buena suerte,*" he said and turned toward the front door.

"Señor. One more thing."

Grainger looked back.

"Do you still leave an ace of spades on the bodies of the unfortunate?"

Grainger smiled. "I ran out of cards." He pushed through the door and emerged into the sunlight. He wished his confidence echoed his words. This Montezuma was one of the chosen few, one of the 2 percent of the 2 percent with skills that probably matched his. If they exceeded his . . . In any case, there would be no avoiding the inevitable.

Grainger entered his car. Some answers only spawned other questions. Someone had tried to kill him that day in Beirut. The reason why was now coming into focus. The yin and the yang was the question and maybe also the answer. Stoneman's information wasn't entirely accurate. Even Runyan didn't have it entirely right.

He retraced his path back toward Zapata to rendezvous with Rawlings where they had agreed to meet at a prearranged location on the outskirts of town. There were undoubtedly death warrants out by now. They would be shot on sight.

THE old gas station materialized out of the sun. Three black Super Hawk motorcycles were parked in a neat line. Three men had the old-timer triangulated between them and were playing bumper pool with him. Grainger needed gas.

The Dodge pulled into the station and stopped at the first pump. The three doing the shoving stopped to look at him. One held the old man by his neck. They were football-jock types wearing cut-off athletic sweatshirts and Nike and Adidas running shoes. They were Ivy League, destined for a platinum spoon, the executive rest room and country club membership. *My other car is a Learjet.* They were born of privilege, and it was smeared all over their drunk and mean faces. A fullback. Center. Quarterback.

"Fill her up, old man. Ethyl." Grainger got out of the car.

The old desert rat shrugged free and shuffled toward Grainger.

"Hey, Darren," yelled the center, "you know any Ethyl?" He downed the last of his Heineken and threw the can down.

Darren, the quarterback, all six feet, two hundred pounds of him, popped open another can. "Yeah. Isn't she a friend of Lucy's?"

The fullback pointed a finger. "Hey, fuck you, pal. Can't you see our pet is busy?" He looked at the other two and winked. *Another bumpkin to fuck with.*

The old man removed the nozzle and hose from the pump and inserted it into the filler receptacle of the Dodge. "Don't I know you, mister?" he said in a subdued voice.

Grainger nodded. He took the handle from the old man and squeezed the lever, watching the old reel-type numbers roll on the pump.

The three jocks approached with a swagger. "And over here in a huddle we have Desi and Fred," said the center. The three formed a semicircle around them.

"Now, what the fuck is ethyl? Asshole," said the fullback.

The pump pinged once more. The nozzle sprang from the filler spout and showered gas across the three. "*This* is ethyl, numbnuts, or whatever grade of cheap gas this bellyaching old man is selling today."

The center bent over in agony, spitting and coughing. The fullback had his mouth open at the wrong time. The quarterback vomited into the dirt. Grainger jammed the nozzle back onto the cradle and moved to the trunk. He opened it and came out with a yellow cylinder. He squeezed the built-in friction lighter, and the propane torch ignited with a *pop.* Yellow-blue flame hissed wickedly, dancing at the end of the brass nozzle.

The QB was the first to get his eyes open. His mouth dribbled stomach fluid and beer. "No. Mister. We were only having a little fun with this geezer here." The other two were making babbling, Furby noises.

"Geezer?" croaked the old man.

The fullback and the center came on-line. "Jesus," from one. "Christ," from the other.

Grainger kicked an empty grease bucket to the quarterback. "You look like someone with a college education. Hold that bucket for me."

The QB gagged and tried to spit. He limped over to Grainger, carrying the bucket by its wire handle.

"Careful you don't get any grease on your hands, boy," said Grainger. When the jock held out the bucket, Grainger put the gas nozzle into it and filled it with fuel. "Now pour it on the transportation."

There was horror in his eyes. "Not on the Super Hawks, man. They're damned near new."

Grainger pointed the torch. The quarterback ran to the motorcycles. Grainger grabbed the fullback by the neck. "Five seconds, he's a sparkler."

The QB poured the gas on the bikes.

"On yours, too, sonny."

The QB complied with a tear in his eye.

Grainger took two steps toward the bikes and heaved the burning torch onto the motorcycles. The explosion took the form of an enormous *WHOOOOMP* as the gas ignited. The inferno poured black, oily smoke into the air. A gas tank exploded, splintering metal and rupturing another tank, which disintegrated in a roar. Burning rubber fouled the air.

The fullback groaned. "I had a thousand dollars in Mexican Dianabol in a saddlebag."

"I know a DEA agent who told me that shit is illegal," said Grainger. "I did you a favor. Now, start walking."

"Walking? Where to?" moaned the center.

"East Jesus. It's a nice day to walk. One more thing. If you ever come back, or touch this unprincipled old man again, I'll hunt you down and kill you all. Slowly."

The QB rubbed his eyes. "Fuck him. We don't have to take this shit. We can take him. Come on."

The fullback looked at the QB like he was crazy. "You take

him, Carmine." He hobbled off. The QB hesitated, and then ran after him.

Grainger looked around. The old man was back on the porch of his building with his headphones on. Grainger walked over to him. "Hey. How much do I owe you?"

The old man pulled the headphones from one ear. "No charge for the gas."

Grainger nodded. "Sorry about the mess."

The old man looked over at the pyre. "When the fire cools down, I'll clean up. Can't rightly remember when I had so much fun. But I could have taken them. If'n they got a little too rough, I get me out Old Betsy and put some rock salt in their ass."

Grainger laughed. He waved and walked back to his car.

The old desert rat leaned back in his chair, headphones in place. *"Rayando el Sol." Mana. Now that was a group. Singing in Mexican. But they could really carry a tune.*

Grainger pulled out onto the highway and slowed for the hitchhiking trio. As he pulled alongside, the QB dropped his thumb and said, "Shit."

Grainger drove past slowly. "Next time," he said, "buy American."

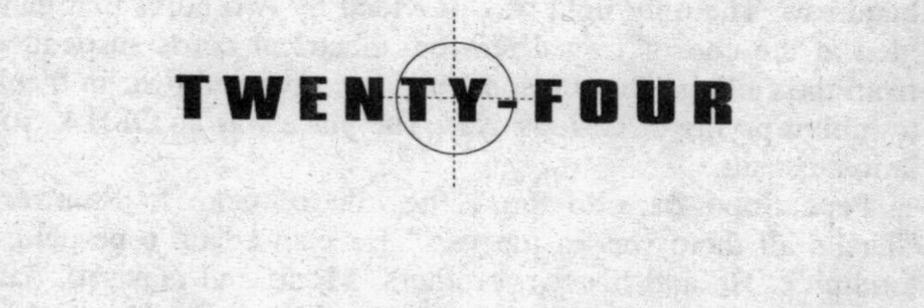

TWENTY-FOUR

"**HERMANO** . . . Lemuel, isn't it?"

Estaban adjusted the swamp cooler on wheels, which was positioned behind him. It provided the only movement in the otherwise dead-still air of the small warehouse. "Such a hurry to leave Zapata? And driving a stolen vehicle. *My* stolen vehicle."

Lemuel stood flanked by the three men who had captured him on the highway. The Barretto brothers: Pepe, the elder; Navarro, his brother with the fingers of his left hand fused together as the result of a catastrophic gasoline burn sustained while cutting up a Mercedes; and Mario, the lesser. Mario was a beast who walked upright. His forehead was a medieval battering ram. Barbed wire body hair poked out from sleeve and collar. His sagebrush eyebrows exploded over the upper regions of his face. His bristly hair was parted in four directions and looked like it had been chopped with a weed whacker. Mario took an IQ test once. The results were negative. The Barretto brothers slunk toward Zapata as one.

Lemuel shivered despite the ninety-degree temperature in the enclosure. The ropes that bound his hands behind his back were cutting off the circulation. Both his hands were numb. The concrete floor of the warehouse was grimy. Workbenches lined the wall. A steel welding table occupied the center of the room. A large vise with gaping jaws was mounted on one corner. There was also a Lincoln D.C. arc welder, a drill press, and a band saw. The only light was provided by two bulbs that dangled at the end of frayed ten-foot electrical cords suspended from the ceiling. The transoms had been painted over in black to inhibit prying or curious eyes. The place was an OSHA violation test site.

Pepe Sopo Barretto threw the kilo of coke to Ramirez. "That's all there was in the van." He chewed on a perpetual toothpick. He and his two brothers, Mario and Navarro, had gotten a call while working on dismantling a new Honda Accord in their transient chop shop. This month's operational disguise for their lucrative business was a used tire store in Rio Grande City. They were able to drop everything. Well, not everything. Nero had said to bring along one certain item they might need. *Anything to help Señor Rios, compadre.*

The Barretto brothers had a place in the FBI hall of infamy. Each of their NCIC records was on accordion-fold paper; stacked high enough that they looked like the first draft of the Texas Penal Code. If there was a Texas revised code or federal statute not contained in their rap sheets, it wasn't a crime: auto theft, possession of stolen property, robbery, assault with intent to commit great bodily harm, smuggling, subornation of perjury, kidnapping, rape, possession of . . . If it was illegal, they possessed it. Mayhem. Mayhem was big and a favorite. The brothers had good lawyers and enough money to pay them a twenty-four/seven retainer. They had been arrested many times, but the DA wasn't making his conviction quotas on them. For every verdict in favor of the people, they walked on seven. The brothers supported the philosophical underpinnings of the criminal justice system in America: "Innocent until proven guilty." Pepe had it tattooed on his arm.

Estaban hated the dank interior of this place. It was not his garden. There was so little light. With Estaban and Ramirez stood Felipe Aguirre, Ramon Zamudio, Rafael Alarcon, and Maximo "Coco" Pedraza. Pedraza was wearing a knee-length white smock. His pale face was expressionless. His mouth was a scar, and his eyes appeared to be only sockets, the eyeballs having been removed with a dull knife, leaving only gaping holes. His ears were pinned against his head. Large hoop earrings dangled from both. His black hair was pomaded and pulled back into a tight, segmented ponytail that extended to midback. He was called *El Cirujano*, The Surgeon.

Estaban opened a small leather briefcase and removed a pair of driving gloves. He put them on, tightening each finger. "I hate the filth and dirt of this place, *Hermano;* but it is fitting for our task today. We have very simple roles here. I ask the questions, and you provide the answers."

"Why have you brought me here?" Lemuel stuttered.

Aguirre slammed a fist into Lemuel's stomach. Lemuel doubled up and fell to his knees.

"Ah, Lemuel . . . There was no question pending. Wait until I ask before you respond. *Comprendes?"* Rios snapped his fingers, and Zamudio brought over a three-legged stool. Estaban sat down. "That's better. Now, where was I? Oh, yes. *Pregunta: Donde esta mi dinero?* Question: Where is my money?"

Lemuel wanted to throw up. His guts churned like an acid pit. Aguirre's fist felt like it was still stuck. Waves of nausea swept over him. "What money—"

The knife edge of Ramirez's hand caught Lemuel in the back of the neck. The impact surged through him like an electric shock. His head snapped, and he almost bit off his tongue. He staggered forward, trying to keep his balance.

"The church has no standards today. Your memory is short. Or you are stupid. Have you forgotten already? *I* ask the questions. Not you." Estaban sprang from his stool and motioned with his open hand. "Come closer." When Lemuel stumbled to within five feet, Estaban put up his hand. "Close enough. Now, I really must impress upon you the vital importance of retrieving certain information. You tell me what I need to know, and you will be taken back to the church." He raised his eyebrows. "Deal?"

Lemuel did not consider himself a brave man. His threshold

of pain was minimal. He remembered once as a boy crying when he impaled his finger with a barbed fishing hook. He wanted to blurt out everything, to tell them all. Why, he would deny Christ and curse his mother. He would revile the Pope and blaspheme God Almighty himself, if it would do any good. He looked around the warehouse and into the dead eyes of the men who stared back at him, and he knew. Lemuel knew that he would die here today, no matter what he said or did. He was a condemned man looking at his executioners, and he understood that as sure as he believed there was a God in heaven. Lemuel drew a long, slow breath and came to his full height. "I can tell you nothing. But I have a request."

"A request?" said Estaban as he felt his men stir in anticipation of their long-awaited release.

"Yes. Kill me quickly."

"You are making it difficult on yourself, *Hermano*. Your confession here today is inevitable. But the price you will pay for your initial silence will be incalculable. You will soon beg to be released from your agony. One more time. Reconsider."

"I have stated my intent."

"Then, *Hermano* Lemuel, make your peace with your God." He motioned to Zamudio and Aguirre. The two men seized Lemuel by the arms and forced him to the welding table. Navarro and Mario Barretto bounded over and grabbed his legs. They slammed him down on the table. Ramirez used nylon belts with ratchet clamps to secure him across his shins, knees, thighs, waist, chest, and shoulders.

Estaban slid over to the immobile Lemuel. "Well, *Hermano*. You look like Gulliver with the Lilliputians. Here, let me introduce you to *el medico*. Brother Lemuel, meet *Dr.* Pedraza. He is called *El Cirujano* and comes highly recommended for this type of . . . operation." Estaban turned to Pedraza. "How long do you anticipate?" He lit a cigar.

El Cirujano blankly regarded Lemuel. When he had been with the FMLN, the *Farabundo Marti Liberación National*, in El Salvador, he had operated once on a soft, pudgy one like this. He had lasted four minutes. He looked up at Rios. "Before your cigar is ash."

Pedraza dipped the strip of rawhide in gasoline. He fastened it tightly around Lemuel's neck. He leaned over until his mouth was close to Lemuel's ear. His lips brushed the lobe. "As the petrol evaporates, the rawhide will shrink. In two minutes you will experience difficulty getting your breath. In four minutes you will start to suffocate. In eight minutes you will no longer be able to speak to ask for mercy. In ten minutes you will be dead."

Lemuel hardly heard him. *The Lord is my shepherd. Hail Mary, Mother of God. Now and at the hour of my death . . .*

El Cirujano was wrong. He said in four minutes Lemuel would start to suffocate. It was only three, and he could feel the constriction on his neck cutting into his carotid arteries and esophagus. His head started to swim. He could only breathe in gasps. *Forgive me my trespasses . . .* Lemuel passed into unconsciousness.

Lemuel awoke screaming. The Surgeon broke the toe of his left foot with a pair of vise grips. The Surgeon had removed the rawhide before it choked the life from him. He screamed again as another toe was crushed. *Take me, Jesus*. The flesh of another toe was ripped free of the bone. Lemuel collapsed into grateful oblivion.

Estaban threw down the butt of his second cigar. "Your timetable is off, *señor*," he said to Pedraza. "Perhaps I was ill advised as to your credentials."

"Patience, Señor Rios. I was only in error in my estimate of this one's constitution. He will break." Pedraza connected the ground cable of the Lincoln welder to Lemuel's foot. He turned on the welder to maximum amperage. It whined to full power. Pedraza took the positive lead and touched Lemuel's leg. His body jolted, rocking the steel table. An inhuman sound emanated from him, unrecognizable. Blood flowed from Lemuel's mouth. His eyes begged for mercy.

Estaban leaned over next to Lemuel. "You cannot take much more, *Hermano*. Talk to me, and I will have The Surgeon send you to God without further pain."

Lemuel's mouth moved. Rios leaned closer. "May God have mercy on my soul. And yours."

Rios stood up. He turned to Barretto. "Pepe. The fire."

Pepe Sopo Barretto welcomed his chance to show his skill. He loped to his truck and removed an oxyacetylene torch with its twin tanks mounted on a wheeled cart. He wheeled the pipe-frame cart with its bent wheel into the warehouse. Finding a piece of heavy, half-inch steel plate on the floor, he slid it over and leaned it against the welding table. He pulled loose a pair of goggles hung around one of the tanks. He slipped them over his eyes, tightening the elastic around the back of his head. He ignited the torch and adjusted the twin knobs until the flame was a pale blue streak of fire three inches long. The torch hissed and popped. He placed the red tip an inch from the plate and let the flame heat the metal into a crimson, premolten mass. He convulsively pressed the brass handle. Pure oxygen shot into the flame. The energized cutting gas ripped through the steel like an erupting volcano, viscous lava exploding from the rear. He looked up and lifted the dark goggles off his eyes. *"Listo."* He dragged the cart toward the patient. The bent wheel beat the concrete like a tin drum. "How you like your meat? *Crudo o bien cosida?"* Raw or well done?

The flame scored a channel up Lemuel's leg, but there was no blood. The fire cauterized as it wended its way. Pain there was; at least at first. One continuous, agonized, animal scream burst from his lungs until he passed out once again.

Barretto threw off the dark welding goggles. "This one is not human." He ran the torch across Lemuel's bare chest, making a large Z. He stepped back and admired his work. "Just like Zorro."

Navarro Barretto idly massaged some waterless hand cleaner into the permanent grime covering his fingers. He watched his brother at work. "Just like a barbecue, no? Except no ants."

Ramirez got up from a box he was sitting on. "Hey, Pepe. Don't forget who you work for."

Pepe Barretto scratched his head and almost burned himself with the still-lit torch. *"Ah, sí."* He turned back to Lemuel and carved an *R* next to the Z. This time, there was no sound from Lemuel. Only the faint smell of the oxyacetylene mix layered over the scent of incinerating flesh and the sizzle of frying meat.

"Enough," said Estaban. "This one will never talk. He is probably dead. Check him."

The Surgeon removed a stethoscope from his case and plugged the tips into his ears. He searched for a place on Lemuel's chest to listen, but could find none. He placed a finger behind the monk's ear, searching for a pulse. "He is still alive," he said with glee. "But just barely. Let me try something else."

Estaban Rios held up his hand. "No more. He is no longer of any value to us for information. Deliver him as a warning."

"Momentito," said *El Cirujano*. "His lips move. He wishes to speak."

Pedraza bent down to listen, but was pulled away by Estaban. "Get back. If he says anything, it will be to my ears." Estaban leaned over. "Speak to me. There is still time. You will be spared." Estaban thought he heard a sound emanate from the torn lips. He put his ear next to them. "Yes?"

Estaban recoiled and stood erect. He backed up, staring at Lemuel's tortured body.

"Jefe?" said Ramirez. "What did he say?"

"Sí, patron," said Navarro Barretto. "What did he say?"

Rios was pale. "He was delirious."

They all were quiet now, looking at Rios. Ramirez inclined forward. "But what did he say?"

Rios stared at Lemuel, unable to tear away his eyes. "He said . . . He said that he forgave us."

The Barretto brothers laughed loudly, synchronized. *El Cirujano* never laughed. Ramirez rubbed his head.

"Was there more, jefe?" said Pepe Barretto.

Rios's eyes were like laser pointers as they swung to engage Pepe. "Yes. He said, 'But Chow Yun-Fat would not.' "

THE old line shack appeared, partially hidden by a rock overhang at the base of a bluff that dominated the desert floor. Like a gigantic ship's prow, a finger ridge ran down from the height of the bluff and plowed into the desert. There, where the ridge met the horizontal plane, somebody had built a small, one-room shack in the middle of nowhere. Prospectors? Cowboys? Outlaws? It was where Rawlings was holding Raoul Rios. It was where Grainger met him in the late afternoon. The Dodge convertible slid to a stop. Grainger swung out of the seat as Rawlings came out from behind a shale outcropping.

Rawlings sniffed. "You smell like gas."

"Pumped my own at the old man's station."

"Figures," said Rawlings. He pointed a finger at the ramshackle structure. "Our guest's inside."

"How'd it go?" asked Grainger.

"I had to scratch two more. But I managed to get our boy loaded up and out here in the pickup. No problem. How about you?"

"Custer's Last Stand. We were the Indians."

"You got all the booty expected?"

"Money. Guns. Dope. Two out of three left." Grainger slapped Rawlings on the shoulder.

They entered the shack. It was dark inside. Spiders and lizards scurried about, ignoring their presence. Raoul was on the dirt floor in a corner, bound and gagged. Rawlings kicked the bottom of his boot. "I got tired of listening to him."

Raoul squirmed and kicked his bound legs. A gurgling noise emitted from his throat. Rawlings snapped out his *Fallschirmjaeger* gravity knife and cut loose the gag with a looping swipe. Raoul expelled a gasp. Then he spat. "*Pinche cabron*. You two are going to pay. Believe me."

Grainger squatted down. "Two guys told my father that one day. They were wrong, too."

THEY unloaded the guns and money and hid them in a shrub-shrouded cache near the line shack. They waited until dark and drove back into Zapata. Rawlings drove Sloane's pickup, and Grainger the Dodge with Raoul in the trunk. Rawlings had shot him with another tranquilizer dart. He would be out for six hours.

They left the Dodge off the highway and motored to the church in the pickup. Rawlings let Grainger out two blocks from the church, and he covered the approach on foot, just in case. Rawlings parked in the alley to the rear.

They slipped through the darkness, checking the perimeter, watching and listening. Rawlings peered into three windows.

All seemed secure. He entered through the rear door. He reappeared a minute later and waved Grainger in. There was no hostile reception party waiting for them. But someone else was.

"Long time, no see," said Stoneman.

"Yeah," said Rawlings. "Last I remember, we were all dangling on a rope together somewhere."

"You need a shave," Grainger said. "Just in the neighborhood?"

"Right. I was thinking about maybe buying some property around here. Great place to retire, I hear."

Sloane stood by the altar. "Annual reunion?" She maneuvered to Grainger. "Mr. Mystery here came in this afternoon and said it was urgent that he talk with you. He said he was a friend, all the way from our nation's capital, too. Is this guy legit?"

"Straight as an arrow," said Grainger.

"Look, Lon, can we talk privately? I came a long way out here—"

"Yeah. Sure." Grainger turned to Sloane and the priests.

"Whatever you say," said Sloane. She retreated with Paul and Leon.

"Do we talk here?" said Stoneman.

"Good as any."

Stoneman looked around suspiciously. He tapped a wall with his knuckles. He was a spook. "I've got some supplementary information."

Stoneman told it all. *Total closure* was the euphemism for "everybody dies" and "the matter was settled in the interests of national security." He revealed how the truth—exposed in Condor—mutated into Tantrum VII, the lie by half-truth and omission: "The Condor report was closely-held, Yankee White. Tantrum VII was only top secret. The third agency rule was engaged. That meant no communication under any circumstances with any other intelligence organ, specifically the DIA. But if someone were digging real hard, they'd find Tantrum and think they hit the mother lode. Tantrum was created ex post facto as a contingency, as insurance and a hedge against a potential Senate Intelligence Oversight Committee inquiry, a serious DIA post mortem, or, the worst-case scenario, some liberal congressperson with a hard-on for the CIA and a deep-seated need to get on prime time, snooping around, armed with subpoenas and supported by some whistle blower or the FOI Act. If need be, the plan was to produce the Tantrum report, admit culpability to a peccadillo or two, and take the slap on the wrist. Everybody leaves the halls of the congressional hearing room happy."

Stoneman took a deep breath. "The Company's only mission that day in Beirut was to safeguard the pending Saleem deal, to make sure there was no interference from the DIA's revenge plot, assuming everything went as anticipated with the State-brokered deal. The soft intel of a sniper stalking you gave the Company a windfall, a needed explanation as to why a Terminex assassination team—code named Yin-Yang—was on station in the first place. That pre-op, stalking-sniper intel they had was originally estimated at just a grade above rumor. Unconfirmed. I don't think they took it seriously until the results were in. No matter. The Terminex team's mission was to execute the contingency—prevent Grainger from killing the mark if Saleem was turned. When your kill shot was made before they could stop you, they rolled over into the alternate protocol: total closure. It's doubtful if the Terminex team was even made aware that maybe there was a threat present from another sniper hunting you." He licked his lips. "There was no indication who the third shooter might have been."

Grainger reciprocated, letting Stoneman know about Montezuma and the Habib connection and that the unidentified assassin was present in Zapata.

"The third shooter? Here?" Stoneman shook his head. "Habib, the Lebanese guide . . . So that's how the shooter knew you'd be in Beirut. A Cuban sniper stalking you nails the CIA in-house hit squad before they can take you out. In-fucking-credible."

Stoneman's stomach was in acidic revolt. "It's all perversely reasonable. The Agency must have had postplan second thoughts about letting Cruickshank close up shop. They didn't want his bullets found in any bodies in case they were later obtained by anyone other than the Company. That's got to be part of the reason why they didn't wait for Cruickshank to execute the finale." Stoneman leaned against a pew. "It was CYA all the way. The Agency was protecting their ass and any remaining Middle Eastern credibility while creating a viable cover story. Everybody dies. Hitting their own man left no loose strings. The false flag wasn't about the Israelis. And dead men don't write memoirs."

"Anything current about the Terminex team?"

Stoneman's eyes darkened. The lines on his face ran deep. "Not much in either version. Like I said before, their code name was Yin-Yang. The shooter himself was really special; code-named The Zen Man; no identity in the files. Heavy backstop. Could be a deniable proprietary of some sort, maybe the leader of a DAGger team, but my guess most likely an annuitant. But I can tell you this; he's alive. His spotter was DOA. The shooter was picked up and exfiltrated by a PM team shepherding a surgeon. The shooter was in Bethesda for six months, but incognito, and no prognosis, status, or disposition was revealed in any of the reports."

It all made sense now, in a senseless sort of way.

Stoneman pushed off the pew. "What the hell you got going on here, anyway?"

Grainger forced himself back. "I don't know yet. Trouble."

"A lot of bad guys are trying to take over the world, and we're raising some serious objections," said Rawlings.

Stoneman shook his head. "If you have this Montezuma character here, you got major trouble." He slapped his leg. "I have to go. It's a long drive back to Corpus Christi and then a red-eye to Houston. I'm continuing on to D.C. I have to be back to work at the center tomorrow afternoon. This was just a little sabbatical."

"U/A?" said Grainger.

"Half and half. I'll find out when I get back. If I make the obits, you'll know I underestimated my power to make friends and influence people." He headed for the door. He stopped and turned around. "Are you up against a lot of them?"

"Human waves of hordes." Rawlings grinned broadly. "We

don't think of it as being outnumbered; more like having extensive target opportunities."

"Not as bad as Somalia, but it'll do," said Grainger. "For everything you've done. Thanks."

"You remember the Camp Perry National Rifle Matches, the year you won?"

"Sure."

"Well, a guy named Tony Castagna said to tell you that if it hadn't of been for a quartering gust of wind from nowhere, you would've been had. I work for him. He got me access. I already thanked him for you."

Grainger remembered. *Castagna . . . Hell of a rifleman. Never did say who he worked for.*

Stoneman needed a receipt. "Are we square?"

Grainger gave him a thumbs-up. "Square."

Stoneman blinked. Satisfied, he closed the church door behind him and looked at the dead street. He wondered if all the bad guys—whomever they were—had wills. *Poor fucks. Where would a town like this bury them all?* He took the steps two at a time. *Maybe Cindy is pregnant. No matter.* He was going to ask her to marry him. The night swallowed him up.

"Talk to him, Father," urged Leon. "Now is the time."

Paul cleared his throat. "We must negotiate a trade. Joey for Rios. I cannot bear to think about that child with those beasts."

"That's not an option. Think about it. Suppose we do trade straight across. We take Joey home and they get Rios. What next?" said Grainger.

Paul shuffled his feet.

"I'll tell you what. They'll come to burn us out before the night's over. *Deal* is a card not in our deck."

"Then, how do we get him back?" said Paul.

"First we retool." Grainger felt his pulse jump. "Then we take him back, Padre. We take him back."

Paul wrung his hands. "When will this war end?"

"When there's no one left but us," said Rawlings.

Sloane led Grainger to her room without shame.

"Tomorrow we plan our finale," said Grainger in retreat.

Leon watched them melt away. He turned to Rawlings. "You might as well stay, too."

Rawlings shook his head. "I'd love to, Leon, but I have a guy waiting for me in a trunk."

TWENTY-FIVE

SONJA got out of bed and slipped the diaphanous black silk robe over her shoulders and fastened the belt around her waist. She would sleep with Estaban, milk his gland, but she would never be found in slumber in his bed when the sun rose. She looked out the open patio doors of his second-story bedroom, which overlooked the garden. The smell of flowers—indistinguishable by individual scent—flooded the room. The sun would be coming up soon. She looked at Estaban. He gave her no particular sensual pleasure. She sought none. To accept pleasure was to admit dependency, even weakness. Others depended on her. Not she on them. She looked once more at Estaban with the satin sheet pulled up around his waist and a look of contentment on a face buried in a goose down pillow. His breathing was stentorian, as it always was after she had drained him. She went out onto the small veranda and listened to the night. . . .

Sonja Ochoa was a Creole from Teriot, Louisiana, a town—if you could call a string of huts surrounded by the Terrebonne Swamp a town—lost figuratively in time and almost literally in space. For local folks, New Orleans was just a name of some place no one had ever been to. County Road 315, which came through town, ended a mile south in an estuary filled with alligators and mosquitoes. Maybe someday, somebody would drain the swamp; but engineers said the Gulf of Mexico would only take its place. And what for, anyway?

Teriot had a permanent population of 637 souls in socioeconomic equanimity but separated by perceived differences of race, religion, and the superiority of national origin. Teriot's population's gross annual income average of five thousand dollars was 40 percent below the national poverty guideline. Half the town poached gators and hunted snakes for their skin and drove twenty-year-old Ford pickups with twin gun racks in the rear window and confederate flag mud guards and brushed their teeth on Robert E. Lee's birthday. The other half of the town was black and planted gardens of collard greens and fished in the swamp and smoked a little of their own homegrown. An uneasy truce existed.

Sonja never knew her father. He was white was all she could ever get out of her mother. Her mother was a self-described mulatto, and, although the term had disappeared from the lexicon of political correctness, she liked the sound of it. Her brother Toby was taken by a monstrous gator known as Bolo one night while Toby was frogging with a gig along the water's edge. Her sister Connie ran away one moonless night, whether to New Iberia or into the swamp, not a soul knew or gave it any thought. Her mother sewed things for people and made a few dollars. No one—not even in Teriot—called it a living. They lived in a shack on the bayou on land nobody claimed.

There was a school of sorts, where Sonja remembered going. Teacher was an ancient black woman who claimed to be an orisha, a transmedium in spiritual contact with the great god Olorun, the owner of heaven. She taught people to count and to make their sign and even how to read a little. But her inspiration was Santeria, her religion, sometimes referred to as La Regla Lucumi or, in the native pejorative, as Macumba.

Santeria was a melding of tribal primitive religions of West Africa mixed liberally with a pantheistic vision. From Nigeria and Benin, its progenitor was exported to the New World and underwent a continuing evolution as slaves were brought over and baptized as Christians. Plantation owners believed their possessions were being pious, worshipping Saint Barbara, when in reality they were praying to Shango, the lord of lightning and fire, for the death of their temporal masters. The emerging religion also adopted the rites of voodoo from Haitian, Cuban, Trinidadian, and Brazilian influences. The one constant was ebo, offerings. Blood sacrifice.

Sonja took to her education eagerly. She absorbed everything the old woman, Yoruba, taught her. She became the chosen one. She passed through her rites of passage, her initiation and training. She wore white for a year. Nor did she look into a mirror for that year. She wore no makeup, and she disavowed sexual relations, although she was tempted by the sleek, liquid sexuality of the swamp hunter who had an airboat and stalked only at night. The few times she had seen him, she became aware of her budding womanhood and emerging sexuality. Although he looked at her with undisguised lust, he seemed preoccupied. One day she was told he never came back from the swamp. She still thought of him at night sometimes.

At twenty, she passed from Iyawo—an initiate—into a santera, an orisha, the head guardian. She could see the future, interpret the past, and influence the present. She gathered her collection of sacred botanicals and predictors of the future: chicken bones, the wings of a bat, the teeth of a cat, the fangs of a water moccasin, the claws of a rat. She kept them in a leather bag around her neck. When it was time to make the transitioning sacrifice, she rowed Yoruba out into the swamp at midnight in a dugout. After chanting to Oshzn, Yoruba removed her amulet from around her neck and passed it to Sonja. The withered and wizened woman stood up in the unstable boat with perfect balance and drew a knife she kept on her belt. She raised it high over her head and without hesitation plunged it into her skinny chest. She toppled over into the water and instantly sank from sight. Sonja remembered listening. She could not recall a splash. She remembered looking at the tranquil surface of the water reflecting the full moon through the mist blanketing it like a skin. It was unbroken. Oshzn, the goddess, had taken her.

Two years later, a biologist came to the swamp to study the unique ecology. The pagan beauty of Sonja Ochoa took him. She had never met a man who bathed every day and smelled like flowers. When he left, he took her with him to Baton Rouge, where he entered her into private tutoring. She took extension courses from LSU. She read extensively. Two years hence, she could say, "How now brown cow" and "The rain in Spain goes mainly down the drain" with the best of them. She learned manners and etiquette and how to be coy and coquettish when necessary. Civilization captivated her. One day she learned that Roy, her man—they had never discussed marriage—had another lover. He informed her that her tenure was up. She would have to move. Veronica was coming to stay.

Roy died that night from a poison concoction assembled by Sonja. She had served the evening meal dressed all in white, and Roy had said that she had never looked lovelier and he was glad she was being a good sport about the whole thing. She left him on the floor of the bedroom, took all the money she could find, and walked out the front door, leaving it open. She thumbed a ride with Henry and Madeline, a newlywed couple on their honeymoon. They headed west on Interstate 10. They crossed into Texas, and she stayed with them all the way to San Antonio. They offered to let her sleep in the same room with them, but she declined. She had some of her own money. She blessed them the last morning and predicted they would be happy for a full year. At the Alamo, as Henry was looking to see where John Wayne had died, she slipped away. For no particular reason, she caught a bus headed for Laredo. It was just the next bus leaving. The following day she was riding on Highway 83 in a black limousine seated next to Estaban Rios. He had seen her at the bus station and something had compelled him to stop. He confessed he didn't know what. Or why. Sonja knew. Obatala, source of spirituality, father of creation, guider of destinies, had taken her. And him. She soon became referred to as La Alma Negra, *The Black Soul.*

SONJA heard Rios stir, and she slipped easily on padded feet to his side.

Estaban rubbed the sleep from his eyes and looked out the twin doors to the veranda. The first streaks of dawn appeared, like slivers of light in the black finger of night. *She is still here.* He propped himself up on one elbow. "Our bed smells of us."

"Your bed, Estaban. I am a transient. An artifact."

"You are my pleasure."

"I am your instrument of pleasure. You are your own pleasure."

Estaban considered the response. He didn't know whether to be pleased or disappointed. "Then to business. What now shall I do about my money? My brother? My revenge?"

Sonja sat on the bed. "Taking the boy has not been enough. They will not negotiate for your brother. You must now give them more than the warning to be provided by the Brother, Lemuel."

"Yes? What must I do?"

"Provide spectators to your lessons. The Chinese say a picture is worth a thousand words."

"Yes," said Estaban. "Of course."

"And, if the intended witness the picture being drawn—"

"Yes. Yes, of course," said Estaban Rios as he reached for her. But, his priestess, his *Alma Negra,* was gone. He looked out the door to his veranda. The sun was shuffling off the night. *Maybe she is a vampire.* That was all right, too. Estaban understood the need for blood.

"**HOW** serious is it?" said Rawlings. They were seated on a log in the shade of a Joshua tree outside the line shack, a deck of cards between them.

"She's important to me." He threw down a card on the pile.

"Eight changes suit, Lon. What do you have most of? Hearts?"

"Diamonds," said Grainger.

"Important, huh? Now, that's what I call a real political word. Guarded like. Says everything and means nothing. Is that what you meant?"

"No," Grainger said, slapping down a jack of spades onto Rawlings's jack of diamonds. He dropped his cards on the ground in front of him. Crazy eights was too mind-boggling for now. "Can you watch Rios for a while?"

"Yeah, sure. You're not going back for a nooner . . . nothing like that?"

Grainger looked back, unsmiling.

"Hey, I was just kidding and maybe just a little jealous. So . . . Where you going? Just for the record."

"I've been smelling a lot of flowers around lately."

Rawlings looked around. "Flowers?"

"Flowers. Lilies. It's time to look for the coffin."

GRAINGER found Runyan in the back. The dog didn't even bark as he drove up. The German Shorthaired Pointer sniffed the air until he was satisfied. The dog escorted Grainger back to the rear of the cabin, where he found Runyan looking out over the arroyo that ran down from the rear of the property.

" 'Bout got it figured out how you're going to accomplish it, Mr. Grainger?" he said, hobbling back from the cleared edge of his land.

"Not quite. There's been a few complications."

"Yeah. I heard. Need anything? If I have it, you got it."

"No, nothing like that. Just some talk. Mind?"

"Not at all. Join me on the porch. I'll mix up a batch of mint juleps."

"Just water for me," said Grainger.

Runyan disappeared inside. He reappeared and limped back to the chair on the porch, forgoing the mint julep. He held two glasses of water.

He fell heavily into the wicker chair. "Speak."

"You were with the DIA."

"Is that a question or a statement?" said Runyan.

"I was just wondering. Something's been bothering me about our last meeting, but I wasn't able to put my finger on it."

"You having second thoughts, Lon?"

"No. My thoughts were running more to the yin and the yang."

Runyan stared right through him. "Who?"

"Funny. Most people would have responded, 'What?' "

Runyan shifted in his chair. "Okay, then . . . What?" He laughed a tinny sort of chuckle.

"A spook I know had some interesting information on Beirut. He actually had better intel than you."

"How's that, Lon?"

Grainger fixed Runyan with his eyes, taking in every breath, every quiver and heartbeat. "He said that it wasn't Montezuma who killed Cruickshank."

Runyan took a sip of water. "Really? That's interesting."

"Aren't you curious who did?"

Runyan finished the water in one motion and set the glass down on the floor of the porch. "I'm sure you're about to tell me."

Grainger petted the pointer, who had come up onto the porch and laid down next to him. He scratched his back, and the dog's back leg kicked in involuntary spasms of doggie delight. "It was The Zen Man."

Runyan stared out across the front yard, his eyes tracing the dirt road to where it disappeared around a bend, heading for the highway. "Do you know where you can find this Zen Man, Lon?"

Grainger ran his finger around the rim of his glass. "I think I do, Mr. Runyan."

Runyan returned from the study of the terrain to Grainger. "Things are rarely what they seem, Lon."

"I'll buy that."

"How'd you figure it out?"

Grainger inclined forward in his chair and stretched his back muscles. "You should have told me you worked for the Company instead of the DIA."

"Did it matter?"

"Something called the Third Agency Rule was invoked. The DIA didn't know a thing about the State Department/CIA deal with Saleem or the Company Terminex team on site. You did. You also knew about Mogadishu and the connection with the shooter. It was all a mystery to them. You knew what you couldn't have known."

"Maybe I forgot. Could have been the CIA I worked for. I've been getting senile lately."

"Did you also forget how you knew that Cruickshank was going to kill us when he got himself perforated?"

"No, I—"

"That's how I finally put it together. I remembered what you said, the first time we met here. That I was 'lucky that he nailed Cruickshank when he did.' It didn't sink in until today, thinking about it. Lucky about what? No one knew about the *what,* Mr. Runyan. Not the DIA, not the CIA. We never revealed that information to anyone. Only people who knew that were myself and my partner. And the man who shot old Liberty Cruickshank."

Runyan let out his breath. His dog crawled over to him and nuzzled his hand. "I don't suppose it would do any good to offer that I learned that from the report."

"Would that be Tantrum VII or Condor?"

Runyan wondered if the bullet would take him in the head. He could try for the Walther PPKS tucked under his shirt but estimated it would just be a waste of effort. Long range was his forte. "I guess I underestimated your intelligence skills. You're more than just a shooter. I should have also considered that you would have had some outside perspective—from the inside."

"You had me going with the dead wife story. Real convincing. Estaban Rio runs her over . . . You ought to be on stage. What was the plan?"

"It took me a while to identify Lorca and make all the connections. The Agency eventually figured it out, but it wasn't revealed in any documents. After six months in Bethesda, I was discharged. They retired me. Revenge kept me going. I moved here shortly after learning Montezuma took up employment with Rios. I was going to do him myself. After a while, I knew it wasn't going to happen. You know the rest." He was calm now. "You going to kill me?"

"I thought about it all the way out here."

"What are you thinking now?"

"That it was just a job. Well, wasn't it? You were just following orders. Right? Just, doing your duty, like the rest of us? Nothing personal." There was a razor edge to his voice.

"I guess so. You know about following orders. And killing. What would you have done, Lon?" He wasn't begging.

Grainger didn't have to answer him. He knew about following orders. And he had already answered that question for himself. The answer explained why Runyan was going to live. "Can I see the tattoo?"

"What?"

"Your tattoo. The yin-yang."

Runyan reached across his chest with his right hand and slowly raised the khaki shirtsleeve of his left arm. The inked circle of faded dark and light appeared. *The Zen Man.*

Grainger got up from his chair and headed for the door.

"If you're going to shoot me, make it good."

Grainger stopped at the open door. "I don't think there's any need."

"You quitting on me?"

"You said you wanted a surrogate. You got one."

Runyan struggled to his feet and hobbled toward the door and out onto the porch. His relief at deliverance from death was palpable. He watched Grainger cross to the car. "Lon."

Grainger had the door handle in his hand. He turned around.

"Death has always been close behind both you and me."

"Yeah. And he's catching up." He opened the door and eased into the worn seat.

The Dodge rumbled, and the transmission engaged with a lurch. The car was moving. Through the rearview mirror he saw Runyan standing on the porch with his dog, the yin getting smaller and smaller.

Runyan watched the car fade away. The sniper was right. There was no need to kill him. There was nothing left inside of him but hate and loathing. He was already dead.

TWENTY-SIX

" 'THE Lord is my light and my salvation. Who shall frighten me?' " Paul Teasdale removed the host from the monstrance and gazed up at the cross. Christ's dolorous eyes stared back at him. In the candlelit church, the shadows of night played off the walls, giving a true cathedral effect. It could also be a dungeon. He was saying Mass for two.

" 'The glory of the Lord will dwell in our land.' " Sister Felicia echoed the responsorial. She knelt next to Humberto, her father, whose hands were folded in prayer.

Father Paul genuflected. " 'The Lord is the defender of my life. Who shall make me tremble?' "

"Allow me the opportunity, Father Paul."

Paul came to his feet, his stomach colliding with his heart. He turned around. "Estaban Rios." The words spilled from his mouth, somewhere between a quake and a growl.

Ramirez, Felipe Aguirre, Ramon Zamudio, and Rafael Alarcon flanked Rios.

"In the spirit. And the flesh." Estaban strode toward Paul, his hands running along the tops of the pews on both sides of the aisle.

"Why have you come here?" barked Paul.

Rios slammed his palm onto a pew. "*Why?* Why have I come here? You insult me. You steal my property. You take my brother from me. You kill my men with impunity; and you ask why have I come here?"

Paul's chest heaved convulsively.

Rios stalked forward to the communion rail. He leaned on it, looking at Paul. "I have recently assumed a new role: that of teacher." He spun around, facing his men. "But, in answer to your question," he said, slowly pivoting back, "I have come for you."

Ramirez and Ramon Zamudio rushed bull-like to Felicia and Humberto, ripping them from their seats.

Aguirre and Alarcon vaulted the rail and grabbed Paul.

"Perhaps I will redecorate this place and make this my newest *casa de putos.*" Rios maneuvered toward the door, scanning the barren walls of the church. "Come. Come, children. Class is in session."

RIOS had a Land Rover. A real Land Rover, not the Range Rover export model that you were lucky enough to keep running on the expressway. His was a real African model with skidpans, roll bar, window grating, four-wheel drive, Warren winch, and rubber gun ports in the windshield. The Land Rover led, driven by Pepe Barretto, who was accompanied by his brothers and Alarcon. In the trailing limousine rode Estaban, who sat in the sequestered rear facing Paul, Felicia, and Humberto on the opposing seat. Nero Ramirez lounged next to Estaban, a Beretta M-12 submachine gun seesawing from knee to knee. Aguirre drove with Zamudio riding shotgun. The interior of the limo was soundless, with barely a sensation of movement.

Paul's hands remained folded on his lap. "What is this all about, Estaban?" Cold eyes and silence told him.

The vehicle stopped moving. Paul looked out the window and saw the moon silhouetting a giant Joshua tree.

Rios got out and opened the door on the opposite side. "This is about lessons, Father; in respect as well as a contemplation of modified behavior, an anticipation of renewed fealty and of course a recognition of authority." He extended his hand to Felicia. "But, if nothing else, then an exercise in the politics of pure terror." He yanked Felicia from the vehicle.

Ramirez motioned with the Beretta. Paul and Humberto staggered out.

"A beautiful night, no?" Estaban did a pirouette on the dirt road.

Paul shivered, even though the night air was hot. They were somewhere in the desert. The lights and engines were shut down on both vehicles, and darkness enveloped them. Only the full moon provided illumination. It even appeared benevolent for a moment. A coyote howled, off in the distance, and the moon suddenly seemed more sinister and conspiratorial.

"A beautiful woman," said Estaban.

Paul recoiled. "Anything you want, Estaban. Ask or take what you want from me."

Pepe Barretto took Felicia by the arm and looked to Estaban for a sign.

Estaban regarded Paul with a grim smile. "You have nothing my men want."

Humberto charged Pepe Barretto. Navarro and Mario clubbed him to the ground.

Rios nodded to Aguirre. He and Alarcon seized Paul by his arms. Paul struggled inconsequentially as Ramirez stood to his front, balancing the M-12 SMG over his shoulder, mocking his efforts. Pinned, Paul stopped resisting. Ramirez slammed the extended stock of the weapon into his stomach. Paul saw it coming and managed to tighten his abdominal muscles to accept the blow. It still collapsed him.

Someone turned the headlights back on the Land Rover and repositioned the vehicle so it was facing the limousine, offset, to provide an arena. They dragged Paul to the front of the Rover and lashed his arms to the bumper and grill. Aguirre kicked Humberto in the stomach and pulled his inert form to the front tire of the limousine, where he was tied.

"There," said Estaban. "All of our guests are seated." He cupped his hands over his eyes. "Turn off those headlights, please. I prefer subdued lighting for drama." He turned to his party. "She is yours. Take her, *muchachos. Mi regalo para usted."*

Paul caught Felicia's imploring eyes. He looked at her for a moment, and then turned his head. He felt the bile build up in his stomach; tears of helplessness and rage escaped from his eyes.

Ramirez bowed to Estaban. "The honor is yours, jefe."

Ah yes, le droit du seigneur. *The right of the lord.* Rios returned the bow theatrically. "I defer to your expertise in these matters."

Pepe Barretto held Felicia as Ramirez approached. He reached for her habit and in one motion, tore it from her body. He held the brown cloth in his fist and put it to his face. He inhaled deeply. He pulled Felicia from Pepe and pushed her roughly down onto the dirt of the road.

Felicia's eyes were wild, desperate. She comprehended what was occurring intellectually. She had an understanding of what was happening as an academic construct, but she was transitioning fast into the real nightmare. Her undergarments of modest white cotton stood starkly contrasted against the dirt of the road where she lay. Ramirez straddled her and reached down for the remaining clothing. He first tugged, then, meeting the resistance of the cloth, tore them from her. A piece of her long slip remained in her hand. She was naked. Felicia attempted to hide her shame. She covered her diminutive breasts and her sex as best as she could.

The Barretto brothers stalked over to watch. Ramirez frantically pulled at his belt buckle. His filthy black pants fell to his ankles, and he stumbled on top of her. He reached down and touched his appendage of which he was so proud. He was bigger than the biggest *hombre negro*—of that he was sure—and would fill her with him. He manipulated her almost hairless receptacle like he was petting a dog. He looked at her face. It was disconnected. He kissed her hard. There was no reaction. He rocked on her and slapped her face. His tool remained limp. His hardness depended on her struggle. He hit her again.

"Fulfill your duty, or let a man in," Pepe Barretto taunted.

Ramirez rubbed his manhood against her and at last felt

himself grow rigid. He would show these amateurs. He pressed down into her cleft.

Felicia's scream was inhuman, emetic. Paul had not heard anything like it before. His stomach heaved, and the ejecta erupted. He made no attempt to direct it away from himself. It was a mark of his disgrace and his eternal shame.

Ramirez tore through her membrane. *A virgin. She is a virgin. When I took her she was just a trail in the desert. When I pull my flesh from her she will be a highway.* Ramirez ejaculated convulsively twenty seconds after entering her. He stood up and pulled up his pants. "See if you can do better, *compadre.*"

Navarro Barretto started for her, his loins shaking with lust. Pepe shoved him away. He mounted her and thrust wildly without removing his trousers. When his zipper pinched him, he struck her. He spent quickly and got up.

Ramirez was smoking marijuana. "I lubricated her for you, no? Perhaps you could not feel the sides after me?" Pepe waved him off and went to urinate behind the limousine where he could have some privacy.

Sister Felicia lay in a state of delirium. She had felt the pain and had smelled their foul breaths and stink-sweat. She had endured. She had felt her center tear. Then another one mounted her. He put his hands over her eyes so she could not see him. Her eyes were open, but she did not see any of them. Novitiate Sister Felicia Anaya believed in God; not God the reward giver, but God the dispenser of divine justice. She believed in Hell and damnation and that retribution came to those who escaped this life untried and unrepentant. She barely felt the surge of the penetrating force that violated her again. She concentrated on the moon. It was balanced on a cactus and looked like it might fall.

Aguirre covered her face with his hand. He didn't want her looking at him with those eyes. He managed a partial erection but then lost it a minute later inside her. He gave a covering grunt and backed off her. The others would never know, and she wouldn't tell.

Ramon Zamudio was next. Alarcon waited in queue. Ramon

made his way to her still form. *"Ahuevo!* I will wake you up." He put his hands around her throat and shook her. "Rise to me, you whore." He let her head drop to the ground. He took her, but he had experienced more excitement stroking his own lizard.

Rios came to Paul and knelt down. He turned his head and watched Zamudio listlessly flailing at her form. He turned back to Paul, whose head had dropped to his chest. "Watch. You have a most personal angle of vision. You may learn something."

Alarcon pulled Zamudio away when he was too slow to rise. He was not going to insert himself where so many had gone before. He would hole her elsewhere. He rolled Felicia over onto her stomach.

Rios still knelt next to Paul. He reached down with his hand and grabbed Paul's jaw, ripping it to the left. "I said watch. It is not often you are given the opportunity to witness martyrdom."

Felicia managed somehow to curl herself into a fetal position. Alarcon put his boot on her back and kicked her back onto her abdomen. Her white buttocks reflecting the moonlight excited him.

The unspent others stirred, too. Even Rios focused his attention. Pepe whittled on a stick at the back of the limousine.

"You are a beast, Rafael," grunted Mario Barretto as he cupped his crotch.

Alarcon gazed down at Felicia. He kicked her legs apart in order to get a better view of her mounds. Still contemplating the next five minutes, he unbuttoned his pants and stepped out of them completely. *Yes. This little Mexicana is a sweet little flower.* He knelt down and put his hands under her hips and pulled her up to him. His swelling bobbed in front of him as he guided her onto him. After brief forward entry, he removed himself from her and in one swift convulsive thrust impaled her, imbedding himself in another place.

Felicia bit her tongue. She had thought she had experienced all the pain possible. But this was like having a stake driven deep inside of her. Blood filled her mouth, and she cried out for the first time since the beginning. It did nothing to relieve the torment or the lacerating presence within her. She saw the cactus spear the moon. Then she passed out.

Humberto regained consciousness. He sobbed softly, pulling against his restraints. He choked, breaths coming as tortured gasps. "Please. Do not do this. If it is a death you want, take me."

Rios pitied the old, ignorant fool. "Please do not do this? It is done, old man. And, it is not a death we seek specifically. It is education."

After Alarcon there was Navarro, who climaxed before he entered her. He beat her savagely with his fists as an alternative.

Mario Barretto was last. But he had masturbated while watching the others. He shrugged. *"No mas."* The others laughed.

Estaban Rios tapped his watch. "Nero. Check her."

Ramirez fastened his belt buckle and shuffled over to Felicia. She lay spread-eagled in the dirt, ashamed no longer. He nudged her with his foot. She gave the tiniest of moans. He rubbed his hands across his lower jaw. "She's still alive."

Estaban took out a handkerchief and patted his forehead as he moved to Paul. He sat down, his back against the bumper of the Land Rover. "Did it excite you?"

Paul stared catatonically.

Rios leaned over and examined the priest closely. "You have soiled yourself. I would have thought you were tougher than that. I have actually watched you fight a time or two. I lost heavily betting against you the first time but then doubled my money on the *El Perro de Michoacan* fight betting on you." Rios hugged his knees. He watched his men straggle about, pulling up their pants or just standing there like imbeciles. "Come. Tell me. You felt a little stirring. No? Your loins burned, with curiosity if nothing else?"

Paul managed to raise his head off his chest and look over at the supine Felicia. He shifted his eyes to Humberto, who was still tied to the wheel of the limousine. He appeared dead. "You are a monster. She was just a child."

Estaban raised his hands to cup his chin and hold his head. "A child no longer, eh? Perhaps it was her fantasy. They say rape is every woman's secret desire."

Paul gagged, and flecks of bitter stomach detritus dribbled from the corner of his mouth.

Estaban shifted his eyes to the nun, who stirred a bit. "I will ask you once, *Cura*. Where is my money? What have you done with my brother?"

"Let her go." The words fell from his tongue with no direction.

"Ramirez."

Ramirez rambled over, kicking the dirt with each step. *"Sí, Patron?"*

"Otra vez mas?" Estaban threw his head in the direction of Felicia.

Ramirez grinned at his boss. "Hey . . . No jefe. *Muchas gracias.* Once is enough for me."

"Very well then, decorate that cactus over there."

Paul's head snapped around. He strained against his bonds. "In the name of God Almighty, don't do this."

Ramirez shrugged his shoulders and yawned. He pointed to Felicia. Alarcon and Zamudio picked her up under their arms and pulled her toward the large saguaro cactus. Two crooked horizontal arms gave it an appearance of a crucifix assembled by a drunken carpenter.

A guttural cry of despair arose from Humberto's throat, transitioning into a long, continuous wail.

"Callate." Rios shouted at Ramirez. "Shut that old fool up."

Ramirez picked up the M-12 where he had left it and trudged over to Humberto.

"Temporarily," warned Rios. "We need him to speak of this night."

Ramirez heaved back and struck Humberto in the head with the buttstock. Humberto slumped over into semiconsciousness.

Zamudio and Alarcon stood the nun up in front of the cactus and glanced over at Estaban.

"Well. What are you waiting for? Tack her up."

The two men raised her off the ground and in a coordinated motion thrust her onto the cactus. The shriek of agony that was released from her throat froze them all. Her scream lasted the duration of one breath, but its echo seemed to linger for minutes.

Zamudio slipped his belt from his trousers and used it to secure her to the cactus.

Estaban murmured something inaudible.

"Que, jefe?" said Ramirez.

Estaban shivered. "I said, cut them loose." He pushed himself off the ground and stood up.

Pepe Barretto drew his boot stiletto and cut the ropes that secured Paul. Navarro did the same to Humberto.

"Well? Stand them up."

Mario jerked Humberto to his feet.

"Go, old man. Join your daughter." Rios motioned with his head.

Humberto sobbed quietly and prayed as he shuffled to Felicia. He looked up at her face, but in the dark he could see nothing. He touched her feet. He allowed the tears from his eyes to wash her.

"Father . . . ?" It was not a voice Humberto recognized. It was a distorted croak, a rasping grate.

Ramirez slid a revolver from his belt and snapped open the cylinder. He dropped out five cartridges into his hand and slapped the weapon shut. He handed it to Rios. Estaban strode stiffly to Humberto.

Paul came to his knees, arms outstretched.

Rios took Humberto's right hand and laid the firearm on his palm. He closed Humberto's fingers around the handle and guided the hand with the gun until it pointed at Felicia. "Do not let her suffer any longer."

Father Paul lurched clumsily to his feet, his legs numb and uncooperative, his wrists throbbing as the blood flowed back into his extremities. He charged for Estaban. Four guns flashed, accompanied by the *click* of hammers being drawn back.

"No!" Estaban raised his hand.

Paul ripped the gun from the combined grip of Humberto and Rios.

"So. You wish to stand in his stead? *Bien.*" Estaban shoved Humberto away.

Paul gripped the gun tightly. He turned and twisted the steel thing, studying its ugly neutrality, considering its willingness to serve any master.

"There is but one bullet, so if you are thinking of shooting me . . ."

Paul's chest heaved in uncontrollable emotion, his body racked by pain. His heart condemned him. He looked back at Felicia. Her head hung, resting on her thin chest. A drop of blood fell on his hand. She was still alive. Her body stirred and shifted as a few spines of the cactus broke. Her eyes were open. They were imploring him. They were begging him. They were forgiving him.

The gun went off without conscious volition. There was a flash of light that illuminated the image of her tortured face. Paul dropped the gun at his feet. He heard Estaban, somewhere in the distance. "You see Priest . . . You were right. Our monsters are us."

Humberto broke loose from Mario and stumbled to the cactus. He touched her feet once more and caressed them absently. He laid his bloody hand on his cheek. Humberto looked at a transfixed Paul. "It is what I would have done had you not." He maneuvered to Estaban. "I will wait for you. By the river."

Estaban stepped away. "Go to the river, old man and take this night's vision with you." He turned to Paul. "And for you, *Cura,* you have two days to deliver my money and my brother, or—"

"Estaban Rios." The voice was still a croak; but it also growled. "You had better kill me now."

Estaban reached into his waist and withdrew a chrome pistol, its silver gleaming in the moonlight. He cocked the hammer and placed the barrel between the priest's cold eyes. He studied the unflinching face over the sights. He shook his head, letting his thumb guide the hammer back slowly as he depressed the trigger. He lowered the gun. "No, Priest. I will not provide you that peace."

PAUL knelt under the crucified body of Sister Felicia Anaya. He didn't pray. He didn't think. He just knelt. Humberto had disappeared into the desert ten minutes, a half hour, a century ago. Paul came to his feet. He released the restraining leather belt as he reached up and took her arms. Her body slid easily off the cactus spines, dropped and folded into his arms. Rigor mortis was just detectable. He placed her facedown and pulled the spikes from her body. He counted them: 108. He found the tattered remnants of her clothing and covered her as best he could. He smoothed her hair. In the moonlight, it was auburn. He could not ever remember seeing her without her head covered. He sat for a while holding her cold hand; then he picked her up and carried her off the road into the desert. He found a spot where a moonbeam seemed to point, filtering through a solitary cottonwood tree. He scratched at the dirt with his hands and a rock that he found. He laid her to rest in the shallow depression and covered her with the dirt he had excavated. Then he prayed: *"O salutaria Hostia, Quate caeli pandis ostium: Bella premunt hostilia, Da robur, fer auxilium . . ."* He prayed for the gates of eternal heaven to open to receive her soul; that she had been taken by the very foes who now pressed in from every side. "Thine aid supply, thy strength bestow."

Paul returned to the road. He had no idea where he was. He began the trek back, following the tire tracks that had brought him to this infamy. *Estaban Rios, Nero Ramirez, Felipe Aguirre, Rafael Alarcon* . . . He repeated their names. He knew who they were. And he swore to Almighty God that he would not be alone in remembering this night and what it wrought. As he walked he flung away the spines of the cactus; one for every ten steps he took. He pricked his hand with each. When he had hurled the hundredth, he stopped. Eight he saved.

He stumbled blindly, moving without seeming volition, sloshing aimlessly in a slough of despondency. *"Our monsters are us."*

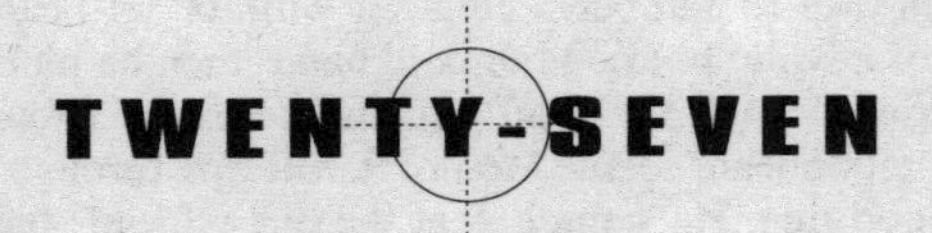

TWENTY-SEVEN

"**SOMETHING** is terribly wrong."

Leon paced the length of the communion rail wringing his hands. Sloane slumped in the first row of pews. Grainger stood in the aisle and looked at his watch. Rawlings stood guard by the door and yawned. It was getting late.

"We'll have to assume enemy action," said Grainger.

Leon wrung his hands. "Felicia? Humberto? They have nothing to do with this. I cannot forgive myself if something has happened to them. Father Paul was right. We do not know the end of this."

Grainger checked his watch again. "It's almost zero three hundred. Three A.M. If we don't hear—" He turned in response to Rawlings suddenly flinging open the door, his gun in hand.

Paul stood framed in the doorway. His hassock was torn and his face blackened. He staggered inside, a feral night creature maddened by the light.

Leon made the sign of the cross. *"Madre Dios."*

Paul stumbled forward, his eyes shrouded and glazed over. He moved like a robot, a deranged leper.

Rawlings slipped outside to look, then returned and shut the door. "Negative," he said.

Paul came to rest in front of Sloane.

"Father Paul! What happened to you? Where have you been?"

Paul looked at her curiously. "Been?"

"Father . . . ?"

Paul shook his head, trying to remember. "Been? Yes. I have been with Satan."

Leon eased cautiously forward. "Humberto? Felicia? Where are Humberto and Felicia?"

Paul swayed unsteadily, moving wavelike from side to side. "Humberto. Yes, Humberto. He is by the river."

Leon moved closer. "The river? And Sister Felicia?"

Paul had drained himself of tears in the ten-mile walk back. He looked up at the crucified Christ. "At peace with the Father."

Leon swallowed and brushed back an inchoate tear. "She is . . . dead?"

Paul's hands descended onto Leon's shoulders with a resounding slap. *"Dead.* Defiled. Desecrated." He collapsed into the pew. In a quieter voice, almost a whisper, he added, "Raped by beasts and crucified on a cactus." His head rose. He sprang to his feet and vaulted the rail, confronting the cross. "Why? Why Lord?" He fell to his knees, mumbling. "She was just a child. They made me watch. With my own hand, I killed her." He wept, but no tears came.

FATHER Paul retold the night's story in fitful bursts and painful recollections. When he had no more to tell, Leon looked at the cross. *"Jesus Christo.* What have we wrought?"

A thud shook the front door. Grainger and Rawlings rotated guns into their hands and sprinted for the door. Rawlings threw it open while Grainger covered. A dark bundle, leaning low on the door, fell across the threshold.

Sloane walked slowly up the aisle toward the door, her clenched fist half devoured in her mouth.

"You'd better stay back," said Grainger.

"Why?" she asked, trancelike.

"Because," he said, "it's Lemuel. And he's not like you remember him."

Sloane covered her face and ran to Grainger. She looked at Lemuel, but his face was almost unrecognizable. It was burned black, and his hair was gone. His body was near naked, burned and torn. Small canyons of singed, ragged flesh cut across scorched skin and dried blood. An obscene *Z* and an *R* were carved in fire. "My God," she said. "My God."

Leon came up, both hands supporting his face. The smell of burned flesh drifted, inundating the room. He gagged.

"Yes. My God has found it necessary to take Brother Lemuel, too." Paul looked back at the cross. "Perhaps he is not my God." He stalked up the aisle. His voice was clear, even resonant.

"What are you saying, Father?" said Leon. "Your mind has become unsettled."

"No, Leon. My mind is the clearest it has ever been."

"He's still alive," screamed Sloane. "Jesus. Get a doctor. Somebody."

Grainger felt for a pulse. He didn't have to recall too much of his medical training at Fort Sam Houston to know Lemuel was on the brink of extinction.

Leon stepped back, propelled by some biological aversion to death so near and imminent. His words tangled in his mouth. "What kind . . . kind of . . . beast? Beast would do this to a human being?"

Lemuel's arm moved, more a twitch, a spasm of a life expiring and not wanting to quit. A croak emanated from his throat. His mouth did not appear to move. "Father? Father . . . Help me."

Paul hovered over Lemuel and bent down. He extended his arm and touched Lemuel's swollen hand. Lemuel blinked in recognition. Paul bent lower, looking directly into Lemuel's eyes. "I am here, *Hermano.*"

"Help me." The voice receded into a synthesized gurgle.

Paul reached and drew the .40 caliber Smith and Wesson tucked into the waistband at the small of Grainger's back. Grainger swung his arm to avert the loss, but was too late.

Grainger stood up. "Give me the gun, Padre."

Paul dropped his eyes to Lemuel. "Not yet." He knelt down next to Lemuel and took his hand. He pressed the muzzle of the weapon against his heart and pulled the trigger. The weapon's report was muffled. Lemuel's body jerked slightly and then was still. The eyes stared at Paul.

Grainger reached over and took the gun.

Paul relinquished the weapon without resistance. He stood up, his eyes moving from Grainger to Rawlings. He shifted his gaze and locked onto Sloane. Her face was contorted as if she was being actively tortured. Her mouth was moving, but no sound came out. Paul pivoted his head to Leon. Leon's lips quivered, and his hands were shaking as if palsied. His eyes blinked like Morse code, but they would not focus. Paul returned to the still body. "I have become experienced at this." He looked at Rawlings and Grainger. "Soon I will stand with you." He blinked and sniffed once. "Besides. I know Lemuel. That was not Lemuel."

THE toll from the hand-inlaid-with-ivory grandfather clock had been expected, but it still startled Estaban. He jumped. He tried to conceal his response with other movements.

Estaban's reaction did not escape Sonja. "It is the hour, Estaban," she observed.

Estaban wrung his hands. He had washed them three times since returning from the desert. He focused on the clock. "Yes. Midnight."

Montezuma sat at the edge of a black leather couch, feeling its butter-smooth texture with his hand. "The night went well, then?" he said.

Estaban circled the oak table, which dominated the study. "Yes. It went well, as Sonja envisioned. We have delivered our messages. Twice. They should also receive the brother soon. They will succumb. I will have my money and the return of Raoul." He turned to Sonja. "Is that not right, my seer?"

The clock tolled solemnly again. "The hour is right for prediction and revelation," she offered.

Estaban stepped to the oak table. "Join us, my nihilistic friend, and behold your future."

Montezuma regarded Estaban with contemptuous curiosity. *An educated man giving credence to nonsense.* He pointed a slender finger at Sonja. "In Cuba, witch, you would be identified and arrested. Then you would be drawn and quartered and your dismembered pieces burned, for promulgating your peasant superstitions."

Sonja smiled. "Perhaps, Federico. In Cuba."

"Well?" said Estaban.

"Why not, Señor Rios. If for nothing else than to prove to you the emptiness of her promises and the blindness of her vision."

"Then come, join us."

Montezuma made his way to the table. Sonja withdrew her knife, a stiletto with a needle point. "Your finger, Señor Lorca." When Montezuma made no move in response, she smiled affably. "It is just a drop of blood. Perhaps you can only shed that of others?"

Montezuma seized her wrist and pulled her close to him. He wrested the knife from her grip. "If I am to shed my own blood, it will be I who administers the cut, not some charlatan practitioner of black arts." He jabbed the point into his thumb. A single drop of viscous, crimson liquid formed and dropped onto the table. He handed the instrument back, blade first.

Sonja reversed the blade and inserted it into her mouth. She closed her lips over the steel and slowly withdrew it, cleansing the metal as it emerged. Then Estaban produced his hand, and she pricked his thumb. A second spot of blood fell to the table. Sonja removed the leather pouch from around her neck and spilled the contents, scattering them across the blood spots: a rat's tail, the leg of a frog, two thin chicken bones, the intestines of a pig, a scorpion's barb, a rooster's beak, the fangs of a water moccasin.

Estaban sniffled. "Does Oggzn favor us? Do we please Olorun?"

She stared at the patterns. The scorpion's barb had fallen over Estaban's blood. The rat's tail superimposed itself, bisecting the elliptical drop of rapidly drying blood. She moved a delicate finger across the two chicken bones. She traced a pattern over them while humming to herself.

"Well," inquired Estaban, "what do they tell us?"

"They tell *you* nothing," she said.

Estaban blinked. "And you?"

"What do you perceive? About your blood? What are the superimposed omens?"

Estaban stared at the icons. "I see a rat's tail and what appears to be a scorpion's barb."

"And what do you see when you look at Lorca's blood?"

Estaban moved closer. "I see two thin bones of a chicken making an *X* over them."

"That is not an *X*."

"Then what," said Montezuma, "would you, in your vacuous shaman wisdom, call it?"

The santera circled the table. "A cross."

"A Catholic cross?" asked Estaban.

Sonja's teeth flashed. "No. Not a Christian cross."

"Enough of your games," shouted Montezuma.

"Yes. Tell us what you see," begged Estaban.

"Death is coming."

Estaban laughed, an apotropaic little titter. "To be sure. He comes to do our bidding, no—"

She lanced Estaban with her look. "Neither you, Estaban," she turned slowly to Montezuma, "nor you, Señor Lorca, have summoned him this time."

"Lies!" Montezuma swept the pieces of animal artifacts from the table with his arm. "You witch! I will swallow none of your fantasy superstitions. It is *I* who command death."

La Alma Negra retrieved the pieces that lay scattered on the floor and returned them to the leather container, all except the two chicken bones. She held them aloft in front of Montezuma's face. She chanted something, which she knew neither Lorca nor Rios understood. Her hands closed on each other, the two bones drawn to each other as if compelled. They merged at right angles and appeared locked, a cross dividing his face into quadrants. "You, Señor Lorca, shall see death coming."

TWENTY-EIGHT

THE sun rose from the depths of *el rio* and struggled momentarily, overcoming the resistance of a darkness bitterly refusing to yield. It sprang forth, as if propelled by a gigantic force, and lodged itself in the sky. Or so it appeared to the border patrolman who watched the river. He tried to be here in the morning, at his favorite spot, as often as possible. Sunrise always held more promise than sunset. You could almost be an optimist at six A.M. But there was another reason he was here this morning: the old man. He had seen him late last night through his Starlight Scope; the old guy sitting on a driftwood log at the water's edge when the mosquitoes were armed and organized into hunter-killer squadrons. He thought maybe the man was out jacklighting deer or fishing for sturgeon. So he stayed and watched. At two A.M. the old man was still there when the border patrolman packed it in, still wondering.

In a fifty-caliber ammunition can the patrolman had a tuna sandwich and a small thermos of sun tea he had brewed for himself. He wasn't some bleeding heart who picked up stray dogs or dropped guilty quarters into tin cups, but there was something about this guy. So, he found himself sliding down a sand berm toward the old codger with his ammo can filled with tea and tuna. The old guy was still there. *Maybe he's dead. A fella could die sitting up. Like that wet up in Lajitas back a few years ago. Remember him? Died on the shitter, sitting erect like he was just constipated or something.*

He circled around from a decent distance. *You never know. The guy might be one of those crazies who wants to commit suicide by cop. No sense taking a chance.* He carried the can in his left hand, his right free and brushing the Glock in its holster. His approach was circumspect. "Nice day, huh?" There was no response. *"Tu hablas Ingles, hombre?"* The old man shook his head. The border guardian nodded. *"Ningun problemas? Hambre?"*

Humberto turned his head. *"No problemas. Hambre? Sí. Poquito."*

The border patrolman set the ammo can at his feet and opened it. *"Para usted."*

Humberto looked up at him. There was a "thank you" somewhere in the grimness of his face.

"Digame, Señor. Que paso? Que estas asiendo aqui?"

Humberto turned back to the river, watching the somnambulant flow. *"Esperando,"* he said.

Waiting? Half the world is waiting for the other half or for its ship to come in. So, if this guy wanted to wait for whatever, more power to him. The interrogation was over.

Humberto Anaya looked down at the olive drab steel container. *"Muchas gracias por el almuerso."*

"Por nada, Señor."

THE border patrolman's boots sank deeply into the sand with every step on his return to where he had parked his truck. *Now I'm running a catering service, doing humanitarian rescues for the destitute. Christ!* The sand scoured the last bit of polish from the leather. *Well, I don't have to stand inspection. I must be getting soft and full of mushy sentimentality. What the hell. It was only some tea and a tuna sandwich on multigrain bread.* But he'd have to get that ammo can back. He kept his gun-cleaning equipment in there. He headed back to his house trailer to take a little siesta. It had been a long night, and he was up early.

* * *

IT was called *La Mercado Latino*. A small mom-and-pop store that carried items like consecrated candles and story magazines with titles like *Corazon Roto y un .45:* "Broken Hearts and a .45." A single overhead fan spun lazily, barely circulating the fetid air. The vegetables were wilted, the milk sour, and the bread stale, but the woman behind the register spoke *Español,* which was more important than whether the *Cheez-Its* were baked in this decade. Besides, it was better than anything available across the river.

The woman held a package of *tortillas de maize* in her hand, inspecting them for freshness. Satisfied, she dropped them into the plastic basket she carried. She moved to another shelf that displayed *salsa picante.* She picked up a bottle of *chile piquin.* Another hand reached for the bottle next to it.

Sloane McKenzie looked sideways up and down the aisle. There was no one around. *"Buenas dias, Rosa."* Rosa Fuentes put the bottle back. She was looking for another label. She unfolded her right hand and reached for the bottle of Tajin brand lemon-pepper seasoning. Then she moved laterally down the shelf. She seemed to be unaware of any presence.

When she had disappeared around the corner, Sloane picked up a piece of folded paper where the bottle had been. She palmed the paper and left the store.

Outside, Grainger was waiting for her. His eyes scanned the street, like a surveyor looking for irregularities. *So this is how she gets her intelligence.* He wondered if it was a dead drop or a contact. Sloane didn't say. He didn't ask. There was no need to know or to jeopardize agent security.

She came and stood alongside him. "I got what we need." They moved off, walking apart by ten feet. Grainger had asked her to keep separated, just in case.

Rosa Fuentes paid for her few purchases. She left the store. She was due to serve *almuerso,* across *el rio,* and Estaban Rios brooked no tardiness.

"**WE** can wait for the snake, or—"

"Or we can behead the viper in its nest," said Paul Teasdale.

Sloane let out her breath. "Yes." The *s* extended into a hiss.

"Then, if we're agreed, the operation's a go. The information we've obtained is thought reliable. Joey is being held in a room in Rios's whorehouse—brothel—across the river. The bulk of Rios's people will also be there celebrating their . . . successes. It's going to be payback time. We're going to have to hit them hard before the deadline Rios gave Paul runs. We can't let them get organized. We have to take it to them. The 'best defense' theory here happens to be correct. They outnumber us between six and ten to one, when you consider that this Warden Duran character has his riot suppression unit at Rios's disposal."

Sloane and Paul nodded in agreement.

"Myles will bring Raoul to the church tonight. Father Leon will make sure he stays comfortable and hidden. We'll move all the kids from the orphanage into the rectory until it's over. We've been immune from retaliation from Rios up to this time because of the Raoul insurance policy, but we can't count on it much longer. We hit the whorehouse tonight and minimize collateral damage as much as possible."

" 'Vengeance is mine; I will repay, saith the Lord,' " Paul shouted like a TV evangelist.

"Have we all gone mad?" said an apoplectic Leon. "Father Paul; is that you I hear? Where has reason fled?"

"Fled with the soul of Lemuel. Buried with the body of Felicia in an unmarked grave in the desert. That is where, Father Leon." Paul shook with a new intensity.

Leon trembled convulsively. The vision of last night had not left him. The horror overwhelmed him still. But now, it was only he who cautioned and preached discretion. "There must be other options to consider."

Paul snorted. "There are. We may kill some. Or we may kill many."

Leon reeled back. "Father. You are a man of God, a man of peace. Surely the Lord will understand your actions last night and forgive—"

"I am a *man*," Paul shouted. He tore his vestal collar from around his neck and dropped it on the floor at his feet. " 'Where now are all your high resolves at last?' Was it not you, Leon, who just a few days ago, counseled action, who was so eager to join in this adventure? Who accepted violence and embraced destruction? Was it not your voice raised in defense of the offense? Was it not you who entered this folly so lightly? Have you forgotten Exodus 21:12, Genesis 9:6, Romans 13:4, and Proverbs 6:17? Well, now I am your man of war. I have sold my garment for your sword. I am now your convert."

Sloane removed her badge and ID case from her pocket. She turned the black leather wallet in her hands. It fell down next to the collar.

Paul looked at her. "You know we have always known who you are."

"Yes. But today I also know who you are as well."

Leon looked at the collar and the badge. "Those are more easily removed than replaced."

Rawlings came through the front door of the church. He shrugged his shoulders and nodded.

Grainger waited until he had joined them. "I've got to look at a few things. I need to borrow your truck."

Sloane tossed him the keys.

"Final brief at twenty hundred. That's eight P.M.," Grainger said.

"I've got me some business to attend to myself," said Rawlings. "But I'll be back by dusk. Then we can get ready for the sudden death overtime."

"There is much to prepare," said Paul.

Grainger took a step toward the door but turned back. "Last night, Padre . . . You said Humberto was 'by the river.' What did you mean?"

Paul studied his swollen fingertips. "The Mexicans have a saying, a belief: 'If you wait by the river long enough, all your enemies will float by.' That is where Humberto waits."

Grainger nodded and headed for the door. *There wasn't going to be any overtime. Just sudden death.*

HE crossed the bridge unnoticed, driving Sloane's old pickup. Rios's gate watcher was half asleep under a banyan tree and failed to note his passage. *He's probably looking for the Dodge convertible*. A mile out of Punta Roja, he left the cratered paved road and drove onto the rutted dirt path that headed out into the Mexican desert. A thirty-minute drive brought him to La Vista Grande, *la ciudad de los muertos.*

Grainger parked the car and surveyed the ghost town on foot. He climbed the water tower for an overview. He inspected the buildings. He sighted avenues of approach, likely assembly and deployment areas, and potential lines of departure. He determined dead space and locations that offered cover and concealment. He selected tentative positions and alternate sites. Three hours later, he completed what he had come for. He returned to the pickup truck and left for the Devil's Boilers.

TWENTY-NINE

"**GODDAMN** it, Butler, did you leave the door unlocked again?" Buck Downs rattled the doorknob and pushed open the back door to the police station.

"No way, Buck. I locked it," said Officer Levon Butler. *I'll be damned. I'm never going to call the son of a bitch "Chief."*

Buck fell heavily into his creaking swivel chair that was crisscrossed with duct tape. "Sit down, boy, and take a load off your mind." Buck grinned. *You just need to know how to talk to his kind.* "Now, like I was saying, Butler, you going out there and shoot those two bastards down on sight like they was a broke-dick dog. Hear me?"

"I hear you, Buck. But what you're asking is wrong. If they broke the law, let's arrest them."

Buck surged to his feet. "Listen to what I'm saying, nigger. I ain't asking. I said, like mangy curs. It's open season. Our employer wants them dead, not alive."

Levon Butler's head throbbed. *This motherfucker would be burning crosses on lawns if he wasn't on a leash.* "I thought the *people* employed us."

Buck fell back into the chair. "Well, think again."

"They have a right—"

"To fuckin' die. Now, get out there and find them. Start at the church." Buck chewed on his inner cheeks. "You with me, Negro?"

Levon Butler backed out the front door of the station, his temples pulsing, barely containing a need to smash Buck's face.

Buck Downs grunted and looked up at his wall where he mounted all his trophies and memorabilia from his gunfighter contests. His gaze moved down the row of certificates of recognition and awards for the fastest draw. He had beaten some of the best. Down in El Paso he bested Richard "Tequila" Young on the balloon bust. And Young was one of the best. Out Fort Worth way he fired up Hunter Scott Anderson in the showdown and managed to edge that quick-shooting son of a gun. Nobody fanned a Peacemaker like old Buck. Buck squinted. One of his fast-draw rigs was missing from its peg: a black Buckheimer Vaquero with a four-and-three-quarter-inch Colt SA in its holster. Buck rocked forward in his chair, studying the empty space on the wall. *It better be just misplaced, or that jerk Butler is going to pay for it.*

In the adjoining jail, Rawlings listened to the exchange between Downs and his officer. He heard Butler leave. He listened to Buck creak back and forth in his chair. He heard him off-gas once loudly and after give a big satisfying sigh. A belch or two was followed by an off-key hum of an old Billy Ray Cyrus song. *Hell. All Billy Ray Cyrus songs are old.* Rawlings eased the connecting jail door open silently and watched Buck nodding off in his chair, feet on his desk. An RC Cola and a jar filled with peanuts sat on his desk next to a half-eaten Moon Pie and an open bag of pork rinds. "Howdy, Sheriff."

Buck Downs opened his eyes incrementally as his brain computed the information. When recognition came, he bolted from his seat and spun around. "You. You bastard. Now you're mine. You're fucked."

Rawlings's grin extended to the farthest expanses of his mouth. An unlit cheroot was clamped between his teeth. "No, Sheriff. You're fucked. But I'm here to see you get unfucked."

Buck's eyes followed the gravitational flow but stopped at Rawlings's hips. Buck's Buckheimer fast-draw rig and Colt were strapped on and tied low. Buck's face glowed, and his teeth shone dull yellow. "So, you want to give it a try, huh? Is that it?" Buck he-hawed. "I eat punks like you for breakfast."

"Hope you're real hungry, Sheriff." Rawlings motioned to the other revolvers and cowboy rigs that hung on the wall. "I didn't take your favorite, now, did I? I was hoping for an Ojala, but see you've got no taste."

The knowing mention of Arvo Ojala flashed in Buck's mind for an instant. It should have told him something; but nothing dampened his enthusiasm. He turned and walked to the wall. "You ain't gonna shoot me in the back like Bob Ford, that dirty little coward that shot poor Jesse James, are you?"

"Not till you've had the opportunity to eat breakfast, Sheriff."

Downs slid a holster and a Third Generation Single Action Army Colt revolver from the wall. It had Colt Custom Shop ivory grips with a nice patina. The trigger was tied back. Buck was a fanner.

Downs buckled on the fast-draw outfit and tied the holster low on his leg with the rawhide thong that dangled from the holster. "Let's step out back into the alley. I don't want your blood all over my newly decorated office."

Rawlings bowed and waved his arm toward the back door. "*Apres vous.*" Buck edged to the door, and Rawlings followed closely, not wanting to lose sight of him. He let Downs walk down the alley. Twenty paces out, he turned back and faced Rawlings. Myles stepped away from the framing doorway. He flipped off the holster's leather loop that secured the hammer. "Your move, Sheriff." The cheroot slid across his mouth from left to right.

Buck stared at his opponent. He didn't appear scared. But that was only because he just didn't know who he was dealing with. His tongue parted his thin lips. He knew he was fast; but he hadn't really killed anybody. Yet. Well, today was the day. *It couldn't be any different than killing a lame horse.* And Buck had done that a couple of times. *Anyway, this is going to be worth lots of brownie points with Rios.* Buck glared at the gunfighter. *He still looks calm.* "You ready to die, mister?"

Rawlings's arm hung loose, his fingertips just brushing the leather of the holster, palm nudging the knurled grips. *No. I'm not ready to die. Leastwise not today.* He spat out the cheroot. "Slap leather, Wyatt."

Buck bent at the knees a split second before his gun hand seized the Colt and pulled it from the holster in one smooth, synchronized motion. He brought the gun level while swinging his left hand across his chest, moving in the opposite direction. Pushing his gun hand forward and his fanning hand rearward, the palm of his left hand caught the serrated hammer and moved it to full cock. But the trigger was tied down. As Buck's left hand continued on past, the unlocked hammer started to fall. Someone punched Buck in the chest—hard—just as the .45 Long Colt round fired.

Rawlings keyed on Buck's version of the Paladin combat crouch. His own hand molded over the revolver's grip, and he began the withdrawal sequence. But, instead of leaning forward, Rawlings leaned back. He didn't need to push the gun forward to meet his other hand. His thumb had cocked the weapon before it cleared the holster. As the front sight emerged from the leather, he leveled the gun and pulled the trigger. Rawlings's 250-grain, high-tin-content lead bullet, which Buck himself had cast from melted-down old tire balance weights, was en route before Buck's hammer caused primer ignition.

The heavy slug impacted Buck Downs's center mass, knocking him backward. His gun fell from his hand, and he sagged to his knees. Blood spread in a widening stain on his shirt, and bubbles ruptured through the star-shaped hole. Tiny red balloons dribbled from the edges of his mouth as Buck sank back onto his haunches.

Rawlings spun the gun around his trigger finger, catching it with a full grip. He stepped in front of Buck, who was wheezing now. A hideous whistling sound emanated from his chest; a fatal sucking chest wound. Rawlings spun the six-gun's cylinder.

Buck struggled to a kneeling position and placed his hand on his chest. Blood flowed unstemmed from between his fingers. His eyes weren't focusing. "You killed me."

Rawlings nodded.

Buck's groan of disappointment transitioned into a death rattle as he fell forward into the dirt of the alley.

"Hold it right there. Don't move. Drop the gun," said the warbling voice.

Rawlings dropped the gun back into the holster.

"I said drop it, not reholster."

Rawlings turned. "Sorry. I hate dropping a firearm in the dirt. Deputy Butler, right?"

"*Officer* Butler. And I said drop it. Take that gun out of your . . ." He used his other hand and arm like a torsion bar to keep from shaking. "*No.* Leave it."

"Officer. You heard what his orders were. He was going to have my partner and me shot down like dogs in the street. Is that your way? In the back?"

Levon's Smith and Wesson .357 Magnum Model 28 Highway Patrolman revolver wobbled in his hand.

"He drew first, Officer. Come on. You've seen *Gunsmoke* reruns."

Levon found himself nodding in agreement. He frantically groped for reconciliation, searching logic for salvation. *This doesn't look or sound like self-defense, not exactly, anyway. No, it's something else.* Then it came to him. Maybe it wasn't part of the Texas Criminal Statutes, but he was making it controlling law. *Levon's Law. That's what applies here, and it's a complete bar to prosecution. Justifiable homicide. The deceased needed killing. They should codify that and call it the Needs Killing Defense. People—leastwise in Texas—could understand that.* He lowered the gun.

Rawlings unbuckled the gun belt and let it drop. "I'll be going now, Officer. I guess you're the new chief." He turned and walked down the alley, disappearing into the shadows.

Levon expelled a pent-up breath. "Hey," he yelled. "What should I do with Buck?"

The voice floated back to him from the shadows. "Bury him with his trophies."

Levon circled the body. He began humming a song that came to him. His hum took voice, and he was singing; maybe more like the recital of a prose poem in the clipped rhythms of rap. "He shot the sheriff; but he did not shoot the deputy down. . . . Yeah." He removed Buck's gun belt. *Have to drag his fat ass out of the middle of the alley. Don't want Jepson's Feed and Grain truck to run over old Buck before the county coroner gets a chance to have a look. "Shot down by an unknown assailant."* That was the way he figured it and the way the report was going to read. *Buck just made the big mistake of drawing down on the Grim Reaper, and he came in second. Second was always the first loser.*

THIRTY

RIOS'S house of ill repute stood alone, a quarter mile past the edge of the shanties and shacks of Punta Roja. Surrounded by desert on three sides, and all things considered, it was well maintained and landscaped nicely. A circular driveway graced the exterior, and two pillars framed the front entrance. Labor was cheap and replenishable. The overhead was low, the profits high and, best of all, the competition was nonexistent.

"*Compadres. Bienvenidos* to the finest little whorehouse in all of Mexico . . . *Mine.*"

There was a smattering of obligatory laughter. Estaban Rios sat on top of the bar. Behind him, Jaime Escalante lethargically wiped bar glasses. Sonja, Montezuma, Servando Chavez, Warden Duran, Ramirez, the Barretto brothers, and Maximo "Coco" Pedraza aka *El Cirujano:* all the king's men turned to the sovereign.

"You have done well, and soon we will be back on track. Tonight, your money is worthless. My beverages and my hospitality are yours, in anticipation of the return of my money and, of course, Raoul. The house is closed tonight to all outsiders in your honor." He bowed deeply. There was more applause and a few "Bravos" heard from the claque. "Enjoy yourselves, *muchachos.* I release you to your pleasures."

Montezuma's contempt was mixed with amusement. Rios's minions were barbarians when sophisticated tacticians were needed. When the showdown came, they would be cannon fodder, target practice. He ambled to the bar and demanded Pernod with orange juice.

Escalante groped under the bar for the dusty bottle of Pernod liqueur. Montezuma was the only one who drank the licorice-accented beverage. Escalante had previously concluded only a *maricon* would drink the stuff; but then there was this Lorca. Jaime had changed his mind. As he mixed in the *jugo de naranja,* he thought he might even give it a try himself.

Estaban motioned for Ramirez and Duran to join him. "Have you seen my *comandante de policia,* that police chief impersonator? It is the best police department money can buy, and where is he?"

Duran shrugged, and Ramirez shook his head.

"I pay that *baboso* Downs far too much for the services he delivers. He knew about tonight's festivities. His absence speaks richly of the disrespect I have noticed from him lately."

"Perhaps, Estaban, it speaks richly of other possibilities," said Montezuma, materializing like a ghost.

Rios focused a jaundiced eye toward Montezuma. "Oh? You have other theories?"

"Certainly, Señor Rios. I have theories. But you do not pay me to theorize. Perhaps you might inquire of your . . . theorist." He shifted his gaze onto Sonja, who sat at a table in the corner. "She specializes in . . . theorizing."

Estaban did not want confrontation, even intellectual confrontation; at least not tonight. The night was young. "I shall, Señor Lorca. I shall do that." He pursed his lips. "But what do you think of our successes so far? Of tonight's celebration?"

Lorca took a sip of his drink. "Successes?"

"Yes," said Estaban. "We have taken effective action by delivering our messages and our ultimatums. It is a matter of time; as in, tomorrow."

"Celebrate when your enemies are cold and buried. I see your actions as nothing but desperate reactions. You are playing a game of catch-up. They lead, and you follow."

"We've clipped their wings," fired Estaban.

Montezuma bellowed a laugh. "You've clipped their toenails, señor."

Estaban felt the stomach acid churn, but he betrayed none of his emotions. *If he were anybody else, I would have him flailed. But this one . . .* "If you are so confident in your predictions, why not a little wager?" He waited for a reaction from Montezuma. There was none. "Well. I propose doubling your stipend for two months. If we do not have everything accomplished within two days from now, you win." He examined his fingernails. "On the other hand, should we accidentally be successful . . . Then, I profit. You relinquish your compensation for that same period as token atonement. That is, unless you feel less than confident."

Montezuma rotated his hand swirling his drink. *El Dedo del Diablo is still alive. It isn't a wager. It's theft.* "Done, señor." He moved his fingertips to his brow and flipped them outward in a mock salute, memorializing the arrangement. *Perhaps Servando and I will be hunting soon.*

Estaban tipped his glass to Montezuma, consummating the bet, before turning away. Estaban rethought about Buck Downs's nonappearance. Perhaps he deserved the benefit of the doubt. *Downs may have been successful in hunting down and killing those two. That better be his excuse.* He turned to find Sonja, but she was gone. Estaban rallied himself against all doubt. *Yes, tomorrow is the day.* He crossed the floor of the whorehouse. *A brisk walk to the hacienda followed by a stroll among the lilies in the garden.*

SONJA Ochoa unbarred the cross member that secured the heavy oaken door. It creaked on rusty hinges as it opened. She entered and descended the steep ramp to the dank bottom. It was an old wine cellar. Moisture condensed on the moldy walls. Empty bottles and trash littered the floor. Joey sat in the middle of the room on a throw rug, manipulating a pencil on some paper. He looked up when she entered and then went back to working on the paper.

Sonja stood over him, peering down at his drawings. She considered the series of circles. Each contained two bisecting lines, perpendicular to each other. The circles were superimposed over figures; stick figures for the most part, but several were fleshed out with puffy arms and bigger-than-life legs. Some had hats; most had poles or weapons.

Joey ignored the woman. He had seen her on several occasions since he had been kidnapped. They fed him regularly, and the food was at least as good as at the orphanage. He was lonely, but was used to entertaining himself with a bare minimum. He would be returning; of that he was sure. She just stood there, so he said, "Hello."

"Are these the things you see when you dream?" Sonja said.

"I just draw because I'm bored. Jaime said it was okay. He gave me the paper," he added quickly.

She studied the drawings. "They are very interesting."

"I'd just like to go home."

"You are home."

"I don't live here. I'm sort of scared being by myself."

Sonja looked once more at the circles and crosses with the crisscrossed figures. "We are—each of us—all alone together." She turned and moved back up the ramp. Halfway to the top, she was stopped by the voice.

"Hey!"

Sonja turned around.

Joey held up a sheet of paper to her. His index finger lay across one of the more elaborate and detailed figures encircled by the ring and superimposed with the cross. He smiled at her in innocence. "This one is you."

"**SLOANE** will stay with what she's familiar: the Beretta and the MP-5. Myles will take the under-folder AK and the Remington 870 (Witness Protection) cut-down twelve-gauge in the shoulder holster. I go with the M-4." Grainger shifted to Paul. "This material is a little out of your line of work."

Paul looked over the firearms laid out on the rectory floor.

This was all new to him, but he burned with an unrelenting fury. Given a choice, he wished he did not exist. But, if wishes were horses, beggars would ride. So, he pointed to an exotic-looking thing that looked space age. "How about that one?"

Grainger picked up the green, synthetic-stocked Steyr AUG assault rifle. "Okay; it's a good weapon. The caliber is 5.56 mm, and it has an overhanging bolt principal—similar to the Uzi—which makes it compact. The rifle has selective fire, available by manipulating this square piece here. Halfway in is semiautomatic, and pushed all the way through is rock and roll, full auto. The safety is all the way to the right. You can use the one-point-five power dot-reticle scope or the iron sights." He hefted the piece and handed it to Paul. "I'm sorry there won't be any time to practice."

"Not to worry. God will guide his bullets," Leon snorted.

Paul seemed not to hear.

Rawlings came through the back curtain. "Didn't start without me, did you?"

"Ordnance distribution only, partner. How'd it go?"

"You know, there is a certain satisfaction unobtainable anywhere else, beating a man at his own game."

Grainger suspected what Rawlings had intended. "So, you paid your respects?"

"I just adjusted the world's balance; covered our six."

"Any problems?"

"Nope. But we've ushered in a new era of law enforcement in Zapata."

GRAINGER lay on Sloane's bed. He had asked to be alone, so she stayed with the children. A small table lamp illuminated the room. He held two pieces of paper in his hands: the external ballistic tables for the .338 Lapua Magnum. His eyes were closed, but his mind was active: *Zeroed at five hundred meters. Bullet trajectory: ten inches high at one hundred meters, sixteen inches high at two hundred, fourteen inches high at three hundred meters, ten inches high at four hundred meters. At six hundred meters, eighteen inches low . . . one thousand meters, one hundred eighty inches low.* Grainger's recitations were more than an exercise in memory enhancement. Every worthy sniper is capable—given sufficient time and opportunity of configuring—"doping in"—his scope so he can hold directly on the target at any estimated range. However, in a fluid, target-rich environment, the capability to shift and engage multiple targets rests with the shooter's ability to hold over (or under) the target, while compensating for the fluctuating ranges and environmental data as they are presented to him, all with his computerized mind. It's known as Kentucky windage.

Grainger understood that the line of sight is an absolutely straight line into infinity—or as far as the eye can see, unaided or assisted. But a bullet responds to other influences. In order to hit the target, a bullet is lobbed, i.e., it rises and then falls into the target. It has a trajectory. Thus, knowing the midrange trajectory is important. That is the highest point a bullet will rise on its way to the target. The fired projectile intersects the line of sight twice. Depending on the zeroed range, but at approximately twenty-five meters from the muzzle, the bullet rises up into the LOS. It continues to rise and falls back, intersecting the LOS the second time (hopefully) at the zero point. Even with the flattest shooting rifles, at a thousand meters, the trajectory of the bullet resembles more a rainbow than a bowstring.

Grainger lay there memorizing, recalling, and factoring: *Minutes of angle. Up/down compensation formulas. The mil-dot is measured from center to center and equals 1/1000th the distance to the target. Quarter-half-full value windage hold-offs. Moving target holds and leads.*

"Walking lead, three hundred meters—add seven inches for ninety-degree angle with a three mph pace." He was speaking out loud.

The door opened with a creak.

Sloane peered in cautiously. "I've been listening at the door. It sounded like you were talking to yourself. Can I come in?"

Grainger sat up. "Sure. And I was."

She shut the door behind her. "You sound like the *Cincinnati Kid.* Remember Steve McQueen going over the card mathematical probabilities?"

"I think so. Wasn't that with Jackie Gleason or something?"

She sat down on the bed. "No. That was *The Hustler* with Paul Newman. It was about pool, not cards."

"Oh, yeah. That's right."

"I'm scared," she said.

He swung his legs onto the floor. "I'd be worried if you weren't." He touched her on the arm. "I'd still prefer if you weren't coming along."

"No. I'm coming. But I'm petrified. I'm so scared that my guts turn to Jell-O every time I think about it. But right now, it's the only thing that interrupts my nightmare seeing Lemuel like that and picturing Sister Felicia."

"Push it back in your mind."

"Is that what you do?"

"No. But they tell me I'm one of the two percent."

"Two percent?"

"Military psychological version of the two percent theory. Two percent of advertising solicitations receive response. Two percent of the people will buy anything if it's packaged right. Two percent of motorcycle riders are outlaws—"

"What's the military version?"

He ran his hands back through his hair. "Just some shrink's speculation that two percent of military men—or about a tenth of a percent of the general population—are unaffected by pangs of conscience or incapacitating fears of death and death dealing. They have an innate disposition—"

"A killer instinct?"

"I think that was the phrase they used."

"Is that you?"

"I just like to think of myself as a—"

"Survivor?"

"Prevailer."

"Maybe you need one to be the other." She got up. "I'll leave you alone. I know you have things to do. I'm going to finish loading magazines."

"Okay. We'll be leaving out around twenty-one hundred. Nine o'clock."

She opened the door. "I'll try to be ready." The door closed behind her.

He lay back down. *Range times velocity of the wind divided by ten equals the number of one-half-minute clicks for a full value crosswind . . .* The computer filed another entry.

"WILL you get Joey back?" Ponce stood in front of Rawlings. It was Lemuel's room, and the only word that described it was *stark*. The centerpiece was an unfinished wooden bed with no box springs, a flattened mattress, and a single wool army blanket. On the opposite wall hung a picture of Christ staring down at a chipped pine dresser sitting on a cracked floor.

Rawlings slipped another round of twelve-gauge number four buckshot into the elastic loops on the canvas bandolier. "We're going to give it the old college try."

"You are going to come back. Right?"

Rawlings slipped another red shell into the loop and placed the belt down on the bed. "I'm going to try real hard in that department, too."

"I wish I was old enough to go with you. I'd like to kill them all."

Rawlings grabbed Ponce by the arm. "It's not like a computer game, son. Maybe you'll be lucky and never find yourself having to make these kinds of decisions."

"I'm not afraid, Mr. Rawlings."

Rawlings released his grip on Ponce's arm. "I never thought you were. Dealing with the fear is the easy part."

Ponce sat at the edge of the bed. "Are you afraid of dying, sir?"

Rawlings picked up a loose shell. "Did you ever watch *The Twilight Zone*? I used to watch reruns in the day room at Bragg sometimes."

"Brag? Day room?"

"Fort Bragg, North Carolina. Day room is kind of a recreation spot when you're off duty. They have cable television and all."

"We don't have cable."

"Yeah, I guess not. Well, anyway, *The Twilight Zone* . . . You know . . . 'There is a fifth dimension beyond that which is known to man. A dimension of sight and sound.' " He gave it his best Rod Serling, but Ponce looked vacant. "The only episode I really remember was one with Robert Redford—he's an actor.

This old lady lives alone in a New York tenement, and it's snowing; cold and a real blizzard. She's afraid of dying and won't open her door to anyone. Then she hears shots and a noise at her door. It's a cop, and he's been shot. He's hurt real bad—dying maybe—and he begs to be let in to get out of the cold. The old lady is afraid. She suspects the truth, I think, but she's not going to let the policeman die on her stoop."

"So, what happens?" asked Ponce.

"She lets him in."

"She saved the police officer?"

"It wasn't a policeman. It was Death in disguise."

"He cheated the old woman?"

"No, that's where you're wrong. It was just her time. He consoled her and showed her the way. He calmed her fears. Dying should come as natural as living."

"Then what happened?"

"Robert Redford puts his hand on the old lady, and she goes. She dies peacefully."

"What did it mean?"

"I don't know; maybe that the fear of death and dying is worse than the actual experience. The policeman comes knocking for all of us sometime."

Ponce nodded, considering. "But what if you don't die peacefully, like the old woman in that story? Does the policeman still come for you anyway?"

Rawlings stood up and stretched. "Hell no, son. In that case they send the SWAT team." He cuffed Ponce lightly on the head. "Come on. You have any Cokes in this place?"

"No," said Ponce.

"Okay," said Rawlings, "then I'll buy you a glass of water." He disappeared out the door.

Ponce followed, wondering if one SWAT team would be enough.

THEY gathered in the church: Grainger, Rawlings, Paul, and Sloane. Leon would stay behind. They carried their weapons in cases or wrapped in blankets. Mission essential items only.

"No speeches from *Henry V*, Mr. Grainger?" said Leon.

"No sermons or Knute Rockne pep talks are necessary," said Grainger.

" 'All that is required for evil to flourish is for good men to do nothing,' " said Paul. "Edmund Burke." He knelt at the rail and closed his eyes. "First we pray, Mr. Rawlings. And then we kill."

Rawlings didn't know whether he should bow his head or laugh. The priest looked like he was meditating. *Is he asking for forgiveness or a good body count?* Rawlings was still wondering when the night swallowed up the four of them.

THIRTY-ONE

THE U. S. border patrolman sat on an overturned pail along a hollowed-out sand ridge in the middle of the trail that led to the only shallow-water ford across the river for two miles in either direction. He tapped the crystal of his luminescent watch and then brought up the Starlight Scope to conduct another sweep of the water; for what, he wasn't quite sure. He wasn't looking for anything or anyone. Maybe it was just habit. *Maybe . . . Turn in early tonight. Check out the old man by the river tomorrow.*

He spun around in response to the approaching footsteps. *Friend or foe? Either/or. Nothing in between.* Paul, the priest, was coming toward him with shadows trailing behind.

Grainger made out the form of the border patrolman sitting astride the path to the river ford, the only reasonable access route across the border, except for the bridge. There was no time for circumspection.

Paul led the way to where the patrolman sat. The others stopped twenty yards from the bucket.

"Evening, Father Paul. Nice night."

Paul looked reflexively at the night sky. "Yes. Orion and the Crab are fairly distinct."

The border patrolman looked past the priest, at the three figures standing in the darkness. "You might invite your friends to the party. I don't arrest anybody for sneaking *into* Mexico." He laughed a little. "Say . . . Is there a fight tonight? Are you fighting again tonight?"

"Yes. I am fighting tonight." Paul waved at the three shadows.

The border patrolman struggled up from his bucket and watched the three figures approach. "Howdy."

"Good evening, Officer," said Sloane.

The patrolman tipped his baseball cap. He eschewed the Smokey Bear hat that was the official USBP cover. "Miss McKenzie. I didn't recognize you in the dark." He noticed the hardware the four carried. Although covered in blankets and other coverings, the rifles were hard to miss. "Y'all got something special going on across the river I should know about?"

"Nothing special," said Sloane. "There's a little fiesta going on at El Paraiso. You'll probably hear about it."

El Paraiso? What's a nice female like this . . . ? Shit! She's carrying at least one long gun or shotgun . . . Damn! I'm an officer of the law; I should do something.

"We have to go," said Paul, taking a few tentative steps toward the river.

"The bridge is a lot drier, I hear," offered the patrolman. He shifted his balance from one foot to the other. Indecision racked his brain.

"We prefer the river," said Paul.

"I guess I was just worrying about you a little, Father Paul."

Grainger slipped slowly past the border guardian, one eye tracking him.

Paul entered the water. When ankle deep, he turned around. "I wouldn't worry. God is with us tonight."

The border patrolman watched the four dematerialize into the undulating waves of mist that rose off the water's surface. The great river was prehistoric. He rested his hand on the handle of his holstered Glock 17. *Fight? My ass. They're going to war.* He took two steps toward the river and stopped. He remembered what he'd been told: "It's a Mexican national problem. Mind your own business and focus on your job description." He smiled to himself and retreated to his bucket. He shined his flashlight on his watch. According to his own flextime schedule, in ten minutes he would be off duty. *Fuck it.* He sat down and lit up a Marlboro.

"**THEY** call me Duster, amigo. You know why they call me Duster?" Jaime Escalante was sampling his personal creation alcoholic concoctions in large quantity tonight. On an ordinary evening Señor Rios would have had him flogged for that breach; but tonight had been declared a fiesta. He swayed, a bit unsteady on his feet, standing on the wooden platform that kept his feet out of the water behind the bar.

"Let me think . . ." Pepe Barretto leaned across the bar, flanked by his two brothers. "Okay. I got it. You work as a maid in your spare time, no?"

Mario convulsed with laughter and slapped the wet bar with a huge open palm. Water spurted into the air, splattering Jaime Escalante.

"Like holy water," shouted Pepe.

Navarro Barretto held up his fused left hand. "Hey, Duster, bring me another *cerveza. Por favor.*" All three brothers laughed.

Pepe pointed a crooked finger at Jaime. "Do I get another guess?" He punched Navarro in the shoulder and winked. "Hey. This time I guess it for sure." He whirled back to Escalante. "You put flake up your nose. Angel dust."

Mario's hand came down again, shaking the bar.

Escalante scowled and backed away to the cooler. He removed a Pacifico beer and slid it across to Navarro. They were all *babosos*. Slugs. Idiots. Not worth his time. He left the brothers chortling among themselves. Escalante straightened his shoulders. He was called Duster because he had killed a man in Guadalajara "for insulting my lady," as he told the story. The truth was, a drunk had looked at his scarred face and called him "Hiroshima." Escalante had, in his words, "canceled the *vato;*"

blasted him with a shotgun, his weapon of choice and similar to the room broom he kept under the bar.

Jaime "Duster" Escalante's reputation was self-proclaimed and self-perpetuated. *Fuck the Barretto brothers.* He turned and watched as Montezuma crossed the room and went down the stairs to where the boy was kept. Watching the kid was Jaime's job. But he wasn't going to say anything to that man under any circumstances. *Not in this lifetime.*

Ramon Zamudio, Felipe Aguirre, Rafael Alarcon, and Nero Ramirez played poker at a round table in the center of the room.

"Flush." Ramirez grinned. He slapped down his hand and swept the four thousand pesos from the table into his sombrero. "Another lesson from the headmaster."

"You cheated," scowled Zamudio.

"Smile when you say that, *compadre.* I have killed men for less." Ramirez could have been smiling.

"Hey, Zamudio. He didn't even deal the hand, so *callate,*" said Aguirre.

Ramirez stood up. "Since the *panocha* is on the house tonight, I will indulge myself. And leave your measly pesos as a tip." He headed up the staircase to the second floor.

"She won't be as tight as that little beardless clam last night," yelled Agurrie.

Ramirez waved him off. *Theresa in Room Three.* She was his favorite, and tonight *libre.*

Two other of Rios's men entered the bar through the front door. Raymundo Bolano and Chuy Santee were called *Los Centinelas,* The Sentinels. They were, along with Escalante, the bouncers for El Paraiso. Large, mirthless men who thought nothing of breaking the arm of a harmless drunk or the neck of a combative one, they sometimes provided personal security for Estaban Rios. They were both particularly proud of that fact. Tonight, because there were no regular patrons to cower before them, they were off duty. Santee brought a bottle of bourbon to a table. "Bring me a woman," roared Bolano.

A diminutive female in a peasant dress slid down the banister. Bolano watched her through narrow-slit eyes. He stroked his mouth with the back of his hand. It was going to be a good night.

Jaime wiped his hands on his apron as Montezuma reappeared from below. He had that kid with him and was leading him out. "Hey!" The exclamation escaped his mouth before fear triggered discretion. Montezuma stopped and fixed him with an icy glare. Escalante swallowed, shrugged, smiled, and shook his head. He swore that Montezuma's eyes glowed red, like the Terminator in the video he had seen. He shivered. *Good riddance. You take care of feeding the kid. Maybe that Montezuma was a pederast. Probably was. His type always is something.*

Montezuma pulled the boy again to the front door, looked back for a moment, and then was gone.

Escalante slid down the bar to *El Cirujano,* who was drinking alone at the end of the bar. "Are you a real surgeon, hombre?"

Maximo "Coco" Pedraza threw down his whiskey in one gulp. *"Sí,"* he said. "A doctor of the truth. Some deliver babies; I deliver pain." He lifted his empty glass in a mock salute.

Escalante turned away. Pedraza was no better than the Barrettos. Someone yelled, *"Musica!"* Jaime marched to the jukebox, plugged it in, and kicked the device. Madonna started to sing some song about *La Isla Bonita* and Spanish lullabies, all with an atrocious accent. "Kill the *gringa,*" shouted Raymundo Bolano.

Mario Barretto rose up and grunted. His chair flew back and tipped over. He made a circle with his thumb and index finger of one hand. He poked the middle finger of the other hand in and out, pumping the hole. Navarro glanced up at him as the mammoth Mario rumbled toward the stairs. "Try not to soil your *pantalones* this time, little brother."

The Barretto brothers laughed. They always laughed together.

The swinging doors at the front of the bar parted slowly, and a man stepped into the room.

Escalante balled up his soiled towel and threw it onto the bar. "Hey hombre; can't you read? *Cerrado.* That means closed in your language."

Zamudio drew to an inside straight and got a deuce when he needed a ten. He cursed under his breath. He folded his cards and looked over at the gringo. *Brown Yanqui cowboy hat. Gray duster. Scars. Don't look like no tourist.*

The tall man strode to the bar, head down, hat covering the upper half of his face.

"Maybe he don't speak English," said Zamudio, expelling a cackling laugh.

"Maybe he just don't speak," said Navarro Barretto, leaning back in his chair. "Hey, gringo. You deaf? Dumb? Or both? What you want?"

Grainger raised his head and scanned the room. "A drink," he said, edging to the bar.

"What you want, *Americano?*" said Escalante.

Grainger's eyes focused on the neon beer signs hanging behind the bar. "Superior. In the bottle."

Escalante looked past Grainger toward the others, for advice. Ramirez would know, but he was upstairs. Aguirre shrugged. Jaime found a bottle of Superior and set it in front of Grainger.

"You gonna open it?"

Escalante flashed a crooked smile. "Ooh. You want an *open* bottle of beer? Why don't you say so?" He put the bottle opener on the cap and sprang it at the gringo.

Grainger batted the cap away and watched the foam ooze out of the bottle.

"Anything else you want? Amigo." *The motherfucker thinks he's Clint Eastwood.*

Grainger jerked his head toward the jukebox. "Yeah. Can you play 'La Bamba'?

Escalante stopped his fidgeting. "We don't play no 'La Bamba.' "

Zamudio stood up slowly.

Grainger pushed away from the bar. "No 'La Bamba'? Now, that really chaps my hide." He watched the room behind him in the mirror. The one standing up was easing his coat back. He spun with a fluid motion, sweeping the duster aside, and shot the hostile threat six times with the M-4 assault rifle on semiautomatic. The 5.56-millimeter bullets ripped through the chest cavity.

Zamudio tumbled backward over his chair, a spray of blood covering the almost straight he was holding.

Escalante's heart stopped in midbeat. *The motherfucker is Clint Eastwood.*

Then came the explosion.

RAWLINGS listened at the back door. He heard Grainger's voice. He opened a cardboard suitcase and took out three pieces of Styrofoam, each two feet by two feet, hinged together with duct tape into an accordion tri-fold. Affixed to the foam was detonating cord they had brought with them all the way from California. The primacord, as it was referred to in its civilian form, ran in reversing parallel lines across the breadth of all three sections that formed the prepared expedient door-breaching demolition charge. Rawlings twisted the exposed ends of an electrical line running from a Claymore generator to an M-6 military blasting cap itself tied in to the detonating cord at a bight. He stuck the Styrofoam to the locked back door utilizing duct tape, which was folded in half to create two-sided adhesion. He pressed the boards into place on the door. "Get around the corner. When it goes, we go. Remember, don't mask each other's fire."

Sloane's heart pounded fiercely, as if it would burst the bounds of her chest. She clutched the Heckler and Koch MP5-A3, its collapsible stock now extended and cradled under her arm. *God. I'm scared.*

Paul wiped his forehead with the barrel of the AUG. Two pistols were tucked into his belt. His mouth trembled but not from fear. He didn't know what he was doing. It didn't matter. There was a trigger and there was his finger. *Nero Ramirez. Ramon Zamudio. Felipe Aguirre. Rafael Alarcon. The Barretto brothers . . . Judgment Day.*

Rawlings heard the six rhythmic shots. He took a breath and depressed the Claymore generator. The explosion sent a ball of fire cascading into the main bar area. Then it recoiled, boiling back to its point of origin as if retracted by a steel spring. The wooden door splintered, sending shards of razor slivers hurtling through the air. One of them impaled Raymundo Bolano in the forehead. He staggered back, looking like a devolved unicorn. Rawlings fired his twelve gauge, killing the screaming man. Bolano's chest absorbed forty number-four buck pellets that passed on through, blowing out his back. Rawlings rolled with the recoil and pumped three rounds of buckshot into a lone figure standing at the far end of the bar.

El Cirujano crashed among wood splinters and flying glass.

Sloane followed on Rawlings's heels. She saw her first target standing next to the first one Rawlings dropped at the card table. He was pulling a pistol from his belt. She squeezed the trigger on the MP-5. Some of that old DEA training was coming back to her. The submachine gun rattled briefly, then quit. *Malfunction! Say it isn't so, Lord.* Sloane dropped the gun on its assault sling strapped around her neck and shoulders. She transitioned to her Beretta M-92F even as she realized there had been no malfunction. She had emptied the thirty-round magazine, more or less, into the target.

Chuy Santee lay sprawled on his back, his head a grotesque pulverized rag, wedged against the bar. A dozen playing cards fluttered down over his body. His mother wouldn't have recognized him.

Sloane hurled over a dead body that blocked her path of advance.

Jaime Escalante's muscles wouldn't respond. Still behind the bar, he stared at the back of the *gringo* who had just killed Zamudio. He eyed the twelve-gauge coach gun that lay on the shelf under the bar. His eyes flicked back and forth. Then the explosion and the *Yanqui* disappeared from sight. Jaime dove for the decking. He reached up and retrieved the shotgun. Cocking both exposed hammers, he reared back up. The gringo was also up and shooting at someone in the room. His back was again toward Jaime. Bodies were falling. Figures were running. Jaime raised the shotgun.

Paul squeezed the trigger on the Steyr. Nothing happened. He pointed the assault rifle at Felipe Aguirre and tried again. Aguirre dove behind the opposite end of the bar.

"Safety's on !" Rawlings screamed at Paul as a bullet plowed up the table in front of him.

Paul jammed his finger onto the safety and thrust it all the way to the end. He turned the gun and shot the wounded Rafael Alarcon in the head with a twenty-round burst. Alarcon had been crawling along the floor. He collapsed, arms and legs splayed out like a scarecrow. Paul forgot how to eject the magazine. He sat on the floor, struggling with the rifle.

The man came through the open front door on the run and panting heavily. He raised the Winchester Model 94 .44 Magnum lever action rifle to his shoulder and got off a snap shot at the first person he saw whom he hadn't talked to that night.

The .44 Magnum slug caught Escalante in the right temple. One microsecond before he was anticipating hammer fall and the pleasure of killing the *Yanqui.* A brilliant flash of celestial light filled his head for the briefest of moments. Jaime Escalante spun three times and corkscrewed down onto the floor of the bar, the middle part of his head missing. The telephone under the bar was ringing.

The border patrolman levered out the smoking case from the Winchester. He closed the action and fired at another Mexican who had crawled behind some boxes stacked at the end of the bar.

Nero Ramirez pushed his whore away and swept up his M3 "Grease Gun" SMG from the floor by the bed. Naked, he burst through the door of Room Three and rushed to the balcony. Through the gunfire and smoke he recognized friend and foe and shot at both in hopes of killing someone who might kill him. Then he saw the gringo in the *uniforme verde. La migra? Here? Is this a raid?* He let off a burst toward the *Americano.* The weapon sounded like a worn-out Hungarian washing machine in need of repair. It seemed to gasp and chug as it fired.

A row of bullets stitched a neat line up the wall behind him. A .45 caliber projectile struck the border patrolman in the shoulder. The Winchester flew from his grip. Blood gushed down his arm. He rolled over on his back behind a roulette wheel and tried to stem the flow, his fingers turning crimson.

Ramirez! Paul pushed the AUG aside and drew his Ruger P-85, nine-millimeter pistol. He rolled on his side and fired up at Nero Ramirez without apparent effect.

Grainger swung the M-4 up and rattled off a burst at the naked figure leaning over the balcony firing a Grease Gun. The assault rifle emptied. He opted to transition to his secondary armament rather than to change magazines. Kneeling down, he placed the rifle on the floor. Drawing his Swenson Custom Combat .45, he searched for the naked man, but he was gone. Instead, he fired at some ankles wearing Mexican-crafted riding boots he saw under a desk. The boots' owner screamed, a guttural, vulture's screech.

Rawlings discarded the Remington shotgun. It was too slow to reload in the midst of a close-contact firefight like this. He spun to see a man scramble up the staircase, hobbling on one leg, bleeding from what looked like a bullet in the calf. The man was firing over his shoulder with a .38 revolver. Rawlings emptied the thirty-round magazine from the AK-47, following the target up the steps. The bullets splintered the railings, steps, and walls behind, but the target made it to the top unscathed. Rawlings flung the AK down, disgusted with himself.

Rawlings drew his SIG he had recovered from Buck's office. He alerted to a close proximity threat.

Pepe Barretto leaped up from behind the pool table and threw a pool cue at one of the intruders before opening fire with twin Taurus 99s; one in each hand, each canted ninety degrees.

He's seen too many John Woo flicks. Rawlings dropped instinctively for a moment. Springing to his feet, he returned fire with a cadence of rounds designed to obtain fire superiority and to put the opposition on the defensive. Seven rounds into the volley, the weapon ceased firing. *Stoppage.* Rawlings shifted immediately into the Delta IAD—immediate action drill—called "Rack-Slap-Assess." He tilted the weapon over and *racked* the slide back. He shook out the expended—but failed-to-extract-and-eject—round. He released the slide, and it slammed back into battery, carrying a live round into the chamber. He then *slapped* the magazine to insure a lock. Finally, he *assessed* the condition to reengage as he watched the target. At no time did he take his eye off Pepe Barretto, who was maneuvering around for a better firing angle. Time elapsed: two-point-five seconds.

Pepe Barretto fired again at the elusive figure no more than thirty steps from him. He still held the guns sideways, the way all the *vatos loco* did in the cinema. Both slides locked back. *Empty. No effect.* The *cabrón* was still standing. *This fucking gun might as well be making only noise.* He pressed the magazine release and fumbled in his pocket, looking for loaded ones.

Rawlings came into the Weaver combat stance and blasted four rounds into the hostile as he stood fishing for other magazines. *Gunfighter Rule Number One: Count your rounds. Rule Number Two: Have a round in the tube while you change magazines for emergencies. Corollary: If your piece has a magazine and/or grip safety, disconnect it. Rule Number Three: Don't shoot your weapons sideways like some Superfly idiot. Use the sights unless you want to be every SWAT team member's wet dream. Live and let die.*

Pepe grunted as the first bullet hit him. He had found a spare magazine and was attempting to place it into the magazine well of the Taurus pistol he favored. He couldn't breathe and found himself sitting on the floor. He didn't remember sitting. *This damn clip won't fit.* He made one more effort before the magazine in his left hand fell to the floor. The Brazilian Beretta slipped from his hand, the empty magazine still inserted. He stared at the gun, blood smeared and mocking his listlessness. *Vato huevon. Lazy balls. Get up!* Pepe was tired. He closed his eyes for a little rest.

Mario Barretto lay sprawled across the bed in the room where he had fallen asleep after ejaculating between the sumptuous cheeks of Maribel Quintero, a two hundred pound trollop recently imported from Uruguay. After he had fallen asleep, she searched his pockets for *la propina*—a tip—as Mario snored. When the gunfire erupted below, she hid on the small iron veranda before lowering herself over the rail to the ground below. She wasn't being paid enough for this kind of abuse. She was going back to Montevideo.

Mario sprang up and rubbed his bleary eyes. The sounds of gunfire confused him. *It isn't New Year's.* His first reaction was to ignore it and go back to sleep with his big, cozy slut who giggled all the time. But she was gone, and the shooting continued. When a round pierced the door, Mario jerked erect. He struggled into his trousers and found his gargantuan Ruger Bisley Vaquero .475 Linebaugh revolver. It was a massive handgun weighing four and one-half pounds. It drove a 445-grain bullet at 1,350 feet per second and made Dirty Harry's Magnum seem like a squirt gun by comparison.

Mario let his massive girth spill over his belt as he stepped out into the hallway. Gunfire and shouts competed. Gunshots were winning. Mario stumbled to the head of the staircase. He saw Pepe lying at the foot of the steps staring up at him. Mario Barretto let out a roar. For all that he wasn't, Mario Barretto was a brother. He cocked the Bisley and took the first three steps in a single bound.

Felipe Aguirre was hit. A bullet penetrated the boxes he was using as cover. He learned the difference between cover and concealment the hard way. He fell against the boxes, pushing them out onto the floor. He saw the woman first and touched off a round in her direction. It went wild.

Grainger fired his .45 three times.

One of the shots shattered Aguirre's left elbow. Splintered bone protruded through the skin. His adrenaline level was so high he barely felt it. He angled away.

Sloane whirled around, realizing she had been taken under effective fire. She shot back toward the bar. Her bullets shattered the fifteen-foot mirror behind the bar and broke a bottle of Pernod. She dove onto the floor, shaking. Her mouth felt like the Sahara.

Rawlings kept his weapon leveled on the fallen Pepe Barretto. Watching him jerk spasmodically on the floor, he concluded the man was dead. Just to be sure, he dumped two more rounds into his prostrate form. He turned toward the sound of the guns to see a shooter firing at Sloane. With both eyes open, his weapons-platform body turned and focused on the threat.

The sights framed the target. He squeezed the trigger twice, obtaining twin body cavity hits. Shift. Another shot.

The bullet tore through Aguirre's cheek. Teeth and blood in an indistinguishable mix of gore splattered the top of the bar.

Grainger shot the enemy an additional five times as he was going down.

Father Paul Teasdale saw Mario Barretto bounding down the stairs like a runaway cattle truck. He struggled up to a sitting position and brought the pistol to bear. His first round went high, over the head of the raging bull.

Grainger, Rawlings, and Sloane whirled to confront the new threat. Simultaneously they opened fire on Mario.

Mario was hit. He was vaguely aware that his limbs felt heavy. He fired the big Bisley again; the sound was like thunder. It masked the puny sounds of their toy guns. He flung himself down the stairs to be at his brother's side. He would save him.

Sloane fired the Beretta pistol at the great beast that thundered toward her. Her face and hands were blackened by residue gunpowder, burned gun oil, and barroom dirt. She saw her Winchester Ballistic Silvertips gouge big, red tunnels into the Beast; twelve rounds and most of them hits. The slide locked back. She had no more left to give. She dropped the empty gun.

Rawlings shot the behemoth four times. *The motherfucker is still coming!*

Grainger shot the giant in both kneecaps and watched him cascade like an avalanche down the last six steps. The monster raised his hand cannon to fire but couldn't seem to hold it up.

Mario fell at Pepe's feet. He crawled up his inert form. He patted Pepe's head. "Pepe? Pepe . . . ?"

Grainger came to his feet. Rawlings came to his side, gun pointing at the top of the stairs.

Mario looked up. "You killed my brother. *Chenge tu madre.*" Blood oozed from multiple wounds. He sank lower onto his brother's chest.

The bullet tore through Mario's right eyebrow and ripped out the back of his head. Paul lowered the Ruger pistol to his side. He limped to Mario's body. He kicked him in the ribs. "You killed my brother, too. But, we are still not even."

Nero Ramirez retreated back to Room Three. The shooting had stopped. He managed to slip on his pants and shoes. His whore cowered in the corner, moaning. "*Callate,* you *pinche* fucking harlot. You didn't make near that much noise when I was fucking you." He pointed his gun at her, and she rolled over in a terrorized ball. He considered his options. He also considered the bullet hole in his thigh. He was bleeding like a sacrificial pig.

Navarro Barretto examined his left arm where the spent bullet had struck him. It was already turning black and blue. A little blood escaped from the puncture. This was no more than an abrasion. The hole in his calf was a little worse, but not bad. He had endured worse. He would be back to stripping cars tomorrow with the big Rios bonus. His serving wench was hiding in the closet. He opened the door and pulled Angelica Suarez from her hide. He might need her.

Sloane stumbled over to the border patrolman and dropped down on both knees. "What in the hell are you doing here?"

"You know, I was thinking about asking you that same question. Besides, is that the thanks I get for getting my boots soaked crossing the river and risking an international God-damned incident?" He groaned as Sloane touched his shoulder.

"If the Mexican police find you on this side of the border . . . An American, federal law enforcement officer . . ." She found a pressure point. "In uniform." She collapsed next to him. "You kill anybody?"

The border patrolman groaned. "Yeah. The slimeball behind the bar, I think. He was going to shoot . . ." He stretched his neck as Grainger and Rawlings approached. "Him."

"He's right. The gunsel with the sawed-off had me. He saved my life."

"Don't mention it. But if y'all would just assist me back across to my jurisdiction, we'll just call it even." He grimaced. "Of course it would help if somebody could tell me why we just shot the living shit out of a Mexican whorehouse, assisted by the Catholic Church?"

"Because it was way past due," said Sloane.

The border patrolman grunted. "That's good enough for me."

Grainger looked up the stairs.

"Party's not over yet," said Rawlings.

The patrolman eased to a more comfortable position. "Have at it, boys. With this busted wing, I think I'll just watch from here. I just realized I'm allergic to death." He shifted in pain. "Someone fetch me my Winchester. Just in case you have a problem resolving the issue in our favor."

A shot rang out. Paul shot Mario again.

"That's enough, Padre. Save your ammo for the live ones. There's still some upstairs waiting for you."

Paul's face was streaked with dirt and sweat. "Good. We are missing one called Navarro Barretto and one other."

"Nero Ramirez," said Sloane. "The last of the NRA."

Grainger looked up the stairs. "We've got to finish this quick. Reinforcements could be coming. There's no time to finesse it. Kick and shoot."

Sloane was the search team. She was to check the cellar where Joey was supposed to be held. She would then return and stay with the wounded patrolman.

Grainger and Paul climbed the stairs; Rawlings covered from below. Once reaching the landing, they waved him up.

The first room was empty. The second had a catatonic woman sitting on the edge of the bed in a tattered bathrobe clutching a rosary. "*Vamanos.*" She sprinted out the door and down the stairs. The room was empty. *Nada.*

The third room was locked. They splintered the door and entered high and low. A babbling girl ran to them trembling uncontrollably. She pointed to the open window. A heavy blood trail ran to the sill. Paul told her to get out and find another line of work.

Rawlings eased to one side of the final door and tried the door. *Locked.* Grainger joined him at the opposite side. He motioned for Paul to again watch the hallway and other rooms.

Grainger looked over at his partner. It was just another door. They had done lots of doors and a lot of bad guys behind them. He motioned with his hand, indicating a wraparound technique on this one. Rawlings nodded back. Grainger stepped back and aimed a kick just beneath the doorknob. His boot impacted the door. It came off at the hinges and propelled into the room.

Rawlings stepped through. The room was dark.

Navarro Barretto heard them at the door. He had no illusions. If they were rattling his door, that meant everybody on his side was dead. He pulled his favorite whore in front of him and waited. He knew it wouldn't be long.

The shot was followed by another with four more coming in rapid succession. Grainger plunged through the doorway.

The man coming through the door seemed confused for a second. Navarro shot his semisilhouetted enemy. Then he shot him again. The man shot back, but Barretto had his shield, and she absorbed all four rounds. She sagged onto his left arm. He shoved the dead woman away. Six hammer blows struck between the belt and the throat, and he flew back against the foot of the bed. He wobbled, momentarily considering what had happened. Navarro Barretto concluded that they had killed him. The bullet hit him between the eyes. He catapulted backward onto a pillow that smelled of sweat and sex.

Grainger moved forward and dropped to the floor. "Target's down."

Rawlings staggered out into the hallway.

Paul took a step toward Rawlings.

Blood dripped steadily down the front of Rawlings's shirt. He spat some from his mouth. "It's not a job for the emotionally disturbed, huh, Padre?" He found a wall and slid down to the floor. A bloody map pointed the way to the bottom.

Paul knelt down next to Rawlings, his hands spread in supplication, not knowing what to do.

Grainger shot Navarro once more in the head before sprinting from the room. His throat constricted. "Myles . . ."

Rawlings smiled weakly. "Gut shot for sure, partner. I'm thirsty as hell." Blood gushed from between his fingers, pulsing in spurts from his perforated stomach.

Paul staggered up. "Help. I must find some help. A doctor—"

Rawlings grabbed Paul's leg. "Sit with me and Lon, Father. They couldn't do anything for me if I was on an operating table at Walter Reed. And we're in Mexico." His giggle became a wet gurgle as he drew his next breath. A viscous drool ran from the corners of his mouth. He slid his right hand up to his chest. "Lon. The son of a bitch tagged me in the lungs with a nine-millimeter. Lucky fucker. Did we grease him?"

Grainger sat down against the wall next to Rawlings. "We got him. They're all dead."

"Got 'em all, huh? We musta done something right." Rawlings slipped lower on the wall. "I guess we should have tossed in a grenade first. If," he coughed quietly, "we had a grenade."

"Myles . . ." Grainger lost the other words.

Sloane mounted the stairs in slow motion, knowing what she'd find at the top.

"Yeah, I know. Lot of water under the bridge." Rawlings turned to Paul. "You ever think about dying, Padre? I mean, where you go and what you do when you get there?"

Paul hung his head. "I believed once that there was life everlasting and that the righteous took their seat at the right hand of God the Father."

Rawlings reached for the priest. "Believed once, Father?"

Paul took his hand.

"You ought to hold on to that. I kind of like the image." Rawlings coughed again, spitting a large globule of blood. "My lungs are filling fast." He hacked once more. "For me, all I see is darkness waiting."

Paul squeezed his hand. "Do you want Reconciliation?"

Rawlings lurched forward and settled back against the wall. "I think it's too late for that. Still, I got no fear—you know? No regrets either." He had to force his eyes open. His breaths became wheezes. A frothy blood fouled his nostrils. "Shit. I'm fading fast. Crossing over soon." A falsetto giggle preceded his words. "I always said I wanted to die in a Mexican whorehouse."

Paul sobbed. His chest heaved in great, convulsive movements.

"Hey Padre. You know the Twenty-third Psalm?"

Paul fought for control. He brushed the wet from his face and nodded. " 'Yea, though I walk through the valley of the shadow of death, I will fear no evil.' "

Rawlings pulled himself away from the wall and seized Paul's arm. "For I am the toughest motherfucker in the valley." His fingers loosened and slid down Paul's arm. He reached for Grainger. "Tell that kid Ponce the policeman was right." His arm fell to the floor. Myles Rawlings died with his eyes open, watching where he was going.

Grainger stared straight ahead. Death had come. He and Rawlings had talked about it sometimes, mostly when they were drunk and experiencing the soldier's inevitable melancholy, waxing with maudlin sentimentality about the warrior's lot and fate. They had always concluded that you should never feel sorry for a soldier going to the Big Reunion in the Sky. He was the check, and it was just being cashed. You live by the sword, you can expect to die by the sword. It wasn't a bad thing. There were worse ways. Dying a natural death was for pussies, they had joked. Grainger felt none of that bravado now, just an immense emptiness. He had a cavity within. He checked his sorrow and brought it up short. Rawlings had said it before: *"The best thing you could do for the dead is to not join them."* He rocked to his feet. "Let's go," he said. He picked up Rawlings's body and slung him across his shoulders. He headed down the staircase. *"The second best thing you can do when the dead was your friend is to send as many as possible of the motherfuckers who killed him to Hell."*

THIRTY-TWO

SLOANE had been unable to find Joey. All she discovered was where he had been. There were only his pictures of the stick figures superimposed with circles and crosses.

Grainger placed Rawlings's body in the van they had seized at the airstrip, which had been retaken from Lemuel by the Barretto brothers. The wounded border patrolman was assisted into the back.

HER name was Consuela Jimenez. She was found cowering behind a desk on the bottom floor. She didn't remember anything except sliding down the banister and sitting on a man's lap. Then the shooting started, and she had crawled behind the desk for cover. She stood before the conquerors and shivered.

"What do we do with her?" said Sloane.

Grainger grabbed the prostitute by the arm. "Ask her if she's seen the boy."

Sloane translated into Spanish. The woman's head bobbed like a spring, first up and down, then sideways. "She saw a young boy taken to the cellar a few days ago and saw him when they brought him out to go to the bathroom, but that was all."

"Tell her to go to Rios and inform him he's got till tomorrow to deliver Joey, or else."

"Or else what?"

"Or else is enough. Go on. Tell her."

Sloane translated

The woman nodded continuously. *"Sí. Sí. Sí. Sí . . ."*

"Go on," said Grainger, motioning the woman out the door.

The terrified woman ran from the room.

"We're going to burn this place to the ground," said Grainger.

"Good," said Paul, "but first I want to remove the bodies."

" 'Remove the bodies?' What for?" said Grainger. "We're running out of time. An army could be coming down on us any time."

Paul stared blankly. "Go on. I will do it myself."

"Goddamn it, Padre, we don't have time for this."

GRAINGER helped Paul drag the last of the bodies outside onto the driveway. Paul arranged them in his own order: The Barretto brothers, Zamudio, Alarcon, and Aguirre. They lay side by side. Santee, Bolano, Escalante, and Maximo "Coco" Pedraza aka *El Cirujano,* were kept in a separate group.

"Whatever you're going to do, Padre, do it fast," said Grainger.

"These stay," he said, pointing to Bolano, Santee, Escalante, and Pedraza. "The rest go."

"In the van, Father Paul?" asked Sloane. "With us?"

Grainger thought about what he had been previously told, and he understood. "All right. They go."

Sloane looked at Grainger like he was a coconspirator in Paul's madness-sponsored insistence on transporting the dead, and dead scum at that.

Grainger found a cardboard box and ripped it apart. Using a marking pen uncovered at the bar, he wrote his message, placing it on the bartender's chest with Escalante's dead fingers grasping the edges. He found a shovel leaning against a wall and threw it into the van before going back inside, behind the bar. Those bottles of alcohol not already shattered by gunfire, he hurled against the wall. He found a box of matches and lit them all. Placing the burning box on a pile of paper, he watched until he was sure there was positive ignition. The back of the wood bar burst into orange flame. He watched the fingers of fire lick at the woodwork and understood—as he always had—that there was a bit of the pyromaniac in everyone. He headed for the door. Some said every man was also a potential rapist. And you could scratch the corner druggist and find an SS man. But what he had become could not be found within the potentials of regular men. A blast of heat rolled over him as the alcohol fed the flames. He emerged into the darkness.

GRAINGER told him not to stare at the conflagration, but Paul watched the flames devour the building. He turned away. *Night blindness.* He would need his night vision acuity. Paul had told them he would not be immediately returning. He still had an accounting. The blood spoor in Room Three leading out the window had to be Ramirez. The animal was hit badly. Grainger had said that the wounded man would probably never make it back to Rios's hacienda. He was losing too much blood. He had also said Ramirez would tire fast and go to ground, like a wounded antelope. If you had to track him, it would be best to wait and follow up after he was in total shock, after the adrenaline had worn off; after he lay down to die. Ramirez might not make it, but Paul intended to make sure. He stepped off on the trail.

NERO Ramirez used his belt as a tourniquet, securing it around his wounded leg. The bullet had ruptured his femoral artery, and he was bleeding to death. He probed with a finger here and there, trying to find a pressure point to stem the bloody flow. It wasn't working. He cinched the trouser belt tighter, which only seemed to accelerate the bloody eruption. The hacienda was a good mile and a half away. *It don't look good, hombre.* Ramirez had to rest. He backed up to a tree, straightened his leg, and slid down to the damp ground. Mosquitoes attacked him, and night flies buzzed around the blood. Then he saw the flames.

* * *

PAUL halted and turned around in response to a rumbling explosion behind him. Something had detonated inside the building. In the light of the consuming flames, he confirmed the bloody spoor.

IN the flash of light that attended the explosion from the house, Ramirez thought he saw a man standing, a hundred meters from him. He slipped his nickel-plated Smith and Wesson pistol from his belt and rested it on his knees. He wished he had the M3, but couldn't carry or manipulate the clumsy thing after he was hit. *No matter. Man. Beast. Ghost.* Nero wasn't afraid of anything.

THE flash faded, and Paul squatted down. He thought he saw a reflection, like tinfoil. *About one hundred yards ahead, by that tree.* He got up and moved laterally, off his direction of travel.

COME *on. Come on, you puto Americano.* Maybe it was just his imagination. Maybe they weren't *Norte Americanos.* Maybe there was nobody. *A la mejor.* Ramirez waited in pain.

PAUL caught the gleam from another angle, and he knew it wasn't Mother Nature. He slipped through the darkness, converging on the shining, hoping he didn't step on a dry branch.

RAMIREZ was tired now. The blood still ran from his leg, although it appeared as if it had slowed down a little. It should have coagulated, but oozing rivulets flowed like red lava, sometimes even spurting in a gusher. If he had been whole, he may have alerted. As it was, his pain-numbed mind didn't catch the telltale sounds. But he still was able to detect and interpret the cold, hard object that rested against his left temple. It was definitely a gun.

"Nero Ramirez."

Ramirez attempted to turn toward the sound of his name. It was painful. He considered—for a fleeting moment—attempting to shoot his way out of this, but thought better of it. He was almost paralyzed. He doubted if he could even get up without assistance. A hand reached down and jerked his pistol away. He strained to see who it was. "You come to help?"

Paul kept his gun pointed at Ramirez as he came around the side of the tree. He stood in profile, the light from the burning building reflected off his face.

Nero Ramirez looked up at the face. *The priest.* He believed his luck held.

"She was only a child."

Nero Manolo Ramirez knew then he was a dead man. *"Lo siento, Padre."*

"I am also sorry," said Father Paul Teasdale in a flat, emotionless voice.

Ramirez never heard him. A bullet had excavated his brain.

Paul struggled to heft the dead weight of the man he had killed. He slung him over his shoulder like a sack of maize. It was a long walk to the river.

RIOS stood motionless on the balcony, watching the flames from his burning *casa de putas* shoot skyward like an erupting volcano. He had watched and listened for a half hour, ever since the explosion and gunfire had erupted. He had tried to call the bar, but with no response. He turned around. "What do you make of this, Lorca?"

"I'd say they have burned down your whorehouse. Wouldn't you?"

"Rios's face was red in the glow of the distant fire. "You don't seem surprised? You anticipated this? You never counseled me."

Lorca laughed sharply. "Señor Rios. You sleep with your counsel. Besides, did I not say that I felt your celebration was premature?"

Rios turned back to the distant conflagration.

"I am sure your oracle predicted that this man Grainger would act preemptively. Who did you think you were dealing with?"

Rios faced around and ran his finger along his mustache. "I estimated we had won a victory."

Montezuma shrugged dismissively. "Your mistake was in believing the battle was the war, señor." His hands formed a pyramid on his chest. "You underestimated your enemy and have now paid the price."

Rios pointed a crooked finger. "Perhaps I overestimated you, Señor Lorca."

"That, señor, and with all modesty," said Montezuma, "is not possible. You will yet call on me to save you."

"They came for the boy," said Sonja.

Montezuma clapped his hands together. "Brilliant and most perceptive as hindsight. But in that they have not succeeded." He looked once again at the glow in the sky. Embers shot like fireworks, and the crackle of combustible material being consumed provided orchestra. "What will we watch tomorrow night for entertainment?" He chuckled and strolled away.

"The boy?" yelled Rios.

Montezuma didn't turn. "I have him now."

GRAINGER stopped the truck on the Mexican side of the river and unloaded the bodies near the water's edge, where a copse of cottonwoods stretched their roots toward the dampness of the riverbank. It was where Paul had requested they meet, after the border patrolman had revealed that he had seen Humberto downstream from there. They waited in the dark, by the great river, hypnotized by the water's murmur and lulled by the fragrance of wild lilacs and honeysuckle.

Grainger stared out over the river, listening to the frogs croaking in concert along the banks and to the chirping crickets in the reeds as they dueled with each other for supremacy. A steady buzzing of grasshoppers provided a sonic overlay to the concerto. An unseen fish jumped somewhere out on the river. He felt disconnected from everything: past, present, and future.

Sloane sat against a tree and watched Grainger drag the dead from the back of the van. She was too spent to help. The Beretta jabbed her in the side as she sat, a constant reminder of its presence. She had rewound the events of the past three hours in her mind a dozen times, and her mind gave no indication it was growing weary of the endless reel. She flinched as she conjured firing her gun, watching a head explode and the picture dissolve to red. This was a nightmare with personal credits. She was La Femme Nikita. *Be careful what you wish for . . .* She longed for something else.

The border patrolman saw that he had stopped bleeding, but his shoulder throbbed mercilessly, each heartbeat producing a knifelike thrust into the muscle. He couldn't help unload the carcasses and didn't even offer, so he just drifted in thought. *Yes. This madness is all connected. The old man sitting alone at Gumtree Bend, a half-mile downstream from here. Rios. The Game. The crazy priest. Even me! Let somebody else call it a circle of life.*

PAUL staggered in from the blackness, an apparition. He heaved the inert form of Nero Ramirez onto the ground next to the others and collapsed alongside Sloane against a crooked tree whose roots protruded from the barren soil.

Sloane felt him there but didn't look. *A priest with a gun and the dead man he just killed.* "Are you okay?"

Paul looked from Grainger to the border patrolman, both men standing there in the darkness. "I just am." He listened to the night birds call to each other. When he was rested, he helped Grainger cover the bodies with branches and debris they found in the dark. Finished, he entered the van, his body aching and his soul missing.

GRAINGER stopped the van in the middle of the track that ran off the Jeep trail they had been using. "Are you going to make it?"

The border patrolman grunted. "Yeah. I'll take an aspirin and call the sawbones in the morning and tell him I shot myself while cleaning my gun."

Grainger got out and moved in slow motion to the rear of the van. He had witnessed—and sponsored—the ends of lots of worlds. But this was his friend. He opened the door. Rawlings's boots stared him in the face. He took them in his hands and pulled. There was no dignity in death and no one goes gentle into any good night. He carried Rawlings like a mother carries a child. He staggered out into the desert. Fifty yards off the track, he laid the body down and returned to the van.

Paul watched Grainger, unsure of his role.

"Can we help?" said Sloane.

Grainger removed the shovel from the back. "Give me some time, then . . ."

She nodded, and he went back into the darkness. In the moonlight, he could be seen in silhouette, digging and hacking at the stubborn ground. Twenty minutes later, he leaned on the shovel, and she knew it was time. Wordlessly, she headed for him. Paul and the border guardian followed.

The grave was only three feet deep. He had hit impenetrable hardpan. Grainger was covered with a dirty film of sweat. With Paul's help, he lowered the body into the hole.

"Can we do this?" said the border patrolman. "I mean, bury the man in an unmarked grave in the desert? What about notices to the next of kin? Law enforcement investigations? Post mortems? Death certificates? The legal stuff?"

Grainger pulled the shovel out of the dirt. "You're a law enforcement officer, aren't you? You investigated, didn't you? Cause of death? Multiple gunshot wounds." He threw a shovel full of dirt into the grave. "And not knowing when to quit and go home." He continued to shovel mechanically.

"What about next of kin?"

"I'll let somebody know."

"And the death certificate?"

"He already died. Years ago. The government killed him."

"What?"

Sloane took the border patrolman gently by the arm. "I'll explain on the way back."

Grainger finished filling in the dirt. He tamped the mound with the back of the shovel, then stepped back. The four of them stood at the corners of the grave. "You might want to say a few words, Padre," said Grainger.

Paul's throat constricted. *Padre? Father? Was he talking to me?* He bowed his head. "Oh Lord. Receive the perfect soul of an imperfect man. Forgive him his trespasses against Your commandments and his blasphemies against Your word. If he detoured on the path to You, absolve him. He died unreconciled, but justly. Let my words be his. Forgive us both." He stared down at the burial ground.

"I guess he wasn't much of a Catholic," mumbled Grainger.

Paul bent down and grasped a fistful of dirt. He scattered it on the grave. "That's okay. I wasn't much of a priest."

GRAINGER motored across the international bridge. On the United States side, he drove down to the river where the border patrolman had parked his truck. "You sure that shoulder is going to hold?" He had done his best to patch him up. He owed this guy.

The border guardian got out of the van stiffly. "Yeah. I'll be fine. First light, I'll drive up to the federal facility at Laredo and get into ER."

"What are you *really* going to tell them?" said Sloane.

The border patrolman suppressed a groan. "Oh, that I followed a bunch of loco people into Mexico, got involved in a shoot-out, killed a Mexican or two, burned down a whorehouse, and passed out my business card to anyone who asked." He emitted a grunt as a spear of pain lanced him.

"The truth, the whole truth, and nothing but the truth, huh?" Sloane mocked gently.

"Okay. How about, 'Shot by a coyote who was bringing over a batch of wets?' Doing my job. Probably get a medal." He hobbled toward his truck. At the door he turned around. "Nice working with y'all. Have a nice day."

He got into the truck, started the engine, and turned on the headlights. *After the Statute of Limitations runs, I'm going to tell my grandkids about this night. Until then, I'll be satisfied with telling them how Grandpa could see the future along a bend in the Rio Grande, when he stood alone on the frontier, guarding America's inviolate borders.* His truck bounced over the broken ground and dropped over the top of a sand berm and was gone.

"**SEÑOR** Rios. Señor Rios." Servando Chavez brought Consuela Jimenez out onto the veranda.

"You bring a whore into my home?" shouted Rios. He glared at Montezuma's factotum.

Chavez dropped his eyes. "Señor Lorca instructed me that you might want to question her. She came from the house."

Rios stepped in front of the woman. "Speak to me. What do you know?"

Consuela folded her hands. "*Nada,* Señor Rios; only that they killed everybody. I saw no survivors. One of their own was killed. An *Americano.*" Her breathing was erratic. She trembled as she spoke to *El Salvador.* "They gave me a message . . . for you."

Estaban regarded her condescendingly. His eyebrow rose. "A message?"

"The tall *Americano* said that you had until tomorrow to give him *el niño.* 'Or else.' "

" 'Or else' what?"

"He did not say. There was only, 'Or else.' " Consuela shivered violently. *"Todos estan muertos.* They are all dead. All dead . . ." she mumbled.

Rios pulled her chin up, examining her face. *"Como te llamas?"*

Consuela swallowed with difficulty. "Consuela. Consuela Jimenez. From Sinaloa."

Rios smiled. "No, Consuela Jimenez from Sinaloa. You are wrong. *You* are still alive."

"Oh, *sí, patron.* Except for me."

Rios dropped her chin. A chrome Walther pistol appeared in his hand. He shot Consuela in the forehead. "But now, Consuela, you are right." Rios turned back to the flames. "I hate the bearer of bad tidings. It is senseless to slay the messenger. I understand that, at least intellectually. However, the Roman emperors Hadrian and Augustus did it as well as the Persians Darius and Xerxes. And you know why?" He twisted toward Sonja. "You feel better after. Do you approve?"

Sonja rotated away and turned to the flames. "Upon returning to Rome from the barbarian wars, the exultant Roman general stood in his chariot in splendor. But beside him rode a slave who whispered in his ear, 'You are mortal.' " She turned around. "There are better ways to sacrifice."

Estaban watched the fires lighting the sky. He needed to think. He would gather his thoughts and sleep on it. Tomorrow would have answers. "Will you come to me tonight, Sonja?" She looked particularly serene. Nothing fazed her.

La Alma Negra shook her head. "This night is another's."

She was an enigma. Estaban watched Chavez drag the whore's body. Her head left a scar of bloody brain matter on his terra-cotta tile. *They can not be dead. Not all of them. Surely Nero survived. He could not be killed so easily.* He heard a single gunshot. It seemed to echo and linger out in the blackness of the desert. *"You are mortal." Indeed.*

THIRTY-THREE

THREE A.M.

A dog barked somewhere, answered by another. The streets were deserted; but the streets were always deserted in Zapata. Paul stayed with Grainger for a while as he did a security check around the premises and then let himself in the back door with his key. Sloane entered the church through the front. She found Leon preparing to conduct Midnight Mass, at three in the morning. Leon was mad. *In all this chaos he is attempting to portray normalcy?*

Paul climbed the stairs to his room and slipped through the door like a thief.*What can I say to Leon to explain my conduct? To defend my actions? What can I say to myself? To my God . . . to justify this murderous aberration?* He turned on one low light. He looked at his kaleidoscopic image in the cracked mirror, broken earlier by his fists. He held his hands out for inspection. They were crusted with blood. His face was caked with more blood and dirt. It looked burned, with cracks that ran in zigzags, like visible fault lines. *This is the real me.*

Paul undressed. He entered the shower and closed the door.

He turned on the water and let the hot liquid cascade over his battered body. Reconstituted blood, now brown and black, washed from his skin and swirled around the drain in dizzy circles. He leaned against the opaque glass shower wall for support.

FATHER Leon genuflected in front of the cross. "Many are the sufferings of the just, and from them all the Lord has delivered them; the Lord preserves all their bones, not one of them shall be broken. Alleluia."

Sloane knelt in the first row and answered. " 'Our soul has escaped like a bird from the hunter's net.' "

PAUL pushed away from the shower wall and leaned on one arm, his head hanging down, watching the water carry away the evidence of his perfidy, disavowals, and transgressions. He stood erect and let the hot water hit him in the face.

LEON turned around and made the sign of the cross with the knife-edge of his hand. "We stand naked before the Lord and cannot hide from his judgments. But, to ignore evil is to sponsor evil. And the blood of the victim becomes our blood."

PAUL turned off the water and stood motionless, listening to the final drips from the showerhead. He pushed open the door and groped for a towel in the semilight of the bathroom.

LEON looked at Sloane, her head bowed. He moved to the small podium. "A reading from the Book of Psalms. 'He that fleeth from the fear shall fall into the pit; and he that getteth up out of the pit shall be taken by the snare. And many are the sufferings of the just, and from them all the Lord has delivered them. So sayeth the Lord.' "

"Blessed be the Word of the Lord," Sloane mumbled.

"And from John . . . 'I tell you solemnly, unless a grain of wheat falls on the ground and dies, it remains a single grain; but if it dies, it yields a rich harvest.' "

* * *

PAUL found a towel and dried his hair. He wrapped the towel around his waist. The voice came to him from that place where his mortal dreams and spiritual fears collided.

"My name is Sonja Ochoa."

LEON turned back to the crucified Christ and raised his hand in supplication. " 'Who knoweth the spirit of the man that goeth upward, or the spirit of the beast that goeth downward, into the Earth?' "

PAUL stood transfixed.

She unbuttoned her soft cotton dress slowly, one button at a time.

Paul watched each wooden button slip from its restraint.

Sonja slipped her shoulders free of the dress and let it fall to the floor.

"I cannot do this. I am a priest."

"No," she said. "You were a priest. You left your past in Mexico."

SLOANE arose from her pew. She wasn't even Catholic. She had cursed and cried, killed and prayed. Now she was just too tired to think anymore. But she realized she tottered on the edge of madness and reconciliation, and which way she would fall was unfathomable. She made her way toward her room in a trance. There was no exit from this.

GRAINGER stood in the darkness outside the church watching and listening, in case Rios mounted an immediate counterattack; but more than that, he needed to be alone.

SHE extended her hand toward him. Paul found himself responding involuntarily. He rose and sought her. The wet towel around his waist parted and fell to the floor. Their hands folded around each other, and she pulled him to her. "Let your inhibitions stay behind you." She sank onto the bed, pulling him with her. "Do not think, but feel only. I will guide you to where you have always dreamed of being."

Paul responded, clutching her to himself. He inhaled her feminine musk and buried his head between her breasts.

Sonja lay couchant, purring softly, feeling him rise against her. "Yes, you will do just fine."

Father Paul, the priest, incinerated in her fires. Paul the man arose.

HE lay staring blankly at the ceiling as she dressed. He was only partially conscious of her movement, but fully aware of her presence. The ceiling fan above his head rotated in a wobbling parabola. It hypnotized him, or maybe just insured the stupefaction. He felt anesthetized.

Sonja buttoned her dress the way she had unbuttoned it, languorously, sensuously manipulating each button until it slipped through the loop. She looked down at her supine consort, her conquest. She felt no malevolence toward him, but also no pity or other emotion.

Paul stirred. "Why have you done this to me?"

Sonja fastened the last button. "*You* chose to break your commandments, not I." She slipped on her shoes. "What now torments you more? That I carry your seed within me, or the vision of the souls you sent to the next world?"

Paul gripped the wet sheets.

Sonja came and stood over him. She leaned down and kissed him on the mouth, her tongue caressing his. He was unable to deter her. "With some practice, you could be a champion."

Sonja Ochoa, santera, *La Alma Negra,* shut the door behind her. It was almost dawn. There were better ways to sacrifice.

THIRTY-FOUR

THE rising sun quickly vanquished the night chill even before becoming fully exposed over the horizon. The sun's color was more burnt umber than bloodred, but it was still early. A smoky haze hung over the ruins of the brothel. The dead bodies lay on the circular driveway. The cardboard held by Escalante's dead fingers read, "YOUR BROTHER AND THE MONEY FOR THE BOY. IN LA CIUDAD DE LOS MUERTOS."

"Buck Downs is dead, Jefe," reported Refugio Duran. "Shot down in the alley behind the police station."

The embers still smoldered. Here and there a hot spot flared up as a cross member collapsed, feeding fuel to the dying fire. "Downs was as a condom, Señor Duran," said Estaban. "When you are done, you peel it off and throw it away. He is as replaceable as a pair of socks."

A few scattered peasant spectators stood off at a respectful distance and marveled how this edifice could so quickly be reduced to ash.

Estaban walked the perimeter of his destroyed brothel. Warden Duran walked next to him without objection from Rios. Servando Chavez trailed them, carrying a canteen of ice water.

"I had Carrara marble in the foyer." Estaban turned to Refugio Duran. "Did you know that?"

Duran didn't know marble from masonry. "Ah, no patron. I did not."

Estaban reached the back of the burned-out building. Sonja was standing with Lorca at the front. He wondered what became of her last night. He stepped over a pile of slag and kept walking. Now there was no question of restraint or consideration of potential consequences. *I should have taken action sooner.* "Now is the time, Refugio."

"Time for what, Estaban?"

Estaban placed his hand on Duran's shoulder. "*Capitain* Vargas."

Duran smiled widely. "Of course. *Capitain* Vargas." The final solution. His stock was going up.

They stopped in front of Sonja and Lorca. The limp wind tugged at Sonja's simple peasant dress with the row of wooden buttons down the front. *She looks particularly beautiful this morning.* Estaban considered the body of his *cantinero,* Jaime Escalante. He swiveled over to *los centinelas,* Chuy Santee and Raymundo Bolano, lying like unwrapped mummies. Next to him was *el Cirujano,* no colder in death. *But where are Ramirez, Zamudio, Aguirre, Alarcon, and the Barretto brothers?* He knew where they had gone for their eternity; of that he was sure. The implications of their physical absence could have terrified him, but there was *Capitain* Vargas. "*La ciudad de los muertos,* Refugio! Why are you still here?"

GRAINGER left before dawn, driving the van into Mexico, across the bridge no government cared about monitoring. He had charted this path in his mind before. He swerved to miss the bomb crater–size holes in the pavement and endured the axle-jarring impacts of those depressions he couldn't avoid.

"It is too bad, really," purred Raoul.

Grainger downshifted to swerve around a washout in the road.

"I feel somehow this is going to be our last ride together." The words came lubricated, slipping easily from his practiced mouth. Raoul Rios was tied to the passenger's bucket seat of the van, his arms pinned behind the backrest. The seat belt kept him immobile.

The van bounced off the last of the disintegrating concrete onto the hardtack surface of desert dirt. "Actually, Señor Whomever-You-Are, I am glad I will be there when my brother kills you. Then I will be the first to piss on your body to season it for the vultures." Raoul's laugh turned into a grunt as the van ran over an old tire that lay in the middle of the trail. He turned his narrow-nostriled face to Grainger. "Where are you taking me, *cabrón?*"

Grainger didn't answer him. The rising sun was coming up behind *la ciudad de los muertos.*

"**ATENCION!**" *Capitain* Vargas exhaled the order. He slapped the riding crop he used as a swagger stick against the sides of his riding trousers. His patrician nose flared. His thin lips drew into a straight line across his lupine face. There was a ragged, shuffling response as twenty-one hard-looking men came roughly to attention. They stood in three ranks of seven, each facing *Capitain* Jenteno Mosquera Vargas, commandant of the guard, leader of Refugio Duran's prison riot and special suppression unit. The sun hadn't risen yet. A night chill still persisted; but the false dawn promised a day of intense heat.

Montezuma was up early, as he always was. He stood next to Refugio Duran, who beamed with pride as he surveyed his special troops.

"Magnificent, no?" Duran said.

"No," replied Montezuma to the obviously disappointed warden.

Vargas called for "open ranks" so he might inspect his unit before conducting this morning's training exercise. He walked slowly down the first rank of men. *Yes, they are smelly, vile, uncouth, and despicable. But they are mine.* He turned into the second row and slapped the squad leader on the arm as he passed.

Vargas had been an officer in the Mexican Army, a graduate of the Chapultepec National Military Academy, until cashiered for brutality and for what the military euphemistically termed "misconduct." To be drummed out of the Mexican Army for "brutality" took some doing. However, his reprisal actions during the Chiapas suppressions were excessive, even by the standards of an army that considered the enemy *untermensch.* He had burned, bayoneted, and decapitated in the name of the eagle and the snake, and they had rewarded him with the humiliation of public dismissal. His superiors stated they understood, but . . . *"Lo siento."* He was gone. Now he was a *capitain* again with better pay and more tactical freedom; and no excess was excessive. He had proven that numerous times, burning, bayoneting, garroting, shooting, and amputating limbs with machetes of those prisoners who failed to get with the program or who participated in any form of rebellious or antisocial behavior.

Capitain Jenteno Vargas made a sharp ninety-degree turn, pivoting on the balls of his feet, and entered the third row. *Of course they are drunkards, sadists, and killers, but loyal, responsive, and courageous drunkards, sadists, and killers.* He took the FN FAL rifle from the last man in the rank and flipped it around in a theatrical inspection. He smiled at the man and threw his weapon back to him. *Capitain* Vargas was happy.

Vargas strode proudly in front of his men and turned to them. "At ease, *compadres.*" He spun on his heel and toe and moved stiffly in front of Duran and Montezuma.

"Well done, as usual, *Capitain,*" said Duran. "You predict we shall be home by noon? That is good."

Vargas brushed a fly from his face with his swagger stick. "All of this for one man, Señor Duran? How profligate of Estaban."

Two large, canvas-covered GMC trucks ground their way toward them.

"We shall see, *Capitain* Vargas. We shall see," said Duran.

Vargas waved his riding crop over his shoulder, bouncing it there rhythmically. "These men have put down riots, suppressed insurrections, and enforced order in your prison against the worst breed of men in Mexico."

Duran nodded, acknowledging all that was being said.

"Now you send them against one man? You insult them with this pettiness."

Montezuma erupted with laughter.

Vargas snapped around. "What is your problem, señor?"

Montezuma's laugh subsided to a snicker. "Oh, I have no problem, *Capitain.* I was just wondering."

"Really?" replied Vargas. "And what would you be wondering?"

"I was just wondering where you will," he said, flipping his head toward the assemblage, "dispose of all this trash?"

The GMCs' squealing brakes brought them to a dusty halt in front of the group.

"Ignore him, *Capitain,*" said Duran, "He is an eternal pessimist; a naysayer and gloomy fatalist. He is not a team player."

Vargas nodded, his dead, Paleozoic shark eyes coldly calculating the grinning man in front of him. He let it drop. He turned his head toward his men. *"Abordar!"*

After the twenty-one men had distributed themselves and climbed aboard the two trucks, Duran and Vargas both entered the cab of the lead vehicle. "Besides, Vargas," said Duran, "Estaban is paying for it all at time and one-half; plus a large bonus for you and me when this is done."

Vargas was placated. He dismissed this Montezuma character as some simpering, jealous, quality-assurance observer for Rios. He would deal with him later.

The driver ground the gears, searching for compound-first. The big GMC lurched forward. *"La ciudad de los muertos,"* said Duran. The driver grunted, and they were off.

Montezuma stood alone in front of the prison, watching the trucks rumble out onto the main road. "We shall see, Vargas," he mocked, in his best imitation of Warden Duran. "We shall see."

GRAINGER drove through the ghost city. Surveyor stakes still marked where the last crews had worked and abandoned their labors. Trenching excavations prepared for sewage lines were intermittently collapsed. Otherwise, the partially completed buildings were remarkably intact, thanks to the arid climate. He drove to the far edge of the development and parked the van in plain sight, where he knew it would be seen. He got out and opened up the side sliding door. Two wide eyes stared at him. Ponce.

"Wrong bus, son. What the hell you doing here?"

"I came to help. To watch you shoot. I'm going to be just like you and Mr. Rawlings."

A helper. Exactly what he didn't need. He had loaded the van in the dark and had no reason to check it for stowaways. It was too late now. "Get out of there, boy."

Grainger opened the door for Raoul, who slid out awkwardly. Raoul swept the area with his eyes. "As good a place as any for you to die," he said.

Grainger took Ponce to an attached underground storage room that looked like a Midwestern tornado shelter. He put Ponce inside with a canteen of water. "Stay here until I come and get you." He closed the creaky doors that covered the storage room.

Grainger pulled Raoul back to the van. There, Grainger removed the rifle and a duffel bag, which contained all his other accessories and equipment. He nudged the still-bound Rios with the cased rifle. "This way." He escorted Raoul to a shed next to a framed structure that looked like it was intended as a community center. He pushed Raoul inside and put him against a wall. Grainger pulled out the tranquilizer gun from his bag.

"Please don't shoot me with that," Raoul simpered.

"You should almost be immune to these by now." Grainger pulled the trigger. The tranquilizer dart lodged in his neck. Raoul collapsed onto the floor. *"Hasta la vista,"* Grainger muttered, closing the door behind him.

He climbed the circular metal stairs to the top of the church bell steeple. It was the highest elevation in the development. From here, visibility was virtually unlimited. Every avenue of approach was visible. There was little dead space. He could interdict every advance from this location; and where he couldn't, there were other solutions in place. He didn't know how many would be coming, but he knew it would be plenty. *Maybe not Montezuma. But enough to make it hairy.* He placed his gear down and retraced his steps to the van. He had other things to do until company arrived.

* * *

AN hour and forty-five minutes later he had completed his tasks. He checked Ponce and Raoul. Now, back in the bell tower of the church, he removed the rifle from the case and leaned it against the wall. On his first reconnaissance trip here, he had prepositioned a small wooden table, among other things. It was there that he placed his ammunition and his handgun. He would need little else. Grainger had packed the walls of the tower with hundreds of end pieces of two by fours that had been cut and left in a pile by the carpenters. They were pinned in place with plywood and plasterboard he had scrounged. They served as a field-expedient armor belt.

The tower afforded a panoramic view of the area. Grainger understood what drew men to the desert. It was beautiful; at least from a distance. Now, he was only interested in the tactical considerations of the landscape. He checked the rope that hung out the opening on the south side of the tower to his rear. The 120-foot nylon climbing and rappelling rope dangled to the ground beneath the 100-foot structure. He looked at his range cards he had drawn on his first sortie to this place, one for each quadrant. The range cards contained preplotted information: distances to potential targets, location of his force-multiplier booby traps, obstacles, and likely enemy positions. They provided a quick reference and guide. He reoriented himself to the information he had previously memorized zero-eight hundred. He settled down to wait. *Maybe Rawlings would still be alive. The string just played out. Some races are relays. You pass the baton. Every road has an end, except I brought him here.* He was at war with himself.

A spiraling plume of dust announced the approach. Grainger watched with detachment as the dust became connected to what he identified as two American Jimmy deuce-and-a-halves. They came straight on without hesitation, and he knew then that Montezuma was not among them. The two trucks stopped nine hundred meters out, parking parallel to each other just forward of the limits of the development. He watched the dust dissipate and settle. For a few moments there was no movement; then men burst from the backs of the two trucks and began to assemble in robotic fashion. They looked like battle droids from one of the *Star Wars* episodes. He counted their numbers. They hadn't come to bargain or trade. *At least everybody understands each other.* Then he heard the music.

"**CORPORAL** Lopez! Play our theme song." Vargas stood like Napoleon at Waterloo, chest thrust out, arms folded behind him, popping his swagger stick against his gloved hand.

Ruben Lopez put the tape into the machine and pressed Play. After a scratchy lead, a booming trumpet, brass, and drum ensemble roared from the external speakers. "El Deguello."

Vargas loved the music. *Deguello* meant literally, "decapitation." *Generalissimo* Antonio López Miguel de Santa Anna had played this stirring piece before he reduced the Alamo by storm. *Of course it is dramatic. But men respond well to drama.* The ringing, traditional Mexican martial exhortation announcing that no quarter would be given was appropriate here today. There would be no prisoners. The bombast continued. Vargas was impatient. He wanted to get out of his sweaty uniform and be in the shower. Perhaps even before noon.

Warden Refugio Duran sidled up next to Vargas. "'El Deguello'? We take no prisoners today? Give no quarter? Eh, Vargas?"

Capitain Vargas regarded Warden Duran, his ostensible boss, with condescension. "That is what it means, Warden Duran."

"Then," said Duran, "does it also mean that we neither expect any quarter?" He raised his eyebrows.

Vargas regarded the oh-so-serious Duran with a barely concealed contempt. Then his face dissolved into a bemused grin. He couldn't help it. *Capitain* Vargas broke out laughing. "El Deguello" drowned him out.

"**AVANCE!**" Vargas's command voice boomed. He watched his line of skirmishers surge forward into the dead streets of La Vista Grande. He put his binoculars to his eyes and scanned the structures. "He has probably reconsidered the folly of his challenge. If he is here, he is most likely trying to hide. We will flush him. Like a rabbit."

THEY were all within range, but Grainger waited for the fruits of his labor. He didn't have to wait long.

"Who fired?" screamed Vargas.

A man came running back down the street toward them. "Cortez is dead. Booby trap. Trip wire tied to a shotgun."

"Get back with your squad," yelled Vargas. "Pay attention."

GRAINGER identified the sound as coming from the bartender's sawed-off shotgun. It was still working. He made a check mark on a range card. An M-16 went off, followed by a thirty-caliber rifle. The set-guns were working out fine.

"**PARDON** me, Señor Duran, I must see to this personally, it seems." Vargas sprinted up the street to where the lead elements of his men now hunkered down in disorganization.

GRAINGER loaded five rounds of .338 Lapua and set the variable power scope at ten power, a good compromise between field of view and magnification as well as accessing the mil-dot and stadia ranging scales calibrated at this setting. Zeroed at five hundred meters, here, at these ranges and target density, he would have to utilize Kentucky windage and elevation. *Hold under, mostly.* The first figure appeared, cautiously advancing up the street. Grainger shot him in the head. A second man burst from concealment and ran to pick up his fallen comrade. The .338 slug took him in the side, bowling him over. The recoil of the rifle was substantial but went unnoticed.

The rattle of undirected automatic weapons fire responded. Bullets cut through uprights and spent themselves against pilings. Grainger looked at a range card and identified a plywood wall where he estimated some would attempt to take refuge. He sent two bullets crashing through the three-eighths-inch wood, killing two more of Vargas's men hunkering down on the opposite side. A leader of some kind tried to rally his subunit. Grainger shot him through the chest. The impact of the heavy bullet catapulted him three feet back. He hit the dirt with finality.

Grainger calculated they had not yet identified his position. He was hard to pinpoint. The visuals and sound signatures of his firing were muted and dissipated by and among the carapace of buildings. It was one of the defender's advantages engaging in MOUT. When the inevitable happened, and they finally located him, he could not let them surround him; hence, the rope. He moved to another opening and took an oblique shot at two men running toward him in tandem. He shot the farthest one, followed by the one in front, who never realized his comrade had been killed.

"**SPREAD** out. Spread out." Vargas exhorted a squad of five remaining men huddled together for psychological protection behind a water trough.

A man sprinted toward Vargas. "*Capitain. Capitain.* We need reinforcements. There are too many . . ." The bullet took him just under the armpit, traversed through his body, and plowed into the dirt of the planed roadway. The man skidded to a stop in front of Vargas, his dead eyes blinking in post mortem reflex.

Vargas pushed the dead man away and leaned back behind the wall. He knew where the sniper was.

GRAINGER momentarily lost sight of active targets, so he shot the two drivers of the trucks as they sat in their cabs, nine hundred meters away. It was just like Mog. *Except Rawlings isn't here.* He wished he had an M-21, or at least a Weatherby Mark V action with its fifty-four-degree bolt lift to shorten reloading time, instead of the ninety-degree one on Runyan's custom bolt action. But he made it work, killing another face that made the mistake of looking over a wall instead of around it, at the bottom.

"**THE** church tower, *muchachos.* That is where he is hiding."

A squad leader looked askance at Vargas. "He may be in the tower, *Capitain*, but I don't think he is hiding." The squad leader had three men left.

"Take your squad to his flank, Sergeant," cried Vargas. "You, Corporal, set up a base of fire here to pin him down. You, Sanchez, take Escobar and maneuver to the right and take him by assault."

Duran slid down the wall next to Vargas. "Still think we'll be home by noon? *Capitain?*"

Grainger saw the men running and dodging between cover below him. They had his position. He shot one more who failed to crouch low enough. The head exploded in a grisly shower of red bone splinters and smashed brain. He set his surprise and went out the window and down the rope with rifle and bag.

PRIVATES Escobar and Sanchez made it to the base of the church. Their breathing was labored and stentorian. They looked up the winding staircase. The fusillade of shots was impacting the tower as they made the climb, alternately covering each other up the spiral. At the top they faced the closed door that accessed the tower. Sanchez nodded, and Escobar shouldered the door open. They fell inside shooting and lived long enough to experience some extrasensory cognition of doom. The Claymore mine shredded them as 200 ball bearings spewed out. The explosion froze their comrades, who watched from below. Sanchez, struck below the waist, managed to shoot himself to end the torment. Escobar was blown out a window. His body hit the ground, still smoldering. The attackers fell into silence.

ON the water tower one hundred meters away, Grainger lowered the rifle. His bullet had closed the electric circuit gate of the mechanical ambush he had set. An M-18 Claymore command-detonated mine had been positioned in the room facing the door where he knew they would come. He had rigged the simple device by wrapping tinfoil around the ends of a clothespin. A blasting cap's positive lead ran from the cap in the mine's priming well to one leg of the clothespin. The cap's negative lead ran from the well to a lantern battery. A circuit-completing positive line connected the other leg of the clothespin and the battery. The clothespin was clipped over a piece of broken mirror hung over the door, serving the twofold purpose of keeping the circuit open while giving him observation of the doorway. When the two soldiers entered the room, he shattered the mirror with a bullet, releasing and snapping shut the clothespin, thus connecting the circuit. It was over. He didn't dwell.

Grainger had been without sleep now for thirty-two hours. He was only now tapping his energy reserve. The zombie zone and he were acquainted. He turned to search for other targets.

Bullets cracked and whipsawed, although now more sporadic. Grainger found a target standing an unknown distance away. He was fully erect behind the skeleton frame of a one-story building. The distance and the maze of frames must have given him a sense of security if not invulnerability. He had binoculars and seemed riveted on the dead body lying at the foot of the church. He seemed mesmerized by the gruesome spectacle. Grainger framed him in the scope and fixed him between two vertical mil-dots. Center-to-center, a mil-dot subtends one meter at a thousand meters. The space between the first and second dots covered approximately thirteen inches of space, i.e., from belt buckle to the horizontal line of the target's shirt pockets. Range: three hundred meters. Bullet impact: sixteen inches high. Angle to target: forty degrees from his elevated position. Subtract six inches from the POA for the down angle. He fixed the crosshairs ten inches under his intended impact point. The man's belt buckle was the aim point. The rifle slammed rearward. The bullet tore out the target's lungs. He flew violently back into the dirt and lay motionless. Grainger ejected the smoking case and moved laterally along the tower's walkway to another position in case he had been observed.

Sniper marksmanship is an extension of fundamental rifle marksmanship. Accurate delivery of a bullet on a target depends upon what is known as the "integrated act of firing one round." Lon Grainger was a master of each of the individual components of this applied skill that was part science, and part art, and—beyond a point—Zen.

This integrated act of shooting—for a sniper—consists of four elements: proper breathing, trigger control, correct sight (scope) picture, and solid body position. He employed the "empty lung" technique, that is, purging his lungs before each shot, thus minimizing or eliminating body movement resulting from the chest expanding and contracting during the inhalation and exhalation cycles. Scope picture: He obtained the exact same eye relief (distance from the eye to the ocular lens) each time he fired, insuring—shot to shot—a maximization of light transmission and field of view, while minimizing the phenomenon called parallax, the tendency of the reticle to move, shifting the point of impact, as the shooter moves his head.

Grainger's trigger control was absolute. While the average rifleman strives to obtain a state of proficiency wherein trigger break is unanticipated, the sniper develops the opposite, i.e., the ability to precisely determine the instant of discharge, in order to be able to deliver precision fire. It is the essence of long-range shooting, a virtual sine qua non. Grainger had here disabled the single set trigger. The set trigger allowed the shooter to set the trigger with a preliminary pull. The subsequent pull then became a hair trigger. However, where multiple targets of opportunity presented themselves in rapid succession, the set trigger was an encumbrance.

Body position is critical to successful long-distance shooting. The proficient sniper learns to adapt to less than ideal situations, where precise body attitudes are impossible. Bone provided the basis of rifle support, not flesh. Whereas most people can be taught to hit a target with reasonable certainty from a perfect position under ideal conditions, combat rarely affords those luxuries. In battle it was the ability to adapt, improvise, extemporize, and invent that ultimately identified and set apart the sniper from the average infantryman. Grainger could deliver accurate fire ambidextrously, in the prone, the kneeling, the sitting, the Hawkins, offhand, and even the "rice paddy prone" position, a modified squat. No matter how he was configured, he was able to obtain the natural point of aim, which in turn insured his lethality.

As he observed from his position, he saw a man come to the kneeling position and motion furiously at unseen allies. The man's movement identified and betrayed him as a leader, a prime sniper target. Grainger swung the butt of the rifle into the hollow of his shoulder utilizing a "hasty sling" to obtain the proper support and muscle tension. His target filled the scope picture. The safety slid off. The first third of his right index finger rested lightly on the trigger. His breathing was normal as he adjusted the rifle's position on the folded jacket he was utilizing as a field expedient rest. At times he had also used the rifle's integrated bipod, chairs, crisscrossed sticks, anything to support the fore end of the weapon.

The crosshair reticle centered on the target's chest. The range calculation by mil-dot was four hundred meters. *Hold: eleven inches low. Minus nine inches for the down angle to the target.* He adjusted his point of aim. He wasn't head hunting. The bullet would hit the chest. If this had been his only target, he would have dialed the range data into the elevation adjustment to account for the one hundred meter-short-of-zero range. But this was a profuse target environment. There was no time for that. It was hold over/hold under and the reason he had memorized the ballistic tables for this particular caliber. He was shooting in Kentucky. Here the wind gusting at five to eight knots would normally have to be accounted for. But the buildings served to attenuate the effects, and thus it wasn't a factor.

Grainger took out the slight slack in the trigger. He maintained a tight spot weld, his cheek buried into his thumb at the small of the stock. His next inhalation was deeper, as was his exhalation. His hold was steady now. He held just below the pocket line. The trigger pull was straight to a clean break at the instant he forecast. The rifle recoiled, more an aggressive shove than a battering ram. He absorbed the recoil, rolling back into position. He watched the immediate effect of the hit. The man jerked backward like a broken puppet and lay sprawled in the dirt. No one came to his aid. He worked the bolt for "invisible ejection," utilizing a practiced motion to eject the empty case downward. Grainger maintained his follow-through by continuing to focus on the target and immediate environs. His finger barely brushed the trigger. He reset the safety. You can teach technique, but you can't teach feel, to feel when is the precise time to fire, when all factors are aligned. That was what separated Grainger from all but a very few snipers. He looked for another target.

"**DURAN!** Duran! My men are being slaughtered like cattle." *Capitain* Vargas slammed back against a small wall, his breathing coming in great torn gasps.

Refugio Duran had his face in the dirt as he crawled toward Vargas's location, which seemed to offer at least a modicum of cover and concealment from the murderous fire. He made it into the covered position and huddled next to Vargas. "When," he stuttered, "do you estimate we will flush the rabbit? *Capitain?"*

Vargas's eyes were primordial, wild. Desperation controlled him. His dilated eyes darted back and forth, and his mouth worked without words being spoken. "Water. I must have a drink."

Duran panted, spent in the relentless heat and stress. *"No hay agua.* Remember, we were going to be home by noon."

"I have only five men left. *Cinco,* damn you. Who is this devil?" said Vargas, his voice shrill and cracking. A single shot cracked, its echo ricocheting. Vargas leaned away from the wall and chanced a peek around the corner in time to witness another man spin around like a top and go down into the dust. He fell back against the wall. "Make that four." He buried his face in his dirty hands. "What shall I do? What can we do?"

"We, *Capitain?*" Duran scowled. "I do not wish to insult you with my pettiness, Vargas, or preempt your military prerogatives. Please proceed."

Vargas had stopped sweating. His skin was dry, his vision blurred, and his parched throat raw. He stood up and yelled at the four men who huddled behind a concrete abutment. "*Muchachos! Adelanto*. Follow me." He sprinted forward, firing his Galil assault rifle like wielding a garden hose. *"A la carga—"*

A bullet took Vargas at the junction of the neck and shoulders and cut right through him. For ten feet, he was a dead man running. His body collapsed, like a duck brought down over decoys. The sound of the kill shot ricocheted around the city of the dead. And for a moment there was silence.

THEY were in headlong flight when the first pitched forward and rolled three times, slamming against a mailbox stanchion. Another stopped and returned fire, maddened by the heat and fear. He fired his Kalashnikov assault rifle aimlessly until empty. Flinging the weapon away, he plunged back across an open expanse, making ten feet before dying.

Ruben Lopez flattened his back against the wall of a small garage. The man who sat next to him bolted up and ran for the trucks, two hundred meters to the rear. He ran in an irregular pattern like an open field runner in the World Cup. In the middle of the field he was upended and inverted by some unseen force. The sound of the gunshot rumbled over Ruben Lopez like a freight train. He put his hands over his ears and prayed for deliverance.

GRAINGER worked the bolt and ejected the empty. The barrel of the rifle was flame hot as he scanned the expanse of land in front of him. He looked at his range cards and counted the tick marks. There were two hostiles left. The bolt closed on another .338 Lapua belted Magnum cartridge.

The lifeless body of *Capitain* Vargas, lying twenty meters from him in the sun, transfixed Refugio Duran. The flies were already feasting. He rolled over and could see the feet of another survivor at the end of a building that looked like it might have been intended as a garage. *At least there's company.*

Lopez regarded the rifle on his lap like it was the mark of Cain. He slid it up to his knees and pushed it off into the dirt. He was resigned. There was no escaping this massacre. He came groggily to his feet and stumbled out into the open, his arms outspread. *"Hombre! Estoy desarmado. Yo me entrego. No despare."* I am unarmed. I surrender. Don't shoot. He wavered there, expecting to die.

GRAINGER brought the rifle to bear on the man standing on the graded path that maybe had been intended as a sidewalk. He appeared to be saying something, although at—he looked into the scope—700 meters, he couldn't be sure. The crosshairs fell across the ragged scarecrow. He thought of Rawlings. He thought about Paul. He thought about Sloane. He thought about himself. Grainger engaged the safety and looked up from the rifle.

LOPEZ stood facing into the late morning sun. He was blind. *Like looking into the mouth of Hell.* He shuffled from foot to foot. He had been standing here for five minutes, and he was still alive. *The Virgin of Guadeloupe! She protects me today!* He lowered his arms and collapsed against the same wall, too spent to move.

Duran watched the soldier with more than passing interest. *Entreaty. Submission. Surrender. Those were the keys to surviving this nightmare.* Duran wobbled to his feet and wiped his mouth with the back of his arm. He stepped out into the open. *Remember the words: "Hombre! I am unarmed. I surrender. Don't shoot." Those are the magic words. And better yet, in English.* Warden Duran smiled broadly. He stood there, expecting to live. The 250 grain .338 bullet exploded like a hand grenade as it passed through his skull. It was noon.

LOPEZ didn't know how long he sat there against the side of the partially completed structure, watching the dust devils and the birds. He counted the yellow jackets as they swarmed around a fence post. He watched a crow, harassed by a blue jay, retreat across an open field. A butterfly circled a potential mate in a choreographed ritual. Ten feet away, a starling methodically pecked at the ground, decimating a line of industrious ants until it was sated. He felt the muzzle of the rifle nudge the side of his head. He looked up at The Devil's Finger.

"Can you drive the truck?"

"Sí, señor," said Ruben Lopez. "I can drive."

"Then go back to the one called Montezuma and give him these." He handed Lopez two things.

Lopez would have gotten up, but the rifle barrel was still lodged against his temple. He reached slowly for the objects. *"Sí, señor."*

"And when you give him those . . ."

"Sí . . . ?"

"Tell him I will meet him at *las Calderas del Diablo*."

Lopez noted that the man standing over him was wearing a brown American cowboy hat that shaded eyes he knew were on loan from *el Diablo*. He fought to stay calm. "Are there any other things you wish me to do?"

"Yes. Tell Señor Rios that *la ciudad de los muertos* has twenty-five new residents."

THIRTY-FIVE

"**COME** on out of there." Grainger held the trapdoor open and yelled inside. A minute later the boy appeared, rubbing his eyes against the bright sun. "Are you okay?"

Ponce nodded and looked around. "What happened? I heard the shooting. Where is everybody?" He saw the first body. "Wow. You killed him!"

"It doesn't look too bad from this distance, huh? You want to be like me, son? Let's take a walk." Grainger led off. Ponce hadn't moved. "Come on." Ponce ran after him.

Grainger stepped over Escobar's body at the base of the church tower. "Claymore got him. Now those two over there . . ."

Ponce pulled loose and vomited in some weeds. He wiped his mouth with his hand. "I want to go back."

"Have you seen enough of what you want to be?"

Ponce nodded feebly and gulped down the water, emptying the canteen Grainger threw him.

Grainger sat down with the kid, his back against a ruptured hay bale found inside the skeleton of a scavenged barn. "Easy on that water. It'll give you stomach cramps."

Ponce eased over closer to Grainger. "Where's Mr. Rawlings? I didn't see him at the church."

Grainger plucked out a strand of straw and thrust it into the ground. *How do you put it to a kid? He got zapped? Checked out? Greased? Taken out? Wasted? Dusted? Bought the farm?* Death had a lot of euphemisms. He felt the texture of another strand of straw. *The kid is looking at me*. Grainger grasped one hand with another and embraced his knees. "He's dead, Ponce. He was killed last night."

"Mr. Rawlings? No. He couldn't be dead. I just talked to him—"

"He's dead."

Ponce's words caught in his throat. He rubbed his eyes and hung his head between his knees, looking at the ground. "He liked me."

Grainger put his hand on the kid's knee. "He had a message for you."

Ponce looked up and wiped a tear from his eye. "He did?"

"Yeah. He said something about 'the policeman was right.' Do you know what he meant?"

Ponce nodded. He leaned back against the straw and stared out at the circling birds. *Yes. I know.* He lowered his head.

"Maybe he went to a better place," said Grainger. *A better place? Christ.*

Enrique "Ponce" De Leon smiled. "It's okay, Mr. Grainger. I know he's dead. Wherever he is, I'll remember him."

Grainger smiled back at him. "So will I, son." He stood up. "Let's go get our guest."

Grainger roused Raoul by shaking and slapping him a little. He poured some water on his face. Raoul rotated his head slowly and came into a fuzzy consciousness. He regarded Grainger through hazy eyes and a fog-shrouded mind.

Grainger pulled Raoul onto his feet. "It's time to go."

Raoul scratched his hair and cast about. He counted four bodies but said nothing. He trudged, trussed up like a hog, after the *Americano* to where he had his van parked. Six more bodies appeared, akimbo in death. There was *Capitain* Vargas and two others, fallen close enough together to form an embrace.

"Who did this?" asked Raoul, his eyes wide and mouth quivering.

"He did," said Ponce, pointing.

Raoul raised his eyes slowly, scanning all the way up to where he saw the single military-style truck parked at the entrance to the complex. Tangled mounds dotted the landscape like stricken sea turtles on a barren beach. "This can't be," he said.

"Tell them," Grainger said flatly, "that it can't be."

"**All** dead?" Estaban massaged his face slowly. "Are you sure?" He faced the other man in the courtyard of the hacienda.

"Sí, Señor Rios. I am sure. *Todos muertos,"* said Ruben Lopez again, for the third time.

"How is that possible? How could twenty-five men be dead at the hands of one man?"

Lopez stood firm. "If you would have been there, señor, you would have your answer."

"It is simple, Estaban," said Montezuma. "You sent sheep to be slaughtered. They imposed no burden on him. He dispatched them with the efficiency of an assembly line at a slaughterhouse."

Lopez nodded. "That is what it was like." His eyes turned toward Lorca. "Are you the one called Montezuma?"

Montezuma acknowledged him with a sideways movement of his head.

Lopez reached inside his uniform jacket and withdrew the two items given him by the killer at *la ciudad de los muertos*. "These are for you. I believe he only spared me in order that I could deliver them."

Montezuma took the items from the outstretched arm. "You talked to him? You saw his eyes?"

"He spoke to me; about you, señor. And yes. I saw his eyes. They were glowing in the shadows beneath a hat as worn by *ranchero Americanos*. He said he will meet you at *las Calderas del Diablo*." He bit his lip. "I have delivered the message. If you have no other use for me, I will be going. It seems I no longer have an employer." He turned away and headed for the exit at the arched gate. He stopped and turned back. "If you intend to send more men against this devil, dig their graves now." He disappeared through the gate.

Rios spat and dismissed the survivor with a wave and contemptuous look that concealed his rising trepidation.

Montezuma examined what he had been handed: a piece of folded notebook paper. Inside was a circle with a crosshair. He recognized it as one of the drawings from his young captive. There was also a playing card: the ace of spades. Montezuma snapped the card in his fingers absently, staring off at the distant mountains. The face inside the crosshair hand-drawn by the boy looked nothing like him. He turned to Rios, his pyramided fingertips bouncing against each other. "Is there perhaps something you wish to say to me, Estaban?"

Rios straightened his gaucho tie. "Yes, there is, my dear Lorca. Save me."

"**WHAT** now?" said Raoul. The van bounced roughly in and among the ruts of the trail that led toward the mountains.

Grainger glanced over at Raoul Rios, bound in the passenger seat of the vehicle. "I'm still waiting for your brother to get the picture. I don't think you'll have long to wait."

"Where are we going?" said Ponce.

"Someplace I've been headed for a long time."

ESTABAN watched as Montezuma and Servando Chavez crossed the courtyard, heading for the garages. Montezuma carried his rifle and pulled the young boy. *He has the boy with him! What is he doing with him?* Chavez bore everything else. As they passed beneath the balcony, he called down. "What are you going to do?"

Montezuma rolled his fingertips and looked up at Estaban and his witch consort. "Something that all the others could not. Save you." He jerked his head sideways, and Chavez fell into step behind him.

Sonja Ochoa touched the leather pouch that dangled at her throat and smiled.

* * *

"I am tired of you leading me around like a burro." Raoul Rios stumbled up the path behind the gringo killer tethered by and pulled with a section of rope.

Grainger paused and looked down the slope of the mountain. The vehicle trail they had followed cut diagonally across the valley floor and ended where it butted against the base of the mountain. There, he had parked the van. The twin peaks called the Devil's Boilers were the dominant terrain feature of this monumental edifice that wrapped around the valley with ridges running down from the high ground. The net result was a vast horseshoe of protective mountain superimposed upon a desert valley of cactus and scrub brush. He turned and resumed climbing. Slung across his back was the M-1 Garand rifle he had recovered at the airstrip. An hour later he arrived at a spot he had preselected when inspecting the area days ago. He leaned on a rock and swept the ridges with his binoculars for almost 270 degrees. He checked his watch.

"Time to die, yet?" mocked Raoul.

Grainger pushed Raoul down, placing his back to a rock face, out of sight. He duct-taped his ankles and mouth. He turned to Ponce. "I want you to get down and stay put." He unsheathed the rifle and flipped out the Harris bipod. He smeared dirt on his face; sweat acting as a dissolving solvent. This was going to be a different opponent.

THE vultures rose in a cloud, screeching at the intruders who disturbed their feast. Montezuma drove into *la ciudad de los muertos*, his engine idling. His eyes played across the scattering of bodies passing in silent review. They appeared like small, plastic soldiers dumped out of a toy box. He stopped the vehicle and leaned on the steering wheel. "Fantastic! Beautiful, is it not Servando? Such precision; like the Pied Piper. He led them to the slaughter."

Servando Chavez wanted to roll the window up and turn on the air conditioner. The stench was powerful. "No one man did this. Whatever did is hopefully gone."

"Servando; let me tell you something. That *is* the work of one man; a maestro. What you see out there is art. That is the artist's signature." Montezuma swept his arm. "That is his gallery." He focused on *Capitain* Vargas, who lay belly up; eyes wide open in frozen disbelief. "This is his canvas."

Chavez shook his head. "Are you sure you can defeat such an . . . artist?"

Montezuma laughed. "Oh yes, Servando. I am sure." He gunned the engine, and the Land Rover spun around in the dirt. "You see; it is a relative thing. He paints because he has to."

"And you, Señor Lorca?"

"I paint because it is who I am."

MONTEZUMA parked the Land Rover in a culvert on the far side of *las Calderas del Diablo* and made the climb up its reverse slopes to a location that would afford him excellent observation and fields of fire. The boy kept up, which surprised him, considering the pace he was setting. Even Chavez was breathing heavily as he brought up the rear. Lorca estimated Grainger was by now in place, factoring the head start. And he most likely had at least a basic familiarity with the geography and lay of the land. That was acceptable. It would take more than basic familiarity of local geography to defeat *El Silencio*.

Federico Lorca climbed steadily with a thirst for what was to come. This was to be his boldest stroke, his greatest coup. He was confident, but not arrogantly so. He fully understood his opponent this time was a master. *But soon he will be a past master.* Two hours later he was in position with a commanding view of the entire valley and the horseshoe mountain that sprawled before him. The twin peaks called the Devil's Boilers dominated the terrain. He could see Rios's van parked on the dirt road where the path met the mountain. It was at least eleven hundred meters to the van. *Grainger must be somewhere on the ridges between the van and this position.*

Servando tied Joey Painter to a tree and scurried over to Montezuma. He lowered himself into position and scanned the surroundings with his spotting scope.

Montezuma used 10 × 50 binoculars to observe. Burlap strips hung over the objective lenses to cut the glare and reflection. *He is out there somewhere. I will find him.* He let Servando search while he used the emery board on his right index finger.

GRAINGER positioned himself between two small boulders on a small outcropping. The outcropping fell short of being a promontory and was thus not an eye magnet. It looked like one of many small sections of flat rock platforms that jutted out from the face of the mountain. From here, he could see the entire portion of the range he was concerned with. A thick patch of creosote bush acted as a natural screen to his front, its oily leaves shining like they had been recently varnished. He had created a tunnel for observation and field of fire through the rich, green leaves. From here, he could control the horseshoe terrain all the way around the far bend without moving his body position perceptibly. From where he lay, the van could be seen three hundred meters below him and six hundred meters to his right front, on the track. He enabled the set trigger and rotated the magnification knob to twenty-eight power. He was as ready as he would ever be. He slid back away from the hide.

"I've decided to let you go."

"That is perhaps the only wise thing you have done so far," growled Raoul. "Untie me."

Grainger snapped open his Emerson CQC7 folding fighting knife. He cut Raoul's rope bonds and helped the unsteady Rios to his feet. "The keys are in the van. It shouldn't take you more than twenty minutes to get there from here. You can see it when you clear the lip of the ridge."

Raoul rubbed his wrists. "You plan to shoot me in the back? Is that it?"

"If I wanted to shoot you, I would have done it a long time ago."

Raoul's lips curled into a sneer. "*Bien.* I may even put in a good word to my brother for you. That way he might kill you quickly instead of slowly."

"You do that." Grainger brushed the dirt from Raoul's shirt.

"You're getting red. I guess you're not used to this outdoor life. You better wear a hat. The sun will cook you." He slapped his brown cowboy hat onto Raoul's head.

I'll roast in Hell before I wear that filthy gringo hat. But he said, "Your concern overwhelms me." He straightened the hat.

Grainger threw him the M-1 Garand. Raoul caught it and stood in suspension. "Don't worry. It's unloaded. It belonged to one of your brother's late helpers." He threw Raoul an eight round en bloc ammunition clip. "Just in case you encounter any snakes or other venomous creatures on your way back to the van. Don't lock and load until you're well down slope or . . ." Grainger shrugged.

Raoul gripped the rifle. *This* pinche *gringo is loco, but at least he understands he can't keep fucking with me.* He looked at the rifle, the clip, and at the .45 Auto tucked in Grainger's waistband.

Grainger shook his head. "You'd be dead before your hand touches the bolt handle."

Grainger led him down the ridge, a hundred yards away from their position, before allowing Raoul to cross over the crest and begin his descent to the roadway.

Raoul slipped on the loose shale and lost his footing. He slid down the detritus for thirty feet before regaining his balance. He looked momentarily back up the slope, then at the van. He pulled back and locked the bolt open and inserted the clip. The bolt slammed forward with authority. Raoul thought about charging back up the slope and killing his tormentor but came to his senses and bounced down the ridge toward the road.

THIRTY-SIX

"I see him," said Lorca, in response to Chavez's exhortation. Montezuma peered at the stick figure sliding down the shale through the Nightforce 5.5-22 × 50 NXS rifle scope. He couldn't utilize the integral range finder that jutted into the sight picture from the bottom of the lens. It was beyond the capacity of the system. Lorca didn't need it. *Eleven hundred meters to the road and . . . six hundred meters beyond.* It was at least seventeen hundred meters to the juncture where the man would meet the desert floor. Waves of shimmering mirage came off the sand, even in the waning sun of the afternoon. Montezuma watched the man pick his way down the slope, winding past the green trunks of the paloverde trees. *The brown cowboy hat. Yes. He is carrying a rifle.* Of that, he was sure. The rest was indistinct, a shimmering, computer-generated pixel headed for the van. *Did he forget something? Does he estimate I'm not in position yet?*

"It is him," offered Servando, unable to contain his excitement as he observed through the twenty-power spotting scope. "It has to be. Who else would be out here?"

Montezuma worked his way into a solid position as his mind

worked on a shooting solution. *Yes. It is the Distant Death. I will take him as he comes over that small swell in the land, one hundred meters from the van.* He intuited the wind on the valley floor from looking at all environmental factors presenting evidence. He adjusted for the minutes of angle deviation for the wind factor. He listened to the clicks as he turned the elevation knob to compensate for the extreme range of twelve hundred meters to the knoll, factoring for the twenty-five-degree down angle from his position. The Devil's Finger came on. *El Silencio* was ready. He observed through the scope. *A stick figure.*

"He threw away his hat! Did you see that?" said Servando. "Why would he do that?"

Montezuma didn't answer. The 7.82-millimeter Warbird Magnum beltless cartridge slid effortlessly into the dark recess of the chamber. He rotated the bolt handle of the Lazzeroni-Sako down to the locked position. "I will take him as he crests that small upheaval in the ground. Do you see it? Between my target and the vehicle?"

"I see it."

"Good," said Montezuma. "I will call the shot. Watch for the impact."

RAOUL flung the hat away. "Stinking fucking trash," he muttered. He cocked his closed-fist right arm and embraced it with his left across his chest. He turned back to the mountain and jerked it upward in a motion of universal defiance. "*Chenge tu madre. Pinche cabrón.*" He started up the slight rise in the ground. He was almost to the road. *I've tripped.* He became suddenly very dizzy and could not breathe. He was looking up now for some reason, and the sun was blinding him. He tried to close his eyes, but it was no use. It was all right now. The pain was subsiding rapidly. Lying there on his back, Raoul considered getting up. The sound of thunder rolled over him, and he saw his blood flowing like a ruptured dam from his chest. He blinked once. Then he neither heard, nor saw, nor thought any longer.

* * *

"**CENTER** of mass hit. High chest."

"I confirm. *Magnifico!* That shot was incredible. I could barely make him out in the spotting scope. It was fantastic." Chavez bubbled with admiration.

Montezuma returned to silence. He continued to observe the dark mound that lay still among the crucifixion thorn, the creosote, and chaparral on top of the rolling incline.

"You have killed the one known as the Distant Death. *El Dedo del Diablo*. You are the undisputed master."

Montezuma remained motionless behind his rifle, tapping the side of his rifle scope with a hypnotic rhythm.

"Pasa algo, companero? Is anything wrong?" said Servando Chavez.

Montezuma rolled over onto his back. "How far would you say it is to that small promontory, on the ridge, above where we first sighted the descending target?"

Servando stood up and stretched. He gazed out over the desert floor, shielding his eyes from the oblique sun. "A long way; sixteen, perhaps seventeen hundred meters. Far beyond rifle range."

Montezuma stared at the bleached-out sky.

Chavez spun around, flinging blood with centrifugal force in an arc. He fell to his knees facing Montezuma, a look of incredulity masking his features.

Montezuma remained inert, rolling to one elbow. "Yes, Servando, there is something very wrong." The rumbling low and angry boom crossed the valley.

Chavez pitched forward into Montezuma, who shoved the body away, displacing the annoyance. The corpse slid down the rock and skidded a body length, where it came to rest down slope, against a senita cactus.

GRAINGER ejected the brass cartridge case from the rifle. The man he had just killed was not Montezuma, not that it mattered. The Cuban was next. He had nothing personal against the killer Montezuma, but the man was hunting him, looking to kill him in some mad personal ego lust. Although he had been reluctant to admit it, Montezuma had been right when they talked at El Boondocks. They *were* a lot alike. Maybe Montezuma was more honest in assessing and admitting to himself who he was. However, he was the enemy now, and Grainger had no qualms about killing him, although he recognized that the man had saved his life in Beirut. It was a collateral effect, to be sure, but who questions the motivations of the lifesaver when the life saved is yours? He couldn't afford to consider that now.

The past *was* only prologue here. It brought them to this spot, but that was it. Just like the last shot, it was only the preliminary. Now it was the main event: *hombre a hombre.* He looked down at Raoul's dead body that lay on the elevated mound of desert far beneath him. The gentle wind rippled Rios's clothing and blew the cowboy hat across the field until it became impaled on a cactus. Grainger felt only ice water course through his veins. He closed the bolt on the next round. The solution was simple, and ageless. *Kill or be killed.*

MONTEZUMA admitted to himself that he had been outwitted, at least initially. *Deception is all, and I have been deceived.* His lair had been discovered. Yes, he could disengage and make concealed movements, stalk his prey, but the hour was getting late. Even the summer sun would be gone in two hours. *I will defer this day to another; perhaps issue a formal challenge to meet Grainger on The Game's range, with spectators to witness my kill. Yes. But this day must not end without some small victory.* Montezuma eased back down the reverse slope, then made his way to where Joey was tied to the tree.

Montezuma untied the ropes that secured Joey to the trunk. "You're a fine young man. I remember your father. He ran well." Lorca pulled Joey toward his shooting position.

"Are you the one who killed my dad?"

Montezuma knelt down in front of Joey. "Yes. I killed him. He was fleet of foot, but not worthy enough to have sired a fine lad like you."

"He was my father." Joey pushed away. He looked at

Chavez's body and then back at his father's killer. "You're gonna die today."

Montezuma picked the boy up in his arms. "You are not the first to predict my demise. Nor will you be the last." He stepped up and put his footprints into the dirt where Chavez had stood looking out across the valley. The afternoon light was fading. "Look, *chico,* you can see forever from here." He held Joey up, facing the desert.

GRAINGER'S eye came away from the scope, and he felt himself tremble. An electric shiver ran from his neck to his ankle. Bile built in his throat. He couldn't breathe. He couldn't swallow. All he could see was Joey in the scope. *Or is it another boy like him?* Grainger raised his head. He lifted the bolt handle and drew it to the rear, stopping just short of the ejector snapping the round out. *Beirut. I will do whatever is necessary.*

JOEY squirmed and writhed, but it was no use. The grip was viselike.

"No matter, *niño.* Enjoy the spectacle. Life is very short." Montezuma's voice was soft and edgeless, even soothing.

Joey stopped struggling and looked down. His body shielded the man who held him. He concentrated his gaze out across the fields, searching for something.

GRAINGER'S eye moved back to the scope's ocular lens. He saw the same picture and felt himself drowning. He was being mocked. Challenged. Condemned. He had nothing. He heard a silent voice speak to him. *You always miss the shot you don't take.* He backhanded some forming moisture in his right eye and eased the bolt forward, watching the missilelike cartridge glide into its silo. He rotated the handle down and positioned himself. *Range: seventeen hundred meters. One mile.* He had previously dialed in the elevation correction into the turret and set the deflection for the windage adjustment preceding his first shot. He pulled the rifle into his shoulder and looked back into the scope. He squeezed the set trigger and heard the rifle speak to him softly, telling him it was ready.

MONTEZUMA bounced the boy a bit. *Like nobody ever did for me.* "I think your torment will soon be over. Mr. Long Ranger. It will soon be I who stalks you." Lorca talked as he stood there. He loved this torment. He reveled in this small triumph, savoring the agony it must surely be producing in his opponent. A little psychological warfare was good. Lorca caught a momentary glare from the sun. He reached into his jacket for his yellow shooting glasses. Something fell from the pocket as he removed the glasses. He watched the object separate into two parts and fall to the ground. He stared at them: Two small bones. Chicken bones. They had fallen together into a geometric shape that stared back at him. *A cross.* On the spot where he had lain. *A damned cross. The witch . . .*

GRAINGER pulled the trigger straight back the second time and willed the rifle to fire. *Now.* The recoil rocked him back.

ACROSS the valley floor, past the road where the van faced the mountain, over the dead body of Raoul Rios, and up the slopes of the Devil's Boilers, came a wink of light from the shadows. Joey saw the twinkle of light. Montezuma did also, but it was a cognition not fully computing as his mind recoiled from the vision of the bones at his feet.

One second. Across the expanses the bullet came. The stabilized projectile rotated in flight, one full revolution every twelve inches of flight. Joey was still held immobile. *Two seconds.* Joey twisted sharply at the waist, and inclined to the left.

Montezuma knew he should respond. *Do something.* He couldn't. He was paralyzed. He could feel the onrushing missile crossing over the expanses of eternity. He could feel the building pressure wave, an invisible tsunami rushing toward him.

Three seconds.

You shall see Death coming. He saw her cursed face. The bullet came over the top of Joey's right shoulder and blew straight through Federico Lorca's throat. Montezuma maintained his hold on Joey as he sank to the ground. As he came to his knees, Joey's feet gently touched the earth. Montezuma relinquished his grip. A large, ragged hole in his throat showed light from both sides. He fell forward into the dirt, his dead eyes staring at the two undisturbed chicken bones, which lay across each other, forming a perfect cross.

Joey stepped over the body and headed toward where he had seen the wink of light. "He was my Father."

GRAINGER and Ponce made their way down the slope of the mountain to the floor of the desert. They crossed over the knoll and bypassed Raoul's contorted body lying in the chaparral. At the van they could see Joey coming toward them. Ponce looked at Grainger, who nodded. He sprinted out to meet his friend. Grainger grinned. Joey had remembered: the time to target.

"I think next time I will have more bonsai trees on the terrace." Estaban Rios fingered a rosebush, alternately touching a petal and a thorn. He kicked idly at a small mound of ants that had reappeared in his henbane. The garden was such a peaceful place. He looked wistfully at Sonja. "Are they all dead?"

The crunch of footsteps made her turn. Sonja watched the two figures enter the garden. "Not all, Estaban."

Estaban rotated his head to see the approach of the priest and the woman nurse from the church. "Ah. It is Paul: orphan, avenger, God's emissary, and sometimes even priest."

Paul stalked to where he stood in front of Estaban. "I am an orphan, but no longer a priest." He raised the Glock in his hand. "Avenger? Yes. And emissary, too; but not God's."

Sonja stared at Sloane.

Estaban focused on the gun. He touched his chest. "Have you come for me?"

"I have come for Brother Lemuel. Sister Felicia. Señor Rawlings." He stepped in, the gun pointing straight at Estaban.

Estaban held out his arms. "Surely not in cold blood, Father. Your vows of celibacy . . ." he looked over at Sonja, "notwithstanding." He returned to Paul. "You cannot take a life; at least not without offering absolution." The priest was within arm's reach. Estaban relaxed. There was eye contact. They had bonded in the knowledge that life was too precious to be taken so cavalierly.

Paul fired one round into Estaban's chest.

Estaban reacted with a small backward step and a look of mild surprise. He put his hands where it hurt a little. Bright blood seeped through his fingers. He looked up at the priest. "You—"

Paul fired again. The bullet struck, high in the chest. Estaban fell to his knees, both hands on his chest. "Consider yourself absolved."

Estaban pitched forward across the reconstructed ant mound that flourished in his henbane. The ants swarmed over the intruder.

Sloane snapped back, facing Sonja. She had come to kill. She raised the gun. She was getting good at it, and it was easier than she thought. Her finger tightened on the Beretta's trigger. The priestess's impassive eyes stared back. *Not in cold blood.* She lowered the gun. "You're under arrest, you voodoo bitch."

Sonja's eyes sparkled. "Arrest? In Mexico? Under whose authority?"

Who am I kidding? And for what crimes committed on American soil? She had no legal authority. But she needed to have her in custody to run her through the FBI's NCIC system. *She has to be wanted for something.* Then it came to her. *The gun.* She was holding "authority." Sloane swung the pistol up and pointed it at Sonja. "Judge Pietro Beretta."

Sonja's face registered no reaction. Her eyes closed and opened once. Her features softened, to open to all observers. Her aura became benign. She drew her knife from her waistband.

"Give it up, princess. Drop the knife."

Sonja Ochoa cut the leather strands that held the pouch to her neck. She opened the mouth of the pouch and turned it over, shaking out the contents onto the dirt: rattles and scales, teeth and nails; all except chicken bones. She raised the knife to arm's length over her head and thought for a moment about Yoruba and how they would walk together again forever. Her gaze fell from the knife to the woman. "I belong to the dead."

The knife plunged down of its own volition and took her in the chest. She fell silently among her icons, a frozen serenity on her face.

Paul held the gun in his hand. It felt like it belonged there. He loathed the feeling. He found himself standing over Sonja. His feelings pulled him in every direction, tearing out his center. He recognized Sonja represented everything that he was not, or at least used to be. Her gods were alien, not his God. But, whatever her intentions, she had brought him something more than just her flesh. He knelt down next to her and pulled the knife away. There was an absence of blood. It was as he expected. He touched her forehead.

Sloane holstered her weapon. "Did you know her, Father Paul?"

Paul stood up. "It's Paul. Just Paul." Sonja riveted him. "Yes. I knew her."

The last ray of light faded, and night came on hard.

THIRTY-SEVEN

THE headlights materialized out of an uncharacteristic fog that had risen from the river.

Paul and Sloane waited at the junction of Rios's private street that connected the hacienda and the public road. The van stopped, and Grainger got out. Sloane ran to him and threw herself into his arms; holding on to him desperately and feeling the tears of emotional release flow freely.

Ponce and Joey burst from the back and ran to Paul. He grabbed them both, the Glock still in his hand. Joey looked at the gun. Paul laid the gun down, and his fingers clutched them both.

Grainger looked at the bodies. "Do they go with us?"

Paul heaved Estaban Rios over his shoulder. "He goes."

THEY stopped by the copse of cottonwoods on the river. Grainger and Paul unloaded Rios's body and placed him by the others who had been deposited there after the raid. Paul inspected each of them. The features of the first seven were now bloated and stinking from lying in the sun. He reached into his pocket; his hand closed into a fist. Moving to the bodies, he plunged a cactus spine into the throat of each. It was a small thing, but it was a promise.

Paul slid the bodies of the eight men into the waters of the Rio Grande and watched as each floated down in the turgid current, like logs at a jam that had just broken free. The moon was rising, and the bodies reflected that light. The processional of eight dead men floated in single file down toward the narrows at Gumtree Bend.

HUMBERTO sat in the darkness under the lean-to he had constructed from pieces of cardboard, canvas, and cloth that had come to him, blown by the wind. He had found food by his side when he had awakened from a short nap. *La migra must have left it for me. The man is a saint.* Humberto knew that God would not fail him. They would not have passed during his short slumbers. He rubbed his eyes and returned to his vigil.

He saw something in the river. He got up stiffly and hobbled to the river's edge, wading out until the water covered his knees, then his thighs, and on to his waist. The first body twisted in the water as it passed by him closely. Little fish nibbled at the decaying flesh. The body behind bumped it and it surged forward, beyond him. He saw the cactus spine imbedded in each. Rios's body rocked in the water as it passed a ripple caused by an underwater obstruction. The body passed silently, now humbled. Humberto watched them recede into the blackness of the great river beyond. A low, gurgling sound emitted from his throat. He raised his eyes to heaven. He knew they would come. It could not be otherwise. Returning to the rocky shore, he knelt and prayed to God for the deliverance of Felicia and to peace ever after. He got up and started back for the church. There was much work to do. His stomach growled. He was *muy hambre.*

ROSA Fuentes straightened out the serving ladles and trays. She put away the last glass and plate. She took off her apron and lit two candles, placing them on the table. Rosa opened up the propane gas line that fed into the kitchen from the large, white tank outside. She extinguished the pilot light and turned on the oven. The soft hiss of flowing gas came to her. She turned off the lights and closed the door behind her. Tomorrow she would visit her husband's grave and then leave for Reynosa, where she had a sister. Behind her, the hacienda was silent. There was no one left to serve. She had kept her promise to him, who had also run and lost.

"CAN we drop you off somewhere? Anywhere? Laredo? El Paso?" Grainger asked again. The church was quiet in the rectory, but a half-dozen people knelt in prayer in the pews. The congregation was returning.

Paul shook his head. "No. I'll be fine at the bus depot." He straightened a picture of the Last Supper on the wall.

"Where will you go?" said Sloane.

Paul closed his cloth suitcase and snapped down the one hasp that wasn't broken. "Anywhere the bus goes. It doesn't matter. The better question is, where will *you* go, Agent McKenzie?"

Sloane smiled and shook her head. Her assignment was to conduct surveillance on the Rios organization and file reports. Now, there was no Rios organization. She would report back to Washington; but what she would say or do was as yet unknown. The only thing she knew for certain was she was going with this man. Yet, it was a good question and one for which she had no answer.

Paul rotated to face Father Leon. "I will miss you."

Leon lowered his head. "And I you, Father."

Paul placed his hand on Leon's shoulder. "Will you be all right?"

"We will survive. But you have been a part of us for so long, things will not be the same. Will you reconsider?"

Paul shook his head. "There is nothing to reconsider. I have made irreversible choices, crossed and burned too many bridges, broken every commandment, and committed every sin. I've given up my prerogative to speak God's word."

Leon covered Paul's hand. "He is a forgiving God."

"Not for his disciples, and not for my transgressions. They are irreconcilable. I am the unforgiven."

Grainger kicked one of the six suitcases that dominated the

rectory floor. "God has provided, Padre. There is enough to pay the mortgage, rebuild the church, and do the Lord's work as you see fit."

Leon shook his head. "We couldn't—"

"Minus fair compensation for the out-of-state help, of course."

"I cannot. I wouldn't know what—"

Paul dropped his hand from Leon's shoulder. "Please, Father. Do not argue with him. *'El este un hombre muy peligroso.'* He is a dangerous man."

"The money's yours, Padre," said Grainger. "It's God's will. Believe me." He turned to Paul. "How 'bout you . . . Paul? Some of it's yours."

Paul shook his head. "Mine? No. That's not God's will."

SLOANE and Grainger threw the last of their things into the Dodge Coronet convertible. Joey and Ponce came out from the orphanage. Grainger grabbed Joey as he ran up and swung him into his arms. "You remembered, didn't you?"

Joey nodded. "More than just remembered. I think I felt something."

"I felt it, too." He put Joey down. "You be good." Grainger opened the car door. "You and Ponce both take care of Father Leon and the rest of the kids."

"You'll come back, won't you?"

"Might just do that," said Grainger, "God willing and the creek don't rise." He got into the car.

Sloane slid into the passenger side. *"Hasta luego, Padre Leon."* She turned to Paul. *"Hasta la vista, compadre."*

Paul picked up his cloth suitcase and headed down the steps. He didn't know who he was anymore. But at least he knew who he wasn't, and that was a start. He looked back once at his church, then turned and swung out into the street, headed for the bus stop outside Garcia's drugstore. *The journey of a thousand miles begins with but a single step. And it's a long way to anywhere when you don't know where you are going.* But he damn sure knew where he had been.

Grainger and Sloane passed Paul. He raised his suitcase

slightly as they motored by. Sloane turned in her seat and watched him until he was gone from view.

Joey watched the Dodge drive away. He tapped Ponce on the arm. "I told you they would come."

From across the river came a sound like a cannonade.

THE hair on the back of the German Shorthaired Pointer bristled at the approach of the car. A low growl rolled from the dog as it trotted down the steps to inspect the intruder.

Grainger stopped the car in front of Runyan's cabin. The dog's bobbed tail appeared stationary while the rest of the body moved. Grainger got out. The dog sniffed him to confirm, then offered his head for a pat. Grainger obliged. "You want to join me?" he said to her.

"No. Go ahead. I'll wait." Whatever it was between these two was better left alone.

Grainger opened the trunk and removed the cased rifle. He looked toward the house but saw no one. The dog loped for the rear. Grainger followed. Turning the corner, he saw Runyan looking out over the canyon behind the cabin. Grainger watched him for a minute. The pointer romped over to Runyan. When the dog bumped him, he turned around.

Runyan bent over and petted the dog. He scratched his ears, and the animal turned his head sideways appreciatively. He acknowledged Grainger, came erect, and walked slowly toward him. " 'And the hunter, home from the hill.' " He shifted his stance. "I'm sorry about Rawlings. But thank you."

"I didn't do it for you."

"I didn't figure you did; but thanks anyway." His stare was level. "Why *did* you do it? The pay was lousy; the hours were long—"

"There was no one else."

Runyan's face contorted a bit. "That's for sure, but maybe a part of it was the need for redemption, like I was counting on. But I also think you needed to prove to yourself you still had it." He shifted his weight awkwardly to the other leg. "You know, Lon, a man is never happier than when he fulfills his destiny; when he reconciles with himself; when his actions and being match the truth of who he is. You're a hunter, Lon. What you do best is hunt. It's who you are."

Grainger shook his head. "Was, maybe. That's over now." He held out the rifle. "I won't be needing it anymore."

Runyan took the rifle. "It'll be here if you ever need it again."

"Hunting season's over."

THE pointer jumped into the back of the Coronet.

"Take him with you, Lon. His name's Yeager."

The dog's bark turned into a plaintive whine as they drove away. The dog sat up in the backseat and howled at the rising moon. A coyote joined in the serenade. A million stars seemed to be sprinkled in the sky. The warm air felt like a massage. She touched his shoulder. Grainger leaned back. He was glad to be down from the mountain.

Sloane let the wind take her hair and caress her face. Maybe she would ask him if he knew anything about those three burned-out motorcycles at the old gas station they had passed. Maybe someday.

SLOANE Nadine McKenzie honorably resigned from the Drug Enforcement Administration. No reasons cited.

RICHARD Arturo Stoneman became assistant to the DCI as an expert in interagency communication and joint operation coordination.

LAWRENCE Dakes left the CIA and now teaches creative writing at Boston College.

FATHER Leon Ortega managed to pay off the trust deeds held against his church. He also turned down a promotion to bishop and transfer to the Archdiocese of Las Vegas to stay on in Zapata. He burned his sales inventory of audiotapes.

PAUL Teasdale worked at odd jobs, rode the rails, and wandered the country. In Los Angeles, he enrolled at LA Community College, taking classes in real estate and business administration. He resigned from the church and married. Two summers later, in

June, he returned to Zapata, where he settled and became a financial consultant to the local parish. The Zapata Orphan's Trust now owns the bank, the Lemuel Sotelo Memorial Sports Arena, the Felicia Ayala Medical Facility, and the new convention center. During an investigative reporter's interview, Paul told the *Houston Chronicle* they had "invested wisely." Paul fights no more.

THE citizens' committee appointed Officer Levon Butler chief of police after a plebiscite turned out the mayor and city council.

CALLE Verdugo was renamed Rawlings Way.

JULIUS "Jules" Moore is the boxing event promoter at the Sotelo Memorial Sports Arena.

THE border patrolman retired to Livonia, a suburb of Detroit, one-half mile from his grandkids. He finished his book called *The Border Guardian*, which was picked up by a major house. Sometimes, in the harsh Michigan winter, his shoulder hurts a bit. He's waiting for time to pass . . . for the day to come when he can put those kids on his knee. He has one last story to tell them.

JAMES Runyan vanished. He left behind a book of poetry by Robert Service. He had circled a few lines from a poem called "The Men Who Don't Fit In":

> *Till he stands one day, with a hope that's dead*
> *In the glare of the truth at last.*

He also left a note that said he had decided to take the Stoics up on their standing offer.

PONCE and Joey were adopted and live in Cozumel.

* * *

LON Grainger married an unidentified woman and bought a fishing and dive boat operation in Cozumel, along with a house on the beach.

IN the early fall of the first year, the Colombians came. But all they found were ashes.

AH-6 U.S. Army two-pilot attack helicopter.
AIT Advanced individual training.
AMAN Hebrew acronym for *Agaf Modiin*, Israeli military intelligence, comparable to the U.S. DIA.
AO Area of operations.
A-Team Basic U.S. Army Special Forces tactical unit of twelve men. Officially referred to as ODA, Operational Detachment A.
Batman An assistant, aide de camp, military valet (British origin).
BFD Big fucking deal.
BGF Black Guerilla Family. A radical prison gang.
BIA Beirut International Airport.
Big Red One Nickname for the First Infantry Division.
Blow Back Negative repercussions.
BMF Big military fighter (or) big motherfucker. A Buck knife.
BMG Browning machine gun.
Bragg Fort Bragg, North Carolina; home of the Eighty-Second Airborne Division, Special Forces, and Delta.
Camisa Shirt (Spanish).
Charley-Charley Command and Control.
Chupacabras In Spanish, literally "goat sucker." Mexican folklore of a vampirelike beast.
Claymore Command-detonated directional mine.
COMSEC Communications Security.
Cosh Small billy club.
Coyote Slang term for the guides who bring illegal aliens across the border from Mexico.

CQB(C) Close quarters battle (combat).

Crotch Derogatory, internal-to-the-organization term for the Marine Corps.

Curendera Faith healer.

Curlex An absorbent gauze used to stop bleeding.

DAGger Direct Action Group.

DAMA Acronym for demand assigned multiple access (multiplexing).

DCI Director of Central Intelligence.

Dead space A tactical consideration of ground wherein an area or approach lies in defilade and hence cannot be effectively covered by flat trajectory fire. For example, a ditch or large depression.

Deuce and a half Two and one-half ton truck.

DGSE The French intelligence service.

DIA Defense Intelligence Agency (U.S.).

DIAIAPPR Defense Intelligence Agency Intelligence Appraisal (Pronounced *diaper*).

DoD Department of Defense.

E-Ring The outer offices of the Pentagon. The third floor is where all the movers and shakers have their offices.

E-Silhouette Military target of a man from the chest up. A half silhouette.

Estaca, la The stake (Spanish).

Fallschirmjaeger Paratrooper (German).

False flag Operation designed to make it appear another government (or some other entity) is responsible.

Five-fifty (550) cord Nylon parachute suspension line.

FOI Freedom of information.

Frat Boys Incorporated The FBI.

Freak Frequency.

Gladiator Prison slang for a prison sexual predator.

HALO/HAHO High Altitude-Low Opening/High Altitude-High Opening. Advanced free fall parachute training.

Hijab An Arab woman's head covering.

Hoppes Number 9 A cleaning solvent for firearms.

Indig Military slang for indigenous personnel.

INMARSAT International Maritime Satellite.

INS Immigration Naturalization Service.

Jimmy Slang for GMC.

Lance-Coolie Internal organization slang expression for a Marine lance corporal.

LOS Line of sight.

Ma'a assalama Good-bye (Arabic).

MAC-10 A small, high-rate-of-fire SMG originally manufactured by the now defunct Military Armaments Corporation, hence the name.

Manos de piedras Hands of stone (Spanish).

MAU Marine Amphibious Unit.

MH-6 Small, highly maneuverable U.S. military utility helicopter. Known as the Little Bird.

MH (UH)-60 U.S. Army aviation troop transport and utility helicopter. Known as the Black Hawk. The MH is the special operations version.

Migra, la Latino, principally Mexican, derogatory slang expression for the U.S. Immigrations and the Border Patrol.

MOA Minute of angle. An angular measurement equaling one inch at 100 yards, two inches at 200, and so on.

Mossad The Israeli intelligence service, comparable to the U.S. CIA.

MOUT Acronym for military operations over urban terrain.

MP Military Police.

MP-5 PDW Heckler and Koch machine pistol (submachine gun). Comes in many versions. The PDW stands for personal defense weapon. It's issued to pilots, vehicle crewman, and sometimes, snipers.

MRE Meals Ready to Eat, the current U.S. military field rations.

M-60 U.S. general purpose machine gun.

Mujer Woman (Spanish).

NCIC National Crime Information Center, the FBI's computerized system.

NFI No further information.

NMCC National Military Command Center: the Pentagon.

Ofrendas Small funereal offerings erected as memorials to the dead (Spanish).

Ojos de pistola Literally, pistol eyes, translated as glaring eyes (Spanish).

OMON Russian acronym for *Otdel Militsii Osobovo Naznachenyia*; security troops for the Interior Ministry.

OPCON Operation (or operational) control.

OPFOR Opposing force; the aggressor unit in war games.

OPLAN Operations plan.

OSS Office of Strategic Services, the predecessor of the CIA.
Pantelones Pants (Spanish).
PCH Pacific Coast Highway.
Peleador, el The bullfighter (Spanish).
Placa Graffiti particular to the Latino community.
PM Paramilitary.
POA Point of aim.
Push Military slang for radio frequency.
RIB Ribbed Inflatable Boat.
RIP/ROP Ranger Indoctrination Program/Ranger Orientation Program.
Room-Broom Slang for a shotgun.
SA Single action.
SATCOM Satellite communications.
Sat Cong Kill Communists (Vietnamese).
Scorpion The Model 61 Czech submachine gun in 7.65 millimeter.
Screws Inmate slang for prison guards.
SEALs Elite U.S. Navy commando unit.
SEC Securities Exchange Commission.
SFOD-Delta Special Forces Operational Detachment–Delta (Delta Force).
Shabak Israeli General Security Service, comparable to the FBI.
Shayettet Israeli naval commandos, equivalent of the U.S. Navy SEALs.
Shit River The Nahr Beirut as it was called by the Americans.
Shuk Arab open-air market and bazaar.
SIOP Single Integrated Operational Plan. Usually refers to nuclear war strategy.
Six Military reference to the clock system indicating directions. Hence six indicates the rear.
SMG Submachine gun.
SPECCAT Special category; an acronym and euphemism for a CIA operative.
STABO Special operations extraction rig worn as part of the individual's load bearing equipment. It was developed during the Viet Nam War and originally named utilizing the first letter of the last name of the five Special Forces soldiers who conceptualized the apparatus. Now ex post facto called the Stabilized Tactical Airborne Body Operations rig, a name that torments language, defies logic, and ignores the creators.

SWAG Scientific wild-ass guess.

TDY Temporary duty.

Three-humped camel The chaotic result of a joint-agency operation.

Total closure A closed-end operation wherein all participants are targeted for extinction as part of the plan.

T. S. Slip Tough shit slip (slang).

201 File Army personnel service record.

U/A Unauthorized.

Uncle Sam's Misguided Children United States Marine Corps.

Uzi Israeli submachine gun.

Vig Vigorish. The usurious profit margin on an illegal street loan.

Wadi Arabic term for a dry wash or ravine.

Wet work Assassinations and violence; from the Russian *Mokrie dela*.

Wild geese Mercenary soldiers. A term developing out of the war in the Congo in the sixties.

Zapatos Shoes (Spanish).

Zeta Z in Spanish. The Zs were an elite Mexican army parachute unit that deserted and turned to the dark side, becoming first enforcers for warring cartels along the border, then assumed the mantle of drug lords themselves.

ONE

June 1988 New York City

CHLOE Larson was, as usual, in a mad and blinding rush. She had all of ten minutes to change into something suitable to wear to *The Phantom of the Opera*—currently sold out a year in advance and the hottest show on Broadway—put on a face, and catch the 6:52 P.M. train out of Bayside into the city, which was, in itself, a three-minute car ride from her apartment to the station. That left her with really only seven minutes. She whipped through her overstuffed closet that she had meant to clean out last winter, and quickly settled on a black crepe skirt and matching jacket with a pink camisole. Clutching one shoe in her hand, she muttered Michael's name under her breath, while she frantically tossed aside shoe after shoe from the pile on the closet floor, at last finally finding the black patent-leather pump's mate.

She hurried down the hall to the bathroom, pulling on her heels as she walked. *It was not supposed to happen like this*, she thought as she flipped her long blond hair upside down, quickly combing it with one hand, while simultaneously brushing her teeth with the other. She was supposed to be relaxed and carefree, giddy with anticipation, her mind free of distractions when the question to end all questions was finally asked of her. Not rushing to and fro, on almost no sleep, from intense classes and study groups with other really anxious people, the New York State Bar Exam oppressively intruding upon her every thought. She spit out the mouthwash, spritzed on Chanel No. 5, and practically ran to the front door. Four minutes. She had four minutes, or else she would have to catch the 7:22 and then she would probably miss the curtain. An image of a dapper and annoyed Michael, waiting outside the Majestic Theater, rose in hand, box in pocket, checking his watch, flashed into her mind.

It was not supposed to happen like this. She was supposed to be more prepared.

She hurried through the courtyard to her car, her fingers rushing to put on the earrings she had grabbed off the night-stand in her room. From the second story above, she felt the eyes of her strange and reclusive neighbor upon her, moving over her from behind his living room window, as they did every day. Just watching as she made her way through the courtyard into the busy world and on with her life. She shook off the cold, uncomfortable feeling as quickly as it had come and climbed into her car. This was no time to think about Marvin. This was no time to think of the bar exam or bar review classes or study groups. It was time to think only of her answer to the question to end all questions that Michael was surely going to ask her to-night.

Three minutes. She had only three minutes, she thought, as she cheated the corner stop sign, barely making the light up on Northern Boulevard.

The deafening sound of the train whistle was upon her now as she ran up the platform stairs two at a time. The doors closed on her just as she waved a thank you to the conductor for waiting and made her way into the car. She sat back against the ripped red vinyl seat and caught her breath from that last run through the parking lot and up the stairs. The train pulled out of the station, headed for Manhattan. She had barely made it.

Just relax and calm down now, Chloe, she told herself, looking at Queens as it passed her by in the fading light of day. Because tonight, after all, was going to be a very special night. Of that she was certain.

TWO

June 1988 New York City

THE wind had picked up and the thick evergreen bushes that hid his motionless body from sight began to rustle and sway. Just to the west, lightning lit the sky, and jagged streaks of white and purple flashed behind the brilliant Manhattan skyline. There was little doubt that it was going to pour—and soon. Buried deep in the dark underbrush, his jaw clenched tight and his neck stiffened at the rumble of thunder. *Wouldn't that just put the icing on the cake, though? A thunderstorm while he sat out here waiting for that bitch to finally get home.*

Crouched low under the thick mange of bushes that surrounded the apartment building there was no breeze, and the heat had become so stifling under the heavy clown mask that he could almost feel the flesh melting off his face. The smell of rotting leaves and moist dirt overwhelmed the evergreen, and he tried hard not to breathe in through his nose. Something small scurried by his ear, and he forced his mind to stop imagining the different kinds of vermin that might, right now, be crawling on his person, up his sleeves, in his work boots. He fingered the sharp, jagged blade anxiously with gloved fingertips.

There were no signs of life in the deserted courtyard. All was quiet, but for the sound of the wind blowing through the branches of the lumbering oak trees, and the constant hum and rattle of a dozen or more air conditioners, precariously suspended up above him from their windowsills. Thick, full hedges practically grew over the entire side of the building, and he knew that, even from the apartments above, he could still not be seen. The carpet of weeds and decaying leaves crunched softly under his weight as he pulled himself up and moved slowly through the bushes toward her window.

She had left her blinds open. The glow from the streetlamp filtered through the hedges, slicing dim ribbons of light across the bedroom. Inside, all was dark and still. Her bed was unmade and her closet door was open. Shoes—high heels, sandals, sneakers—lined the closet floor. Next to her television, a stuffed-bear collection was displayed on the crowded dresser. Dozens of black marble eyes glinted back at him in the amber slivers of light from the window. The red glow on her alarm clock read 12:33 A.M.

His eyes knew exactly where to look. They quickly scanned down the dresser, and he licked his dry lips. Colored bras and matching lacy panties lay tossed about in the open drawer.

His hand went to his jeans and he felt his hard-on rise back to life. His eyes moved fast to the rocking chair where she had hung her white lace nightie. He closed his eyes and stroked himself faster, recalling in his mind exactly how she had looked last night. Her firm, full tits bouncing up and down while she fucked her boyfriend in that see-through white nightie. Her head thrown back in ecstasy, and her curved, full mouth open wide with pleasure. She was a bad girl, leaving her blinds open. Very bad. His hand moved faster still. Now he envisioned how she would look with those long legs wrapped in nylon thigh-highs and strapped into a pair of the high heels from her closet. And his own hands, locked around their black spikes, hoisting her legs up, up, up in the air and then spreading them wide apart while she screamed. First in fear, and then in pleasure. Her blond mane fanned out under her head on the bed, her arms strapped tight to the headboard. The lacy crotch of her pretty pink panties and her thick blond bush, exposed right by his mouth. *Yum-yum!* He moaned loudly in his head and his breath hissed as it escaped through the tiny slit in the center of his contorted red smile. He stopped himself before he climaxed and opened his eyes again. Her bedroom door sat ajar, and he could see that the rest of the apartment was dark and empty. He sank back down to his spot under the evergreens. Sweat rolled down his face, and the latex suctioned fast to the skin. Thunder rumbled again, and he felt his cock slowly shrivel back down inside his pants.

She was supposed to have been home hours ago. Every single Wednesday night she's home no later than 10:45 P.M. But tonight, *tonight,* of all nights, she's late. He bit down hard on his lower lip, reopening the cut he had chewed on an hour earlier, tasting the salty blood that flooded his mouth. He fought back the almost overwhelming urge to scream.

Goddamn mother-fucking bitch! He could not help but be disappointed. He had been so excited, *so thrilled*, just counting off the minutes. At 10:45 she would walk right past him, only steps away, in her tight gym clothes. The lights would go on above him, and he would rise slowly to the window. She would purposely leave the blinds open, and he would watch. Watch as she pulled her sweaty T-shirt over her head and slid her tight shorts over her naked thighs. Watch as she would get herself ready for bed. *Ready for him!*

Like a giddy schoolboy on his first date, he had giggled to himself merrily in the bushes. *How far will we go tonight, my dear? First base? Second? All the way?* But those initial, exciting minutes had ticked by and here he still was, two hours later—squatting like a vagrant with unspeakable vermin crawling all over him, probably breeding in his ears. The anticipation that had fueled him, that had fed the fantasy, was now gone. His disappointment had slowly turned into anger, an anger that had grown more intense with each passing minute. He clenched his teeth hard and his breath hissed. No, siree, he was not excited anymore. He was not thrilled. He was beyond annoyed.

He sat chewing his lip in the dark for what seemed like another hour, but really was only a matter of minutes. Lightning lit the sky and the thunder rumbled even louder and he knew then that it was time to go. Grudgingly, he removed his mask, gathered his bag of tricks, and extricated himself from the bushes. He knew that there would be a next time.

Headlights beamed down the dark street just then, and he quickly ducked off the cement pathway back behind the hedges. A sleek silver BMW pulled up fast in front of the complex, double-parking no less than thirty feet from his hiding spot.

Minutes passed like hours, but finally the passenger door opened, and two long and luscious legs, their delicate feet wrapped in high-heeled black patent-leather pumps, swung out. He knew instantly that it was her, and an inexplicable feeling of calm came over him.

It must be fate.

Then the Clown sank back under the evergreens. To wait.

THREE

TIMES Square and 42nd Street were still all aglow in neon, bustling with different sorts of life even past midnight on a simple Wednesday. Chloe nervously chewed on a thumbnail and watched out the passenger-side window as the BMW snaked its way through the streets of Manhattan toward 34th Street and the Midtown Tunnel.

She knew that she should not have gone out tonight. The tiny, annoying voice inside her head had told her as much all day long, but she hadn't listened, and with less then four weeks to go before the New York State Bar Exam, she had blown off a night of intense studying for a night of romance and passion. A worthy cause, perhaps, except that the evening hadn't been very romantic in the end, and now she was both miserable and panic stricken, suffering from an overwhelming sense of dread about the exam. Michael continued to rant on about his day from corporate hell, and didn't seem to notice either her misery or her panic, much less her inattention. Or if he did, he didn't seem to care.

Michael Decker was Chloe's boyfriend. Possibly her soon-to-be ex-boyfriend. A high-profile trial attorney, he was on the partner track with the very prestigious Wall Street law firm of White, Hughey & Lombard. They had met there two summers ago when Chloe was hired as Michael's legal intern in the Commercial Litigation Department. She had quickly learned that Michael never took no for an answer when he wanted a yes to his question. The first day on the job he was yelling at her to read her case law more closely, and the next one he was kissing her hot and heavy in the copy room. He was handsome and brilliant and had this romantic mystique about him that Chloe could not explain, and just could not ignore. So she had found a new job, romance had blossomed, and tonight had marked the two-year anniversary of their first real date.

For the past two weeks Chloe had asked, practically begged, Michael if they could celebrate their anniversary date after the bar exam. But instead, he had called her this same afternoon to surprise her with theater tickets for tonight's performance of *Phantom of the Opera*. Michael knew everyone's weakness, and if he didn't know it, he found it. So when Chloe had first said no, he knew to immediately zero in on the guilt factor—that Irish-Catholic homing device buried deep within her conscience. *We hardly see each other anymore, Chloe. You're always studying. We deserve to spend some time together. We need it, babe. I need it.* Etc. etc., and etc. He finally told her that he'd had to practically steal the tickets from some needy client, and she relented, reluctantly agreeing to meet him in the city. She had canceled on her study group at school out in Queens, grabbed a quick change after her bar review class, and had shlepped into Manhattan all the while trying to quiet that disconcerting voice in the back of her head that had suddenly begun to shout.

After all that, she had to say that she wasn't even surprised when, ten minutes after curtain call, the elderly usher with the kind face handed her the note that told her Michael was stuck in an emergency meeting and would be late. She should have left right there, right then, but, well . . . she didn't. She watched now out the window as the BMW slid under the East River and the tunnel lights passed by in a dizzying blur of yellow.

Michael had shown up for the final curtain call with a rose in his hand and had begun the familiar litany of excuses before she could slug him. A zillion apologies later he had somehow managed to then guilt her into dinner, and the next thing she knew, they were heading across the street together to Carmine's and she was left wondering just when and where she had lost her spinal cord. How she hated being Irish-Catholic. The guilt trips were more like pilgrimages.

If the night had only ended there, it would have been on a good note. But over a plate of Veal Marsala and a bottle of Cristal, Michael had delivered the sucker punch of the evening. She had just begun to relax a little and enjoy the champagne and romantic atmosphere when Michael had pulled out a small box that she instantly knew was not small enough.

"Happy Anniversary." He had smiled softly, a perfect smile, his sexy brown eyes warm in the flickering candlelight. The strolling violinists neared, like shark to chum. "I love you, baby."

Obviously not enough to marry me, she had thought as she stared at the silver-wrapped box with the extra-large white bow, afraid to open it. Afraid to see what wasn't inside.

"Go ahead, open it." He had filled their glasses with more champagne, and his grin had grown more smug. Obviously, he thought that alcohol and jewelry of any sort would surely get him out of the doghouse for being late. Little did he know that at that very moment he was so far from home, he was going to need a map and a survival kit to get back. *Or maybe she was wrong. Maybe he had just put it in a big box to fool her.*

But no. Inside, dangling from a delicate gold chain, was a pendant of two intertwined hearts, connected by a brilliant diamond. It was beautiful. But it wasn't round and it didn't fit on her finger. Mad at herself for thinking this way, she had blinked back hot tears. Before she knew it, he was out of his seat and behind her, moving her long blond hair onto her shoulders and fastening the necklace. He kissed the nape of her neck, obviously mistaking her tears for those of happiness. Or ignoring them. He whispered in her ear, "It looks great on you." Then he had sat back in his seat and ordered tiramisu, which arrived five minutes later with a candle and three singing Italians. The violinists soon got wind of the party downtown and had sauntered over and everyone had sung and strummed "Happy Anniversary" in Italian. She wished she had just stayed home.

The car now moved along the Long Island Expressway toward Queens with Michael still oblivious to her absence from the conversation. It had started to sprinkle outside, and lightning lit the sky. In the side-view mirror Chloe watched the Manhattan skyline shrink smaller and smaller behind Lefrak City and Rego Park, until it almost disappeared from sight. After two years, Michael knew what she wanted, and it *wasn't* a necklace. *Damn him.* She had enough stress in her life with the bar exam that she needed this emotional albatross about as much as she needed a hole in the head.

They approached her exit on the Clearview Expressway and she finally decided that a discussion about their future together—or lack thereof—would just have to wait until after she sat for the bar. The last thing she wanted right now was the heart-wrenching ache over a failed relationship. One stress factor at a time. Still, she hoped her stony silence in the car would send its message.

"It's not just the depo," Michael continued on, seemingly oblivious. "If I have to run to the judge every time I want to ask something as inane as a date of birth and Social Security number, this case is going to get buried in the mountains of sanctions I'm going to ask for."

He pulled off now onto Northern Boulevard and stopped at a light. There were no other cars out on the street at this hour. Finally he paused, recognized the sound of silence, and looked over cautiously at Chloe. "Are you okay? You haven't said much at all since we left Carmine's. You're not still mad about my being late, are you? I said I was sorry." He gripped the leather steering wheel with both hands, bracing himself for the fight that hung heavy in the air. His tone was arrogant and defensive. "You know what that firm is like. I just can't get away, and that's the bottom line. The deal depended on me being there."

The silence in the small car was almost deafening. Before she could even respond, he had changed both his tone and the subject. Reaching across the front seat, he traced the heart pendant that rested in the nape of her neck with his finger. "I had it made special. Do you like it?" His voice was now a sensuous inviting whisper.

No, no, no. She wasn't going to go there. Not tonight. *I refuse to answer, Counselor, on the grounds it may incriminate me.*

"I am just distracted." She touched her neck and said flatly,

"It's beautiful." The hell she was going to let him think that she was just being an emotional bitch who was upset because she didn't get the ring she'd told all her friends and extended family she was expecting. He could take what she said and chew on it for a few days. The light changed and they drove on in silence.

"I know what this is about. I know what you're thinking." He sighed an exaggerated sigh and leaned back in the driver's seat, hitting the palm of his hand hard against the steering wheel. "This is all about the bar exam, isn't it? Jesus, Chloe, you have studied for that test almost nonstop for two months, and I have been really understanding. I really have. I only asked for one night out. . . . Just one. I have had this incredibly tough day and all during dinner there has been this, this tension between us. Loosen up, will you? I really, really need you to." He sounded annoyed that he even had to bother having this conversation, and she wanted to slug him again. "Take it from someone who has been there: Stop worrying about the bar exam. You're tops in your class, you've got a terrific job lined up—you'll do fine."

"I'm sorry that my company at dinner did not brighten your tough day, Michael. I really am," she said, the sarcasm chilling her words. "But, let me just say that you must suffer from short-term memory loss. Do you remember that we spent last night together, too? I wouldn't exactly say that I have neglected you. Might I also remind you that I did not even want to celebrate tonight and I told you as much, but you chose to ignore me. Now, as far as having fun goes, I might have been in a better mood if you hadn't been two hours late." Great. In addition to the guilt pangs her stomach was digesting for dessert, her head was beginning to throb. She rubbed her temples.

He pulled the car up in front of her apartment building, looking for a spot.

"You can just let me out here," she said sharply.

He looked stunned and stopped the car, double-parking in front of her complex.

"What? You don't want me to come in tonight?" He sounded hurt, surprised. Good. That made two of them.

"I'm just really tired, Michael, and this conversation i[illegible] it's degenerating. And quick. Plus I missed my ae[illegible] tonight, so I think I'll take the early one in the morning before class."

Silence filled the car. He looked off out his window and she gathered her jacket and purse. "Look, I'm really sorry about tonight, Chloe. I really am. I wanted it to be special and it obviously wasn't, and for that, I apologize. And I'm sorry if you're stressed over the bar exam. I shouldn't have snapped like that." His tone was sincere and much softer. The "sensitive guy" tactic took her slightly by surprise.

Leaning over the car seat, he traced a finger up her neck and over her face. He ran his finger over her cheekbones as she looked down in her lap, fidgeting for the keys in her purse, trying hard to ignore his touch. Burying his hand in her honey-blond hair, he pulled her close and brushed his mouth near her ear. Softly he murmured, "You don't need the gym. Let me work you out."

Michael made her weak. Ever since that day in the copy room. And she could rarely say no to him. Chloe could smell the sweetness of his warm breath, and felt his strong hands tracing farther down the small of her back. In her head she knew she should not put up with his crap, but in her heart, well, that was another story. For crazy reasons she loved him. But tonight—well, tonight was just not going to happen. Even the spineless had a limit. She opened the car door fast and stepped out, catching her breath. When she leaned back in, her tone was one of indifference.

"This is not going to happen, Michael. I'm tempted, but it's already almost one. Marie is picking me up at eight forty-five, and I can't be late again." She slammed the door shut.

He turned off the engine and got out of the driver's side. "Fine, fine. I get it. Some great fucking night this turned out to be," he said sullenly and slammed his door in return. She glared [illegible]im, turned on her heel, and marched off across the courtyard [illegible]er lobby.

[illegible] shit," he mumbled and ran after her. He caught up [illegible]dewalk and grabbed her hand. "Stop, just stop. [illegible]d. I'm also an insensitive clod. I admit it." [illegible]ves for a sign that it was safe to proceed.

Apparently, they still read caution, but when she did not move away he took that as a good sign. "There, I've said it. I'm a jerk and tonight was a mess and it's all my fault. Come on, please, forgive me," he whispered. "Don't end tonight like this." He wrapped his hand behind her neck and pulled her mouth to his. Her full lips tasted sweet.

After a moment she stepped back and touched her hand lightly to her mouth. "Fine. Forgiven. But you're still not spending the night." The words were cool.

She needed to be alone tonight. To think. Past her bedroom, where was this whole thing headed anyway? The streetlights cast deep shadows on the walkway. The wind blew harder and the trees and bushes rustled and stirred around them. A dog barked off in the distance, and the sky rumbled.

Michael looked up. "I think it's going to pour tonight," he said absently, grabbing her limp hand in his. They walked to the front door of the building in silence. On the stoop he smiled and said lightly, "Damn. And here I thought I was so smooth. Sensitivity is supposed to work with you women. The man who's not afraid to cry, show his feelings." He laughed, obviously fishing for a smile in return, then he massaged her hand with his and kissed her gently on the cheek, moving his lips lightly over her face toward her lips. Her eyes were closed, her full mouth slightly parted. "You look so good tonight I just might cry if I can't have you." *If at first you don't succeed . . . try, try again.* His hands moved slowly down the small of her back, over her skirt. She didn't move. "You know, it's not too late to change your mind," he murmured, his fingers moving over her. "I can just go move the car."

His touch was electrifying. Finally, she pulled away and opened the door. Damn it, she was going to make a statement tonight and not even her libido was going to stop her.

"Good night, Michael. I'll talk to you tomorrow."

He looked as if he had been punched in the gut. Or somewhere else.

"Happy Anniversary," he said quietly as she slipped in[illegible] foyer door. The glass door closed with a creak.

He walked slowly back to the car, keys in hand. Damn it. He had really screwed things up tonight. He really had. At the car, he watched as Chloe stood at the living room window and waved to him that all was okay inside. She still looked pissed. And then the curtain closed and she was gone. He climbed in the BMW and drove off toward the expressway and back toward Manhattan, thinking about how to get back on her good side. Maybe he'd send her flowers tomorrow. That's it. Long red roses with an apology and an "I love you." That should get him out of the doghouse and back into her bed. With the crackle of thunder sounding closer still and the storm fast moving in, he turned onto the Clearview Expressway, leaving Bayside way behind him.

FOUR

THE clown watched with wide eyes through parted branches as her luscious legs stepped out of the BMW. Long and tan, probably from some high-priced tanning salon. She was wearing a short and tight, *oh so tight,* black skirt and a pink silk camisole that showed off her full, perky breasts. Over her arm she carried a matching black suit jacket. Pink was her favorite color—and his too—and he was glad she had chosen to wear it tonight. *Mmmm-hmmm . . . pretty in pink!* A slow smile spread over his face and he began to think that perhaps tonight—well, tonight might not be so bad after all. In fact, things were starting to *shape up* quite nicely. He put his hand over his mouth to suppress an escaping giggle.

Her long blond hair met the small of her back in a cascade ... curls and he could smell her sweet, sexy perfume, ... humid air. He recognized it immediately as her fa... No. 5. The perspiration rushed down from the ... king his back and armpits.

... n forever talking with that preppie little

prick of a boyfriend. She didn't look happy. Blah, blah, blah . . . Didn't they know what time it was? It was time to go home. *Time to go to bed.* His fingers drummed impatiently against the black nylon bag. His bag of tricks.

She slammed her door. He, in turn, suddenly got out of the car and slammed his. Down the street a dog began to bark. The Clown's knees quivered slightly. *What if a nosy neighbor woke up?*

But no neighbors came out to play, and Preppie walked fast to meet her on the sidewalk. He grabbed her hand and they exchanged words that he could not hear. Then he kissed her full on the lips. Hand in hand they walked to the front door of the complex. Her high heels clicked on the cement walk, so close he could practically reach out and touch her ankle. Again, he began to panic. *Was the boyfriend going in, too?* That would just ruin everything. Preppie had had his fun with her last night—tonight was *his* turn.

On the stoop of the foyer they kissed again, but then she slipped in the main door of the complex alone. *Not so lucky tonight, are we, Preppie?* The Clown chuckled softly.

Preppie turned, his head down, and walked slowly back to his car, jingling the keys in his hand. Like a good little boyfriend, he waited until the light went on in the apartment and he saw her wave from the living room window before he drove off into the night.

The Clown smiled. *How quaint! The Preppie Prick walks her to her door and kisses her good night. Don't let those bedbugs bite! And he even stays around to make sure that she is safe and sound and that no bogeyman is lurking inside. What a laugh riot!*

Five minutes later, the lights in her bedroom went on, illuminating the bushes. He pulled himself deeper into the hedge. The air conditioner rattled to life above him and condensation dripped through the evergreen onto his head. He saw her shadow bouncing about in the bushes as she walked around the room, and then she closed the blinds and the light grew dim.

He sat completely motionless for twenty minutes af[illegible] the lights went out. Thunder rumbled, louder this ti[illegible] had started. Soft at first, but he knew that would change. The wind gusts were strong now, and the bushes swayed back and forth, dancing a strange dance in the dim streetlight. The storm was almost upon them. She had made it just in the nick of time.

He grabbed his bag of tricks and snaked his way around the corner of the building until he was directly beneath the window with the broken latch in her living room. Then at precisely 1:32 A.M., the Clown pulled his mask on snug over his face. He stood and brushed off his now *very tight* blue jeans, silently lifted the darkened window and slithered inside out of the rain.